AZHEEK

THE RISING

ISBN : 978-1-7770247-8-9

Printed in the United States, United Kingdom, Europe and Australia by:
Ingram Book Group LLC
One Ingram BLVD., La Vergne, TN 37086

i var vala u iorethe ind uron, nim alyeh larha.

tuma fara doha valira, nim ehan.
i var hava u andal.

kalan u te etheliar. i ihv beranok iord u.

ur vala menid ni imoria.

OCEAN OF THE MOON

NORTHLANDS

HIGHLANDS

THE
CRADLE

ZEDA

ILAGA
IVA

AN
LURAN
IVA

SONTAR
IVEL
+

IMOG
IVA

IKRAN
+

FOROS
+

+ OK

ELOA
+

VAIA
+

KAPADUA

SAKHALA
+

JSAN
YAN'ZI

IRENVEL

VORA

THE
DEAD SEA

VOLEHN

ELIZIA

PARADIZ

N OF THE SUN

IANAR

THE BEGINNING

Blood spilled across the earth, lit only by pale streams of red moonlight through the forest canopy. Leaves rustled in the breeze, the only sound to accompany muffled sobs.

Sitting at the base of a tree was a woman, battered and bruised, riddled with unforgiving scars. Her once sparkling green eyes were now bloodshot, her gaze distant and glazed over. Wounds covered her brown skin, many still open and oozing: lashes from whips, cuts from blades, and the flesh about her wrists and ankles raw from rusted shackles. The only cloth that covered her had been reduced to rags, riddled with filth, clinging to her pregnant belly. The blood came strongest from between her skeletal legs.

She could feel her pursuers growing closer. She could feel the pounding of horses' hooves travelling through the ground. The earth warned of their approach, trees whispering to her in fear. She was running out of time.

Closing her eyes, she clenched her teeth. All she could smell was earth and blood: her own, putrid like metal. She could taste it, and no matter how much she tried to swallow it down, it never went away.

Push. *Push.*

A loud cry sounded from her lips, her face screwed up in agony as she trembled.

Then she gasped, air drawing in like a scream, and her shaking legs finally returned to the ground.

The baby cried. With what strength she had left, she pulled the newborn into her arms.

The woman wept, cradling her daughter. She knew she would die here. She could feel her pursuers growing closer and closer. The earth begged her to run. The trees pleaded, every leaf shaking in fear, but her legs could hold her no longer.

Then she sensed someone else: a presence that appeared with no warning. There was someone in the woods, striding towards her.

The stranger emerged through the trees, a long cloak billowing at his heels, hood shrouding his face in darkness.

He reached the woman and lowered to one knee. She looked at him weakly, her gaze then turning to the woods behind him. There were others there, but only just. Spirits. Distant souls from the past.

"You... are not one of them." Her words were barely a whisper.

The man turned slightly to follow her gaze. He could not see the spirits, but he knew they were there. If she could see them, it was too late.

"Please help me," she cried. "Please help my child."

He took the baby, holding it with one arm, looking at it for only a moment. A tear slid down her cheek.

"Your fight is over," he said. His voice was soft. Eerie. "Be at peace."

The man raised a hand and touched two fingers to her forehead.

Her green eyes glazed over, her stare turning distant. Her breathing slowed, her body ceasing to shake. No longer did she tremble in the night.

The stranger rose to his feet, and as the woman's dead eyes began to glow, he turned and walked away.

Green light filled her absent gaze, more colours rising from her. Lights of various greens and gold rose from her body, and soon her brittle bones sank into the ground, skin merging into the bark of the tree.

A thunder of hooves filled the air as her pursuers grew closer and closer, and when riders burst through the trees, yanking on reins, the horses reared and whinnied. Skidding to a halt, the masked riders turned to the disappearing corpse.

Lights of the earth azheek glistened off their metal masks, every one of them cold and unfeeling like the humans who wore them. The baraduhr could do nothing but watch as the last of the azheek sank into the earth, leaving only flora where her body had been. Soft grass swayed in the breeze, tiny green and gold lights floating above the blades.

A rider came from his horse, landing heavily on the ground. His knuckles cracked within leather gloves as he balled his fists, and striding forward, he snarled. He stomped on the azheek's resting place, grinding out lights beneath his boot.

"Fucking bitch."

"Did she give birth?" another rider asked. "Where's the baby?"

"Find it. Now."

The humans dug spurs into their steeds and tore off in every direction, upturning dirt and leaves in their search.

But the stranger and the stolen child were gone.

CHAPTER 1

VERAION

Dry earth cracked and crumbled beneath the soles of a runner racing desperately across a barren grassland. The ground was golden beneath the beating sun, heat rising from the infertile earth, but the woman felt no discomfort in the sweltering rays. Her breaths ran dry, panting heavily to accompany the creaking of leather around her body, but not a bead of sweat appeared on her tanned skin.

The fire azheek ran as fast as her legs could take her. Muscles rippled beneath her clothes, aching in her hysteria. Dirt and dust stirred about her boots, but she never looked back to watch it billow behind her. Her pale green eyes were fixed on the horizon.

Trees. *Shelter.*

Chester's skin glowed beneath the sun, worshipped by the god, her long blood-red hair shining like fire in the light. She wasn't tall, just over five feet, but she had strength built from years of training. Still, her muscles didn't do much to lengthen her strides as she fought to reach the woods.

Her face had been round in youth but age brought sharpened edges, her cheekbones and jaw the most defined features of her otherwise softer visage.

Her pants were tucked into boots, a leather bodice wrapped around her torso, strapping down her breasts to keep them firmly in place as she ran. Daggers hung about her waist, and across her back was slung her greatest weapon.

A sword with two blades, curved near the hilt, encircling a floating crystal. The stone shone white, blue lights wafting from it, floating around the metal that gleamed in the sunlight. An ancient language was engraved along the blades, old runes she couldn't read. But she didn't need to understand them to know the true value of this weapon.

Kara'i steel. Stronger, lighter, unable to tarnish, unable to chip or rust. The water azheeks were the only azheeks to still carry Old magic and their weapons were no different.

If being an azheek wasn't reason enough to be hunted by baraduhr, carrying kara'i steel definitely was.

Chester tore through the grassland, eyes fixed on the forest, but no matter how heavily she breathed, no matter how sore her muscles grew, not a single bead of sweat appeared on her skin.

She spared a second to glance over her shoulder. Masked riders. Seven of them. Baraduhr.

"*Shit*." Her curse was lost among panting.

She continued running. Faster. *Faster*.

Then a crack of lightning split through the sky and a drop of water hit her skin. Then another. The droplets sizzled against her, heat radiating from her body as fire flowed through her veins. As rain clouds thickened, droplets turned to a downpour.

Soon she was drenched. Steam rose from her, and as she yelled, flames burst from her skin and licked down her strong arms. The fire azheek cast flames over her shoulders but took no time to aim, and the pouring rain only fought her element.

Finally she reached the woods, and her flames disappeared.

Chester raced through the trees, ducking under low-lying branches and leaping over fallen logs. The forest was dark now, light blocked by the storm and thick canopy.

Skidding to a halt, she ducked behind a large tree. Her chest heaved and she took a moment to swallow, attempting to moisten her dry throat.

Chester took in a slow breath, fighting to calm her racing heart, and with an exhale, her pupils filled with fire, turning her green irises orange in the light. No water fell into her eyes, for her burning stare turned the rain to steam.

She reached over her shoulder and grabbed her weapon, crystal and runes glowing eerily in the darkness. Giving the hilt a harsh jerk, it extended, turning the sword into a polearm. She took a moment to look at the blue light shining from the kara'i steel and smiled slightly, letting out a sigh.

"Curse the gods for giving me you," she murmured. "But I just don't know how to let you go."

The baraduhr charged into the forest. Chester let her head fall back against the tree as she waited, her heart finding a steadier pace.

She drew a dagger, and the moment a rider rode into view, she threw it. The blade throttled through the air and speared the first rider in the neck. His head lolled uselessly as blood spurted from his artery, body slumping over. His horse continued through the woods uncontrolled.

Chester stayed in her place, hiding as rider after rider tore through the trees. When the seventh came, she raised an arm. Her skin shone bright red as flames leapt from her hand, bursting through the darkness, catching the human. All it took was a single flame on his cloak and Chester yelled, tensing her hands, causing the fire to burst and spread. The baraduhr screamed beneath his mask, falling from his saddle.

The sixth rider pulled on his reins as he heard the screams, leaping from his horse to charge at her.

His sword met her blades. The clash of metal on metal sang through the rain, and as azheek and human fought, their boots turned the earth to mud.

Slamming her boot into his gut, she swung her polearm. The weapon shone in the darkness, blue light eerie among the increasing splatter of blood.

Chester slammed the pommel of her weapon into the man's face, cracking his mask. The metal was thin. Again and again she attacked, again and again until it shattered. With one quick swing, she cut his skull in half, sending brains and eyes splattering through the trees.

A yell rang in her ears as the seventh rider barrelled into her, still aflame. He clawed from behind and she grabbed him by the arms, wrenching him over her head. With a yell she slammed her boot into his face repeatedly, every blow filled with hatred, and even when the metal dented, she didn't stop. Flesh came from his skull, peeled away by breaking metal, and he could barely scream beneath the helmet that caged him in, unable to move his jaw.

Someone grabbed her by the arms, yanking her back. She screamed, bursting into flames to send him away. She grabbed a dagger, wheeling to face her attacker, but before she could act, another baraduhr struck her across the head.

She fell forward. Blood dripped down the back of her neck, mingling with rain. She staggered towards her glowing weapon, crawling through the mud, hand outstretched, and grabbed it. But the light in her pupils flickered.

One of the humans ran for her.

Then a machete spun through the trees, landing with a loud crack in the attacker's skull, the baraduhr flying backwards from the force.

Chester stared in alarm.

A man ran past her wielding a machete in one hand, and as he tore through the trees he slid to the ground. He sliced off another baraduhr's leg, grabbing his first blade as he went. Leaping back to his feet, he lunged for another masked human.

The stranger had long, wild hair, matted with neglect, but as Chester's vision blurred, that was all she could see.

He was fast, moving swiftly through the trees, leaving the baraduhr in pieces. Their weapons were longer than his, their swords giving them more reach, but he was faster. Stronger.

He was shorter than most of the baraduhr but he was aggressive, closing the distance between himself and his enemies, putting himself out of sword range—putting himself right in front of them. He fought with his weapons in mind, machetes no match to block the strike of a longsword, but he dodged blows more consistently than he needed to block. And he knew where and when to move.

With every swing of his blades, limbs came from bodies. With every swing of his blades, baraduhr screams followed.

Chester struggled to stand, gripping a tree, blinking through the rain. The stranger turned towards her.

"Get down!"

She ducked just as he threw a machete, the blade humming inches from her head to land in the chest of the last baraduhr.

Chester collapsed to her knees, eyes rolling back in her head, landing with a splat on the soaked earth.

The man stood in place, hazel eyes scanning the trees. He counted the horses. Seven. He counted the corpses. Seven.

Only once he knew all the baraduhr were dead did he move towards the unconscious woman. He yanked his machete from the corpse behind her and slid both weapons into the sheaths slung in an X across his back.

Slowly he lowered to one knee, rolling Chester over, pressing his fingers to her neck. He didn't need to find a pulse to know she was still alive, for his body filled with warmth: the warmth of a fire azheek. It was comforting in the cold rain, but as his eyes met her face, his brow furrowed. His hazel stare roved over her features, a hand pushing dark red hair from her cheek. She looked familiar, like a distant memory.

"*vu iar u?*" he murmured. His eyes thinned as he thought, a hand running over his scraggly beard.

Then he saw her weapon. His brow furrowed even more. The white crystal shone in the darkness, blue lights calmly dancing in the rain. Rain that would never tarnish precious kara'i steel.

Heaving Chester over one shoulder, he took her weapon with him as he headed from the carnage.

* * *

Chester came to with a groan, wincing as consciousness returned to her. Slowly she sat up, a hand moving to the back of her head, and when her fingers met a sticky substance, she opened her eyes. She was inside a hollow tree, safe from the rain: a large sequoia with space enough for her to lie down—space enough for a fire to be lit in the centre of the hollow trunk. A rabbit was roasting on a spit.

Her weapons were beside her, and on the other side of the fire lay a drenched cloak.

Chester glanced to the muddy green paste on her fingers and gave it a sniff. A healing paste. She wiped it on her pants, already dry.

Rain poured outside the tree, spray wafting in from the opening, but the fire was set up far enough away that the flames didn't flicker.

A figure emerged outside, and Chester watched as the stranger ducked into the shelter, moving to the other side of the fire. He was completely soaked. The rain weighed his hair down, but it was so matted there was still volume in the dark mess. A beard riddled his chin, making it almost impossible to tell how old he was. At a glance, he could have been forty. If he were a human, his face would be wrinkled by that age, but in the firelight his brown skin looked as radiant as hers. If he was an azheek, he was past his prime.

He carried with him two large leaves and plopped them by the fire as he sat down. Without looking at Chester, he yanked off his fingerless gloves, unbuckling the belts slung across his body, and started to pile all of his weapons in a great heap.

"Thank you," Chester said. "For saving me."

The man nodded, not looking up from his work. His cheekbones were sharp, seen only when his hair swayed with movement. The dark locks otherwise hung in his face.

He pulled off his vest and attempted to wring it out. Water poured, but it still didn't do much to dry the thing. He laid it near the fire and picked up his sodden cloak, holding it out.

"Could you dry this for me?" It sounded less like a request and more like a demand.

"What makes you think I can do that?" she said.

He looked at her. His eyes were piercing, the shape angular and naturally intimidating, and in the firelight his hazel stare looked golden.

"You're a fire azheek," he said.

She held his gaze for a moment before taking the cloak. He returned to his work.

Chester ran her hands over the sodden fabric. He pulled his myriad of weapons from their sheaths, laying the leather out to dry.

A gold chain hung around his neck, and as the pendant came close to falling from his sodden shirt, he put it back in. Still, she could see that whatever it was, it glowed white. His pale shirt clung to his form, to the muscles beneath his brown skin.

There was something about him that felt familiar, but she was sure she had never met him before.

"Here." She offered him his cloak, now dry. He took it with a nod and used it to dry his blades, weapon after weapon, machetes and daggers.

"My name is Chester," she said. It took a while before he answered, and he never looked up from his work.

"Veraion."

"Have we met before?"

He stopped for a moment. She felt it too. He glanced at her and then shook his head. He was about to return his gaze to his weapons when he spotted hers. Instinctually, she placed a hand on it.

"Kara'i," he said. "Where on Ianar did you get that?"

"I didn't get it from a water azheek. I killed a baraduhr for it."

"Ah… well, whoever the original owner was, I'm sure they're glad to see you wield it instead."

She nodded.

"How long ago did you come across that weapon?" he asked.

"About ten years ago," she said. "I was in a neighbouring wood. A baraduhr had it."

He nodded. Then he stopped and looked at her. "Ten years ago? How old were you?"

"Uhh… fourteen? Fifteen?"

He squinted. "You killed a baraduhr. When you were fourteen."

"It was no easy feat," she said lightly, not catching on to his bewilderment. "He was good. *Really* good. *Huge* too, possibly the biggest man I'd ever seen, but then again, I was fourteen. I'm sure anyone could have looked big. I'm short now—I was even shorter back then." She smiled to herself. "He was good. I had to blast half his face off and gut him like a fish before I could finally grab the thing. Even when his insides became his outsides, he was still fighting."

She glanced at him and only then noticed his expression. Disbelief. She snorted.

"I've been at this a while," she said simply. "I was raised killing baraduhr. It's my normal."

He shook his head. Then he leaned towards the fire, turning the rabbit on the spit.

"When did you start fighting?" she asked. "You're good. You're really good."

"I was trained in my youth," he said. "But rarely fought off the training grounds. I didn't take a life until a few years ago. I've been hunting baraduhr ever since."

She nodded, understanding. "Who did they kill?"

He paused. Veraion swallowed the knot in his throat. "My ilis."

He took the rabbit from the fire and sliced the meat, dividing it onto the two leaves he had collected.

"I'm sorry," Chester said. He merely nodded.

"Do you remember his face?" he asked. "The man you killed for that weapon."

"No."

He offered her a leaf of rabbit meat and she took it with a gracious nod.

"Thank you," she said.

He sat back and started to eat. He used his fingers to pick up the pieces of meat. Then he watched as Chester rolled her large leaf and turned her meal into a wrap. He looked down at his own inconvenient method and blinked. She noticed and smirked a little.

"Whatever kind of leaf this is," she said, "it's not like we could ever be poisoned by it."

He turned his meal into a wrap.

"Do you?" she asked. "Remember the faces of all yours?"

"You've been killing a lot longer than I have."

"That's a yes."

He chewed slowly, gaze distant. "I remember their last words too. Most of them cry for their mothers."

They ate in silence, listening to the crackling fire and the fall of rain outside.

"There's one thing all humans have in common when they die," Chester said, attempting to lighten the mood. "They all shit themselves."

He snorted into his food. He glanced at her with an amused expression.

"Why were you out there?" she asked. "There isn't a town for miles in this area."

"I was heading north, saw the baraduhr. You?"

Chester smiled to herself, almost bitterly. "I went for a walk to clear my head and ended up being chased by those bastards."

"You said it yourself, there isn't a town for miles."

"Not above ground, no."

He raised an eyebrow at her.

"Foros," she said. He stared.

"Foros? The underground city?"

"That's the one."

"That's here? Near here?"

"Near enough, yeah."

He sat back, eyes wide. "Fuck…"

"Were you looking for it?"

"No, I just… I've heard stories. I've been a lot of places but never an underground city."

"Safety was definitely a perk." She nodded. "Unless you're an idiot like me and go for walks above ground."

He snorted lightly. Then his brow furrowed curiously. "I heard Foros is an earth azheek city."

"Earth azheeks and humans," she said. "Plenty of humans. They're everywhere."

"Hm… you know, you don't really look like a fire azheek."

She smiled to herself. "My features are a little softer."

"And your eyes."

"That's what gives it away. My mother was an earth azheek."

Veraion looked at her quickly. "What?"

"My mother was an earth azheek," she said. "Or so I've been told. It explains the eyes and the softer features. I mean, I've only ever met one other fire azheek, but based off what I've heard, fire azheeks… don't really look like me."

"Yes," Veraion said. "But… *you're* an azheek. You have powers. You weren't born human."

"Yeah," she murmured. "I can only assume my father was a fire azheek, but I still… I still question it sometimes. Cross-breeders always end up with human children—having a mixed-blood child born with a power is unheard of. I'm lucky. I've never met another mixed-blood that wasn't born human."

"Yeah… me too." His gaze grew distant.

"What about you? Earth azheek?"

He nodded, but only just. "Barely," he said. "I never really trained my powers. I'm fine saying I'm human."

She smirked. "Even if you don't use your powers, you're still stronger, faster. Even if you never used your powers, not a day in your life, you'd still never get sick or risk an infection from even the largest cut."

"Yeah, but we don't tell them that."

She smiled and raised her wrap. "And if these leaves were poisonous, and you were human, you'd be dead."

"Are you going to go back to Foros when the rain stops?" he asked. She let out a soft sigh, and this time it was she that became withdrawn.

"I don't know if I want to," she said.

"Are you a runaway?"

"You could say that," she said lightly.

"So you ran away with no food, rations, or a horse?"

"Hey, maybe I like walking."

He smirked and shook his head.

"You said you were heading north?" she asked.

"Sontar Ivel."

Her eyes widened. "*What?*"

"The capital."

"I know what Sontar Ivel is—I'm just surprised, is all. It's far."

"Good thing those baraduhr had horses. Personally, I'm not a fan of walking."

She chuckled into her food. "Yeah, if you plan on getting to Sontar Ivel within the next five years, I'd highly suggest *not* walking."

"Ah, come on, one could probably walk it in about a year. Maybe less if they have long fucking legs."

Chester laughed. "Long legs, I have not."

"You're going to Sontar Ivel now, are you?"

She let out a sigh, gazing at the bark across from her. "Probably not. Sontar Ivel," she murmured. "I've heard so much about the capital… but it always seemed so far away. So… otherworldly. Almost as though it's not even real. Do you think there's baraduhr in the capital?"

His eyes went dark. "There's baraduhr everywhere."

"But in *Sontar Ivel*?"

He merely looked at her, and she sighed.

"Yeah, you're probably right."

"A piece of advice," he said. "If you choose to stay away from Foros and travel above ground, keep that weapon hidden."

She glanced at her prized possession.

"Kara'i weapons are never seen out of the hands of their owners," he said. "Out of the hands of a water azheek. And you know how often they mingle with the rest of us."

"Never."

"Never. If you walk around with that thing on display, you'll attract attention, and not the good kind."

She sighed. "Yeah, I know."

"Whip it out for battle if you need to, but otherwise… keep it hidden."

"Have you ever met one?"

"A water azheek?"

"Yeah."

It took him a moment to respond, as though thinking, deciding whether or not he should say. "My ilis."

"Oh… did they… have the markings?"

He nodded.

"They glowed and everything?" she asked. "You always hear that they still carry Old magic, are still with the Old Ways, but when you never get to see it yourself, it seems so unreal."

"Markings and all," he said.

A twig snapped somewhere outside and Chester perked up, listening.

"It was probably one of the horses," Veraion said.

"Oh, I wasn't worried." She eased back into her original position. "I'm just... expecting someone."

"A travelling companion?"

"Life companion, really. He'll catch up soon." Her gaze remained on the opening of the tree, watching the rain pouring outside. Veraion glanced at her.

"Should I ask? Or..."

"He's a wasfought."

He choked on his food. "*What?*"

"A wasfought?" She looked at him with an amused smile.

"A *wasfought?*" He glanced at the opening. Her smile turned to a dark smirk.

"You're not afraid, are you?"

"Everyone's afraid of wasfoughts," he said. "Those things are insane. You know it's physically impossible to break their bones, right? People use them as clubs. They don't deteriorate over time."

"Oh, Aven's harmless," she said, waving him off.

"Harmless?" he repeated dryly. "It's like the gods wanted to see what would happen if they mixed a wolf with a lion with a bull with a bear and then gave it unbreakable bones and a thirst for blood."

"Okay, harmless is a lie. He's harmless to *me*."

Veraion continued watching her uncomfortably. "Should I leave? You can have the tree."

She laughed. "He wouldn't attack you, not without reason."

"That doesn't make me feel any better."

She continued chuckling as she ate the last of her food.

"How long have you had this… wasfought?" he asked.

She thought to herself for a moment. "Twelve years?"

"You're going to have to explain yourself."

She laughed again. "A group of us were on a hunt. One of our party was killed by a wasfought and it took the rest of us to take it down. That's when we realized she had a cub. She had just been trying to feed her young."

"You didn't kill the thing?"

"He was a *baby*!"

"A wasfought cub is still a wasfought."

"He was innocent. I took him in and took care of him. Raised him."

Veraion watched her like she was crazy. Then his brow furrowed.

"Hold on," he muttered. "Twelve years. That would have made you… twelve? Thirteen? On a hunting party?"

"I was… efficient."

"*aishida*," he murmured. "Maybe you *should* come to Sontar Ivel. I could use a bodyguard."

"My rate is a hundred gold coins a day," she joked.

"Even the gods couldn't afford that."

"What can I say, I'm priceless."

She cast him a smug smile and he shook his head, but he couldn't stop a smirk resting on his lips. It had been a long time since he had smiled.

* * *

When the rain cleared and the sun rose, Veraion returned his weapons to his body and climbed from the tree. By the time Chester came around, nothing remained of the man but for coal where the fire had been and tiny blades of grass poking out of the ground where he had slept. She grabbed her weapons and headed into the morning air.

Droplets of water clung to the trees, twinkling in the sunrise. It made her smile, appreciating life above ground, and she watched a spider as it irritably fixed its web. Every drop of dew shimmered in the morning light.

Then she spotted horses through the trees. Seven of them. Veraion nodded a greeting to her as he approached.

"So are you just really fast or is this a part of your earth azheek thing?" She stared at the horses in surprise.

"Animals like me," he said simply.

"Earth azheek thing." She nodded.

"Pick one," he said. She went to take the reins of the closest, a brown mare, but Veraion pulled her away. "Not that one. We've bonded."

Chester laughed and took the reins of the next closest, a brown-and-white-spotted mare.

"It was nice knowing you, Raion," she said.

He looked at her a moment and smiled at the nickname. "It's been a long time since anyone has called me that. Where… do you think you're going to go?"

"Oh, I don't know." She looked around. "That way?"

From the look on his face it was clear he was pitying her.

"Don't pity me," she scoffed.

"I'm not pitying you."

"You're pitying me."

"I'm just… There's nothing that way. Not for at least a week."

"Well, fuck."

He snorted, placing his foot in the stirrup of his mare, easily swinging into the saddle.

"Any chance I could follow you for a bit?" she asked. "You know where you're going and… you seem nice?"

She raised her foot into the stirrup with great difficulty.

"You just watched me kill people," he said.

"Hey, that's my kind of nice."

"I can't afford you."

"We'll call it even for the horse." She smiled.

He clicked his tongue and the horses started walking. Chester yelped and hopped alongside her mare, one foot in the stirrup. Veraion was doing his best not to smirk, pretending he couldn't see her.

"Hey!" she exclaimed.

"Would you like me to find you a box?"

As she neared a tall root, she pushed off it and managed to haul herself half onto the horse, letting out a long groan as she finally got into the saddle. By then, Veraion was laughing.

"I take back the *nice*." She glared, though there was amusement in her tone.

"What?" He cast her a sweet smile. "I thought you liked walking."

She threw him a dry smirk. "I'll set my wasfought on you."

* * *

When they reached civilization, Chester took the five remaining horses and baraduhr weapons into town, following the bustle until she found a marketplace. She enjoyed the sights, sounds, and smells, all so different from what she was used to in Foros. It was a common town, like so many others above ground, but that was it: she was above ground.

Chester was in no rush and smiled beneath the warmth of the sun. As a fire azheek, the sun god loved her the most. Her water azheek weapon was once more strapped across her back, but the blades and crystals were hidden beneath cloth, only the hilt in view.

There wasn't an azheek in sight here, and Chester smiled as she noticed the human features azheeks could never have. Freckles, moles, scars that healed terribly, and hair that looked limp and lifeless years before going grey. She loved these little differences and never once looked down on them. In fact, she thought it was beautiful.

Humans could look so diverse. It had been thousands of years since the cross-breeding of azheeks resulted in humans, so now azheeks all looked similar. It was easy to tell who was what. She was the only azheek she knew with eyes that contradicted the element flowing through their veins.

Chester sold the baraduhr weapons first, taking her time to say farewell to the horses before handing the reins over. She hid away her bags of coin and headed back to where Veraion was waiting in the woods.

Making her way through town, she passed a tavern, glancing at wanted posters on the walls.

Then she stopped, going back in her tracks until she could see them again.

Wanted. By command of the queen. For the murder of twenty-seven men and women across the mainland. Name: unknown. Age: past prime, thirties or forties. Height: five foot eight. Hair: dark brown. Eyes: hazel. Skin: brown. Species: earth azheek.

The etched drawing had gotten him perfectly, from the long mass of matted hair to the hatred seething in his eyes. Veraion.

"Huh," she grunted.

Chester headed back through town, meeting him in the woods. She tossed him one of the bags of coin and they swung into their saddles, continuing on their way.

She watched him as they rode, and eventually he couldn't take her incessant staring any longer.

"Are you having a stroke?" he asked.

She smiled. "Is there a reason you didn't want to go into town?"

He glanced at her and sighed. "You saw the posters, didn't you?"

"Yeeeeahhh."

"You know that the people were all baraduhr, right?"

"I figured as much, but if they were, why would the queen be against it?"

He smiled bitterly. "Baraduhr wear masks for a reason. They don't want people to know. Humans die and people think someone killed them for fun."

"What, you didn't leave the masks on them?"

"They don't wear them all the time."

She held her creepy eye contact only a moment longer before returning her gaze to the trees.

"You don't have to travel with me," he reminded her.

"I know."

They rode for a day, avoiding another town, listening to the chopping of wood and falling of trees as townspeople sought growth, clearing land for farming and labour.

The night brought with it the red moon, turning the clouds pink, and all through the sky Chester and Veraion saw colours. They billowed thousands and thousands of miles away, galaxies shining with millions of stars: a sight that only azheeks could see, for every star was an ancestor. Humans were so far from the magic of the past, from their ancestors, and farthest yet from the gods. They didn't care about the Sun, the Moon, or Mother Nature, and their lack of care wasn't without reason. There was no use worshipping gods that couldn't see you.

Chester leaned against a tree, standing as she watched the night's sky, smiling to herself. She could never get tired of looking at the sky, at every tiny star she knew was a distant piece of herself, watching over her.

Veraion followed her gaze. He had once felt like she did now, and he hoped that young peacefulness would never leave her.

The skin crawled on the back of his neck and he rose to his feet, grabbing the horses' reins as he stared into the dark wood.

"*Shit*," he said. Chester glanced at him.

"You okay?"

"Wasfought," he said. "Tell me it's yours."

The horses whinnied, snorting fearfully, and Veraion murmured lowly, doing what he could to provide comfort.

Chester took a few steps back and followed his gaze, staring through the trees, and as she filled her pupils with fire, seeing through the darkness, she saw the beast.

With the snout of a wolf and the skull of a lion, its head was massive. A male, shown by the mane that grew from the top of its head, down its shoulders, and to its chest. The wasfought's bristles raised, smelling the horses, tantalized by fresh meat.

Muscle. Pure muscle. If the gods had blessed azheeks with strength, speed, and healing, then someone stronger had blessed the wasfoughts.

The beast moved forward and every gargantuan muscle rippled.

Standing in the woods, it was taller than any wolf, and Chester knew from having her own beast as a friend that should this creature rise to its hind legs, it would stand seven feet tall. But this was not her friend.

The beast had brown fur with black markings across its face and body as though painted for war, a trait every wasfought had. Its eyes were golden, fixed on Chester as she stood forward.

"Tell me that's yours," Veraion said, glancing between the beast and the woman.

"He's not." She spoke with no trace of fear. Veraion stared at her and she raised her arms, blooming flames upon her hands. She sent them down her skin, making them as big as possible, showing the beast very clearly what powers she possessed.

"We're azheeks," she said loudly. "Don't bother."

Veraion's eyes were wide, flicking between her and the war machine through the trees, and as he stared, the beast met his gaze. The forest wasfought looked him up and down before returning its attention to Chester. She gave it a look as though to say, *I'm not lying.*

It turned and walked away, disappearing into the night. Just like that.

Veraion stared at her as she snuffed out the flames, looking at him with a smile.

"They can't eat us—you know that, right?" she said. "We'd turn back into our element. There's no point and they know that. I'd burn the poor thing from the inside out."

"You just talked to a fucking wasfought."

"They're smart," she said simply, taking a seat at the foot of a tree. "You people just don't give them the credit."

"They're pack animals—that thing might come back with more."

"That *thing* will tell the others we're azheeks. Relax, Raion. Climb a tree if it'll make you feel better."

He glared at her. "Have you no fear?"

"Oh, I fear lots of things. Just not wasfoughts."

He shook his head and released the reins he had been clinging to. He flexed his hands. His grip had been so tight, his knuckles ached.

"Stay close," he murmured to the horses. "Stay by Chester. She'll keep you safe."

She snorted.

He sat at the base of a nearby tree, settling into the earth, and let out a soft sigh. She glanced at him and smiled.

"A wasfought tamer and a horse whisperer walk into a bar."

"Ouch."

She laughed, and every time she snorted, he couldn't help but smile.

* * *

The blood moon made way for the sun, and as the sky filled with light, the billowing colours of night changed to a blanket of pale blue. Still, as the azheeks rose, they could see stars here and there.

They continued on their way, their horses walking steadily as Veraion guided them north, trusting his instincts more than the compass he carried.

Into the day they rode, plucking, collecting, and eating fruits as they passed by apple trees, offering the same treats to their steeds.

To sun-high, to the afternoon, and into the evening. They talked here and there but the man was usually quiet, more jaded and less eager to share his life story, but Chester didn't mind. She was happy to be above ground, heading for the capital, waiting for her wasfought to catch up.

The hairs on the back of Veraion's neck rose, his skin crawling as he sensed something—something big. Something was moving towards them. Fast.

He glanced over his shoulder, staring through the trees in fear.

"What is it?" Chester said.

"Wasfought."

"They won't—"

"*Go!*" he yelled, and the mares burst into a gallop.

Chester grabbed the reins and stared around in confusion, searching for the beast. Veraion's eyes were fixed on the trees in desperation, clear panic on his usually calm face. Then she heard it. A deafening roar.

Chester's eyes widened as she looked over her shoulder to see a massive wasfought charging at them: a beast of white, grey, and black. A beast with claws extended and teeth bared.

It leapt off the ground and soared through the air, grabbing Veraion by the shoulder, ripping him from his horse.

Beast and man went crashing through the woods, and Chester yanked back on her reins, falling from her mare as it reared. She landed painfully but didn't spare a moment. She could hear yelling, roaring, and the grisly sound of flesh tearing.

Chester tore towards the fray, flames bursting from her arms, and threw herself into the mass of beast, man, and blood. Both wasfought and azheek yelled in pain, shying away from her fire.

Chester turned to the beast, her pupils glowing bright orange. "Aven! *No.*"

Aven was gigantic. His fur was white, getting darker down his limbs until black at his great paws, claws extended. His mane was tipped with black fur, the bristles down his spine equally as dark. Around his eyes were menacing markings, like warpaint, and in the sockets only one eye remained, an eye of piercing ice blue. Scars scored across his face and body—marks from blade and beast—his snout a mess of scratches, lip permanently fixed in a snarl.

Veraion was bleeding profusely. His face, arms, and chest were shredded from the brief seconds of war, and as he winced, gripping his ribs, Chester knew that at least a few of them had broken on impact. His left cheek was hanging from his face.

One of Veraion's machetes was embedded in Aven's shoulder, but the beast growled, giving his body a shake. The blade fell to the ground with a useless *clink*.

Chester snuffed out her flames with an angry huff. Still, Aven looked past her, glaring at Veraion. The man returned the beast's stare, eyes wide with terror.

"Aven," Chester warned. "Veraion is a friend."

Aven shook his head, his great mane swaying as he moved. He took a step forward and Veraion pulled himself back. Chester raised a hand, flames glowing beneath her skin.

"Aven! *Stop.*"

"Where the fuck did you *get* that thing?" Veraion stared. "That is no common wasfought! The colour of his fur, his mane, his eyes—you cannot tell me you've seen another wasfought like that."

She looked at him over her shoulder.

"That thing comes from the north!" Veraion gasped.

Then came a deep, monstrous growl. Words that were barely human.

"*Stop. Talking.*"

Chester's eyes widened, and she turned in horror to face the voice.

Wasfoughts don't talk.

Aven rose to his hind legs, the beast standing seven feet in the air. Sickening sounds came from inside his gargantuan body: the sounds of bones breaking. His snout shrank back in uneven jolts, limbs lengthening in crunches, transforming to the limbs of a man. His fur shrank to wild body hair, mane shifting to become a thick head of white, grey, and black locks.

With each breath, Aven's stomach pulled in to reveal defined hunks of muscle. With each breath, a growl emitted from his gnarled lips.

"*natura's ma'ale, natur,*" Veraion swore under his breath, his eyes wide—horrified. Chester was as frozen as he was.

This was *impossible.*

The giant that stood before them appeared to be in his mid-thirties, with menacing black markings across his face that looked like warpaint. Only one ice-blue eye remained, and it was fixed on Veraion. His skin was pale as snow, fading to grey along his arms and legs until black at his hands and feet. His long hair was white, though it grew black in some places, and down his chest was a dark V, as though lining where a mane should have been. Thick hair covered his body, wild about his chest, thinning slightly over his stomach only to thicken again. The lower it grew, the more untamed it got, until it was wild between his legs.

The giant was covered in scars, and now, Veraion's blood. He strode forward, pushing Chester to the side, and though he hadn't pushed her hard, he sent her to the ground.

The man moved as though a stranger to his body, the use of his limbs awkward and uncontrolled—all the more unsettling as he advanced on the bleeding earth azheek. Veraion scrambled to grab for his weapons, but the mutant took him by the neck, raising him into the air.

"You hurt her," the giant growled. "I kill you."

Veraion could only stare at him with wide eyes, bleeding onto the giant's black hand. Then he was tossed aside as though weighing nothing.

The mutant turned for Chester and she pulled herself away, arms trembling. He walked towards her, awkward, like a newborn deer learning to walk. She wanted to back away but was frozen, and he took her by the shoulders, picking her up, placing her back on her feet. While he was trying to be gentle, he wasn't. He was not used to this body.

Chester swayed in place, staring up at him.

"Are you okay?" he asked. A low rumble sounded from his throat with every word. She said nothing. "Chester," he pressed.

She swallowed the knot in her throat. "Aven?"

He nodded.

"What the fuck…" She pulled away, taking a step back, staring at him in shock. He clenched his jaw, watching her fearfully.

"Have you…" she said. "Have you always been able to do this?"

"Do what?"

"This." She gestured at his human body.

"No."

She remained still. Frozen. Horrified.

"As soon as I realized you were gone, I followed," the mutant said. "But the rain masked your path, and then I came across an old woman and she gave me blood and now I can do this."

"*What?*"

"I don't know—she asked me to drink it, said it was time, something about brothers. I don't know."

Chester blinked at him, eyes wide. Then came Veraion's weak voice.

"An elder with the power to turn you into a human gave you a prophecy, and all you can remember is *something about brothers?*"

"Shut your mouth," Aven snarled.

"How do you know how to talk?" Chester stared.

"I've always talked. You… you reply. All the time."

"I mean, I understand you, mostly, but you're—you're speaking Common."

"All wasfoughts speak this language, it just comes out different. We understand every word you say."

"I… yeah…"

Chester stared at him a while more, taking another step away. Behind her, Veraion grasped a tree and painfully hauled himself back to his feet.

"Can others… Do other wasfoughts do this?" she asked.

"None that I know of. But I don't know how long this will last. Chester, I heard whispers in the village—this man, he's wanted by command of the queen."

"I know."

"You—you what?"

"I know."

"You *do?*"

"Yeah, Aven, it's fine."

"He killed twenty-seven people!"

She gave him a look. "You and I have both killed a *lot* more than that."

"But he's wanted *by command of the queen!*"

"They were all baraduhr," Veraion snapped.

Aven walked over, shoved his hand into Veraion's face, and sent him back to the ground.

"The queen wants him dead." Aven turned to Chester desperately. "The *queen.* Those people weren't baraduhr."

"They killed her," Veraion rasped.

"Chester's alive, you idiot."

"Not *her,* you idiot. The woman I loved."

Aven raised a fist but Chester grabbed his arm. Upon feeling her touch, he stopped.

"Four years ago the baraduhr hunted us down and killed her," Veraion said. "And for four years I have been hunting them. Before they took Ilia from me I had never killed a man. Now I have killed countless. The twenty-seven that I'm wanted for were men and women of status, but I promise you, they were not innocent."

Aven looked at Chester expectantly.

"We've killed more," she reminded him. He looked displeased.

"He's lying," Aven said. "We shouldn't trust him."

"Azheeks don't lie," she said.

"Well, they… they *can.*"

"It's… rare."

"We should go back to Foros," he said.

"I'm not going back to Foros."

"The elder told me to find you and protect you. You are safe in Foros."

"Not from Yrilim."

His face fell. "Yrilim hurt you?"

"No, I just—I'm not going back."

"Do you want me to kill him?"

She couldn't help but laugh slightly. "Killing isn't always the solution."

This answer genuinely confused him.

"I think I'm going to go to Sontar Ivel," she said. "I was waiting for you to… join us."

His face lit up. "You were?"

She smiled awkwardly, and yet almost fondly. As he stared at her, the seven-foot beast of a man looked so much like a puppy.

"Of course," she said, doing everything she could to still envision him as a wasfought. "You're my best friend—I'd never go anywhere without you."

Aven, human Aven, couldn't help but beam. Veraion watched them in utmost disbelief.

"What the fuck," he whispered to himself.

Aven kept his smile on Chester, lowering to his knees to be a little more at eye level with her. "Can I please kill him?"

"No," she said fondly.

There came a moment of silence. The giant stared up at Chester as though she was his lord and saviour; meanwhile she was still trying to comprehend what on Ianar was happening. Still, she was genuinely touched by the way he looked at her. Veraion glanced between the two with wide eyes.

"*aishida*," he murmured.

"You used to tell me all the time you wished you could talk to me, to really talk to me," Aven said, almost hurt at her clear discomfort with his new appearance.

"I did…"

"Maybe… maybe the gods… made your wishes come true?"

"I mean, I…"

Aven watched her, swallowing the knot in his throat. Chester glanced at Veraion as he clutched at his face, fighting to keep his cheek in place.

"Aven, I'm going to help Veraion now. Don't try to stop me."

The giant's face fell, and he watched as she moved over to the man, helping him to his feet.

* * *

"*Fuck.*"

Veraion groaned through clenched teeth, trying not to move his face as Chester stitched it shut. He had retrieved a vial from his belongings, the last of his potions to help with pain, and drank the whole thing. But he still flinched every time she touched him. He wished dearly he had more.

He was seated at the base of a tree, one hand clutching his chest, holding some of his hanging flaps in place.

Behind Chester was a fire, illuminating the woods as the sun began to set. Near the flames was a small bowl, inside which a healing paste was warming. There was another dish of water close by, a rag draped over the edge. Their mares were grazing, reins tied to a tree to prevent them from bolting whenever Aven turned up.

"Will you stop moving?" Chester muttered irritably.

"My face is hanging off my face." Veraion glared. "You wouldn't be having fun if you were in my place, either."

He groaned as the needle went back through his skin. He squeezed his eyes shut, balling his fists, clutching to whatever he could reach.

"Fuck your pet," he muttered. She cast him a glare. Aven had gone hunting, leaving Veraion free to insult him in his absence.

"He's not a pet," she said. "He's allowed to do whatever he pleases."

"This is what he pleases," Veraion muttered, motioning at his face. "This was five seconds of what he pleases."

"Then be grateful it wasn't longer than that. Hold tight."

She pushed the needle through his skin and he let out a muffled yell. He closed his eyes, gripping his pants as he tried to keep his breaths steady, doing everything he could to not shake as she finished stitching his face together.

"You believe in prophecies?" she asked quietly.

"Of course."

"Why?"

He looked at her. "What do you mean, why?"

"Have any ever come true?"

"Of course they have."

"In our lifetime?"

He didn't respond.

"You really think Aven was given a prophecy?" she continued.

"Something about brothers," he muttered. "I cannot believe that's all he took away from it."

"He's a wasfought," she said with a smirk. "Do you honestly expect him to care about prophecies?"

"Not anymore, he isn't."

The wasfought came through the trees. The horses whinnied, but Veraion raised a hand.

"It's okay," he said softly, wincing as pain shot through his arm. Still, his small gesture was enough to calm the horses until they were just snorting nervously.

Aven dragged his kill with him and brought his offering of a small boar to Chester. He sat down, wagging his tail, and she couldn't help but smile.

"Thank you," she said.

Veraion glared at Aven. Both he and the beast snarled, looking away from each other. Chester shook her head.

"You two," she muttered.

"He ripped my face off," Veraion reminded her. She glanced at Aven and couldn't help but notice the very satisfied gleam in his single eye.

"Alright, what's next?" Chester asked, creating a tiny flame to cut the thread. "Arm or chest?"

Veraion winced, looking down at his blood-soaked shirt. "Chest."

She nodded. Using a dagger to cut the last of his shredded clothes away, she gingerly peeled the sodden cloth from his skin. Veraion could swear the wasfought was smiling.

Veraion's necklace was bloodied, and as the cloth was removed, the pendant came free. A crystal with tiny lights wafting from it, and inside, a curious substance that looked like liquid light. It shone white.

As Chester peeled the sleeves from his arms he winced, and as she pulled the cloth from his chest, she saw a tattoo upon the top of his stomach: the old symbol for a compass.

"Look at this," Chester said, chucking his bloody rags aside. "You should be used to pain. That's not an easy spot to get tattooed."

"Tattoos are consensual pain," he muttered through gritted teeth. She chuckled.

Veraion closed his eyes, leaning his head back against the tree, fists balled as he tried to breathe as steadily as possible. Chester grimaced as she pulled his skin back into place. Aven watched every second of it, never looking away as she stitched Veraion back together. The wasfought enjoyed every wince and groan that came from the man.

"Where's the tattoo from?" Chester asked

Veraion's eyes were closed, his breaths weak. He didn't answer.

Once all of the wounds were stitched shut, Chester took the rag from the bowl of water, wringing out the excess, and wiped away the rest of his blood. When he was mostly clean, she smeared the healing paste over his new stitches. He groaned.

"I'm sorry about all this," she said. "It's only right I tend to your wounds."

Aven huffed.

"Veraion saved me from baraduhr." She gave him a curt look. "And tended to my wounds. He could have taken my weapon and walked away. Kara'i steel is priceless."

He huffed again.

"You're lucky he's an azheek," she said. "A human would have died from this."

Aven snorted as though to repeat the word *lucky* with disdain.

"If not the shock of the initial injury," she said, "I've seen some *nasty* infections. Once we get these shut, we won't have to worry about anything else. Just tearing. So for a while, Aven, we're going to take care of Veraion."

The beast rolled his eye and trotted off to mark the area his territory.

Veraion took in a deep breath, the exhale sounding like a heavy sigh. He shifted in place, groaning loudly. A hand returned to his ribs.

"Are they broken?" Chester asked. He nodded. "Do I need to… reset them?"

They shared a very uncomfortable look.

He grimaced. "I'll be fine."

She started wrapping his chest and arms with spare cloth.

"One of the perks of being an earth azheek," he said. "I heal faster than most. They'll be fine by the time I get to Sontar Ivel."

"I notice a lack of 'we'."

"You really think your dog is going to want to come?"

"That's one big fucking dog."

"Same shit."

"Not even slightly."

"I'll make my way at sunrise," he said. "You don't have to come."

"Are you uninviting me?"

"Technically I never invited you to begin with."

She yanked on the gauze, tying an uncomfortably tight knot. He swore loudly, casting her a glare.

She smiled. "But I'm such great company."

He glared dryly as she finished her work then moved to the boar. He couldn't do much but watch as she prepared it, and when Aven returned just in time to eat the guts, he had to look away.

There came the horrid sounds of Aven's breaking bones, and he glanced back to watch the beast's snout shortening in jolts until a giant, naked man sat in his place.

"Heart, please," Aven said. Chester dug a hand into the boar and cut the organ free, handing it to the giant. She was so used to feeding him bloody carcasses, it took her a moment to realize she had just put it in his human hand. She glanced at him before busying herself with her work.

Aven sat back, fixing his single eye on Veraion, and ate the heart. Blood dripped down his beard and neck, and not once did he break eye contact. Veraion grimaced and turned away.

Chester cooked and they ate in silence. Aven returned to his original form, preferring his wasfought jaws, and the azheeks said nothing, listening to the crackle of flames and song of crickets around them.

When their bellies were full and eyelids drooped, Chester lay by the fire while Veraion stayed in his place, trying to remain as still as possible.

Chester gazed through the forest canopy, at the millions of stars and billowing colours of the night sky. The red moon was full tonight, and she smiled to herself, turning to look at the wasfought beside her. Aven tipped his head back, a long, lilting howl sounding from his black lips. It sang through the trees, and soon he was joined by other wasfoughts. Their howls were distant and echoing, eerie but beautiful—a pack, somewhere far off in the woods.

Chester's smile was fond as she watched the beast. Whenever his howl ended and started anew it was always hoarse, like a singing roar, until it peaked and became a steady cry.

She returned her gaze to the sky. Nights were always tinged a little bit pink in the light of the blood moon.

"Curious," she said. "Azheeks love the gods, and yet, it seems only wasfoughts worship the Moon. Azheeks think of Mother Nature and the Sun, but never the Moon."

Veraion was too weary to say anything.

When the ringing of wasfought calls drew to a close, the beast flopped onto his back, paws sticking up as he stargazed with Chester.

"Aven?"

A low grumble came from his throat.

"What happened?" she asked. "To get this ability. You said something about a woman?"

Then came the loud crunching as his body changed. He was still beside her, and she kept her gaze on the sky, knowing that if she looked at him it would only make her uncomfortable and, in turn, make him sad.

"An old woman," he said. "I thought she was from Foros, but her accent was different."

"An earth azheek?"

"An *old* earth azheek."

"And… you drank her blood?"

"Not her blood, someone else's. In a vial."

"Because that makes it less weird," Veraion muttered.

"We're not talking to you," Aven snapped. Chester snorted.

"What did she say? Blood of the brother? You have a brother?"

He shrugged. "I don't know."

"Gods, you really are a wasfought," Veraion said. Aven glared at him. After a moment the giant returned his gaze to the stars.

"What do you see up there?" Chester asked.

"Black," he said.

"Just black?"

"There are stars too, and the moon, and her blood light, but mostly it's just black."

"Hmm."

"What do you see?"

She smiled. "Thousands of stars. Millions, maybe. Swirling colours of purple and blue."

"Azheeks see more in the sky," Veraion said from his place. "Every star is an ancestor's spirit."

"Nobody asked your opinion," Aven snapped. Chester snorted again.

The giant turned his head to look at her, beaming upon seeing her smile. She glanced at him, uncomfortable, and his face fell.

"I'm just not used to this yet," she said kindly, making a point to hold his gaze. "It might… take a while."

His skull shifted with loud cracks, his body morphing until he was once more a wasfought, and she smiled, laughing softly as he shuffled forward and nuzzled his giant head into her arms.

Aven let out a long sigh that almost sounded like a whimper. She looked down at him and found him watching her, as though afraid to close his eye. She placed a soft kiss upon his forehead.

"Go to sleep, Little One. I'll be here when you wake up."

Only then did Aven allow himself to curl into her more, nodding off. Every exhale brought with it a low grumble from deep in his chest, like a purr as he breathed in her familiar scent. Chester ran her fingers through his thick fur, and when she glanced up at Veraion, she found him with a raised eyebrow.

"*Little One?*" he mouthed silently.

"*He was*," she replied just as quietly. "*Once.*"

Her gaze rested on Aven's giant form, fingers tracing his scars. Veraion shook his head in disbelief, letting out a long sigh as he shifted, trying to find a position that didn't throb.

He was unsuccessful.

CHAPTER 2
THE STALLION

Sunrise brought with it the loud groans of Veraion slowly getting to his feet as Chester gathered their things, tying bags to horses. She glanced at him as he got up, the skin around his broken ribs severely bruised, but as he turned his back on her, she only stared more.

His entire back was tattooed, marked with a tiger and flowing maple leaves surrounded by thick black bars. The piece was huge, continuing into his pants, where even his butt had been marked. But the work was old and unfinished as though forgotten—as though part of a life left behind.

He picked up his shredded vest and gingerly wrapped what remained of it around his body, but it was just as damaged as he was. She glanced at him and tried to suppress her laughter, but it was no use. Half of his chest was hanging out.

"Great," he muttered. "I have a nipple on full display."

"Be glad you still *have* a nipple," she laughed. "I'll find you some clothes at the next town."

Veraion slowly strapped his weapons in place. When Aven appeared through the trees, his body shifting until he was a seven-foot man, Veraion smiled bitterly. "Get him some clothes too."

With a series of curses, Veraion got a foot in one of his stirrups. Chester hurried over, providing support as he clambered onto the horse, his crude slurs never ceasing until he was finally in the saddle.

"*natura's ma'ale, natur,*" he swore with a wince. "*Fuck.*"

Chester smiled at him apologetically, glancing at Aven as she mounted her mare.

"Keep a little distance," Veraion said to Aven bitterly. "You'll spook the horses."

The giant turned away, mocking the man as he went.

With a single command from the earth azheek, the horses started at a trot. Veraion cursed loudly with every bounce, but he gritted his teeth and kept going until they were at a canter, glaring through the trees at the wasfought that ran beside them.

They rode for the day, and while Veraion wanted to keep going, the ungodly throbbing of his wounds forced him to stop and rest. But the moment the sun rose once more, he was back on his horse, clenching his jaw through the pain.

Halfway through the second day, the trio reached a town. Veraion waited in the outer woods as Chester headed in, followed by a seven-foot giant who at least now wore a loincloth. All eyes turned to Aven as they moved through the village.

Chester was quick to find a clothes vendor, searching for a shirt and vest that might fit Veraion. Aven rummaged through the piles of clothing, fishing out a sacrilegious excuse for a blouse. It had far too many frills and just as many colours and he held it up with a grin.

"We should get him this."

Chester took one look at it and burst out laughing. Aven chuckled, gazing over the monstrosity.

"Can you imagine him in that?" Chester laughed. "My gods."

"Please can we make him wear it?"

"I would if we had coin to spare, but we don't."

"He'll have to wear it if it's the only thing we buy."

She took the shirt from him, shaking her head, though she was still stifling her snorts.

"He'd just continue having one tit out, you know that. This one, please!" She turned to the old vendor, holding up a plain white shirt with loose sleeves, similar to the one Veraion had been wearing prior to his assault. Chester continued rummaging until she found a vest similar to the old one, but it was loose, a good choice until his wounds were healed. She passed it to the salesman.

"Do you need anything?" the human asked, beady eyes on Aven.

"I'm good," he said.

"You... sure?" The vendor glanced at his loincloth. Aven followed his stare.

"I don't even like wearing *this* thing."

"Do you have anything his size?" Chester asked.

"Well... not quite," the old man admitted.

"Anything close? A large tunic, perhaps?"

"Let me check." He disappeared behind a mound of clothes and Aven turned to Chester with a pout.

"Why?"

"Have you noticed all the stares? If you want to continue coming into town with me, you're going to have to look a little less... naked."

"I could just be a wasfou—"

Chester whacked him on the arm with wide eyes. He let out a frustrated sigh.

"Fine."

Then the old man reappeared with a giant tunic and a large pair of pants.

"I'm tall, not wide," Aven said.

"Good enough." Chester nodded. "We'll take those, too."

She gave the human his coin and took the clothes, casting him one last smile before heading back through town. Aven stayed close behind, glancing at those staring. He did his best to smile and nod, and Chester watched him over her shoulder. He looked terrifying. She walked into a man.

"I'm sorry—"

Aven grabbed the human by the shoulder, raising a fist to cave his skull in.

"*Aven!*" Chester exclaimed, dropping the clothes as she yanked his arm back.

"Watch where you're going," Aven snarled at the man. The poor human's eyes looked like they were about to pop out of his head.

"It wasn't his fault!" Chester insisted, fighting to pull Aven's fist down. "Aven!"

"He hit you!"

"No, he didn't!"

Finally he dropped his fist.

"I'm so sorry," Chester said, prying Aven's other hand away. "I'm so sorry."

She grabbed the clothes off the floor, taking Aven by the wrist, hauling him away from the village square. The giant let her, but he held his glare, using two fingers to point at his eye before aggressively pointing them at the stunned man. The human stood in place, staring after the odd duo until they disappeared into the woods.

Once they were far enough, Chester turned to the giant.

"*Aven*," she said. "You can't just attack people for bumping into me, and I was the one that bumped into him, okay?"

"But—"

"*No.*"

He pouted, grumbling his way through the trees.

When they reached Veraion, Chester helped him out of his old rags and into his new attire, never once asking about the tattoos he so clearly didn't want to talk about.

Aven shoved his clothes into Chester's bag, turning back into a wasfought.

* * *

North they rode, on and on, losing count of the days. They stopped at night, allowing time for food and rest, but the moment the sun rose, they would be back on their journey. They would hunt at night, and if Veraion caught a rabbit, Aven would be sure to catch a deer. If Veraion foraged a handful of fruit, Aven would bring Chester the whole damn bush, roots and all.

Whenever they reached a town, Chester wandered in to explore, picking up whatever rations were needed. Sometimes Aven came, but even in clothes he stood out like a sore thumb. If anything, putting him in clothes only made him all the more awkward, as he walked like a newborn deer forced into boots with pants riding up its ass.

On occasion, when Veraion needed something specific for his wounds, he joined Chester instead, hood always pulled low, leaving Aven to stay with the horses, much to their dismay.

On this day, Chester headed into town with her giant companion clothed and clomping around in uncomfortable boots. They followed the sounds of music to the village square, enjoying the sights and smells along the way. When they reached the marketplace, they found a festival. Garlands hung from shop fronts, music resonating through the streets, and people danced freely.

The two gazed around curiously, smiling as they watched the townsfolk. There were lots of animals too, grazing in pens.

Aven moved forward with an excited smile, and when he saw a pen of bunnies, he gasped. Chester followed with a fond laugh. A woman was standing by the rabbits, overseeing the children petting them, their parents nearby.

"Can I petf them?" Aven's eyes were wide.

Chester glanced at the woman. She seemed unsure, confused, but was too distracted by how massive he was to say no. Aven crouched down, carefully reaching over the fence, and stroked a rabbit with a single finger. When it didn't run away, joy spread across his face.

"Oh my god," he whispered. "Ohmygodohmygod—Chester, I'm petting a rabbit."

She pursed her lips, trying to fight her smile, but it spread from ear to ear.

"Animals always run away from me," he murmured, gently picking the rabbit up, and as he held it in his arms, tears welled in his eye.

"Aven, are you... crying?" Chester said. He looked at her, and a tear slid down his cheek.

"It's so *cute*," he choked. Chester laughed, crouching to join him, and as he snivelled, staring at the bunny, it was him she had her eyes on. She was trying to not cry over how cute *he* was.

Aven raised the rabbit to his face, and she instantly went to take it from him, but he didn't chomp down on it. Instead, he snuggled his cheek into its fluff.

"So *soffffffft*," he whispered.

Chester smiled and rose to her feet, patting him on the head. She looked over to the petting zoo vendor.

"Thank you," she said quietly. The vendor smiled and nodded, endeared by the giant.

Hours they spent at the fair. Aven played with all the animals he had never before gotten to play with: mice, rats, chickens, roosters, lambs, pigs, sheep, and horses.

When they reached the larger animals, Aven looked back to the rabbit pen wishfully, but when Chester stopped and he bumped into her, he followed her gaze.

"Whoa," they murmured.

A great black stallion. The draught horse was eating lazily out of a trough, ignoring all the eyes that stared.

"Holy shit," he said.

"That is a big fucking horse," she agreed.

"Reckon it could carry me?"

Chester looked to Aven with a mischievous gleam in her eye.

* * *

"We need your help," Chester said, jogging towards Veraion.

"With what?"

"Stealing a horse."

He turned a dry expression her way. "What?"

"We can't afford it, so…"

"Why do you need this horse?"

"It's gigantic. Could even carry Aven's weight, I bet."

Aven grinned, casting the man a thumbs-up.

"What makes you think I could help?" Veraion said. "I'm crippled."

"Come on, you wouldn't have to do much," Chester pressed. "Animals love you. You barely have to say anything and the horses already know what to do."

"You get me a noble steed," Aven said, "and I promise I won't attack you. For at least a month. *Maybe* two."

Veraion glared between the two. "Why do you even want a horse? You barely like wearing clothes. Do you realize how much you'll hate sitting in a saddle? Can't you just run?"

"If you want me to blend in then help me blend in."

"He'll have to learn eventually," Chester said. "A horse smaller than this won't be able to take his weight."

Veraion gave her a dry look. "That horse might be someone's favourite companion. Or a way of life."

Both Chester and Aven gave him puppy-dog eyes, and he grimaced.

"No."

They didn't stop.

"*No.*"

They got closer.

"Fucking *Valduhr*—if I agree, will you stop looking at me like that?"

They nodded.

"*Fine.*"

Chester and Aven raised their arms victoriously, high-fiving. But she immediately regretted it and shook out her hand, clutching her elbow from the force of the collision.

Her arm still stung by the time the sun set.

* * *

Music rang in the night. Aven wandered back into town wearing only a loincloth. He meandered through the shadows and found his way to the square, glancing over at the stallion every now and then. It was easy for him to see over the crowd.

He smiled and nodded to those that passed by, staring up at him, but always returned his gaze to the horse's pen. Occasionally the rabbits, but mostly the stallion.

Then he saw a shadow slinking between the cottages. The cloaked man saw Aven over the crowd and nodded.

Quickly Aven ducked behind a house, ensuring nobody could see him, and morphed into a wasfought.

With a deafening roar, he tore into the marketplace.

Screams erupted and the fair was thrown into mayhem. People ran as fast as they could, away from the beast that raced through the crowd, creating as much fear and frenzy as possible.

Veraion took his cue and ran to the stallion's pen. The poor creature was whinnying in fear, but he opened the gate, raising a hand.

"It's okay," he said. He placed his hand upon the horse's neck. "*tama iris byan.*"

The horse was calm.

He took the reins and swung into the saddle with a pained yell, and with a single command and a light kick, the stallion took to the woods.

Aven roared, racing towards a large man that had drawn a sword. Instantly the brave warrior dropped his weapon and ran. The wasfought chuckled to himself, glancing over at the stallion's pen. It was gone.

Tipping back his head, he let out a victorious howl before turning on his heels, bolting from sight.

Aven raced through the woods, and soon he saw three horses galloping as fast as they could go, two of them with riders. Quickly he took his place beside them.

Veraion sat atop the great stallion, grinning over at Chester, and she laughed loudly, already at home in her mare's saddle.

Chester turned to find Aven zipping alongside them and their eyes locked, a wide smile fixed on her lips, a twinkle of laughter shining in his ice-blue eye.

CHAPTER 3

SONTAR IVEL

By the time the three reached Sontar Ivel, Aven had howled at a full moon two more times. He had learned how to properly ride a horse, had stopped complaining about wearing clothes, and even practiced with a sword a few times. He confirmed he hated it. More important still, Veraion's wounds had healed. His face, arms, chest, and ribs no longer hurt, even when Aven would poke him a little *too* hard.

Aven had stopped trying to kill Veraion, and while he continued to grumble about his company here and there, he had admitted defeat. Chester liked the man. And that was that.

They lost track of the days. Chester stopped counting after week eight, and though she was beginning to doubt they would ever reach the capital, she kept her worries to herself.

Landscapes changed along the way, forests to fields to pastures and villages, and always when they neared a place of humans, fallen trees, burnt ground, and an air to the woods as though hunted and cleared beyond what could be sustained. And yet, all that mattered was that they were above ground, heading north, riding to Sontar Ivel. That alone was enough to keep Chester content, and her content was enough for Aven. He did his best to remain gruff and stoic, but new sights, sounds, and smells were exciting, and unfortunately for him, in his original and preferred form, he had a tail that betrayed his will to look tough. It always informed the others exactly how excited he really was.

The sun was at its zenith as they rode, passing tree after tree, after tree. The air was filled with the familiar sound of their horses' hooves, scattering dirt and fallen leaves in their wake. But Veraion could feel a difference in the land. Something sweeter, richer. Something more magical.

He gazed to the sky and saw a falcon, an Eleonora's falcon, and he smiled. They were here.

The trees thinned and they saw it: the white walls of Sontar Ivel.

When they broke from the woods, their eyes widened. Even their horses slowed. The capital sat on top of a massive plateau. Its outer walls were tall, and though the country was as old as time, the great stones still sparkled in the sunlight. Trees grew from the walls, roots winding down the white rock, and rivers of water flowed down the sides, leading away from the capital and towards the sea.

In the air were floating pieces of land hosting temples and sacred chambers. Some hovered near the outer walls, but they could see more scattered across the sky, sending dancing shadows over the land below. Streams defied gravity and travelled up from the ground, through the middle of the hovering islands to pour from the edges and return to the ground. The smallest streams turned to mist in the air.

There were people gathered at the southern gates, for swarms flocked to Sontar Ivel every single day. Horses, carriages, and carts moved up and down the plateau, and Chester took in a deep breath, her gaze filled with excitement. She exchanged a look with Aven, and it was clear he was just as awestruck as she.

Veraion took in a deep breath and drew his hood. He urged his mare forward and the three rode for the gates. When they reached the crowd of people, they slowed their horses. Chester ensured her kara'i weapon was hidden, and Veraion pulled his hood even lower.

Chester and Aven stared up at the walls as they slowly inched closer and closer to the golden gates, heads tipping all the way back to gaze up at the massive trees that grew from the old, pristine stones. Cypress, olive, and evergreen cork oaks reached to the sky, their leaves brilliant green and swaying in the cool breeze. Flower petals floated through the air, and they listened to the lapping of water as rivers flowed nearby and streams glistened in the sky.

The air smelled so different—so clean, so sweet. It smelled as though they were close to the ocean despite being the farthest from it. They spotted herons, pelicans, and kingfishers that lived on fish, somehow thriving so far from the sea.

They rode through the city gates, and the instant they entered were met by vendors selling wares. Souvenirs, books, food, drinks, tapestries, paintings, carvings, sculptures, and personal services.

Azheeks and humans milled about, diverse and beautiful—a sea of colour. Earth azheeks with dark skin, thick hair, and green eyes, bodies strong and compact. Fire azheeks with hair like flaming coal, eyes like embers, and features just as sharp, their skin from tanned to brown. And air azheeks with sleek black hair and grey eyes, skin sun-kissed and bodies more lithe, streamlined, built to move through the skies with ease, and that they did, floating above to avoid crowded streets.

Chester and Aven stared around with wide eyes, never before having seen so many azheeks, let alone this many so integrated. They had known many earth azheeks in their time, and only one other of fire, and the giant's eye followed an air azheek as she floated by. He excitedly tapped Chester, pointing at the sight.

The two stared around with wide eyes as Veraion guided them into the new world, through the southern gate city. The locals here took advantage of foreigners and visitors that were far too lazy to make the journey into the main capital. There were small cities at every gate: north, south, east, and west.

Veraion guided them through the bustle, nodding politely to every vendor that thrust an item in his face, refusing as kindly as possible. Chester and Aven wanted nothing more than to accept every single offering, but everything came at a price they could not afford. So they followed Veraion and did as he did, nodding, smiling, and avoiding conflict.

When they had made it through the southern gate city, Veraion let out a sigh of relief and their horses hurried to a canter once more.

Past farms and fields growing wheat, corn, potatoes, rice, and sugar beets, they rode by forests and parks, gazing up at oleander, carob, and mastic trees that bloomed flowers and red seeds. The pink blooms of oleander, while poisonous to humans, would never harm an azheek.

They rode through Sontar Ivel's thick forests until they reached the walls of the main city, built of the same white stone that didn't seem to age. Everything was that same white stone. Clean, pristine. Beautiful.

Back in a bustle of merchants and vendors, Veraion pulled his hood lower.

Weaving through streets and wide roads, colour filled the air around them. Flowers grew from walls, wooden beams in place so flora could bloom in canopies above them, dappling sunlight across their skin. Brilliant purples, pinks, reds, oranges, yellows, and white danced among the vibrant greens.

Plants grew from walls as though the rock were fertile earth, and water flowed all through the city to provide fresh, clean drink for those that lived there. Some of the walls held rivers themselves, the parapets vast pools that people could swim in, and many did, floating along, basking in the radiant sun, allowing every inch of their skin to be caressed by the great god.

There were goats climbing walls, ibex and chamois. Lizards, salamanders, and Veraion could sense tiny dormice scurrying in the shadows. Aven spotted a bright yellow bird, a golden oriole, and his single eye zipped around as a colourful bee-eater flew by.

He and Chester couldn't close their gaping mouths.

The air was sweet with ever-blooming flowers: lilies, bougainvillea, and rosemary, made better still by ripe fruit all around the city, fruit so ripe the three didn't just smell it. They could taste it. Apples, oranges, pears, peaches, clementines, melons, and grapefruits, and as they rode beneath a canopy of bright yellow lemons, Chester stared up with an awestruck smile.

There were cafes and restaurants everywhere. On walls to overlook the streets and tucked into cliffs to overlook magical turquoise water. Lanterns and candles were blooming to life as the sun inched closer to the horizon.

They moved further and further into the capital, closer and closer to the castle of Sontar Ivel. The castle built by the gods to be home to the Five— the castle that had been the birthplace of their first Ianar-born queen.

The palace grew larger and larger, and the closer they got, the more they could feel it.

Raw, emanating power.

The castle stood in the centre of Sontar Ivel, on a piece of land connected to the rest of the city in the north and south. To the east and west, it was surrounded by water.

The walls were white, as untouched and pristine as every other building in the capital. Turrets rose high into the sky, sparkling in the sunlight, and open windows and archways allowed fresh air to flow through the palace. Water poured down the walls, breaking over turrets and towers to fall in streams to the rivers below.

The castle was still far away, but they could feel its magic so strongly.

Aven was so enthralled he didn't notice people staring at him.

The giant sat atop his great black stallion, menacing markings a permanent feature upon his face towering over everyone else, and yet, the wonder and awe in his single eye were enough to make him look like a puppy. At least, he looked like a puppy to Chester.

Stray cats and dogs trotted around the city, chasing one another, playing. They all looked well fed, taken care of by the city's people.

As the sun began to set, the riders came to a halt.

Veraion dismounted his mare, giving Chester a nod, and headed for a rickety door built into a city wall. Above the door hung a sign. *Five's Inn.*

"Wait here," he said before disappearing inside.

Chester slid down from her horse, and as Aven came from his, the stallion snorted in relief. Aven looked at the sign.

"F… I… Fi… Five's…"

"You can read?" Chester stared.

"It's been a while—they don't have many signs in Foros. Five's—Five's Inn?" He glanced at Chester to find her watching him in disbelief, both stunned and proud.

"You're the one that taught me how to read," he reminded her.

"What?"

"Remember? You used to read me books, telling me what every letter was. You taught me."

She looked like she was about to cry.

"Are you okay?" He stared. "Is it Veraion? I can kill him."

She laughed. "*Aven.*"

He shrugged. "Was worth a shot."

"You still hate him?"

"Always."

She snorted and shook her head. He was trying so hard to keep the act up.

"Why do you like him?" he said.

"I don't know." She spoke truthfully, fondly. "He's nice. He makes me laugh. He's moody and mysterious, and never opens up, but I feel like… I feel like we're the first friends he's had in a long time."

"Loser."

Chester laughed.

"Do you love him?" Aven asked. She chuckled.

"No."

"Yrilim?"

Her smile faded.

"Do you want me to kill him?" he said. "I'll run all the way back to Foros and kill him."

Chester laughed once more. He beamed. He liked making her laugh.

"You know that wouldn't do anything," she said. "He's my ilis. I'm bound to him for eternity."

"Even if I kill him?"

"Even after death, I'll be bound to him." She leaned her head against his arm, far too short to reach his shoulder. "You know how azheeks are—death isn't really *death*. We go on to Savai, the next world. Even if he dies, I'll still feel him—he'll still be alive, he'll just be... there. And when I die, I'll be right there with him."

Aven smiled sadly. "I'm not an azheek. I won't be there with you."

Chester's throat tightened. She knew this, and though she tried not to think about it, it was the truth. She wrapped her arms around him, as best as she could reach.

"I don't want to think about that," she said.

"Are you crying?"

"Shut up."

Aven squeezed her tight. "You can still love other people, right?"

"Of course," she murmured. "Azheeks can love many, but the *ilis*, that's... How would you even say it in Common? A soulmate?"

"Are they always romantic?"

"No, many are platonic. And most that might begin as romantic usually end up platonic, too."

"Is yours? Romantic?"

"I... I don't know."

He nodded.

They gazed at the colourful sky, watching the sun set. Purple, pink, orange, and yellow—clouds illuminated by the setting sun. Flowers bloomed all around them, the air crisp and sweet, and as they stood there, they could hear music. Someone somewhere was playing a guitar, fingers dancing over every string with ease. They could hear birds calling to one another, but they had no idea what kind of birds these were. Everything was so new, so different.

Aven's voice came as a whisper. "I can still kill him."

Chester laughed. "You've talked to wasfoughts, right? You've met some on our hunts and travels."

He nodded.

"Are they as smart as I think they are?"

He nodded.

"I mean… I know I tried teaching you how to read," she said. "But it never occurred to me that I actually *taught* you how to read. Do they know that people use their bones as weapons? Clubs and such. At least, whenever people can find their bones."

He nodded.

"How do they feel about that?"

"Some like it, some hate it. Personally, I like it. It's nice to know that even after death I can still be caving skulls in."

She laughed. "And the others? Is it true that there are wasfought graveyards? A place they go to die so nobody can find their bones?"

"From what I have gathered, yes."

"Do you know where it is?"

"North, somewhere." He shrugged. "North enough so no one else can get there. People can't survive the harsh temperatures, so the wasfoughts go there."

She nodded. "The further you get from Sontar Ivel, the more inhabitable the world is. The north is freezing and the south, burning. Too far east or west, I hear nothing grows."

Aven leaned over to the wall and plucked a bushel of pink flowers from its place, a look of excitement on his face. "This will grow back, right?"

"That's what I've heard."

Their smiles spread and Aven tucked the flowers behind Chester's ear, plucking another bushel and placing it behind his own.

Veraion emerged from the inn doors followed by a man: tall, slender, with sun-kissed skin and eyes twinkling like aquamarines. His face was angular, with defined cheekbones and a pointed nose, but the features were softer, more feminine. Pale blond hair fell down his back in loose waves, some of it braided to keep from falling in his face. Markings lined his skin, like patterns had been neatly cut into place, winding all over his body. The markings of Old.

Chester's eyes widened and she nudged Aven. "He's a water azheek," she whispered. He stared.

All water azheeks were born with these marks, every pattern unique, but his did not glow or glimmer as Chester had been taught they did.

He looked to be in his late twenties or thirties, just past his prime. He was bound to someone.

"We have a room with three beds," Veraion said. "Theideus will take the horses to the stables."

Theideus wore common clothes, and even though his markings did not glow, he still looked regal.

He stared up at Aven in alarm but pulled his gaze away to be polite.

Standing aside, he waited quietly as the travellers pulled their bags from the horses. They fondly petted their steeds before Theideus started guiding the animals away, but Veraion's mare stood rooted in her place. He chuckled and clicked his tongue, nodding for her to follow the man. Only then did she do so.

Veraion entered the inn, heading down a set of steps leading underground. They could hear voices from inside, and with the door open, the bustle grew louder. Aven followed, but he forgot to duck and walked face-first into the doorway. Chester gasped in concern. Veraion snorted.

Aven rubbed his nose in irritation as he shuffled down the stairwell, bending in order to fit, and the further down the steps they moved, the louder the merriment grew.

Five's Inn was built into the city walls, running underground, and the lower they got, the louder they heard a bustling tavern. Talk and laughter boomed from inside.

"This is one of the original inns of Sontar Ivel," Veraion said. "Hence it being part of the walls."

"Is it true that there's secret tunnels running all through the city?" Chester said. "Underground too?"

"So I've heard, yes."

"I wonder where they'd take you, if you found them."

"They were built to help people escape if need be. This whole city was built to protect azheeks, to protect the Five."

"From what?" Aven muttered, rubbing his face.

"I don't know. Whatever it was, whoever, they succeeded anyway. Only Aishida survived. The Five were all gone, but at least Natura's bloodline continued."

At the bottom of the steps was an entrance room where an old innkeeper was waiting. He was an air azheek, hair tied back in a bun and moustache long and greying. His eyes were a blue-grey, kind and welcoming, turning to half-moons as he smiled. His robes were loose about the sleeves and flowing at his ankles, a sash wrapped about his round belly. The fabric he wore was intricately embroidered.

On the ground beside him sat a dog. Its fur was shaggy, marbled with various shades of brown and tan, darker along its back and paler about its belly. It had large, upturned ears and a blackened snout, and it wagged its tail upon sensing Veraion's earthly energy.

Veraion sniffed curiously, glancing around, smelling a trace of something he recognized but couldn't quite place. Pungent, distinctive. Bitter. It was subtle enough that neither Chester nor Aven picked up on it, for they were too busy inhaling the smell of food wafting from the tavern.

The dog trotted towards Veraion, poking his hand with its nose, and he smiled, lowering to a knee to give the creature a proper pat.

Then it saw Aven and backed away. It was confused, scared. It could feel that Aven was a wasfought, but it could see that he wasn't. Veraion glanced between the giant and the dog.

"What?" Aven said to it as though speaking to a human.

"Sorry," the innkeeper said, coaxing the dog back. "She's normally really friendly."

Aven thinned his eye at the dog as though testing her. *Your move.*

The dog thinned her eyes at him. *Freak.*

"Welcome to Five's Inn," the innkeeper said with a smile. "My name is Tao. I believe you've already met Theideus. We have space for you in room fourteen." He handed Veraion a set of keys. "Would you like me to show you?"

"Thank you, Tao." Veraion smiled. "But that's okay, we'll find our way."

"What's her name?" Chester asked, offering a hand to the dog, and she sniffed it before begging for pets just as she had done with Veraion.

"Oh…" Tao blinked. "We… call her Dog."

"Your dog is called Dog?" Chester laughed.

"I met her one day on the street. Petted her, gave her some food. She followed me here and has been here ever since. We all call her Dog. She responds to it well."

Chester smiled, giving Dog more love than Aven appreciated. He watched them with jealousy seething in his eyes. Veraion noticed this and bit back a very amused smile.

"Room fourteen?" he asked. Tao nodded and pointed at a door. Aven went for it, wrapping his hand around the doorknob. He tore the wood from its hinges. Dog jumped and cowered from the sound, hiding behind Tao's legs. Aven blinked at the planks in his hand.

Tao's eyes widened, but he didn't look angry. He looked stunned, but impressed. Almost *amused.*

"I'm so sorry," Chester gasped, wide eyes turning to the innkeeper.

"We'll… pay for that." Veraion ushered Chester forth, and she cast Tao another apologetic look before hurrying into the corridor. Aven gave the man a sheepish smile before backing into the hallway, gingerly placing the door where it had been.

Room fourteen was cosy, with stone walls and sconces to light the space. Five's Inn had curving ceilings, like caves, and candles lit the white stone to illuminate the space with warm light. There were a few tapestries hanging here and there to decorate the room.

Three single beds lined a wall, spaced out with end tables on both sides. Across from them was a small desk and trunks for clothes.

Veraion entered with a groan and piled weapon after weapon onto his bed. Chester yanked off her outer layers, taking the furthest bed, and Aven threw all of his clothes to the floor. Gingerly, he placed his flowers on an end table.

The giant turned into a wasfought with a series of horrid crunches and landed with a thud on the ground, rubbing his back into a rug. Veraion pulled off his vest, massaging his shoulders.

"Finally," Chester groaned, untying her bodice. She yanked it off, casting it onto her bed. She reached into her bag and pulled on a loose tunic, letting out a loud sigh as her skin could finally breathe again.

Aven flailed around on the floor, growling loudly. Then he started running around. He spun in circles, darting back and forth, ripping the rug from its place, and as Chester laughed, he leapt onto the middle bed.

The frame collapsed.

"For fuck's sake," Veraion muttered.

* * *

The dining hall had the same stone floors, walls, and ceiling. Torches lit the space, and long, colourful tapestries decorated the room. They depicted the gods and the Five, Natura, the first to have all four powers, and her daughter, the first Ianar-born queen, Aishida. The tapestries showed queens that followed as well as other heroes and champions Sontar Ivel had seen throughout the years, one of whom was a large man, depicted with a body as though sculpted by the gods, face half burned, body no less scarred.

Wooden tables and benches filled the tavern, with booths along the far wall. To the right was a bar, and behind this was an opening to the kitchens. Azheeks and humans were everywhere, talking, laughing, and singing.

Veraion, Chester, and Aven shuffled through the bustling hall, dressed in their most casual clothing. Not a single bit of armour was on them, their only weapons small daggers tucked into boots. Chester's hair was up, both she and Aven with pink flowers tucked behind their ears. Veraion's mess of hair was tied back in an incredibly knotted bun, and as he gazed around, stray locks almost hit Chester in the face.

There was a free booth against the far wall, and Veraion pointed at it before heading to the bar for drinks.

Chester and Aven made for the table, looking around in awe. They had never seen so many azheeks and humans intermingling, and the sight of it brought a smile to Chester's eyes. She could never get tired of this.

Then a drunken man stumbled into her. Aven grabbed him by the shoulder and turned to Chester.

"Permission to punch him in the mouth?" he asked.

"No!"

"But he touched you."

"I'm—I'm sorry!" the man stuttered. "I've had one too many drinks! It was my fault, I'm sorry."

Chester smiled and nodded, removing Aven's hand from his shoulder.

"It's okay," she said. "Just be careful, you don't want to hurt yourself."

"Or anyone else," Aven snarled. The man stared at them both before hurrying away, glancing back at the giant with wide eyes.

Chester ushered him to the free booth, onto the bench. She gave him a firm look. "Aven. Stop it. That's *enough*. You have to stop doing that."

"He touched you!"

"By *accident*."

He looked away, disgruntled.

"*Aven?*"

He glanced at her. "Fine."

"*Aven.*"

He sighed. "I won't do it again."

"Thank you." She watched him with a fond look in her eyes and shook her head, taking a seat beside him. "You weren't this protective back in Foros."

"You were safe in Foros."

"And whenever we left? Scouting? Hunting? Our short travels?"

"I killed anyone that touched you." This was true.

"Promise me you won't do that again," she pressed kindly. "We have to lie low—we can't draw any more attention to us. You already stand out enough—threatening every stranger that comes near me is only going to make things worse."

"Or we ditch the *wanted* man, and then you and I have nothing to worry about."

Veraion approached, placing three tankards of ale on the table. He slid onto the bench opposite his companions. Chester took a pint and sipped. Aven wrapped his hand around a tankard and picked it up so quickly ale splashed all over his face.

He blinked. "I thought it would be heavier."

Chester patted him on the arm.

As Aven wiped his face with his tunic, an innkeeper came to their table. She had black hair, messy in a loose braid, a few moles decorating her light brown skin. Her nose was a little hooked, her eyes kind: brown with flecks of amber. She wore a common dress, wrapped with an apron, and though she was covered in ash and soot from hours spent in the kitchen, there was not a trace of sweat on her.

"For three?" she asked.

"Five," Veraion replied, but he was watching her strangely. She looked so familiar to him.

"More coming?"

"He eats a lot." He waved at Aven. She looked at the man in question and he smiled awkwardly.

"Where on Ianar are you from?" she asked. "I've never seen folk like you."

"He's from the north," Veraion said.

"The Northlands?" She stared. "I've heard how tall they are but... wow. Never thought they were *that* tall."

Chester and Aven smiled as convincingly as they could.

"Did the tattoos hurt?" The innkeeper motioned at his markings. Aven glanced at the others.

"Uhhh... yes?"

She looked back at Veraion, who was still watching her.

"Maina?" he asked. She raised an eyebrow.

"Yeah?"

Veraion smiled in disbelief, pulling a silver coin from his pocket, and tossed it at her. "Better late than never."

Maina looked at him, then the coin, then back at him. Her eyes widened and she grabbed his face, staring past his mess of facial hair and scars.

"Holy shit!" She gaped. "Veraion?"

He grinned, rising to his feet, grabbing her into a strong hug. "How long has it been?"

"Seven years? Eight? Nine?" She pulled back just so she could stare at him some more. "You've changed so much! You're all grown up now, aren't you? And by the love of the *gods*, your hair is long, and that beard! I didn't recognize you at all!"

"You look almost exactly the same." He smiled. "Although... you bound? You have an ilis?"

"I do." She smiled. "You met Theideus, right?"

"The water azheek?" Chester stared.

"That's the one," she said fondly. "Not all friendships need words."

Then Aven raised a hand.

"Yes?"

"I'm hungry."

Maina blinked at him, glancing at the other two before heading back for the kitchens.

"You need to improve your people skills," Veraion said, sitting down.

"I'm usually eating them. Or getting pet."

"An old friend?" Chester asked.

"Very." Veraion nodded. "She was an innkeeper at a town that Ilia and I passed through many years ago. She helped us blend in."

Maina returned with a tray of five plates and pushed it towards Aven. She then shooed Veraion further along his bench, taking a seat beside him.

"Where's Ilia?" she asked. Her eyes rested on Aven as he inhaled his food. "By the gods, you eat like a wasfought."

"Ilia is dead," Veraion said softly. Maina's face fell.

"I'm so sorry."

Veraion drank to avoid having to speak.

"I... How?"

"Baraduhr," Chester responded for him.

"I'm so sorry."

"She's been from my arms many years now," he said simply.

"Do you still... feel her?" Maina asked.

He shook his head. "She's... trapped."

Her face fell, and it was clear she regretted ever bringing up the woman's name.

"What about you?" Veraion turned back to her, trying to change the conversation. "When did you come to Sontar Ivel? When did you bind with Theideus?"

"I left town not long after you did," she said. "Your tales of travel were always so riveting, and if there's one place I knew I wanted to go, it was the capital. I met Theideus on the road—he was... lost, so he came with me. He's been my best friend since the day we met."

Veraion smiled.

"Speaking of travel..." She reached into her apron. "Have you always been slaughtering masses across the mainland?" She pulled out a wanted poster. He groaned.

"*aish*," he muttered. "These things are everywhere."

She pulled out another one and handed it to Chester. Chester unrolled it and her face fell.

Wanted by command of the queen. Partner of mass murderer. Name: unknown. Height: five foot two. Hair: dark red. Eyes: hazel. Skin: light brown. Species: fire azheek.

"What the fuck?" she choked. She then started laughing.

The drawing was atrocious.

Aven leaned over and coughed on his food, cackling wildly. "Is that supposed to be you?"

Veraion grabbed the poster and looked at it with concern. "I only went into town once, maybe twice on the way here."

"Someone must have recognized you," Chester wheezed. "And saw me with you—this must have been the day I slept on my face and almost suffocated in my sleep."

"You see how easy it is to be wanted *on command of the queen*?"

"I have nothing to worry about," she said, laughing. "That doesn't even look like me."

"Does that say hazel?" Aven pointed. "Your eyes are green."

"Is it true?" Maina stared.

"It was him." Chester pointed. Veraion glared.

"They were baraduhr," he said. "The ones that took Ilia."

Maina sighed. "Please don't tell me you've brought trouble to my inn."

He smiled over his tankard. "Never."

"Is there a poster for me?" Aven asked.

"No," Maina said. He was disappointed.

* * *

Aven's wasfought slumber was broken by a knock on the door. His ear twitched, but he otherwise ignored the sound. He was curled up on Chester's bed with her, neglecting his mattress and broken mound of wood in the middle of the room.

Knock. Knock. Knock.

His eye opened and he groaned, but he only snuggled closer to Chester. She stirred in her sleep.

Finally Veraion rose from his bed wearing a loose pair of pants and an equally airy shirt. Heading towards the door, he let out a large yawn. When he opened it, he came face to face with Maina. Behind her, Theideus.

"Morning, love," Maina said, yawning. "The queen is giving a speech later, sun-high at the castle. Are you going to check it out?"

He nodded. "I'd like to see what she has to say."

"Okay." Maina tried to enter, but Veraion blocked the way in a panic.

"OH HI MAINA, YOU WANT TO COME IN?" he shouted. She stared at him in alarm.

Back in the room, Aven took his cue and changed form with a series of unsettling crunches. Only once Veraion knew he had returned to human did he step aside and allow the innkeepers to enter. Maina glanced Veraion up and down on her way in. Theideus smiled timidly, following her.

"We have visitors," Veraion said. Chester was still in her place, eyes closed, face half buried in a pillow. She waved her hand lazily, otherwise unmoved.

"What happened to the bed?" Maina exclaimed.

Finally Chester opened her eyes only to realize a naked, human Aven was wrapped around her. She yelped, scrambling from her bed, falling to the ground with a thud.

"Aven!" She stared. "We talked about this!"

"How is it any different?" he whined.

"I'm still just… getting used to—It's just weird."

"Maybe another time, guys," Veraion said.

Maina leaned over to him, pointing at the broken bed. "Were you in here when they did that?"

"It's not—We're not—" Chester laughed. "He's just very big."

"Yeah, how does that feel?"

Chester glared.

"Veraion, you're with Theideus." Maina returned to her mission. "Only he can tame that mammoth on your head. If you're going to see the queen, you're not going looking like that."

He groaned.

"I helped you fit in last time," she said. "I'll do it again."

Veraion shook his head but admitted defeat and allowed Theideus to usher him from the room.

When they were gone, Maina motioned for Chester to sit on Veraion's bed. She glanced at Aven but did as she was told, watching as the innkeeper took a satchel from her apron, pulling on gloves. She stuck her hand inside, scooping out a handful of black goop. Before Chester could react, Maina slapped it onto her head.

"Hey!"

"Hold still, you'll ruin the sheets."

Chester tried to get up but Maina shoved her back down.

"You're wanted, Chester. You're on posters. Do you want to be arrested your first day in Sontar Ivel?"

"It doesn't even look like me!"

"*Hold still.*"

Chester sighed and stayed still, allowing Maina to work the dye into her hair.

"Did you say something about the queen earlier?" Aven asked.

Maina nodded. "She'll be talking to the city later today." Chester and Aven exchanged excited glances.

"Have you seen her?" Chester said.

"As beautiful as you imagine," Maina said with a sigh.

"And… have you seen her use her powers?"

"Yes and no. She mostly has no reason to use them—it's not like she's fighting anyone ever."

"Never in my life did I think I'd ever see the queen," Chester murmured. "White hair, white markings, and powers, and everything?"

"The whole lot." Maina nodded again.

"Reckon if I fire an arrow at her we'll get to see her use her powers?"

Maina laughed. "I reckon you'd get killed on the spot, if not by her or the guards, by everyone around you."

"Is it true the queens have all four powers?" Aven asked.

"That's why her lights are white," Chester said. "Water azheeks are blue, and the rest of us… well… Old magic left the rest of us a long time ago. But… what's Theideus's story?" she asked. "I've never met a water azheek before. To be fair, I'd never met an air azheek before yesterday either, but I thought kara'i never leave their cities."

"He's the only water azheek in all of Sontar Ivel," Maina said. "Probably in all the mainland."

"What brought him here?"

"I don't know, and I doubt I ever will. He can't talk. From what I've gathered, he's cursed. Exiled. It's the only reason he's here and not with the rest of his kind. And for that… I'm kind of grateful."

Chester and Aven exchanged curious glances.

"Is that why his markings don't glow?" Chester asked. Maina nodded. "Does he still have his powers?"

"He does—he's still an azheek, he just doesn't carry the magic of *his* people."

"He's never written down his story?"

"He's never written down anything," she said simply.

"But he understands the common tongue?"

"Yeah," Maina said. "He can understand us, he just chooses not to communicate back. He's very committed to his curse. I think he… feels he deserves it."

"So he's never spoken to you? Not even through writing?"

"Never."

"But the two of you are bound?"

Maina smiled to herself. "Some friendships need no words."

"Maina," Aven said. "What are you?"

"I'm a fire azheek."

"But your eyes are human, and your hair is black, and you have moles."

She smiled. "I wasn't born a fire azheek."

Chester looked back at her in alarm. "What?"

"Relax, I'm no baraduhr. I was first-generation human, my mother a fire azheek from Ikran. She died when I was young, but I was with her when she passed, and when she did, she gave me her powers."

"You can do that?" Aven stared.

"That's so rare," Chester said.

Maina nodded. "I've heard it can only be done between those that share bonds, or family members, or... I don't know. You have to be compatible or something. I'm sure if I was second generation it wouldn't have worked."

"What was it like? The change."

"Honestly?" Maina laughed. "I didn't notice. It was slow. I didn't know for a long time, but then again, human was all I knew, right? It's not like I knew what it was like to have powers, or how to use them. I think it was a whole year before anything happened." She snorted. "One day someone scared me and I burst into flames. It took me a long time to learn how to control it. I burned off all my clothes... in the village square. I wore chainmail for a year after that."

Chester laughed, and Maina chuckled as she continued working the dye into her hair.

"You're bound now," Chester said. "But did you ever stop ageing in your prime? Did you fully *become* an azheek?"

"I was curious about that, but I met Theideus early on in my prime years, so I'll never really know. But... I think I'm still human in the head. Azheeks think differently—you're a lot more... simple. In a good way. No lies, no deceit, you're not conniving like most humans are. Living here, in the capital, it's so different. But back where I grew up… I can't say I miss it, living in a primarily human town. Here it's so easy. So calm. So pure. I think living surrounded by azheeks really makes humans better people. We become more like you."

"Wow…" Chester murmured.

"How about you? Are you in your prime?"

Chester smiled to herself, though it seemed sad. "No, I'm bound."

"Is it him?"

Chester glanced at Aven and smiled, shaking her head. "I wish. My ilis is very far away."

"Why?"

"He uh… isn't bound to me."

"*What?* I thought azheeks could only bind to those that reciprocate their affection."

"I can still kill him if you want," Aven said. Chester smiled.

"Close your eyes," Maina said, and when Chester did, she carefully wiped dye onto the woman's eyebrows. "Done."

Chester rose to her feet, looking at her reflection in a nearby mirror. Aven shuffled over and took her place on the bed, looking at Maina expectantly.

"Are you always so… free?" She glanced at his penis.

"He is," Chester said. Aven continued staring at Maina, then pointed at his hair.

"Oh." She blinked. "You're not wanted—I think your hair is fine."

"But I want to match," he said. Maina glanced at Chester, who smiled. The innkeeper shrugged and lathered black dye into Aven's white hair.

"Is it true there are tunnels that run through the city?" Chester asked.

"Oh yeah." Maina nodded, and the other two exchanged wide-eyed glances yet again. "Don't get too excited—they don't lead to magical lands, just… other places in the city."

"Have you ever found any?"

"A few. Give any kid a coin and they'll show you the closest one. I swear it's all they do in their spare time. But it's also dangerous. Kids get lost in there all the time."

"Do you ever use them?"

"One. I have a shortcut to the marketplace. Means I can sleep in and still get everything before work begins. I can show you sometime! By the way, no drying yourself with fire."

Chester's face fell. "What?"

"The dye, you'll burn it off if you use fire."

"I have to... use... towels?"

Maina grinned. "You're human now. You're going to have to get used to doing human things. Like drying yourself with a towel. And *lying*. I know it doesn't come naturally to you guys—just don't forget, if someone asks, you're human."

Chester nodded. There was a look on her face as though she was just now realizing how much effort being a "human" would be.

Veraion sat cross-legged on the floor of Theideus and Maina's room, head tipped back slightly as his great mass of hair was washed. There was a basin sitting on the ground, catching the water that flowed from Theideus's hands, through Veraion's hair, rinsing out the last of the black dye. They had been silent for the most part, Veraion allowing the other to do whatever he saw fit, which included a very rough and painful brushing. This brought out a few yelps on his end, and soon Theideus gave up and instead cut out the knots with a pair of scissors.

Then the dye went in, followed by a long, awkward silence as they waited for it to soak, and now the water azheek was washing it out with naught but his bare hands and the element he could summon from thin air.

Veraion gazed at the wall ahead. Maina and Theideus's chamber had two single beds with side tables just like room fourteen, but this space was lived in. There were dressers packed with clothes, a laundry basket that was brimming, and decorations all over the walls.

Veraion could tell whose side of the room was whose. Theideus's was neat. Still decorated, but neat. Every tapestry and painting was aligned perfectly parallel to the next, and there were old runes on them: Ancient Azheek, a language the kara'i still spoke. His area favoured cooler colours, turquoise, blue, indigo, and purple, while the other side of the room was ripe with any colour under the sun.

Maina's side was haphazard. Messy. Funny. It suited her. It suited them. She had large tapestries hanging on the walls and ceiling, and dangling trinkets that were made to chime in the wind. They would only chime here if she moved them herself. There were sculptures and pottery and textiles of woven silk. It seemed she spent most of her coin on things that looked pretty—things that reminded her of her mother. He could see Ikrani elephants, peacocks, and horned cows, and intricate mandalas that one could stare at for hours. Maina had never been to Ikran, but here in the capital she could still experience their people and culture, for all walks of life thrived in Sontar Ivel.

There was henna paste on her bedside table, commonly used by Ikrani people to decorate skin, and he wondered how much she'd had to buy in order to dye their hair.

Veraion smiled to himself. Theideus was gentle now that the knots were gone, and the water was cool and refreshing. The sound of it lapping against the basin was calming.

Theideus washed away the last of the dye, and with a wave of his hand, Veraion's hair was dry. Not a drop of water remained, and the man sat up straight, the weight of his wet hair suddenly gone. He glanced back curiously as Theideus waved his hand again, and in an instant, all water in the basin disappeared. All that was left was the black dye, now a dry powder.

Theideus picked up the scissors and showed them to Veraion to let him know he was going to start cutting, and Veraion nodded, turning back around, allowing the man to work away.

Cut after cut, black hair fell into the basin. Cut after cut until Veraion's hair no longer hung halfway down his back in knots and instead fell just past his shoulders in neat waves.

Veraion swallowed the knot in his throat and finally spoke, and the words that came from his lips were words that Theideus knew. Ancient Azheek.

"My name is Veraion," the earth azheek said, speaking in Theideus's mother tongue. *"I don't think I properly introduced myself."*

This was followed by silence, for the scissors stopped snipping. Veraion glanced over his shoulder and saw Theideus staring at him, his eyes wide. Shocked. *Sad.*

"I don't know how long it's been since you've heard someone speak your language," Veraion said. *"I don't know if it hurts or if it's welcomed."*

And then Theideus smiled. Pained, but he smiled. He nodded as though to say *welcomed.* He opened his mouth, debating whether or not to act out a word, unsure as to whether or not he should break his absolute silence. He then closed his mouth and smiled once more. He nodded, as though to prompt Veraion to continue, and the earth azheek returned to his place as Theideus continued cutting his hair.

"Not many people know I can speak Azheek," Veraion said. *"It's not common. But if... if you ever did want to say—or write anything, I can also read and write Sa'uri."*

Theideus moved from his place and took a seat in front of the other man, and there he smiled and nodded as though to say thank you.

Then he set down the scissors and picked up a straight-edge razor. Veraion looked at him, a hand subconsciously roving over the thick beard that had claimed his face for so long. He let out a slight sigh with a smile.

He sat still, gazing at the ceiling as Theideus wiped shaving cream over his chin.

Maina showed Chester and Aven to the inn's wash area before returning to room fourteen. There she waited until the two emerged, towels wrapped around their bodies and about their hair. Chester was having a very difficult time, and Maina couldn't help but laugh.

Then the door opened behind them. Chester looked over and dropped her towel.

It was Veraion, or someone that looked slightly like him. If it weren't for the scars and compass tattoo on his sternum, she wouldn't have recognized him at all. Veraion's giant mess of matted hair had been combed, cleaned, dyed black, and trimmed to fall just past his shoulders. His beard had been shaved clean, removing ten years from his face and exposing a chiselled chin even he'd forgotten he had. The scars upon his left cheek and neck stood out even more now, a feature not on his wanted posters. The only resemblance remaining was his piercing eyes.

He glanced at the others uncomfortably, running a hand over the back of his neck. Behind him, Theideus looked very proud of his work.

"*Raion?*" Chester stared. Maina wolf-whistled.

"Think they'll recognize me?" he asked.

"If it wasn't for the uncanny smell of dirt, I wouldn't recognize you," Aven said. Veraion cast him a dry smile.

"That'll do." Maina nodded in approval. "That will definitely do."

Theideus headed into the room and she gave him a high-five. He inspected Chester and Aven, admiring their new hair. Then he spotted Chester's weapon hidden under a pile of clothes. His eyes were drawn to the blue light, to the blades marked with ancient Sa'uri.

Theideus's brow furrowed. He moved forward, pulling the weapon from its hiding place, and his face fell. Chester started forward, but before she could say anything, he turned and grabbed her by the throat, slamming her against the wall. Maina yelled in alarm and Aven launched forward, hackles rising, but Veraion grabbed him by the arm, hauling back as hard as possible.

Theideus yelled but no sound came from his cursed throat. "*Where did you get this?*"

"I—I killed a baraduhr for it," Chester choked, having to read his lips.

"*When?*"

"Ten years ago!"

Tears welled in his eyes and he released her, taking a shaking step back. He fell to his knees, gripping the weapon. Slowly the man closed his eyes, touching his forehead to the floating crystal.

Maina came forward, looking between Theideus and Chester fearfully.

"Are you okay?" she asked Chester. Chester nodded.

Maina moved for Theideus, wrapping an arm around him as he cried.

"Theideus." Maina stared. "What…"

Chester lowered to her knees. "This weapon," she said. "You know it?"

He nodded.

"You knew the original owner?"

He nodded again. He wiped the tears from his eyes and looked at the sword, the crystal and its lights illuminating his face, eyes sparkling like aquamarines. In the back of the room, Aven yanked his fist out of Veraion's grasp.

Slowly Theideus rose to his feet, and the others followed.

"*You killed the baraduhr?*" he asked silently. Chester nodded.

He breathed slowly, swallowing the knot in his throat. Then he offered the weapon back to her, hands shaking. He looked her in the eyes and mouthed his next words very clearly.

"*Thank you.*"

She looked at the weapon, then to the man holding it.

"I've had this weapon for ten years," she said. "And I love it with all my heart. But if it means something to you…"

Theideus lowered to one knee, bowing his head, holding the blades up for her. She didn't move, and neither did he.

Finally Chester wrapped her hand around the hilt. Only once she had accepted the weapon did he rise. He stood there for a moment, gaze glazed over. Then he left the room.

The others stood in silence.

CHAPTER 4
EINMYRIA

Music and laughter filled the streets of Sontar Ivel as Chester and Aven wandered. The sun shone high in the sky and illuminated the city. Rivers sparkled and leaves shone bright green, the distant castle a glimmering spectacle. The two excitedly pointed at sights, marvelling at the bustling life of the capital.

The air was crisp and fresh, cleaned by the abundance of greenery and filtered by flowing water, sweetened by the eternal bloom of flowers and fruit, thriving in the magic of the ancient keep. But the smells they enjoyed most came from bakeries and restaurants. Fresh bread, cakes, and pastries. Any eatery brought saliva to their mouths—smells of seafood that thrived in the city's waters even so far from the ocean, and of roasted vegetables. Aven had never been one to fuss over greens, but the smells of peppers, zucchini, onions, eggplants, mushrooms, and potatoes were making him question everything. All it took was a little olive oil, garlic, and rosemary, and all of a sudden he wanted to gorge himself sick.

They sampled food and drink, accepting anything that was free to taste. They ducked into every shop they passed, stunned over how many different kinds of bread a baker could make. Chester wished she had money to buy everything.

They meandered through the streets, using only their visual of the castle as a guide to ensure they were at least making their way towards it. Chester was wearing a common dress now, her dyed-black hair pinned up, and though Aven was fully clothed, it didn't do anything to hide his gargantuan stature.

As they wandered, Aven plucked more flowers, tucking them into Chester's hair until there was no more space. They climbed a city wall and sat, gazing over twinkling rivers and pools below, eating lunch they had packed from the inn. There was a group of musicians by the water, plucking and strumming guitars.

While they rested, Chester braided and wove their collection of flowers until she had made two wreaths, placing one upon her head and the other on Aven's.

Returning to the city below, Chester spotted an armoury and nudged Aven, curiously heading inside.

The walls were lined with armour: breastplates, gauntlets, bracers, and pauldrons, cuisses and greaves, and an assortment of helmets. From the back of the shop, behind a counter and through a set of swinging doors, came loud noises. A hammer against anvil.

Aven tapped at a helmet.

"These look really good," Chester said.

"Think they're better than the ones in Foros?"

"Oh, definitely."

He balled a fist and punched a large, curved breastplate. *THUNK*. He left a stark dent in the steel.

"Aven!" Chester gasped.

"Huh… I thought it would be stronger."

"You can't just go around testing your strength!"

Then the clanging from next door stopped. Chester panicked, shoving Aven in front of the armour just in time to hide it.

A human came through the swinging doors, carrying with her a helmet. She was tall and strong, looking to be in her thirties or forties, her skin a deep, dark brown. Scarification marked her muscled arms, across her shoulders, over her cheeks and forehead—scars that mimicked the scales of a crocodile. Her black hair was woven into thick, long dreadlocks, half tied up in a knot to keep it away from her face, decorated with beads. The woman's muscles rippled, strong from her work, her nose wide and lips thick, and as she looked up, her dark eyes locked on the newcomers. On Aven.

"What on Ianar are you?" she asked, her voice deep. She had the accent of Kapadua upon her tongue, a region south-west of Foros, on the coast of the mainland—home to earth azheeks and humans. It explained the scale-like scarification.

"Euhhh…" Aven mumbled. "Nnnorth."

"Northlands? Are they all as tall as you up north?" The armourer stared. "Huge."

The human stared a moment longer before shaking her head, returning to a more professional manner. "How can I help you two today?"

"We were just looking around," Chester said.

"Do you need armour? You both… have a lot of scars."

"Maybe another time." She smiled. "I'm sorry for bothering you."

Then Aven spoke up. "Have you ever made armour for animals? Like a wasfought, maybe?"

"Why would a wasfought need armour?" The armourer laughed. "Those things *are* armour."

Chester smiled, nodding farewell, and ushered Aven from the armoury. The human watched them go. Then she noticed the dent in the breastplate.

The closer Chester and Aven got to the castle, the louder the streets grew. Talk was ripe in the air, and soon all they had to do was follow the horde of people.

A large crowd was gathered at the southern gates, chanting and cheering. Guards, armoured from head to toe in white and gold, stood proud along the castle walls, hands resting upon the hilts of their swords. Air azheek guards patrolled the skies, watching the bustling crowd to the south, keeping an eye on the boats that floated upon turquoise-blue waters to the east and west of the palace.

Through the deafening talk and laughter came a resonating chant.

Athos. Athos. Athos.

"What's going on?" Chester asked as she tried to see over the swarm of heads. Aven bent down and she clambered onto his back, smiling as he stood. Save for the guards above, she had the best view.

People around them stared, but neither she nor Aven noticed. They were used to being stared at. Chester had been the only fire azheek in Foros, and Aven, a wasfought.

Then the crowd erupted as a man appeared on a castle wall. A man with a body built by the gods. A man as muscular as Aven. He stood over six feet tall, his skin tanned and covered in scars. Riddled with mars from blade, beast, and fire. Burns marked his face, chest, stomach, back, arms, and legs. One eye was sea blue, the other blind and cloudy. His dark brown hair was long and thick, braided and cuffed in gold, pooling down his gargantuan back. Facial hair lined his strong jaw, growing in patches upon the left side of his face, hindered by burns.

He appeared in his forties, and from the state of his body, it was clear that the life he had known was a life of blood and bones. A life of war. His gaze was cold, unfeeling, ignoring the sea of faces below that stared up in awe and adoration.

A great belt, pants, and boots were all he wore. Every burn and blemish gleamed in the sun, and where his skin had not been marked by battle, he grew thick body hair.

Athos. Athos. Athos.

Aven looked over at a woman who was sobbing. He shared an amused glance with Chester.

Athos stood on the castle wall, gazing over the flood of faces without a hint of emotion. He was worshipped, he was loved. Revered. People spoke of him more frequently than they did the queen, many flocking to the city just to witness him, but he did not care for their cheers or praise.

Then he saw Chester in the crowd, towering above everyone with the seven-foot giant.

"You clearly do not understand the concept of lying low," came Veraion's voice, and gruffly he yanked Chester from Aven's back. She fell with a yelp, but he caught her and helped her find her footing.

"Lie low," he hissed. "Literally." He glanced at the castle to see Athos watching them, and his gaze darkened. "*Lie low.*"

Veraion looked at Athos only a moment longer before heading off through the crowd, searching for a spot in the shade. He found a space under the awning of a nearby stall.

The crowd roared once more, and his eyes turned to the castle. The queen.

An azheek in her prime with golden skin and long wavy snow-white hair stepped into the sunlight. Her eyes were pale blue and her gaze rested upon her people, a kind smile on her lips. Azheek markings decorated her skin, glimmering with white light, flickering here and there with the calm beat of her heart. It was an extraordinary sight, like a starry blanket caressing her skin.

From head to toe she wore white, adorned with lace and glimmering embroidery, and in the light of the sun, she appeared a goddess.

The city cheered, calling her name, waving in adoration.

Siran. Siran. Siran.

Softly the queen laughed to herself, and as magic carried her voice, they heard it as though she were speaking next to them.

"Sweet fuck," Chester murmured. "She is beautiful."

Siran raised her right arm into the air, her hand open and her fingers gently spread, and as far as the eye could see, every man, woman, and child, single, double, and swapped spirit, did the same. Their hands were outstretched, open, signifying their hearts were equal—prepared to receive, prepared to give. A welcome. Chester and Aven quickly followed suit. Veraion, however, did not. His arms remained crossed, his gaze dark.

"Welcome!" Siran called, and she lowered her arm. The sea of people did so too, though here and there some still continued their signs of love. She laughed and waved her hand, motioning for them to relax. Finally they did.

"Thank you so much for your love and support." She beamed. "But most of all, thank you for being who you are: proud and harmonious humans and azheeks!"

The crowd went wild.

"It is an honour to speak before you once again," she continued. A man cheered from the crowd and she laughed quietly. "I could bore you all with tales from my travels, but we all know why we have gathered here today."

She smiled, and the crowd stamped their feet in unified anticipation.

"The annual tournament of Sontar Ivel!"

The thunder of the audience was deafening.

Athos! Athos! Athos!

Siran couldn't help but smile once more. "Yes, our beloved and undefeated champion will enter the arena once again for all to watch, but not until the rest of you have shown your own strengths! Registry begins now. You have one month to sign up, to train, to prepare, and come summer, the tournament begins!"

The crowd cheered.

"This tournament has been tradition since the Coming of the Five, since the Founding of Sontar Ivel, and I am honoured to be able to witness it continue, albeit... with a reigning champion that doesn't seem to give anyone a chance."

She smiled and looked over to Athos, and though the crowd screamed for him, he didn't react. He didn't even return the queen's gaze. She moved her attention back to the people below.

"Thank you so much for your love and support, and rest knowing I reciprocate it tenfold."

The queen smiled and waved farewell to her thundering people. Her guards surrounded her, guiding her from sight, but one man remained.

Athos stood still, his eyes upon Chester.

* * *

The three sat at their usual booth in the dining hall of Five's Inn, lucky to have gotten there before a swarm of people entered, flocking to the inn for the dish served this night. They could smell it even from room fourteen, and they could tell that whatever it was, it was spicy.

The tavern was packed. The usual patrons were here, but all around the hall were new faces.

Women and men of all ages sat around the tables, some old, some with children, and many appeared to come from the same region of Ianar. Their skin was brown, hair dark, and many were human. Some were earth azheeks, some fire. The women had long hair, braided, woven with flowers from around the city. The skin about their hands and forearms was decorated with henna in intricate patterns, and most of the men had their hair hidden beneath turbans. The headdresses came in different colours and styles, indicating what region of their country they came from, what region of Ikran they called home.

Tao and Theideus were seated at the bar, and as Maina appeared from the kitchens, they stood up and cheered. She laughed as more people joined in, clapping at her entrance.

She was dressed nicely now. Her hair was tied back with flowers tucked behind her ear. She wore a dark red top, embroidered with gold leaves and pink flowers, and a matching skirt, and around her body, over one shoulder, was cloth of sheer pink.

Maina performed an exaggerated bow.

More innkeepers emerged from the kitchens with trays of food and moved about the hall, serving all that waited.

Maina headed through the tavern and received her praise with a laugh.

"Maina!" an Ikrani man called. He was older, beard grey and hair hidden beneath a blue-and-gold turban. His accent was strong. "What will it take to have you come work for us! Little Ikran is nothing without your vindaloo."

Maina smiled from ear to ear and put on an accent as heavy as his. "My *mother's* vindaloo. And you'll have to pay me more than Tao does!"

"You'll never pay more than I do!" Tao called from the bar. The Ikrani man waved him away.

"I will never stop fighting for you." The man wagged his finger. Maina smiled, patting him on the shoulder, and made her way to where Veraion, Chester, and Aven were watching.

"What's all this?" Chester asked.

"Once a month I make my mother's vindaloo," Maina said. "It was just as popular back home, you remember?"

Veraion nodded. "I remember. It's nice you've found such a loyal community here. You know the recipe is good when Ikrani flock to eat it."

Maina winked. "Not everyone can handle it though."

"Handle what?" Aven raised an eyebrow.

An innkeeper swooped by and lowered a tray of five plates onto the table. Every plate had a portion of rice and a heaped serving of something very red. Chicken, from what Aven could smell.

He yanked a plate towards himself, quickly shoving food into his mouth. He chewed. And then he stopped.

His eye widened. A lot. Maina laughed. He spat it out, panting heavily, and grabbed a tankard of ale, chugging.

"Spicy?" Chester laughed.

Aven grabbed Chester's tankard the moment his was empty and chugged that too. Veraion watched him with a smug smile and proceeded to eat his vindaloo. He was used to spicy food, but even he had to admit that this was *hot*.

Aven reached for Veraion's tankard. Veraion smacked his hand away.

"What... is... this?" Aven rasped.

"Oh, just chicken." Maina smiled. "Marinated with vinegar. And garlic. Paprika, ginger, coriander, turmeric, mustard powder, cumin, cinnamon." Her smile grew a little evil. "Oh, and of course a healthy dose of ghost peppers."

"Ghost... peppers?"

"They're only the spiciest peppers on all of Ianar," Veraion said.

Aven smiled at them and then slid from the booth, running for the bar. Theideus had three pints of ale waiting. He'd been watching the entire exchange and could barely breathe through his silent laughing. Tao's laughter boomed through the hall.

"Is he going to be okay?" Maina asked.

"Maybe this is his one weakness," Chester murmured. She watched him, concerned, but he was in good hands. Tao was pouring him a tankard of milk.

Finally Chester tucked into her food. Her eyes widened. "Oh... *wow*."

"One of the perks of being a fire azheek now." Maina smiled. "I can cook as spicy as Valduhr and it won't bother me one bit."

Aven finished downing his milk and made his way back to their booth with two more tankards of ale. He slid into his place, defeated.

"Here." Maina handed him a plate of rice. "Eat this instead."

Aven looked at the plain food with a disgruntled huff.

"Are all these people from Ikran?" Chester asked.

"Mhmm," Maina said with a smile. "I've never been to Ikran, but here... it's like I get to be there every day."

"Is Little Ikran another inn? A restaurant?"

"Oh no, it's an area of Sontar Ivel where most of the Ikrani community live. Lots of temples, eateries—food like this! Jewellery, flowers. And Mustafa's is open all day and night."

"My gods," Chester murmured. "I love this city."

"We have everything," Maina said, raising her hands. "I'll take you! Little Ikran, Zeda Town, Sakhala Street. Sontar Ivel really is the capital, the heart of the world! You can travel all across Ianar within these white walls."

Chester stared at her food in wonder.

"You going to eat these?" Maina asked Aven, glancing at his neglected plates. He shook his head with a small pout. She laughed and took them away, heading back for the kitchens.

Aven let out a little sigh and ate his rice in silence.

Around them the dining hall boomed with merriment as people ate their vindaloo, indulging in the ungodly spice of Ianar's ghost peppers, and yet, over all the noise, Chester could hear Aven's stomach growling.

"I'm going to go hunt," he said.

"And where do you plan on doing that?" Veraion asked. "Find yourself a farm and prey on livestock?"

"There's forests in the south. Not too far. We passed them on the way here."

"There are wasfoughts in those woods," Veraion said. "Even within the walls. I could feel them when we were out there. No packs, but there's some loners."

"Well then, I guess it's a good thing I can handle a wasfought." Aven said smugly. He shuffled from the booth. "Also a full moon tonight. I need to howl."

Veraion laughed, shaking his head. "Is it a compulsion?"

"I don't know what that word means."

"You *have* to howl at a full moon?"

"Yes."

"Why?"

"Because… Fuck you."

"Be safe." Chester smiled.

"Always."

"Bring something back for the inn," Veraion said around a mouthful of spice. "I told them we'd hunt in exchange for shelter."

Aven nodded, transferring his flower crown to Chester's head, placing a kiss on her hair.

When he turned away, he was faced with Dog. She growled at him and he growled right back, baring his human teeth as he moved around her and sauntered from the hall. Veraion watched him go. The moment Aven was gone, his calm demeanour broke.

Veraion gasped and grabbed his tankard of ale, downing as much of it in one breath as he could. Chester laughed.

"*Fuck*," Veraion rasped, shovelling rice into his mouth. "This is *spicy*."

"Were you holding that in?"

He nodded. Eyes watering. She cackled loudly.

"You two." She shook her head. "*Children.*"

"I'm winning though."

Chester snorted. Dog poked Veraion's hand with her nose, and he petted her.

"See?" he said, nodding towards the canine. "Winning."

She shook her head at him again, but she was also laughing. "So… Aven hunts for the inn? That's how we pay?"

He nodded. "And I told them you'd inn-keep."

Her face went serious. She looked at him. He smiled.

She reached across the table and punched him in the arm. He laughed, rubbing the area, trying not to show just how much it hurt.

"Aven gets to hunt and I have to help around the inn?" she scoffed.

"I was hoping you'd get bathroom duty."

"I will piss in your food."

He chuckled. Dog trotted off to join Tao at the bar.

"And you?" she asked. "What's your pay?"

"Starting next month I'll have some gold coming in," he said. "I'm joining the tournament."

She looked at him dryly. "The tournament."

"You earn coin the more you win."

"So much for lying low," she scoffed. "The whole city is going to be looking at you."

"I'll be wearing a helmet, and even if I wasn't, I look nothing like the posters now, thanks to Theideus... and Aven." He motioned at his plethora of scars.

She shook her head. "You're not going to win."

"Ye of little faith."

"Oh, I have faith alright. I have faith in that giant man we saw standing on the walls today. In the giant man hung on posters around the city." She nodded her head towards a tapestry of Athos.

"I don't need to *win*." He shrugged. "Just make it to top ten."

"Why the sudden ego trip?"

"What, can't a man long for gold and glory?"

"You?" She raised an eyebrow. "Gold? Glory?"

"Why not?"

"You're hiding something."

He sent her a smile and continued eating.

"Is that what you came here for?" she asked. "You came all this way for a tournament?"

"Sure."

She sighed loudly. "I'll get it out of you one day."

* * *

Moonlight streamed through the forest canopy, glistening off the blood of the deer Aven tucked into, snout drenched with red. Beside him was another dead stag. The woods were dappled with the warm light of fireflies scattered through the trees, and he took a moment to marvel at them as he chewed.

Through the trees came a wasfought howl, lilting and beautiful, and Aven choked on his mouthful, immediately tipping his head to the sky, answering the call. He coughed, hacking up deer throat, and then returned to howling. Other wasfoughts joined, but they sounded much further away. He always found it beautiful, hearing his kind.

Slowly the worship of the blood moon came to an end and he morphed to a human, taking both deer by the legs. He looked at the gaping hole in the side of his dinner, questioning whether or not this was acceptable to take back to the inn, but he shrugged and brought it along anyway.

He headed through the woods, back for the main city, but slowed as he sniffed the air. His sniffs got stronger, brow furrowing as he looked around. The scent was sweet, like flowers, but tart with expensive oils. He cocked his head in confusion and followed the smell.

Creeping through the underbrush, he laid down his kill and peered through the trees. A rider: a woman atop a palomino horse. She wore a deep blue cloak that streamed over her stallion's flank. Long black hair pooled from beneath her hood in tight waves.

"Elaira?" she whispered, searching the woods. Her horse snorted nervously and Aven glanced at it, well aware that it was probably his presence putting it on edge.

"Elaira?" she called again, louder this time. She looked around, and when Aven saw her face, he couldn't help but sigh.

Pretty.

Human, clear from first glance. Her hair was dark, her eyes hazel, and her olive skin was dappled with freckles. Her face was round, chin and nose small. She looked young, her face youthful and her stature petite, but he could tell from her scent that she was a woman.

Her cloak glimmered almost purple in the moonlight, and all about her, fireflies calmly danced.

Her horse panicked. Its ears flattened against its head and it reared up with a whinny. She was thrown back, landing with a painful thud as her stallion bolted, leaving her in the woods alone.

Aven stared around in confusion. He couldn't have set off the horse; he was down wind. But then he smelled it too. Another wasfought.

Through the trees, on the other side of the lady, was a beast of the forest. Its fur was black, markings light brown, eyes yellow and fixed on the human. Drool dripped from its jaws as it bared its teeth, hackles raised, claws extending. It stepped forward, eyes set on her.

The wasfought charged, and before Aven could think, his body morphed to a beast and he burst through the underbrush, hurtling through the air. Slamming into the other wasfought, they fell to the ground, barely missing the woman as she screamed. The earth shook upon their fall, and she backed away, trembling wildly.

Aven stood before her, growling at the other wasfought. This beast was younger than him, smaller. Its pride made it want to stay and fight, but after scanning Aven's colossal body, it admitted defeat, casting him one last growl before bounding away.

Aven stood in his place, snarling after the darkness. Then he glanced over his shoulder to see the woman frozen, eyes wide and fearful. He swallowed the knot in his throat, forcing his hackles to lower. Still, when he turned to face her, she pulled further away. It didn't help that his face was soaked in blood.

He could taste her fear, stronger than the deer stuck between his teeth. The scent was rank. So he sat down, opened his mouth, stuck out his tongue, and wagged his tail. She stared in alarm, but slowly her expression changed. Aven wagged his tail profusely, and a smile swept across her face. A smile of disbelief.

Aven moved a bit closer. She backed away once more. So he lay down, pressed his chin to the forest floor, and wagged his tail. He shuffled forward, letting out a series of soft whimpers. He had used this manoeuvre on Chester many times.

"Oh my god," she whispered. She raised her hand, afraid at first, unsure as to whether or not she should really do this, but he lifted his head to meet her touch. She smiled as he nuzzled his nose into her hand.

The woman let out a laugh and petted him. His heart fluttered in his chest.

* * *

The dining hall wasn't too busy for breakfast. Chester and Veraion were seated at their usual booth. The earth azheek was dipping bread in honey when Aven burst in, a dead deer in each hand and love in his eyes.

Wearing naught but a loincloth, Aven walked over to their table and threw his kill to the ground, a wide smile on his face, arms spread to welcome Chester with a hug. She stood up and he grabbed her into a tight embrace. Her arms were pinned to her sides as he swung her around.

"I'm in love," Aven sighed, putting her down.

"Are you high?" Veraion said.

"I met a woman last night," he said excitedly. "In the woods. She's so beautiful. I saved her from a wasfought, she petted me—"

"Did she see you change?" Chester stared.

"If the baraduhr get a whiff of what you can do," Veraion warned lowly, "you will be more hunted than any azheek ever was."

"Why?" Aven scoffed. "It's not like they could take my power from me."

"They would try."

"Relax, I know it's a secret. She thinks I'm a wasfought."

"There's a hole in my deer!" Maina exclaimed, and they looked over to see her staring at the carcasses with wide eyes. One was partly eaten, the other with its throat torn out, the wound massive. Both were smothered in blood.

"What do you hunt with, your hands?"

"My mouth—"

"He's kidding," Veraion said quickly. "It was an accident. The next batch will be clean, I promise." He smiled with too much teeth.

"It all tastes the same, doesn't it?" Aven said.

Maina looked at him in disbelief but motioned for other innkeepers to help her carry the kill to the kitchens. She shook her head at Aven before walking away, and Chester patted him on the arm before following.

Aven took a seat, eating Chester's leftovers. There was some egg on her plate, but mostly they dined on freshly sliced vegetables and olives, plucked from farms that would sell the exact same harvest to the inn within a week.

"Chester works here now?" Aven asked.

"Yup." Veraion chuckled to himself.

"She's gonna piss in your food."

* * *

That night Aven left the inn once more, spotting Theideus and Tao upon a city wall. They were doing something, moving slowly as though dancing. Tao led and Theideus copied his movements. Aven cocked his head to the side and watched. He swore that if they increased their speed, what they were doing could have been a fight routine.

As Aven watched the azheeks, he understood how naturally their elements flowed with grace. Water and air, reflected in their movements.

Theideus was elegant, his blond hair flowing in the cool breeze, and Tao had a pleasant smile upon his lips, his long moustache ruffling about his chest. When he spotted Aven, his smile only grew. The giant returned the look.

Dog was seated on the wall, watching Aven with distrust, and the giant waved her away.

"Yeah, yeah."

He moved through the streets in naught but a loincloth, his pace increasing to a jog, and the moment he was out of sight, far enough from the main hub, he turned into a beast and ran, zooming towards the southern woods.

He passed rivers, leaping through them, and when bioluminescence erupted around him, he stopped. The beast forgot what he was doing and sat in the river, pawing at water, splashing at the tiny lights. He bounded back and forth, tail wagging profusely as he played with the glowing stream.

Glancing up, Aven saw fireflies flickering, and a content sigh left his lips. Then he remembered the fireflies from the night before. *The woods.* Aven silently cursed at himself and his absentmindedness and headed towards the forest. But whenever he passed a river or stream, he made sure to run through it and set off the bioluminescence.

The great beast made it to the woods eventually, sniffing the air, looking for food, but when he smelled flowers and expensive oils, he changed course and trotted towards the small clearing where the rider had been the night before. He padded through the trees, ducking into the underbrush, and saw her atop her palomino horse. The stallion was pawing at the ground nervously, no more at ease this night.

The woman's blue cloak glimmered in the light of the red moon, golden hues shimmering from fireflies around her. Aven moved forward but stopped when another rider entered the clearing—a rider that smelled just as royal, if not more so. Her white cloak was draped over her horse's flank, the mare just as pampered, its long hair shining in the moonlight.

The woman in blue dismounted her horse. Her company was apprehensive but eventually followed suit.

"Did anyone see you leave?" the first lady asked, hushed. Aven let out a small sigh as he watched her. But then the second rider pulled back her hood and his eye widened in shock.

The queen.

Siran was stunning, stealing the light of the moon. Her skin radiated even in the darkness, markings glimmering with white light. It was like the starry sky had fallen, twinkling here in the woods. Aven almost felt like he had to look away out of respect, but he couldn't. She was too beautiful. Too mesmerizing.

"Einmyria," Siran gasped, pulling her into a hug. Einmyria returned the embrace, both closing their eyes, gripping the other.

"Nobody followed," Siran said. "But why did you want to meet me out here? We could have met at the palace."

"I'm not allowed in the palace," Einmyria said. "And I... don't think it would be wise. I don't think you want anyone to hear."

"There are spying creatures in the woods. You have a shadow." Siran looked directly at Aven. He froze, but when she didn't stray her gaze, he stepped forward, emerging from the bushes.

"Oh." Einmyria smiled.

The horses whinnied but the women held the reins firmly, and when the queen whispered words of comfort, the steeds found calm. They snorted nervously but otherwise remained still.

Aven came forward and sat beside Einmyria. She laughed softly and placed a hand upon his great head.

"Is this... a new pet?" Siran asked.

"He saved my life last night. When you didn't show."

Siran glanced at Einmyria but returned her gaze to Aven. "A friendly wasfought. The world never ceases to amaze."

Einmyria watched her a moment. Then she broke.

"What on Ianar happened to you?" she said. "To *us*? You never replied to any of my letters. I wrote to you every month for *two years*, still sending letters on your birthday for three after that despite never hearing back, and now that I *am* back... you're queen?"

"I didn't receive any letters," Siran said. "They must have kept them from me."

"They? Who did this? What happened? Have you always been queen? Or is this... Elaira, promise me... you're not one of them."

Siran held Einmyria's gaze, her jaw clenched. Still, there was sadness in her eyes.

"Tell me you're not baraduhr," Einmyria choked. "They capture, torture, kill, all for what, a *possibility* of powers?"

"I am *not* baraduhr," she said sternly, though her voice was cracking. "I am daughter of queen Siran the Second. I have always known I was queen, I just couldn't tell anyone. Not even you. I had to keep it a secret for my own safety."

"I would have known." She shook her head. "*I would have known.* We grew up under the same roof—you were a sister to me."

"I still am." The queen came forward and took Einmyria's hands, but the human stood back.

"Even if you tried to hide your powers, I would have known," Einmyria pressed. "I might be human, but even I know who is an azheek and who isn't."

"You knew I was an azheek."

"Yes, of water. Did you sprout the other powers overnight?"

"I chose one power," Siran said. "The rest had to stay a secret until I was strong enough to fight for myself, and I had to choose water because... they're the only other azheeks with markings."

Aven's gaze flicked between the two women, the wasfought not quite understanding what he was hearing.

"The potions you took," Einmyria said. "To mute your markings. To hide them…"

"Yes. Nobody could know."

"But you told me... you *told* me you were a water azheek. You *showed* me."

"We were kids." Siran smiled sadly. "It was no fun being powerless."

Einmyria smiled bitterly. "And your hair? Your hair that was once blond? Your *name?*"

"I was dyeing it before, for my own safety. Please, Myria, leave it. It's nothing you could understand."

"Then *help* me. Please, I already lost my mother and brother—I cannot lose you too. You were a sister to me. You're all I have left, you and my father."

Siran almost flinched at the word. It was subtle, and it would have gone unnoticed had Aven not been watching her so intently.

"Your father?" Siran said.

"Elaira, I miss you." Einmyria's sad eyes searched Siran's face—Elaira's face—for a trace of her lost sister. But the queen clenched her jaw and nodded.

"I missed you too."

"All this time, all these years I was away… you were becoming queen, and I… I had no idea."

"I'm sorry," the azheek said. "I have to go. Nobody followed, but they'll have noticed I'm gone by now. I had to leave through the old tunnels. If they find them, I'll never be able to sneak out again."

The queen swung into her saddle with ease, looking at Einmyria and Aven one last time before giving a command, sending her horse to a gallop, speeding back for the castle.

Even at night, the castle glimmered. The white walls were radiant beneath the stars, rivers flowing down every side, gleaming with life.

Einmyria closed her eyes, taking in slow breaths as she bit back tears. Aven licked her hand and she smiled, lowering to one knee.

"You are one strange wasfought," she said, gently tracing her fingers over his scars. His heart fluttered as she looked at him, her gaze meandering over his menacing markings.

* * *

Aven reached his friends and dropped two more deer onto the floor. Both of them had bite marks on their throats, bite marks the size of a wasfought's giant jaws, but there was no blood.

"What is this!" Maina exclaimed. Those in the dining hall glanced over at the commotion, and Tao stared with wide eyes from the bar.

"What?" Aven retorted. "I cleaned them! You said clean—they're clean!"

She stared at him, then his friends. Tao came over, eyes fixed on the gaping holes.

"What on Ianar happened to these poor creatures?" he said.

"He's... from the... north?" Chester smiled sheepishly. "It's a... custom. You cut their throats out after you kill them."

Veraion let out a quiet sigh, closing his eyes as he pressed his fingers to his forehead. Chester needed to practice lying.

"These look like teeth marks," Tao said.

"They do that on purpose." Chester smiled with a little too much teeth.

Tao and Maina glanced at Chester, then up at Aven, and shook their heads as they finally admitted defeat. The old air azheek waved a hand and the deer lifted up from the ground, floating after him as he made his way to the kitchens with Maina.

Aven slid into the booth beside Chester, doing a double-take as he noticed Dog watching him from the far corner of the hall. He thinned his eye at her. She thinned her eyes at him. Chester looked between the two and laughed, and hearing her laugh was enough for him to ignore the clever canine and smile.

"Pray tell," Veraion said. "How did you clean the deer?"

"Chucked them in the river."

Chester choked on her food. Veraion snorted and shook his head.

"*What?*" Aven stared between them. "Is that not how people clean things?"

Chester rested her head on his arm as she laughed. He looked at her in confusion.

"I took them to the river and beat them with stones!"

She laughed harder, her face hidden behind a hand.

"Those poor deer," she wheezed.

"Tell me you didn't use soap," Veraion said. Aven glanced at him.

"I didn't have any on me—should I get them back?"

Chester clutched on to his giant arm and shook her head into his skin.

"Aven, I love you," she managed between breaths, wiping a tear.

He finally stopped defending himself and smiled.

Veraion looked between the two and shook his head. Still, there was a fond look in his eyes. He didn't understand how this seven-foot beast of a man could so easily look like a puppy when with Chester.

Aven watched her as she held him by the arm, resting her head on it. She looked tiny. So he petted her like she often did to him, scratching the top of her head. She smiled.

"The woman was there again last night," Aven said excitedly, grabbing a pastry. "Her name is Einmyria."

"Is there a reason she keeps going there?" Chester asked. "Or does she just have a death wish?"

"She met someone last night."

"You watched?"

"They weren't *mating*. She met the *queen*."

Chester's eyes widened. Veraion's chewing slowed, but he otherwise didn't react—or allow himself to.

"I think they were friends," Aven said. "When they were kids. Or they grew up together? In the same house. They kept saying sisters. Einmyria was confronting her about it. I think she went away for a while and never heard from her, and when she came back to Sontar Ivel, suddenly Elaira, or Siran, was the queen. Her name is different too. Siran says she's always been queen but had to hide it until she was strong enough to defend herself. I don't think Einmyria believes her. Chester, I… Siran, *Elaira*, might not be the real queen."

"How would you even fake that?" Chester stared. Then she looked at Veraion, who was chewing his food very, *very* slowly. He didn't look up. Chester squinted at him, leaning in, her gaze roving over his face. "You *knew*."

Veraion glanced at her but returned his gaze to his food. He finally swallowed and took a sip of his drink.

"That's why you're here," Chester said. "You *knew*."

He cast her another glance.

"That's why you're signing up for the tournament." Her eyes widened. "The champions are revered—they can get close to the queen… Athos lives in the castle!"

Finally Veraion held her gaze. He let out a dark sigh.

She laughed. "Fuck your gold and glory. I *knew* you were up to something. Top ten get access to the castle, don't they?"

"Yes."

"Anything else we should know about this tournament?"

"Champions go missing."

"What?"

"Every year, after the tournament is over, at *least* one of the azheek champions goes missing. Never a champion from Sontar Ivel, always a foreigner. Someone that goes missing on the road home."

"How have I never heard about this?"

"Because it's kept secret," he said darkly. "The people in charge of the tournament, the people of the castle, don't want anyone to know."

"Is it connected?"

He gave her a look. "That's what I want to know."

"Why didn't you tell us any of this?"

His gaze went distant, shoulders heavy. "Ilia was one of the only people that knew. She died for it."

Chester swallowed the knot in her throat and nodded. "So is Siran, or Elaira… baraduhr?"

"She said she wasn't," Aven said. "She seemed very adamant on that."

"Then how does she have all four powers?" Chester said. "The bloodline is only passed on by the real queens—direct descendants of the gods."

"Well… has anyone seen her use her powers?"

"I mean, *we* haven't, but the markings in her skin, they shine white. No azheek but the queen has white magic."

"Water azheeks still have the Old markings," Veraion said. "But even so, theirs glow blue. Save for Theideus, because he's… cursed."

"Einmyria said that Siran was a water azheek." Aven nodded. "Or at least, that was the power she chose to use until she was strong enough to defend herself."

"Well, that's a load of bullshit," Chester scoffed. "I was defending myself from a very young age."

"To be fair, your trainer was… a lot. Everyone in Foros was afraid of him. I never even met him, but to this day people still talk about him."

Veraion raised an eyebrow at them.

"The guy that brought me to Foros," Chester explained. "The one that found me when I was born. He came back once a month to ensure I was being trained properly, and always put me through the works when he was there. I never saw his face though, always kept his hood pulled low. He stopped coming after I found Aven."

"Everyone's afraid of wasfoughts." The giant grinned.

"You were a *baby*. I'm sure it was a different reason."

He shrugged.

"We're getting off topic here," Chester said. "The queen, or false queen—I mean, she seems nice?"

Veraion looked disgusted.

"Has she even done anything bad?" Aven asked.

Veraion slammed his fist onto the table, jaw clenched and nostrils flared. His breaths were heavy and he looked at Aven with a piercing glare, hatred seething in his eyes.

He got up and left. The two watched him go in silence.

"I'd take that as a yes," Chester said.

CHAPTER 5
TALES OF OLD

Chester and Aven moved through the city, looking for Veraion. It was early in the day so the bustle hadn't quite hit the streets, but there was still so much to see, smell, and hear. Sontar Ivel was already so alive.

"Where do you think he's gone?" Aven asked. His eyes were on a puffy-haired painter as they passed by, the human working on a beautiful landscape.

Chester shrugged. "Probably gone to drink his heart out."

"You two-legs are strange. When wasfoughts are upset, we just kill things. It's simple."

She laughed. "I doubt we'll find him—it seems he knows this city better than either of us—but it's worth a shot."

"Are you actually concerned about him? Or are you just trying to avoid bathroom duty?"

She cast him a smirk. "Meet me back at the inn by sundown." She tossed him a silver coin. "Have fun, Little One."

She headed away, and Aven watched her go with a fond smile. He had to fight every urge to follow, taking in a deep breath, and headed in the other direction.

Chester wandered, and though she walked until her feet were sore, she didn't see a problem with it. Sontar Ivel was beautiful. She marvelled at the winding walls of the city, turning the capital into a labyrinth of wonder. She stared up at the trees and plants that grew from stone, at the eternally blooming flowers, and at the rivers flowing from the castle, streaming from floating islands. She gazed down at large bodies of clear water, awestruck by the colourful fish swimming below. She smiled every time a gust of wind sent petals into the air, knowing they would grow back within the week. She nodded along to music ringing through the streets, dancing occasionally as people encouraged her to do so.

Her smile spread from ear to ear as she gazed around, taking in deep breaths. She loved that the air always seemed to smell like freshly baked bread. And flowers. And fruit. She could taste it on her tongue. She could also taste salt from water flowing all about the city.

She loved that there was always music. Musicians spaced themselves out along the walls, so no matter where one went, a tune followed.

She approached a tavern, stepping away as a man lunged from inside, spewing onto the ground. She grimaced at him, stepping around his vomit before heading inside. The tavern was moderately empty, with people scattered about the hall. Some were unconscious.

Chester headed for the bar, scanning the area. She couldn't see Veraion. Two young men were seated at the counter, one slouched over a cup of water, but Chester's eyes rested on the barmaid before her, an older fire azheek.

"Hey there." The barmaid smiled. "You looking for a drink?"

"No, actually, I'm just looking for a person."

"In particular?"

Chester raised an eyebrow at her, and she shrugged.

"You never know, people think this is a brothel all the time." She then lowered her voice. "It is, if you need anything."

Chester laughed. "Thank you, but not today."

The other fire azheek gave a light shrug before heading off to tend to a patron that was now falling off a bench. Chester sighed.

"There's a more popular tavern just down the road," the man beside her said. "Maybe your friend is there. It's called Herron's Place. We came here because it's less… noisy."

He had long black hair tied in a loose ponytail, and light stubble over his sharp chin, his eyes dark and bloodshot. His skin looked gaunt. He held his glass of water loosely, looking incredibly dehydrated.

"Rough night?" Chester smirked.

"Rough enough." He chuckled, then winced. "I'm Thalamere."

The other man looked far less hung over, his hair brown and slicked back. He was good-looking and he knew it. "Rendel," he said.

Both Thalamere and Rendel were well dressed, and though they seemed to be dressed down, the indents upon their fingers exposed that they commonly wore rings. Hidden beneath the reek of alcohol was a hint of expensive oils.

"Chester," she said.

"Is that not a boy's name?" Rendel asked.

"I have a twenty-inch cock I keep wrapped around my waist."

Thalamere snorted water out his nose. His head pounded. He groaned. "Oh no, no jokes. Please."

"Wasn't a joke." She smiled. She patted his shoulder. "Take it easy, Thalamere. Death by drink is a sad way to go."

He smiled, watching her leave before returning to his cup.

"Which way to Herron's Place?" she called over her shoulder. Rendel pointed.

Chester continued down the street, spotting another tavern. She saw posters in the distance—Veraion's wanted poster and hers—and chuckled. She would get that monstrosity of a portrait tattooed if she was ever drunk enough.

Then she passed another, a painted tapestry. Athos.

She slowed her pace.

He had been illustrated with care, a clear reflection of his true self. Huge, muscular, and terrifying, covered in scars and burns, his piercing gaze holding any viewer transfixed. The artist had encapsulated his energy flawlessly, right down to the cold, dead look in his eyes. One sea blue, the other blind and clouded.

Chester glanced at the stall next to where the mural was hanging. Tournament registry. A smile crept onto her lips.

Aven stared up at the library doors. They reached four stories high, decorated with stained glass. He had never seen stained glass before.

People milled in and out, and in awe, he wandered forward.

He stood in the doorway, watching colours pooling onto the floor, streaming in through the intricate doors. A small smile rested on his lips as he took one of the great doorknobs into his hand, gently moving it back and forth, sending rainbows dancing across the floor.

"Heeheheeheee," he giggled. Then he spotted a librarian staring at him and stopped, standing up straight, letting out an uncomfortable cough. But when he looked up from the floor, he saw the books. Miles and miles of books, stretching as far as the eye could see, flooding the aisles, reaching to the ceiling. And when he looked up, his eyes only widened further.

Hovering above the library was a map of Ianar. The model was made of crystal, floating magically above the hundreds of thousands of books.

Their world looked like a great vortex, for in the heart of it was Sontar Ivel, and all other land revolved around it. The world never moved quickly—people would not notice a change in their own lifetime—but cartographers never had it easy portraying accuracy. Entire cities could move, countries changing shape over time as the ground slowly circled the centre point.

Aven wandered in, staring up, almost bumping into people as he went. They stared at his size, his height, the discolouration of his skin, but he was too busy craning his head all the way back to notice.

Gold letters hovered above him, naming the cities, towns, rivers, and mountain ranges, and he smiled when he spotted the tiny city of Foros. It was further east than he had expected, for the maps they had back home were old.

As an old librarian approached, a human with a long white beard, Aven pointed at the roof.

"Is this accurate?" he asked. "Real time?"

The human looked at Aven with wide eyes but managed to retain professionalism and nodded.

"Yes," he said. "Like most things in this city, it's magic, linked to Ianar."

"Fuck," Aven murmured, staring back up. "That's amazing."

The librarian smiled.

"Have… have towns or cities ever been ripped in half?"

"The term 'ripped' implies that it happened somewhat quickly," the old man said. "So no. But over time, yes. I do believe. All countries have at least changed shape over the years."

"Sontar Ivel?"

"Never. This is the heart of it all. But everything else, yes."

Aven nodded, still in awe. He could see Sontar Ivel—it was hard to miss—and to the east, in the middle of what looked like tundra, Sirenvel, the city of fire. To the south was the great earth azheek city of Okos, and north-east of Sontar Ivel lay the empire of Zalfur, stretching much wider than he had known.

"Zalfur is *huge*." He stared. "The city in the sky?"

The human followed his gaze. "Zalfur… is an empire. Made up of four cities. Zeda, the capital, Akana, Usan, and the port city, Yan'zi."

"I always thought Sontar Ivel would be the biggest."

"Well… when you unite all three major air azheek cities and then seize a port nearby, you get… big."

Aven glanced at the man. "You sound scared."

"The Zalfuri are scary."

"Why?"

The librarian let out a grim sigh. "Humans used to live in Zalfur, but the day the Red Emperor came into power, he threw all the children from the city walls. Those that came back could fly, and those that didn't… well, he believed they got what they deserved."

"He killed all the humans?"

"Not just the humans. Some air azheeks don't learn to fly until a certain age, others never at all. The day he came into power, he killed off the *weak*. And now… the Zalfuri are an elite race of azheeks."

Aven looked at him, following his gaze to the large stretch of land that had become the empire of Zalfur.

"They're stronger than the rest of us," the old man said. "Faster. And that's only enhanced by where they live and train."

"What do you mean?"

"The altitude," he said. "Everything is harder up there. Every breath draws in less air—less fuel for their muscles. It takes more effort to do even the simplest of tasks, and yet… they still train like maniacs. It changes their bodies. It changes the way they're wired. So when they come down here… they're unbeatable."

"Shit…"

"All Fang'ei train in Zeda, and while it is already the highest of the floating cities, they train in the mountains. It is said the Red Emperor was the first to discover this, and of course he uses it for war."

"Why is he called… the Red Emperor?"

The old librarian cast him a glance. "Because of how many people he's killed. How much blood has soaked the earth, tainted by his rule. And the day he took the throne he got tattoos to mimic Old markings. His hands, neck. Head. He took the throne of Zalfur wearing a crown of his own blood. That is why we call him the Red Emperor."

Aven let out a long, low exhale. His gaze wandered from the Cradle, north of Sontar Ivel, where he knew the empire of Zalfur began. And his eyes moved east, to Zeda, Akana, Usan, and the port city of Yan'zi on the eastern coast.

"And Yan'zi?" he asked. "The port?"

"Once called Amora," the old human said. "The Red Emperor and his Fang'ei killed everyone. They laid waste to the port of Amora, annihilating the Amorai, and rebuilt their own city in its stead."

"Fang'ei?"

The librarian clenched his jaw, gazing up at the great empire. "The Fang'ei are the worst of the Zalfuri. The most insane. Chosen as children and raised by Lord Ezaria, by the Red Emperor himself. They're living, breathing clones. There isn't a person in power that isn't Fang'ei. Zeda, Akana, Usan, Yan'zi, and all through Ground Country. You find someone in charge, and they were trained by Lord Ezaria. You find someone that has any semblance of power, they were trained by Lord Ezaria."

Aven watched him. He spoke with spite, but Aven knew the anger was a mask to try and hide how afraid he truly was.

"And with access to a port," the human continued, "they could build ships. And that they did. And did some more. And now the empire of Zalfur and their silver-haired warlord have a fleet. A fleet faster than all others because the Zalfuri can control wind."

Aven was now as wide-eyed as the old human.

"As I said," the librarian murmured. "Scary."

"All of that was under Lord Ezaria's rule? The Red Emperor?"

He nodded.

"Wow... he's... efficient."

"Well, he's had centuries to do it. Lord Ezaria is two hundred years old."

Aven stared. "*What*? How?"

"He's an azheek," the librarian said simply. "And he never bound to anyone. No ilis. He's been in power for over a hundred and fifty years."

"There's never been a coup?"

"There have been many assassination attempts but none have been successful. Even the Northmen don't go near Zalfur anymore. And the Highlanders."

"The Northmen? The... tall guys?" Aven pointed at himself. The librarian glanced him up and down and nodded.

"The Northmen tried to take Ground Country many years ago. And the Emperor painted the icelands red with their blood."

"Okay..." Aven said. "I see what you mean."

"Scary."

Aven nodded. "So the port wasn't originally an air azheek city?"

The librarian shook his head.

"And they killed everyone?"

"Every man, woman, and child."

"If none were left alive, then how does anyone know what happened?"

The librarian blinked. "The... perhaps there were some survivors."

Aven nodded, gazing up at the map. He cocked his head. "Where are the water azheek cities?"

"Usually in the eastern ocean somewhere," the old man said, relieved the conversation had moved along. "They move around on their own—sometimes I swear they do it just to give me a headache." He squinted, searching the plethora of islands to the east of the mainland. He pointed. "There. Paradiz, Volehn, and over there, their capital, Elizia."

Aven gazed at the map, watching every shard of crystal twinkling. His brow furrowed, head cocking some more. "Is it just me, or does everything seem to be moving east? Zeda was once directly north of Sontar Ivel, no? And Foros used to be further west?"

"It does seem that way," the librarian murmured. "Is this your first time in Sontar Ivel?"

"How could you tell?" Aven smiled, staring up in awe.

"The map always draws this reaction from newcomers." He smiled.

"What's that?" The giant pointed at the eastern sea. There was some kind of vortex in the middle of it.

"Ah, the Dead Sea." The human let out a long, fearful sigh. "There isn't a real whirlpool, I don't think. But cartographers draw it like that on every map as a warning. It didn't get that name for no reason. No one sails into the Dead Sea and comes back."

"Why?"

"No one knows, do they? Nobody has survived to tell the tale."

"What makes you think they're dead?"

"Well… the shipwrecks at the bottom of the ocean say so."

"Oh."

The librarian let out a long, wonderous sigh. Aven glanced at him.

"If no one comes back from the Dead Sea, how do you know there's shipwrecks at the bottom?"

The old man looked at him. "You ask very good questions, my boy."

"Do you have answers?"

"Not this time. Perhaps the water azheeks have seen it. Shipwrecks. Perhaps its rumours."

Aven nodded.

"Well, I have to get back to work," the librarian said. "But if you have any more questions, feel free to ask."

"Thanks." Aven smiled. "I appreciate it."

The giant watched the glimmering map and completely forgot that he had once been adamant to return to Foros. He had heard stories of Sontar Ivel, of the magic and wonder of Ianar, but he had never quite believed it. But here and now, staring at the map above, he sighed. There was so much to the world he hadn't experienced.

Finally he pulled his gaze away and wandered through the library. Aven traced a finger along shelves, gently feeling the bindings of books. They all felt so different, some so new, some so old he yanked his hand away out of fear he'd break them. But not a speck of dust touched his skin. The library was immaculate.

He opened a book and smelled it, closing his eye to take a deep inhale. A smile spread across his lips. He turned the first page and was met with words. So many tiny, tiny words.

Aven grimaced and put it back on the shelf.

The giant milled about, wandering down every aisle, completely forgetting that he was supposed to be looking for Veraion. He found himself in the children's section. Spotting a large book, he pulled it off the shelf and opened it, enjoying the crackling of the leather binding and old paper.

Pictures!

Aven took a seat, slowly reading the big letters, enjoying the artwork. He knew these illustrations.

On the first page was a drawing of a woman with dark skin and brilliant green eyes, her hair winding like roots. Her stomach was swollen, pregnant, the child inside her the world of Ianar. Rivers streamed from her breasts like milk, and inside, the umbilical cord connected the Mother to Ianar, leading right to Sontar Ivel. A channel between their world and the next. This was why the capital never changed, never moved. It was connected to their Mother god.

Beside her was a man, a man of bright fire. His long hair billowed behind him, one hand upon the bottom of her belly, streams of his light blessing Ianar. The land too close to his touch was unhabitable, too hot to survive.

On the woman's other side, climbing over her shoulder, was a child. A young girl with a pale glow, reaching down to place her hand on the top of the woman's belly, providing light where the man's could not reach. The land closest to her, furthest from the sun, was too cold to bring life.

The gods. Mother Nature, the Sun, and the Moon. But the Moon had her original colours, a paler and colder reflection of her father.

Mother Nature had created Ianar before the light of the Sun and Moon, but her child had been lifeless and empty. So she searched for ten thousand years until she found him, the Sun searching the galaxies with his daughter, and when the three came together, they were whole.

Mother Nature and the Sun fell so madly in love they bound, the binding of their love and light creating life. It was said they loved one another so much, it was the reason they ensured their favourite children, azheeks, would find true love in their lifetime, going as far as to prevent them from ageing until they found their ilis. Sometimes this love was romantic, as felt between the Mother and the Sun. Sometimes this love was platonic, as felt between the Mother and the Moon, and sometimes this love was familial, as between the Sun and the Moon.

Aven turned the page to see another familiar figure. Natura, the first queen, the first to host all elemental powers. Golden-brown skin, white hair, glowing white markings, and brilliant eyes that changed colour in the light of her father. By her side were the four lords: Atesh, the first lord of fire, Dunia, the first lord of earth, Awera, the first lord of water, and Ongji, the first lord of air. Together, they were the Five.

Aven smiled, a finger tracing the drawings.

Azheeks had thrived for years on Ianar prior to the Five, but the gods had sent them to guide the others, and the day they had come had been the longest day of the year, now celebrated as Five's Day. Natura had emerged in the heart of the mainland, the lord of earth to her south, lord of air to her north, fire to her east, and water to her west. And in Natura's place, the castle rose. Where the four lords stood, the ground was lifted into the air, to float over the stronghold of Sontar Ivel, with temples upon them built by the gods for the Five. To protect them. To protect azheeks.

Aven smiled, carefully turning the pages. He adored the illustrations, so vibrant and colourful, so much like the country around him, and excitement flooded him as he realized he would get to experience Five's Day in the capital.

He gazed over depictions of the Five. They had come to Ianar in their prime, every one of them two-spirited and two-formed. No matter who they bound to, they could produce offspring. But Natura was the only one to have a child before their demise. Natura gave birth to Aishida, the first Ianar-born queen, a two-spirited girl. Her birth decided the future of the bloodline, for after her, all queens were two-spirited women.

He turned the pages to the fall of the Five. Nobody ever spoke of what brought them down, what killed them, for whoever did it had been forgotten. Whoever had killed them had been erased from history.

The greatest insult was to be forgotten, and forgotten they were. The gods had removed them from the world, from anyone's memory. All Aven knew was that the day the Five were killed, the world changed. Magic changed.

The day the Five were killed was the longest night of the year. This day was once one of mourning, but thousands of years had passed and the people of Ianar had found a way to make it lighter.

The Day of Giving, they called it. For much of Ianar, the longest night happened in the heart of winter when rations were scarce, so the Day of Giving became a day when they would trade supplies. At least, that was how it started. Now, people gave each other gifts they didn't truly need. Still, it was a way to show love and appreciation, and he was sure the gods preferred a day of loving exchange to a day of mourning. Because there wasn't a single day that went by that the people of Ianar weren't reminded of the Five's murders.

Humans. They hadn't existed before the fall of the Five. Before then, azheeks could cross-breed and their children would be born of either of their parents' powers. But the day the Five were killed, the world changed. Magic changed. Magic *left*. And it left mixed-blooded children powerless.

Aven sighed. It couldn't have been easy for the first humans. But it had been thousands of years and humans were so common there were more of them than there were azheeks. There was a balance to azheeks, only ever becoming pregnant when the gods intended it, only ever producing enough offspring to replace the deaths of others, for always there was a balance of elements on Ianar. But humans, humans could breed like animals, and that they did.

Aven turned the page and found the Moon, depicted older now, a teenager. But she no longer had her pale light and had become the Blood Moon. She had changed that day, the day the Five were killed—the longest night of the year. Her light turned red, stained with the blood spilled.

Aven marvelled at the drawings, at the depiction of his favourite god. There was something about the Moon he found so beautiful, so haunting, as though he sought her approval more than the others'. A child god, a young god, a naïve god. Perhaps that was why he liked her. There was a lot he could relate to.

The man was so immersed in the illustrations he forgot he was in the library.

Down the aisle, a woman appeared, her gaze upon the book in her hands. She was deep in thought, lost in the writings, but when she heard Aven sigh, she glanced up. Her eyes returned to her book.

She stopped. She looked back at him.

Aven could feel someone watching him, and when his eyes flicked up to meet hers, he panicked.

Einmyria.

He yanked up his book, shielding his face from view. He winced behind the pages.

Slowly Einmyria approached, looking at him over his picture book. He put it down and smiled nervously.

"Hello." He cast her an uncomfortably toothy grin.

"Hi…"

"I… should go." He rose to his feet, using a shelf for support. It snapped under his weight, sending books toppling to the ground.

Einmyria stared up at him with wide eyes. He stood almost two feet taller than her.

"Fuck," Aven exclaimed, trying to catch books as they fell. "Shit— fuckshit—god damn it." He chuckled awkwardly, glancing at her as he hastily grabbed them, piling them neatly on the floor.

Aven sidled away, covering his face with his hand. She stared after him.

* * *

Night came and Veraion was still gone. Maina got off work early and took Chester through the city—through a hidden tunnel, a shortcut to the market. There she guided her through the bustling streets of Little Ikran, whisking her off to venture through Zeda Town, and they wandered into the great temple at Sakhala Street. Chester wanted to stay—she could explore for hours—but their stomachs grumbled and Maina took her to one of her favourite restaurants. It was pricier, but Maina was willing to pay. What they paid for was the view—a view of the castle.

It was truly a taste of Sontar Ivel. The restaurant was carved into a rocky cliff, overlooking the water that led to the castle. Lemons grew above them, the air sweet and crisp as it always was, and there were musicians playing in the slowly setting sun. Guitars, bandurrias, vihuelas, accompanied by a softly beaten tambourine and a set of castanets.

They ate breaded salads, cheese, and pesto. They had grilled slices of bread topped with vegetables, rubbed garlic, and tomato, and even more bread—baked, topped with caramelized onions, olives, more tomato, and basil leaves, covered with grated cheese. They drank wine made from red and white grapes, and by the time they returned to the inn, Chester was stuffed, content, and ready to pass into a food-induced coma.

She found Aven in room fourteen, sitting on his broken bed, disgruntled. He had been forced to eat dinner with Tao and Theideus, which would have been fine if Dog hadn't spent the whole time nipping at his ankles just to piss him off.

"You abandoned me," he huffed.

"I didn't abandon you," she laughed. "I got back before you did and Maina swept me away. She told me she left a lot of meat for you!"

"Dog stole some."

Chester laughed. "Well… I got you a gift!"

Aven perked up.

"You've been human for a few months now," she said. "And I figured it was time I finally gave you *this*."

AZHEEK : THE RISING

His face fell. What she held in her hand was thin, with a wooden shaft, bristled on the end.

A *toothbrush*.

He bared his teeth.

"I know you hated it when you were younger," she said, as though speaking to a child. "I still have the scars. But you're a big boy now. It's time to start brushing your teeth."

He took the toothbrush between his index finger and thumb, grimacing at it. He grumbled.

"I even got you special toothpaste," she continued in the same tone. "It's *meat* flavoured."

She held up the small tube and he took that too, between his other index finger and thumb, holding both toothbrush and toothpaste at arm's length as though they had just crawled out of a toilet and had eight legs.

"It's your choice," Chester said. "But your breath... might be... a little... reek-of-a-thousand-corpses-y."

Aven glanced at her, still wearing a grimace, and sighed. "Fine."

She smiled, patting his arm. He ducked his head so she could reach and she petted that too, ruffling his hair.

She couldn't help but laugh at how disgruntled he looked, still holding his "gifts" with straight arms, and she kissed him on the forehead, giving his dyed hair another ruffle before she headed to her bed, pulled off her clothes, and collapsed.

* * *

The wasfought returned to the woods. His dyed-black mane swayed about him as he trotted through the trees, through the light of the blood moon and dancing fireflies, heading for Einmyria's clearing. She was already there.

Einmyria sat in the grass, gazing through the forest canopy at the night sky, enjoying what stars she could see as a human. She had a rucksack with her.

Aven came forward, unable to stop his tail from wagging. Her grazing horse snorted upon seeing him but seemed to otherwise be unbothered in his presence.

"Hello." She smiled. He moved to nuzzle his great head into her, but she backed away. Reaching into her bag, she pulled out a book. The same picture book he had been reading earlier that day.

Aven sat straight up. His mouth opened and closed a few times, his eye wide.

"I don't know what you are," she said. "But…"

There was a long moment of silence. Then he transformed.

The loud cracks and crunches of his bones made her flinch in alarm, watching with wide eyes. His body morphed and his skull shifted until he sat before her as a human, albeit an incredibly huge and discoloured human.

She stared at him. Shocked. Terrified. Perplexed.

Then she glanced at his bare penis.

She gulped, looking away, and unfastened her cloak. She handed it to him. He didn't know what it was for, but after she gave him a couple of obvious glances, he shoved it between his legs. Still, she was blushing.

"How did you know?" he asked.

"Your scars," she said. "Your markings. The fact that you're seven feet tall. I have never heard of someone like you, but there have been a lot of things lately that I cannot explain."

"Please don't tell anyone."

"I won't," she said. "Are there more like you?"

"Not that I know."

She nodded. She fiddled awkwardly for a moment. "Thank you for saving me the other night."

"Any time."

She glanced at him. "Why are you following me?"

"Technically, I'm here to hunt. You just... keep turning up."

She smiled. "Why do you keep coming to say hi?"

"You're pretty."

"Oh."

He smiled at her. She glanced at him, shy, but eventually her smile returned.

"Do you want me to stop saying hi?" he said. She shook her head.

"You're pretty, too."

Aven smiled. "You should see me in a flower crown."

* * *

Morning rose over Sontar Ivel, every river and canal twinkling turquoise in the light of the sun god. People milled about the streets, many sleeping in, and others ate breakfast in the open air, in cafes and eateries overlooking the city. The air was sweet and fresh, never smelling otherwise; lush greenery and blooming flowers grew as far as the eye could see. Music softly resonated through the streets, but from where Veraion sat upon a city wall, overlooking one of the rings of the city, he listened to the lapping of water and calling of vendors. This ring acted as a wide canal, fish of all shapes and sizes swimming here and there, some moving quickly, others slowly—as slowly as the gondolas that floated above. Oarsmen worked with ease in the morning light, calling the names of the food they had for sale as they passed the open windows and doors of the houses built into the city walls.

Veraion smiled as more and more boats came into view, bringing with them a floating market. Those that lived close to the water leaned out of their windows to buy produce, food, and drinks, and those that lived higher up lowered baskets by rope, containing the coin needed to buy what they wanted.

Sandwiches, pastries, and coffee brewed from beans that grew all around the warmer regions of Ianar. A nearby gondola carried a vast array of cheeses, another yoghurts from goat milk, and as more boats passed, he saw food from other places in the world.

A dark-skinned human was selling bread and beans, and fried triangle-shaped dough with fruity dips. Breakfast from Okos. An air azheek sold coconut rice topped with sugar. Breakfast from Zalfur. And as a brown-skinned earth azheek came within earshot, Veraion's eyes lit up.

"Taho!" the vendor called. He was old, his hair predominantly grey, skin aged with life, and he wore naught but pants in the morning light. His belly was large from years of drinking but his limbs were strong from years of work. Over his arms and chest were old tattoos, geometric shapes of hexagons and triangles, in rows and in patterns, and Veraion knew that every mark and every placement had meaning. This man was from the Vaian Islands.

The vendor had with him large buckets and stacks of cups. Veraion couldn't stop the smile that lit in his eyes.

"Taho!" the man called again. The air was ripe with every vendor calling.

Veraion looked around for a way to get to the water and headed for a rickety ladder. It creaked with his weight but he moved with purpose, waving to the vendor as he got close.

"Good morning!" Veraion smiled.

"Morning!" The taho vendor beamed and steered his boat over. He pushed his way through the water with a long bamboo pole, careful where he placed it—careful not to damage the coral beneath.

"Are you from the Vaian Islands?" Veraion asked.

"I am!"

A light rested in Veraion's eyes that hadn't been there for a long time. "I haven't had taho in over twenty years."

"Twenty?" The old vendor stared. "I could never survive."

Veraion laughed. "I don't know how I did either. One, please—actually, make it two." He gave the man some coin. "Can I—can I please watch?"

The Vaian man smiled and moved his boat a little more, and as he took the lids off two buckets, Veraion smelled the brown sugar syrup he had long forgotten about. One bucket was divided in two, with syrup filling one side and chewy pearls made from the pith of sago palm trees in the other. The second bucket was filled to the brim with silken tofu.

The vendor took a wide spoon in one hand, holding two cups in the other, and swiftly scooped pieces of tofu into them.

Veraion smiled. Memories rushed back to him, memories of the taho vendor that came by his childhood home every morning. He had loved watching them scoop the silken tofu; there was something so satisfying in how quickly and skilfully they did it. He had had taho every morning, not because he particularly liked the way it tasted, but because he absolutely adored the way they scooped that tofu.

When the cups were mostly filled, the vendor closed the tofu bucket and moved to the other, using a deeper spoon to scoop sago pearls on top. Then he finished them off by pouring over a generous amount of brown sugar syrup.

He dipped the spoon in and around to properly mix the ingredients.

"Thank you." Veraion smiled, nodding respectfully as he took the cups.

"Thank you!" The old man beamed. "Are you from Vaia?"

"I am."

"Long live, brother."

Veraion only smiled more. "Long live."

He watched the vendor go, floating down the canal, and laughed softly as a child reached out of her window with a giant glass jar, greeting the Vaian man with a wide smile.

* * *

"This isn't any better!" Maina exclaimed over Aven's kills. The deers' throats were intact, but now there were holes in their chests from where Aven had ripped out their hearts with his gigantic fist.

"What?!" He stared.

"Why are there always holes in your hunt?"

"I needed to kill them somehow!"

"Are their hearts missing?"

"Did you need those too?"

Maina clapped a hand to her forehead, closing her eyes in frustration.

"It tastes the same." Aven glared. "Go do… inn-keepy things. Just… rub some chili on it." He waved her off. Chester was eating breakfast nearby and was choking on her food, laughing. He couldn't help but smile as he sat beside her.

Maina let out a sigh and other innkeepers rushed over, helping her take Aven's holey offering to the kitchens.

Aven and Chester looked up as Veraion entered the dining hall, carrying with him two cups of taho.

"Morning." The earth azheek smiled, taking his place across from them.

"Well, good morning, Veraion," Chester said.

"Try this." He gave her one cup. She looked at it, then him.

"Any chance you want to tell us what happened yesterday? Where you went? Where you slept?"

"I slept in a tree."

"A what—a *tree*?"

"It was quite big, don't worry."

"Veraion."

He sighed. "I'm sorry. I shouldn't have snapped. I just… I needed time. I needed air. And apparently… I needed taho."

"Ta-what?"

"Taho." He smiled, raising his cup.

"You didn't get me one?" Aven grunted.

"I get the feeling you won't like it." Veraion picked up a spoon and Chester followed suit, taking a good bite of the syrupy tofu. Chester smacked her lips a few times as she assessed the taste.

"It's... different."

Veraion nodded slowly. He looked confused. "Has it always been this *sweet?*"

"What is this?" Chester held it out for Aven to try, and just as Veraion expected, the giant made a very confused face when he did. The texture was foreign to him, the soft tofu seemingly disintegrating upon his tongue, accompanied by chewy pearls of sago palm pith.

"Taho," Veraion said. "From the Vaian Islands."

"They have it here?"

"Sontar Ivel has everything. I'd honestly forgotten about this." He smiled to himself and kept eating. Chester watched him for a moment, a fond look in her eyes, and shook her head.

"Yeah, fine. I accept your apology taho."

She and Aven shared her cup, though he kept making faces, and eventually she had to turn away from him to stop herself from laughing.

Maina re-emerged from the kitchens and Veraion waved her over, offering the treat.

"What did you do yesterday?" Chester asked Veraion. "Apart from eat sweet things and sleep in a tree."

"Walked around, signed up for the tournament."

Maina froze. "What?"

"What?" He raised an eyebrow at her.

"You're joining the tournament?"

"Yeah."

"You can't." Her face fell.

"Why not?"

"You'll be destroyed," she said fearfully. "Everybody knows you can't win the tournament, not now that Athos reigns. He's the undefeated champion, ten years in the running. He's been number one since the day he turned up. He has the strength of a thousand men."

"Exactly one thousand?" Veraion snorted.

"This isn't a joke," she snapped. "What happens if you face a fire azheek? They could burn you alive."

"Killing isn't permitted," he said. "Plus azheeks are only allowed to use their powers once it comes to the top ten champions, you know that."

"Accidents happen all the time," she pressed. "You know people have a hard time controlling their powers in moments of panic and desperation. People *have* died, and most of them have died because of Athos's *accidents*."

"As in underhand means of victory?" Chester asked.

"No," Maina said. "He *accidentally* kills them. He's too strong. He can barely control it. That man was made to kill, not to fight for show. He punched a man once and his heart stopped beating."

"Even I could stop a heart if I hit someone the right way," Veraion reminded her. "You could too."

"How many has he killed?" Chester asked.

"His first year, a lot," Maina said. "Every year after that, not too many because he only fought in the final game. Some people compete until they gain champion title, one of the top ten, and then they back out. You have no idea how many people don't even *bother* trying to fight him. And the ones that do… I am telling you, anyone that faces him comes out *seriously* injured, if not maimed for life. I think some of them die when they leave the city to return home. I've heard whispers that champions go missing."

Veraion cast Chester a foreboding look.

"What does he do?" Chester asked. "Apart from the tournament, what does he do? He lives in the castle, right?"

"He… Honestly, I don't know," she said. "Most of the year he's not even here. He comes for the tournament, watches, looks bored, annihilates the champions in the final game, retains his title, and then leaves. He does what he wants. No one can control that man. I think the castle *wants* him to be a member—I think they *want* him to be an adviser or to train the queen's men, hence him having quarters there—and he seems to be invited to all their important events, but… that man does as he pleases. He has more freedom than the queen—more respect among the people."

"Respect?" Veraion retorted. "Is he loved? Or is he feared?"

"Either way, he has power. Please don't sign up," she said desperately. "*Please.*"

"How is he still allowed to be champion?" Chester asked. "If he's killed so many people… by *accident.*"

"Everyone signs waivers when they register for the tournament," Veraion said. "Just in case."

"Just in case," Maina repeated darkly. "You're going to die. Or at least lose a limb."

"I'll be fine," he said laxly. "I'll be giving the inn my coin, by the way."

She sighed in frustration. "You're going to need armour. *Good.* Armour."

Chester nudged Aven with a smile. "I know a place."

* * *

Veraion, Chester, and Aven moved through the city, and though the tournament was still weeks away, people were already training openly on the streets. Blacksmiths and armourers were everywhere, taking advantage of the yearly event.

Chester headed for the armoury they knew, and Aven held the doors open for her. He went in after and let the door swing shut in Veraion's face. The man rolled his eyes before heading in on his own.

The armourer was standing behind the counter, wide-eyed, staring at a customer. The man was huge, over six feet tall, and though his back was turned towards the newcomers, they could tell just from the broadness of his shoulders that he was a mass of muscle. Scarred muscle, from blade, beast, and burns. His brown hair was long and thick, pooling over his back.

Veraion's gaze grew dark in the man's presence.

Athos. The undefeated champion of Sontar Ivel.

Athos turned and his eyes landed on Chester. Though he directed his cold gaze to her companions, he eventually rested his stare back on her. Aven's skin crawled and he instinctually balled a fist.

"Welcome back!" The Kapaduan armourer smiled, seemingly out of breath. "What can I help you with?"

Veraion finally took his glare off Athos. "Armour."

"Everyone is joining the tournament this year!" She chuckled nervously, glancing at the champion. He looked at her, a very slight change of expression upon his cold face. Conceit.

"I guess this is all our lucky day," she said. "We get to meet the champion in the flesh!"

Veraion cast her a very insincere smile.

"Will you be joining the tournament?" Athos's deep voice took everyone by surprise. He was looking at Chester.

"Me?" She blinked.

"Of course."

Veraion stood between them, his glare dark. He had to look up at the champion, but it didn't intimidate him.

"I'd never let my little sister get in harm's way," he snarled. Chester rolled her eyes. Athos held the man's glare, and after a long moment, he smirked.

"Good luck."

He left, his gaze never leaving Chester as he passed by.

The moment he was gone, the armourer let out a sigh of relief as though she had been holding her breath the whole time. Chester looked at Veraion with a raised eyebrow.

"You okay, *brother?*"

"He's not right," he said. Both he and Aven were still glaring at the door.

"Are you jealous?"

"Chester, that man is *not right*. There is something horribly wrong with him. I can feel it."

She smirked. "Are you sure you're not just a *little* jealous?"

"Whatever that man is, it is the last thing I would ever want to be."

Aven was still frowning at the door. "What is he?"

"Human," the armourer replied. "Proof that azheeks are not always the superior species."

Chester was genuinely impressed.

"He comes from a city far from here," the armourer said. "Mahr Ivel, he called it. The Iron City."

"Mahr Ivel," Veraion repeated darkly. "Mahr Ivel isn't a real place. That man is hiding something."

"And you've been to every city on the face of the planet," Chester said dryly.

"No, but I know of them. I know Ianar. I know empires, cities, towns, and villages. I know mountains and rivers. Mahr Ivel doesn't exist."

She shook her head at him, looking to the armourer. "You make Athos's armour?"

The human laughed. "I'm flattered you think so, but no. Athos... does not wear armour."

Chester let out an ominous sigh, glancing at Veraion, who was still glowering. She returned to the armourer. "What's your name?"

"Zaiera." She nodded. "Have you come back to pay for my broken chest-plate?"

They followed her gaze to the dent Aven had left.

"*aish.*" Veraion let out an exasperated sigh. "Yes."

Aven looked at him in surprise.

"I'm joining the tournament," Veraion said. "I can only give you a little now, but as the tournament goes on, I'll give you my coin. I will cover the cost of my armour... and Aven's stupidity."

Aven mocked him like a child, but neither Veraion nor Zaiera saw it. She was too busy looking at the earth azheek dryly.

"He's good," Chester said. "Really good."

Zaiera scoured him over, then glanced at Aven, who gave her a wide smile and a thumbs-up. She returned her gaze to Veraion, taking note of his scars. "You survived a wasfought attack?"

He nodded. Chester was about to remind him he only survived because she intervened, but she held her tongue.

Zaiera let out a sharp sigh. "Okay."

CHAPTER 6
BLOOD AND SAND

Excitement flooded the streets of Sontar Ivel. For weeks the buzz was growing, more and more people flocking to the city from all corners of the land, and as the tournament's commencement date rolled closer and closer, every inn in the capital was packed.

The tournament grounds became a market most of the year, but for the duration of summer, the stalls and huts were cleared. Small fight rings were constructed, stretching out as far as the eye could see.

The tournament commenced on the first day of summer, the longest day of the year—Five's Day. Talk, laughter, and music boomed through the capital and merchants shouted, waving their wares. This was the best time of year for them, for the streets were packed with foreigners, drawn in by the prospect of celebrating Five's Day in Sontar Ivel—by the prospect of the tournament that had been founded by the Five themselves.

Every man, woman, and child wore a smile, couples holding hands and friends laughing loudly, arms around the shoulders of their companions. Hands were occupied, exchanging coin for garlands and woven flower crowns, silver for clothes sewn in the city, but most of all, hands were busy holding street foods sold on every corner. Crisp rice balls stuffed with gooey cheese, peas, and minced meats. Battered and fried seafood, squeezed with lemon juice. And for those that wanted the taste of something sweet, they ran to the stalls selling deep-fried balls of dough filled with custard, cream, chocolate, or jelly, dusted with fine sugar.

The smell of food filled the air even through the tournament grounds, where vendors weren't allowed to sell.

Sunlight beat down on the city, bringing sweat to bead on all skin but that of those who held fire in their veins. The smell of food was thick in the air, but as spectators wandered into the tournament grounds, the smell of dry dirt was just as strong.

Over the grounds hung a great tapestry with the names of every contestant. Hundreds of names littered the cloth, embroidered in gold, and at the top of it all was sewn the largest name of all. Athos.

Veraion moved through the grounds in Zaiera's armour. It was lightweight for agility but strong for protection, fitting perfectly. His black hair was tied back, but it didn't do much to stop sweat from glistening upon his neck.

He and Aven headed through the crowd, reading the names hung above each ring. Veraion found his and greeted the referee as Aven poked a toothpick into his food: breaded olives stuffed with spiced meat. He ate one, then another, and then flicked the toothpick away to tip his head back and take a solid mouthful instead.

In the middle of the grounds was a watch tower where only one man stood. Athos's thick brown hair barely moved in the breeze.

Veraion leaned against a post and looked around. "Where's Chester?"

"She said she was going to meet us here," Aven said around a mouthful of food. "I thought you knew where she... Oh."

Veraion followed his gaze. Through the crowd, at a nearby fight ring, Chester was seated on the fence. Her dyed hair had been braided away from her face, a simple sword propped against the railing. She was wearing armour similar to his, eating a custard puff, and when she saw the boys looking at her she gave them a lax salute with sugar-dusted fingers.

"*aish*," Veraion muttered. He moved through the throng, followed by Aven, and when he reached her, she gave him an expectant smile. She was wearing a wreath, some of the flowers pink—the exact flowers that had grown back in place of the clusters Aven had plucked the month before.

"Have you lost your mind?" Veraion hissed.

"No more than you." She smiled as Aven stole one of her dough puffs. Veraion shook his head in disbelief.

"What?" She laughed. "It's just fun."

"I'm not in this for fun."

"You aren't, but I am," she said simply. "This is what I do, Raion. And if anyone is to blame, you're the one that informed me we'd get paid for this. Between kicking ass and scrubbing toilets, the choice was easy."

He shook his head, though there was a smile on his lips. He took a custard puff. "You've been planning this since you first found out."

She winked as he ate. "Gold and glory, my friend."

"Are you registered as—"

"Human, of course."

"Your weapon?"

"What weapon?" She nodded to the common sword beside her, another strapped across her back. "I don't know a single person that owns kara'i steel." She smiled. He raised an eyebrow at her.

"You're getting better at lying."

She looked proud. "Are you still using machetes?"

"Not for this. They're good for kills, but if I need to properly block a swing, I'm better off with swords."

She gasped, her voice cooing. "Don't tell me we have matching dual blades."

He snorted. "It appears we also have matching armour. Did you make the same deal with Zaiera?"

"Same as you, brother. Shall we be fighting twins? I bet the crowd would love that."

"Considering there's about a ten-year age gap between us, I don't think that angle would work."

She smirked. He glanced to the tapestry above her ring and raised an eyebrow. Her name wasn't on it.

"What name did you register with?"

"Mahriel," she said. "My trainer used to call me that. It's more chantable than Chester. *Mah-ri-el, Mah-ri-el, Mah-ri-el.*"

"Your mentor called you Mahriel?"

She nodded.

"Are you aware it means Iron Heart?"

She blinked. She hadn't known that. She wasn't sure if she liked it. "What?"

"Your mentor expected a lot from you," Veraion said.

Chester turned her perplexed look to the name hanging above her ring. "Iron as in brave? Or as in cold and unfeeling..."

"Too late to change it now." Veraion smirked, patting her leg. "Have fun, *Iron Heart.*"

She threw him a middle finger and he laughed, making a move to leave. Aven stopped him, a hand on his shoulder, and then used his free thumb to wipe powdered sugar from Veraion's lip.

Veraion withdrew with a startled noise, staring at the giant, and Aven held eye contact as he licked his thumb clean. It was Chester's turn to laugh.

Veraion grimaced. "Why are you like this?"

Aven blinked slowly with a mischievous smile. Veraion's look of confused discomfort only grew.

"What is that? Why are you doing that?"

Aven did it again. "I'm winking."

There was a moment of silence.

"Aven," Veraion said. "You only have *one* eye. You can't wink... Either that or you're... always winking."

He shook his head at Aven the whole way back to his ring.

Chester handed Aven the last of her snack, pulling off her crown of flowers and placing it upon his head. Veraion watched them from his place, and though he didn't know it, there was a fond look on his face. He leapt over the fence.

"Are you ready?" his referee called. He nodded, pulling on his helmet. The referee raised a hand into the air, and slowly, one by one, the others followed suit.

All eyes turned to Athos on his watchtower. The champion gazed down at everyone. It seemed he was already bored. He raised a hand, though it was slight. He didn't care enough to waste any more energy. Then he flicked his wrist and all referees threw down their arms. Horns blared and the tournament grounds rang with the clashing of metal on metal.

Veraion's opponent lunged at him and he ducked out of the way. Dust stirred into the air as their boots scuffed the earth, scattering dried dirt at surrounding spectators.

Low drums began beating, vibrating through the bodies of the crowd.

Veraion drew his swords and his opponent wheeled around, lunging once more, but he parried the attack, kicking him in the chest. The other man staggered back and Veraion lashed out quickly. He slammed his blade against the man's helmet. Once, twice, three times, and when he stumbled, Veraion punched him. The man fell to the ground.

Veraion waited for him to get back up, but he didn't. He cocked his head.

"Is that it?" the referee called. Veraion nudged his opponent with his foot.

"It appears so."

Those that had been watching cheered and a guard climbed into the ring, dragging the unconscious fighter away. The referee yanked down the tapestry with the man's name.

"Don't get too confident," he said. "These first few days will be quick to remove weak competitors. The real fighting happens once they've been picked off."

Veraion nodded and climbed onto the railing, gazing over the crowd to see Chester.

Neither she nor her opponent had their weapons, but that wasn't stopping her. She leapt into the air and drop-kicked the man, sending him careening backwards. Aven cheered loudly. Her opponent stumbled to his feet, reaching for his weapon, but Chester lunged at him, slamming him to the ground from behind. Quickly she wrapped her arms around his neck, squeezing, and he choked, eyes wide. He fought to grab his sword but Chester grabbed him back.

The more he struggled, the harder she squeezed.

At last, he threw a hand to the sky, his index and middle fingers raised to indicate surrender. The crowd cheered and Chester laughed, releasing him.

Rising to her feet, she offered a hand. He glared but accepted her help, and when he stood, she shook his hand with a smile.

The man hobbled away, picking up their weapons as he went. He chucked Chester's swords at her and she caught them swiftly, throwing her arms up in victory. Aven yelled loudly, encouraging others to do the same. Some spectators reached over the railing to pat her in approval.

"Yeah." She grinned. "This is much better."

Chester looked over the crowd to where Athos was watching, holding his gaze for a moment before turning back to her audience with a smile.

Chester and Veraion rose victorious again and again, ploughing through the first day of the tournament. Aven watched in the crowd, cheering loudly, egging on others, and when he noticed money exchanging hands, he decided to join in. He placed his bets on Chester, and while he'd never admit it, he also bet on Veraion.

Aven started the day with a single silver coin. He ended with a satchel.

Veraion fought quickly and accepted his praise with only small nods. Chester fought loudly and with many theatrics, yelling for her audience, basking in their love with a shit-eating grin.

At long last, down fell Chester's last adversary. She threw up her arms and her crowd cheered, jeering at her opponent as the guards dragged her from the grounds. Chester's referee came forward with a smile.

"You will go far, I can say that for sure." He beamed. She smiled, out of breath, giving a nod of thanks. "Let's hear it for Mahriel! Mahriel of— Where are you from?"

She looked at him, chest still heaving. Glancing up at Athos's watchtower, she smirked. "Mahr Ivel."

The referee's eyes widened. "Oh my! Let us hear it for Mahriel! Hailing from the hometown of our very own champion, Mahr Ivel! Mahriel of Mahr Ivel!"

The crowd went wild. People chanted her name.

Athos was still watching her, a gleam in his piercing eyes, so she raised a sword and pointed it at him. A grin crawled across her lips, and as the audience chanted her name, Athos smirked darkly.

* * *

The boom of the Five's Inn tavern was heard even down the hallway in the bathing rooms, and Chester sat in her bath, listening. She couldn't help but smile. There were many stalls and she always took the one on the far end. Theideus summoned water from the rivers above to fill the tubs, and she never had to wait for the bath to heat up, for she could do that herself.

She loved the smell here, the damp air bringing out a strong essence of birch and pine from the panels of wood that made each tub and divided the bathing areas. The air was thick and steamy, humid, filling her lungs, and she closed her eyes, breathing slowly.

She sat in her place, splashing water over her shoulders, sweaty hair tied up. She was careful, always washing her hair last to avoid turning herself grey.

She could hear people talking about her, about Veraion, and when she heard Aven loudly boasting about how great they were, her smile returned. There would be festivities all through the night, celebrating the tournament and Five's Day, and while she would have loved to experience it, she was far too tired.

She had a lantern in her stall, the only thing lighting the steamy booth, and she watched the flames dance.

Slowly her smile faded. Fire always reminded her of him. Yrilim. It had been weeks since she'd spoken about him, hoping the others had forgotten. But she never did.

Chester let out a quiet sigh and closed her eyes, sliding further into the bath.

Lower she sank, lower and lower until her face disappeared beneath the surface, water muffling the sounds of the inn around her.

Quiet. Naught but the beating of her heart.

And yet, it almost sounded like there were two heartbeats. It wasn't just hers she was listening to.

Veraion sat in his bath, and though Chester didn't know he was right beside her, separated by a thin wall of steamed wood, he could feel her. He could feel her sadness.

He splashed water over his neck, pushing fingers through his messy hair.

He could feel her so strongly, and in the time she had sat beside him, he had felt her go from happy, to peaceful, to heartbroken.

He reached into the water, picking up his necklace, and gazed at the glowing crystal. Veraion clenched his jaw and swallowed the knot in his throat, looking at the wall separating him from her.

Chester listened to Yrilim's heartbeat. He was calm. The tempo of his heart matched up almost perfectly with hers. She emerged from the water and let out another sigh.

"God damn it," she murmured. Azheek bonds were both a blessing and a curse.

A trickle of dye-stained water travelled down her face.

She came from the bath and untied her hair, crouching to dunk it into the water, scrubbing at her scalp.

* * *

Chester wore only a towel as she headed back for room fourteen. Drops of black dye dripped from her hair, trickling down her back and into the cloth wrapped around her.

She could smell the rich pine and birch from the bathing rooms, and the food wafting from the dining hall, but as she stood in the corridor, she smelled something bitter. It was pungent, foreign to her, and she glanced around curiously. It was coming strongest from the far end of the hall, from where she knew Tao's quarters were.

Maina appeared from her chambers and Chester quickly forgot about the curious smell.

"I quit." Chester smiled. Maina chuckled.

"I should have known. That's why you never complained."

Chester shrugged. "You never asked me to clean a toilet."

"You get a pint on me tonight!" Maina laughed, heading towards the tavern. "I heard you did well. Try not to die, yeah?"

Chester laughed and gave a salute before heading into her room.

Craning her neck from side to side, she arched her back and stretched.

The door opened and closed behind her as Veraion entered, a towel around his waist. His wounds from Aven had long healed, but both he and Chester were covered in bruises—bruises that would only grow darker and more painful.

"Do you smell that in the hallway?" he asked, glancing back at the door. "I swear to the gods…"

He shook his head, pushing the thought away.

Chester was looking in a mirror, at her black hair, and she smiled. "You know, I like it. The black. It almost suits me more."

He stood behind her, looking at their reflections. "It does."

Chester's smile grew sad. "Do you think… do you think this is what my mother looked like?"

He looked at her, then to her hair, and smiled to himself. It was sombre, and he pulled a speck of dust from her wet hair. He looked at her in the mirror. "Yeah. Probably."

He headed to his bed.

"You did good today," she said, finally turning from the mirror. He looked at her with a smirk and threw his arms into the air, re-enacting her behaviour.

"I'm Mahriel! Look at me! I'm so great!" He spun around.

"Fuck off," she laughed. "You'd do it too if you weren't wanted by command of the queen."

"You aren't?"

She waved him off. He ran a hand through his wet hair, groaning from the long day, and her gaze rested on his necklace. It shimmered, soft white lights wafting from it. Mesmerizing.

"Could I… see your necklace?" she asked. He glanced down and became withdrawn.

"I'd rather you didn't."

She nodded. "I respect that."

Then she picked up another towel, taking a seat at the edge of her bed, beginning a battle with her wet hair.

Veraion watched her for a moment. He glanced at his necklace, clenching his jaw, and lifted it over his head. He came forward, dangling the pendant in front of her. It took her a moment to see it, and when she did, she stopped, peering at him through her black hair.

"You sure?"

He nodded. She placed down the towel and took the pendant into her hand, draping the gold chain over her fingers. He took a seat beside her as she stared at the crystal, circling a thumb over its smooth surface. White lights rose from it, and inside the stone there was a substance that looked like liquid light, dancing like smoke. The crystal was cool to the touch, but comforting.

She looked at him. His gaze was on the ground.

"It was hers, wasn't it?" she asked. He nodded. "Four years, you said?" He nodded again. "I'm sorry. I can't imagine."

He finally looked at her and smiled slightly. "I've accepted it. Took a while though."

She nodded. Then she rested her head on his shoulder, looking at the glowing pendant in her hand. It reminded her a lot of the crystal in her water azheek weapon.

"Where did you grow up?" she asked. "Where are you from? Vaia?"

He smiled to himself, sadly. "Originally, the Vaian Islands. But baraduhr came and laid waste to my village."

She let out a long sigh. "I'm sorry."

"I only survived because my mother hid me in the cargo hold of a small boat and pushed me out to sea. She told me not to look back, not to come up, not until I couldn't hear anything but the lapping of water against the hull. I didn't move for three days. Even long after the screaming stopped, long after the smell of the burning flesh left, I was too scared to move."

Knots had built in both their throats and she took his hand, giving it a light squeeze.

"I'm so sorry." Her words were quiet. She felt him nod.

"It is what it is."

"Both orphaned by baraduhr," she said. "It's no wonder we get along."

He smiled a little. "Yeah. That's the only reason."

She nudged him with a snort. "Shut up." She couldn't see it, but she knew he was smiling. He rested his head upon hers.

"How old were you?" she asked.

"Six."

"Is it harder? Because you knew your parents? I never knew mine. I have nothing to miss."

"I bet your parents were wonderful," he said. "Loving. Kind. I bet they were brave. I'm sure they fought till the last breath." A tear slid from his bloodshot eyes and he swallowed the knot in his throat.

She squeezed his hand again, smiling sadly. "You're just describing your parents, aren't you?"

He didn't reply, not with his words, but he closed his eyes and nestled his head against hers some more.

"What happened after that?" she asked. "Unless… unless this is too hard. You don't have to say."

"After that… I was taken to Zalfur."

"*Zalfur?*" She pulled away only to stare at him. "The… the *empire?* The cities in the sky?"

He smiled slightly, understanding her reaction, and nodded.

"I—Okay," she said. "Maybe I'm just going off stereotypes and rumours. But I've heard it's all rock and snow, and… and that they're kind of… scary."

He snorted softly. "It's not all ice and snow—it's quite beautiful, actually. Plenty of mountains, yes, particularly in Zeda, and the castle is very high up, but Zalfur is a huge country, and you can't categorize all of it into a box."

"How about the people?"

"Like every place, there's good ones and there's bad ones."

"Like… the Red Emperor… and his Fang'ei."

He smiled to himself. "Everyone knows about Lord Ezaria."

"Yeah, how can we not? Only the strong survive in Zalfur."

"I'm sure that's the easiest way to sum it up," he said.

"It's not the truth?"

"It is, but there's more to it. And there's always two sides to a story."

"Where did you live?" she asked. "Which city?"

"Zeda."

She let out another sigh. "I hear the Zedai are the craziest. And Zeda is where the Fang'ei train, right? The best of the best? The… worst of the worst."

He laughed. "It's funny how far the Zalfuri reputation travels. It's why I don't talk about it. It raises so many questions."

"I thought Zalfur was home to air azheeks and air azheeks alone?"

He nodded. "Ilia and I were the only ones there of different powers. But it's hard to train as an earth azheek in a country of air."

She looked at him. "You keep saying you're practically human—why?"

He smiled to himself a little. "My powers were… stunted. I could barely access them. I got teased a lot."

"Were you always like that?"

He looked at her and she nodded, understanding.

"Trauma?"

He nodded. "I was a regular azheek as a kid, playing with powers. But after my parents were killed… it's like my body shut down. And never woke up."

Chester watched him and a smile appeared, on her lips and in her eyes. Knowing. "You've woken up, Veraion. Just because you can't control trees or summon roots from the ground doesn't mean you're less of an earth azheek. You make grass grow in your sleep, you know."

"What?"

"I noticed it when we were riding north. Every morning, when you'd get up, there would be grass poking out of the ground beneath you."

He blinked. "That's… new."

"And I guess you haven't noticed *that*." She pointed towards his bed and he followed her gaze.

Near his pillow, hidden between the wooden bedframe, growing from the rock walls, was a hint of green. He blinked.

She nudged him. "Barely an earth azheek, my ass."

"That's… very new."

Then Chester cocked her head, a thought occurring to her. "I've heard that Zalfuri speak both Common and Ancient Azheek—is that true?" He glanced at her sheepishly and she stared. "You speak *Ancient Azheek?*"

"*Ancient* is not very accurate," he said. "The kara'i have spoken that language for thousands of years—for them it's the only language. And the Zalfuri have had it in their curriculum for almost two hundred years now."

"Because of the Red Emperor, right?"

He nodded. "Ezaria respects the Old Ways. He wishes to restore them."

"Hence the human baby murder," she murmured. "I can't imagine being alive for two hundred years... *two hundred* years and not a single bind. What a loveless life. It's no wonder he's so cold."

Veraion smiled slightly, uncomfortable.

"But what you're saying is that you do speak Azheek," she pressed.

"Yeah."

"You can read and write it?"

"Yeah. I understand Sa'uri. The Old letters."

"Fuck... well, that would explain why you swear in it. I notice you tend to say... expressions."

"*aishida?*"

"Everyone knows Aishida."

"*natura's ma'ale, natur?*"

"That's the one." She smiled. "What does it mean?"

"Natura's mother, Nature."

"Oh... makes sense."

He smiled. "*baraduhr* means 'masked men', *barad* meaning 'masked' and *duhr*, 'human'." He paused. "It also means 'nothing'. *uhr* means 'all', and *duhr*, 'none', as in... 'azheeks with no powers'."

"Oof. Ouch. I can see why they're so bitter."

He nodded.

She smiled. "Tell me, how would one say 'kill them all'?"

He smirked. "*kyale dehen uhr.*"

"*kyale dehen uhr,*" she repeated. "I like that."

They sat there for a while, in silence. Then Veraion spoke.

"Who's Yrilim?"

She snorted. "Took you four months to ask."

"I didn't want to pry."

"Didn't want to pry? Or didn't care to know?"

He smiled. "Back then? Both. Now… I'll listen if you want to tell."

She watched the swirling crystal in her hand for a moment before speaking. "He's a fire azheek. He turned up in Foros one day, in the river. Ended up there by accident. He was unconscious, on the brink of death. Aven and I saw him and dragged him out. Then you know how it goes. You fall in love, you bind, you're fucked for all eternity."

He laughed. "Where is he now?"

"Still there, I assume."

"Why… did you leave him behind?"

She smiled sadly, letting out a sigh. "Because Yrilim is bound to someone else."

Veraion's brow furrowed. "That… can't be possible. A one-sided bond?"

"Apparently."

He thought this over. It didn't make any sense, but he didn't want to press the matter. "How are you doing?"

She looked at him with a fond smile. "I'm doing good, and with this tournament, I think I'm going to be *real* fucking good."

"Good."

"Hey," she murmured. "If you can speak Azheek, and read it, do you know what my sword says?"

She handed Veraion his necklace and moved over to where her water azheek weapon was wrapped up and hidden, pulling it free. The blue lights swirled, her crystal glowing white. The old runes glimmered and she ran her fingers over the gleaming blades, sitting beside Veraion once more.

"*kanaua'a iord volehn,*" he murmured. "*fa'ale iord kara, madia.* Protector of Volehn, daughter of water, Madia."

"Volehn? That's one of the water azheek cities, right?"

"Yeah." He nodded. "So now at least you know where it comes from." Then his brow furrowed. "*Madia*... I know that name. I know that name..." He cocked his head, tracing a finger over the old language. "*Madia*..." His eyes widened and he sat up. "Madia! Madia was a lord—the daughter of the lord of Volehn."

"*What?*"

Chester and Veraion stared at one another.

"Madia," he said. "Daughter of Madias. She was a lord. Or she would have been... if she hadn't disappeared."

"Theideus knew a lord?"

"Theideus knew one well enough to choke you when he saw you had this," he said, sharing at her shock.

"He's a *lord?*"

"Let's not jump to conclusions—he could have just worked in the castle."

"You're right... You know what, anyone from Volehn would have known who Madia was—you did, and you're not even from Volehn."

He nodded but was still enthralled. "You don't just have a water azheek weapon, you have the weapon of a *lord*. A kara'i *lord*."

"Fucking Valduhr..."

"How long ago did you get this?"

"About ten years."

"Lines up," he said. "She went missing about a year before that."

Chester let out a long sigh, gazing at the weapon in new light. "You think she was killed?"

"Probably. There's no other reason why someone else would have that weapon."

"So Theideus is from Volehn," she murmured. "I think we now know more about him than Maina does."

"To be honest, I had a feeling he was from Volehn. I hear the Volehni have paler blond hair and lighter blue eyes, and it checks out."

"Don't they all have blond hair and blue eyes?"

"Yes, but there's differences. The Volehni have lighter hair, skin, and eyes, and they speak Azheek with a softer tone. They also pronounce the Rs differently from the Elizi. Different accent."

"I never thought about accents within Azheek," she murmured.

"Elizia is the capital. The Azheek I speak is from there—the Zalfuri learned from them. Their hair is blond, but not as light as the Volehni, skin a little darker, and their eyes usually have a green tint—sea blue."

Chester nodded in interest, tracing the runes that were so foreign to her.

"And Paradiz," Veraion said. "I've never met someone from Paradiz, but I've been told their hair is a little more copper-blond, eyes almost purple-blue."

"Whoa, that sounds cool."

"Their skin is more tanned, too. They spend a lot of time in the sun, so eventually their hair does turn lighter, but it's not that way naturally. And their dialect... It's different. And they speak almost entirely in slang—or in what the others consider slang."

Chester smiled. "Nice."

"Apparently Paradizi can understand Elizi and Volehni with no problems, but if I met someone from Paradiz... apparently I would have great difficulty understanding *them*."

"Accent?"

"Whole different dialect."

"Like a different language?"

"It's still Sa'uri," he said. "Or Ancient Azheek, as some people would call it. But the sentences are structured differently. And the intonation, the way they speak, it's very... specific. To Paradiz."

"You've never met a Paradizi, yet you know all this?"

"We've been warned about the Paradizi."

Chester laughed. "Just because of the way they speak?"

"We've been warned that if we ever meet someone from Paradiz, we'll probably think they're trying to start a fight. Just because of the way they speak. But… that's just it. That's just how they speak."

Chester watched him with a smile. "I like the sound of Paradiz. Do you know any of the Paradiz dialect?"

He sat back and thought to himself. "Only one thing… *dahveh?*"

"What does that mean?"

"Do you want to die?"

She laughed again.

"In Elizi you would say, *tu u vend do dahv?* Literally, 'Do you want to die?' But in Paradiz, it's just… *dahveh?* 'Death, huh?'"

Chester smiled, looking at him fondly. "You know so much."

He snorted. "Yeah… maybe."

"Do you know what the islands are like?"

"Paradiz? I hear it's a series of islands, turquoise waters, and they're all so… relaxed. You know, from what I've heard, it kind of reminds me of home. The Vaian Islands. Or the Eloan Islands, north of Vaia. Apparently Paradiz used to be close with those islands, but they left when the Five died to prevent the creation of humans."

Chester nodded, thinking to herself. "You said Ilia was a water azheek, right?"

He let out a soft sigh and nodded.

"Where was she from?"

It took him a moment to respond. "Elizia."

"What's Elizia like?"

"Very green," he said. "It's more mountainous—thick jungles, waterfalls, lagoons, and of course it's an island, so beaches all around."

"Do you know about Volehn?"

"Rocky, limestone formations. There are still beaches, of course, but not as flat as Paradiz and far more rocky than Elizia."

She watched him with an amused smile. "Do you know everything?"

He laughed. "Is it wrong that I feel like we're invading Theideus's privacy?"

"No," she sighed. "I feel that way too. He could easily communicate with Maina, with us, but he chooses not to. I feel like if he knew that we knew, it might make him uncomfortable. We should probably... leave it."

He nodded. "Agreed. Not until he wants to talk about it."

They both sighed, eyes resting upon the glowing crystals in their hands, and after a moment, Chester's head rested upon Veraion's shoulder once more.

"How do you say 'fuck'?"

He laughed. "*mida.*"

* * *

Aven returned to the woods as he had done every night for the last month. He wouldn't tell anyone, but he even brushed his teeth. Every day. And when he ran out of his tube of meat-flavoured toothpaste, he started using Chester's. It always left his mouth feeling like he had sucked on a block of ice, but for the first time in his life he was experiencing the very human emotion of feeling self-conscious. He didn't want Einmyria to think his breath reeked of a thousand corpses.

He sat in the grass, admiring lazy fireflies around him, gazing at the stars with a smile. Then he pulled off his oversized tunic and turned into a wasfought with a series of unsettling crunches.

He tipped his head back, howling at the full moon. He had come by horse the last few weeks, and his stallion snorted irritably, but it had grown used to him and his strange ways.

Through the trees, Einmyria approached. She smiled as she saw him, listening to his wasfought song. She could hear other beasts in the woods, but they were all far now. He had marked their territory well and his reputation had grown in these woods. No wasfought wanted to bother with the mutant beast and his tiny human companion.

Aven rose to his feet, his body shifting as he went, and draped his tunic back over his head.

"That was beautiful." Einmyria smiled. He offered a hand to help her, and when she drew her legs to one side, he picked her up. Einmyria gasped, laughing as he spun her around. She swayed in place when he finally let her down.

"Don't do that again," she said, though her voice was kind.

"Sorry."

"You seem happy—did you have a good day?"

"I did." He beamed. "I have friends participating in the tournament and they made it through without a single loss."

"That's impressive. Did you not join?"

"I'm not a fighter." He shrugged.

Einmyria glanced up at him and his gargantuan muscles. She smiled to herself and looked away.

She was wearing her cloak, blue and iridescent, and beneath it her mid-length dress shimmered in the light of the blood moon. Shiny. He wanted to touch the fabric. She could tell.

"Peace silk," she said. "It's very smooth."

"Peace silk," he murmured. "I need some peace silk."

"You can… touch it, if you want to."

He smiled a little and stroked the fabric at her chest with a single finger, careful not to touch her inappropriately. She bit back her smile.

The giant's clothes were linen, baggy, oversized, and for the most part made it look like he was wearing a potato sack. But Einmyria still found him very pretty.

"Is there a difference between peace silk and… silk?" he asked.

"All silk used to be peace silk," she said. "When it was azheeks making it. But humans like to cut corners and do things fast and easy, even if it means hurting others. So now we have to differentiate by name."

"What… what do they do?"

"They boil the silk worms alive."

"Oh… that's not very nice."

"No, it's not."

"Peace silk." He nodded. "*Peace silk.*"

She smiled.

"I have something for you," he said. Reaching into a rucksack he had tied to his saddle, he pulled out a vibrant bouquet of flowers. Einmyria blushed, accepting the present with a smile.

"Thank you, they're beautiful." She smelled the bouquet as they sat in the grass but was careful not to get too close to the blooms.

"Flowers were always my favourite part of the city," she said. "I never realized how good I had it here until I left. We get seasons here, but the plants, they thrive all year round no matter what. Eternal colour. Eternal life. It's beautiful. You know… away from Sontar Ivel, people refer to it as the City of Flowers. I love that. I never knew until I left."

He watched her as she kept her hazel eyes on the bouquet in her hands.

"Where did you go?" he asked. "How long were you away?"

She sighed. "My brother and I travelled around for his work. He worked for my father. I didn't want to go, but my father said it would be good for me to see the world, so I left my home behind. We were gone for… five? Six years?"

"It wasn't worth it?"

She smiled sadly. "I saw the world. And I lost my brother."

Einmyria let out a small sigh and gazed around the enchanting forest, at the fireflies dancing lazily around them. "The years I spent away… they felt so empty. All I wanted was to come back. But now that I am… it just doesn't feel the same." There was so much sadness in her words. "It doesn't feel like home anymore."

"What happened to your brother?" he asked.

She smiled sadly. "He was killed."

"God damn. I don't think I know a single person that hasn't lost a loved one."

"Have you?"

"Technically, my mother, I guess."

"A wasfought?"

He nodded. She watched him for a moment, and a smile appeared on her lips.

"Is it weird that I really want to know what you looked like as a cub?"

He took a bushel of pink flowers from her bouquet, tucking it behind his ear. "I was fucking adorable."

Einmyria laughed, her smile spreading from ear to ear, and he couldn't help but beam upon seeing it.

"You know what else I discovered?" she said. "While I was away from Sontar Ivel... Turns out I'm allergic to pollen."

"To what?"

"Pollen. It's what trees, grass—it's what flowers release to pollinate other plants of the same species. The plants here don't release pollen because they grow through the magic of the city, but outside the capital... Turns out I am very allergic."

"Oh..." He blinked. "I never would have thought of that."

"Aven," she said. "I'm allergic to tree sex."

He looked at her in confusion, and she laughed.

"Pollen," she said between wheezes. "It's essentially... it's..."

He had no idea what she was talking about, but he found himself laughing anyway. Her cheeks puffed up when she smiled, her nose scrunching to make her face all the more youthful. He couldn't look away.

She let out a long sigh as her laughter subsided, though she chuckled here and there.

"What's the reason you come to the woods every night?" Aven asked. "I come to hunt, you came for... the queen. But you've continued coming. It's not safe here."

Her smile turned sad once more. "I… have nowhere else to go, really. The inner city just doesn't feel like home anymore. With my brother dead and my sister suddenly queen, it all just… The beauty of the city, it's… too much of a contrast to the way I feel."

"I'm sorry you feel that way."

She looked at him fondly. "But when I'm here, with you, I don't feel that way."

Aven took another bushel of pink flowers from the bouquet and moved to tuck them behind her ear, but she withdrew in a panic.

"Oh," he stammered. "I'm sorry."

"No! It's okay." She smiled. "It's just… oleander flowers are poisonous."

He blinked at her, then at the flowers in his hand. "Oh…"

"Maybe not to wasfoughts," she said. "Definitely not to azheeks, but to humans. And animals. Humans are animals."

He smiled sheepishly and threw them over his shoulder.

"How about these ones?" He picked out a bushel of smaller purple flowers. She bit back a smile.

"Bougainvillea flowers are okay," she said. "But the sap is mildly toxic and if ingested in enough quantities, can lead to illness. Leaves are fine, but if a human is pricked by the thorns we can get reactions. Pain, itching, sometimes even burning skin and blisters."

He stared at her with a wide eye and dropped jaw. "But these are everywhere! These and the—the pink ones!"

She laughed. "Yes."

"Why would people grow them if they're a hazard to humans?"

"Well, once upon a time Ianar was only azheeks. When Sontar Ivel was created by the gods it was only azheeks."

He huffed. "You'd think people would want to keep one another safe though?"

"They tried," she said lightly. "But it's Sontar Ivel. You pluck a flower, it grows back. You trim a bush, it grows back. You cut down a tree, it grows back. Everything is as it always was. Nothing has changed—nothing *will* ever change. It's why it's so beautiful. If it were up to humans the forests would probably be gone by now."

He tossed the bushel of flowers over his shoulder. "Fuck."

She watched him with a smile. "It's sweet that you care."

"Of course I care," he muttered, glaring at the bouquet in her hands. She laughed lightly.

"This." She pulled a large flower from the batch. Its petals were orange, white at the tips, with bright green leaves and little red buds. "This is my favourite."

"And it won't kill you?"

"It won't kill me." She smiled.

"It won't... make you... itchy?"

"No," she laughed.

"Okay. What is it?"

"Pomegranate. Pomegranate flower."

"Okay. Pomegranate..." His brow furrowed. "Can you eat these?"

"You're thinking of the fruit. I mean... you could probably eat the flower, but I wouldn't recommend it."

He nodded and took the orange bloom from her hand, raising it as though to ask if he could tuck it into her hair. She smiled and nodded, leaning forward a little, and he gently pushed a wavy lock of black hair from her face, tucking the flower into place. She averted her eyes with a blush.

"You know a lot about flowers," he said. "You're smart."

"All humans that grow up here know a lot about flowers." She smiled. "We learn fast. Either we listen to our parents or... we learn the hard way."

He smirked. "You learned the hard way, didn't you?"

"I did," she chuckled. "I can confirm, oleander flowers are *very* poisonous. The whole plant is."

"Stupid plant," he muttered. "Can you... can you teach me? I'd like to know which ones are safe and which ones aren't."

"I think you'll be okay—you're a… wasfought." She nodded at the oleander flowers he still had tucked behind his ear. He chucked them over his shoulder.

"But you're human," he said. "I want to know which ones are safe for *you*, and which ones aren't."

She smiled and averted her gaze again. "Okay. I'll teach you. Maybe… maybe if you don't want to keep meeting in the woods… we could meet in the city? During the day? I was going to watch a few of the tournament games but I got caught up with Five's Day. Perhaps I could see you there sometime?"

Aven coughed, panic flashing through him. Veraion and Chester still didn't know that Einmyria knew of his abilities. He hadn't yet told them, knowing they wouldn't take it well.

"I—uhh… maybe later?" He smiled a grin that was too toothy. "My friends would kill me if they knew I told someone they were fighting. They, uhh… they don't like attention."

"Oh… okay, we can meet here."

He glanced at her a few times. "Or… maybe… we could meet in the city away from the tournament? We can look at flowers. And I can punch the ones that are poisonous."

Einmyria laughed. "I'd love that."

CHAPTER 7

THE CALL

Chester yelled to the exultant cheers of her audience, arms in the air, revelling in the attention.

Mahriel. Mahriel. Mahriel.

She wheeled around and charged for her opponent, leaping back into battle. In the next ring, Veraion attacked his challenger with unforgiving speed. They both fought with a sword in each hand and moved so swiftly, so similarly, it was like a dance. With their hair dyed the same colour and their fighting styles parallel, it wasn't hard to believe they could be siblings.

As the tournament went on, the rings got bigger and the opponents got better. The crowds got thicker and louder, with more and more money exchanging hands as everyone placed bets on their favourite fighters. Aven never missed an opportunity to bet on his friends, and as the days went on, his bag of gold got heavier and heavier. Soon he no longer wore linen and was dressed from head to toe in peace silk—in open robes and loose pants that billowed with every movement. His skin breathed freely in the Sontar Ivel air, almost like he wasn't wearing clothes at all. He liked that.

It was a sight to see, a seven-foot giant with menacing markings and the muscles of a god, wearing floral patterns and designs, every colour as bright as the blooms around the city. On the occasion he decided not to wear an elaborate pattern, he wore baby pink.

On most days Aven had at least one flower tucked into his hair. He made flower crowns, wearing all of them on his head, gradually giving them out to those in the stands around him.

Zaiera, Maina, and Theideus made a point to attend most of Chester's and Veraion's games, and they cheered loudly with Aven—save for Theideus, who couldn't make noise. Instead, the water azheek brought pots and pans, clanging them together, much to the dismay of those around him. Zaiera always informed people that Veraion and Mahriel were wearing her armour.

And above the grounds, watching from his tower, Athos's unfaltering gaze remained on Chester.

Aven started meeting Einmyria in the city, on the days his friends weren't fighting. They'd meet at the library and she'd read him books, taking him around the city to point out and name every flower, informing him exactly how poisonous some were.

Aven held up his promise on punching them. Lightly. Enough to garner a laugh from the woman.

Sometimes they met in the woods at night and sometimes he brought back hunts for the inn, but mostly, he paid for his stay in coin.

With the progression of the tournament, the small rings were taken away and a larger fighting pit was built. Various levels of seating lined the walls, places where people could stand or sit, but most remained on their two feet. The new grounds allowed far more space for battle, drumming up anticipation for the day when the tournament would be taken to the great arena of Sontar Ivel.

The fights grew more intense, and it was increasingly common for azheeks to use their powers in moments of panic, earning them instant disqualification if it gave them an upper hand in the match.

Veraion and Chester now only fought once or twice a week, and though it left them time to do other things, they could do nothing with their days off but recover. Bruises and cuts covered them, their muscles barely having enough time to stop being sore before they were back in the ring.

But the ring was where Chester loved to be.

* * *

Chester sat front row with Aven and Zaiera, all of them with a crown of flowers upon their heads and panicked looks in their eyes. Her knuckles were white as she clung to the railing, eyes fixed on Veraion. He was on his back, swords raised in an X over his face as his opponent slammed her longsword down again and again.

"Fuck," Chester muttered. "Get up. *Get. Up.*"

Veraion gritted his teeth and kicked his adversary in the gut, thrusting his swords up to catch her own, then back to send her flying over his head. She was a human, tall and muscular—much more so than Veraion. She came from the Northlands and lived up to the reputation of the Northmen.

Quickly he scrambled to his feet, panting heavily, and though he couldn't see her, he could feel her. He could feel her coming at him. One of the few earth azheek abilities he had was sensing others—azheeks, humans, animals—and with a helmet obscuring his vison, this came as an incredible advantage.

The woman ran, braided hair whipping behind her, weapon raised above her head, and he wheeled around, kicking her in the throat. A loud ring of uncomfortable horror sounded through the audience as everyone winced, watching as she staggered back, clutching her neck, wheezing.

Veraion raced forward, ducking as she swung, and before he knew what she was doing, she grabbed him and threw him right into the railing. Those in the front row jumped and leapt back, but Chester grabbed the edge and stared down. Her wide eyes flicked between her friend in a heap on the ground and the giant northerner racing towards him.

"*Get up!*" Chester yelled.

"Yeah," Veraion choked. "Got it."

He dove to the side as the woman struck down her sword, and raced back to the middle of the ring, taking in deep breaths as his body screamed for rest.

They tore at one another. Veraion ducked as she swung angrily, weaving around her as she tried to keep up. It was like watching a badger fighting a bear.

Soon he found an opening and dove under her arm, grabbing her sword hand, hurling her to the ground. They went tumbling across the pit, dirt rising all about them. Yanking her sword from her grasp, he threw it away and slammed the hilt of his own into the side of her helmet. She yelled, grabbing at him, wrapping her massive hands around his throat, but he flipped his weapon and brought it down.

The tip of his blade stopped half an inch from her neck.

Chester leapt to her feet and cheered, arms flying to the air. The fallen lady glared at Veraion, seething, but finally raised her two fingers to admit defeat. The audience went wild and Aven howled with excitement.

Veraion flopped to the side, lying on his back, staring at the sky. His chest heaved, lungs struggling to find air. Sweat dripped from him, causing his armour to slide grossly over his sodden clothes, and every one of his wounds stung. Blood was splattered across the sand, and he knew that a fair amount of it was his.

His opponent rose to her feet, aided by guards that rushed in, and she cast Veraion one last glare, spitting on him before she limped from the ring. He waved a weak goodbye.

Chester leapt over the railing and raced over, hauling him to his feet. The audience cheered.

Veraion. Veraion. Veraion.

Chester grabbed his hand and forced him to throw it into the air. He laughed, shaking his head at her. With a wince, he draped an arm around her shoulders for support, and she helped him hobble from the ring. Aven and Zaiera had moved to the shade of the holding area.

Veraion yanked off his helmet, letting out a loud groan as his skin could finally breathe.

"*natura's ma'ale, natur.*" He winced, running a hand through his sodden hair, shaking sweat out of his eyes. Chester laughed as he landed heavily on a bench.

Outside, the crowd was starting to chant her name.

"It's your turn now," he said. "I'll be right here… watching." He already looked half asleep.

"Sure," Chester laughed. She took off her flower crown and rested it on his face. He didn't react, too exhausted to do so.

Chester pulled on her armour as the crowd stamped their feet. Zaiera rushed over, helping her fix the plates, tying them securely. Aven glanced across the pit as her opponent entered the ring, raising his arms.

"Looks like you're fighting a fire azheek," he said.

"Easy." She winked, picking up her swords. She fist-bumped Zaiera before running into the sunlight.

Exultant roars filled her ears as she appeared in the pit, and she grinned from ear to ear, spinning around to address everyone that watched. Aven and Zaiera moved back to the stands, shooing away the people that had taken their front-row seats.

Chester yelled, encouraging the crowd. With every syllable of her name, they stamped their feet.

Mahriel. Mahriel. Mahriel.

There was a podium in the audience, a private area for lords and nobles to watch, and she wasn't surprised at all to see Athos. Who she was surprised to see, however, was the queen. People cheered and waved at the queen, and she smiled fondly, though she returned her gaze to the pit below.

Then the horn sounded and Chester charged for her opponent. He was taller than her, very much so. He was more muscular, too. This would not be a battle of strength, for if it was, he would win. It was her job to make this about endurance and speed.

Chester tore towards him and he yelled, raising his sword, swinging as she grew near. She dropped to the ground, sliding by his legs, slicing his calf. The man screamed, wheeling around, pupils already glowing in anger.

"I could have cut your leg off, you know that, right?" she called. "Technically this match should be over."

He snarled, and she swore she could see steam rising from his helmet.

He charged at her. In his other hand he carried a shield, and he held it up in front of him like a battering ram. He tore for her as fast as he could go.

"Shit."

She lunged out of the way, but as she did, he burst out from behind the shield and swung his sword, slicing her across the stomach. His blade tore over her armour, *through* her armour, and blood flicked from the tip of his blade onto the sand.

Chester staggered back with a yell. She glanced to her spattered blood. It was sizzling, burning the sand. Quickly she stood on the red to hide it from view. She glanced to the holding area to see Veraion leaning against the grating, his eyes wide. He had seen it too.

Her opponent lunged and she swung her swords. Parry, attack, parry, attack. The clash of metal on metal rang in the air, screaming over the roar of the audience.

Chester used her speed to stay a safe enough distance away, darting in to attack and darting back out to ensure she wouldn't get pummelled.

Then she threw one of her swords. It went spinning for her adversary and he ducked in alarm. In the second he was distracted, she charged at him, kicking his sword from his hand, quickly discarding it far to the side. He stood with naught but his shield, his teeth bared.

"Fucking *bitch*."

He swung his shield and she leapt out of the way, but the pain in her gut was growing too strong. She staggered.

He slammed his shield across her back.

Splinters went flying and so did she. Chester flew forward, quickly tucking in her chin to roll, but she landed on her back. As her legs hit the ground, stretching out the slash across her gut, pain shot through her. Her eyes widened with a scream.

"Move!" Aven yelled. "*Move!*"

She rolled out of the way just in time to avoid a shield to the face. The man struck it into the ground so hard it got stuck. Her eyes were wide as she stared, knowing very well it could have been her skull caved in and not the earth.

Chester kicked him in the face. He staggered back with a yell, and as she scrambled to her feet, teetering to the side, he threw up a hand and blasted flames at her. Chester threw herself back to the ground. Fire roared past her head.

A horn blared. He was disqualified.

The man yelled, swearing at the referees. Soon he was having a full-blown argument with members of the audience, flames licking over his arms. Aven's yells sounded like a roaring wasfought, but nobody noticed, for everyone else was screaming just as loud as he. Zaiera was shouting at the fire azheek, her voice growing louder, angrier, and deeper the closer the man got.

Chester staggered, falling backwards, but someone caught her on her way down.

"Don't move," Veraion said. "Your hair..." He was behind her, using his body to shield her hair from view. He dragged her into the shade of the holding cell.

"Are you okay?" He stared. "Your stomach!"

"I'll be fine," she said, wincing. "Fucker sharpened the shit out of his blades. Fucking ass. You don't need sharp weapons!" she called out of the cell, but there was no way the man would hear her, for Aven and Zaiera were yelling directly into his face.

Veraion helped untie her breastplate. Not a drop of sweat beaded upon her skin, and for a moment, he felt so incredibly jealous.

Chester pulled her hair over a shoulder and saw what he meant. Large chunks of dye had been burned away, exposing her true blood red underneath.

"Shit." Her eyes widened. "Do you think anyone saw?"

"I don't know," Veraion said.

Aven and Zaiera were making their way to the holding area, still yelling at Chester's opponent across the pit. With every step, Aven's peace silk flowed about him in a vast array of colours as he spewed profanities.

"Yeah?" Aven shouted at the fire azheek, his voice deep and hoarse. "Well you can eat my ass the day after I've had Ikrani food! It's gonna be *wet*!"

Chester snorted loudly.

"AND *SPICY!*" Aven yelled. Then he turned to her with his eye wide, concern ripe on his face. "Are you okay?"

"I'm good," she laughed. "Ikrani food really doesn't sit well with you, does it?"

Zaiera backed into the holding cell, finger pointed at the fuming fire azheek still fighting with the audience.

"Look at my face, you stupid man!" she yelled, motioning at her scarification. "You think I am afraid of pain? I did this for fun!"

She threw up a middle finger.

"Chester!" Zaiera turned to her, and her brow furrowed. "What happened to your hair?"

Chester quickly cast it back over her shoulder. "Blood," she said. She winced as she tried to yank her breastplate away, and Zaiera rushed forward, helping her do so. They grimaced at her reddened shirt.

"Are you sure you're okay?" Veraion lowered to a knee.

"Oh, I'm fine." She smiled weakly. "I love my abs so much I keep them protected by a layer of fat."

The man snorted.

"Still fucking hurts though," she admitted.

"We have to get you cleaned up," Zaiera said. "Right now." She stood and started yelling for a medic.

"I'll be fine." Chester winced, but she spotted Veraion giving her wide eyes, desperately mouthing the word *human* on repeat.

"Auuhh yeah," she said, glancing at him. "Yes, please, medic—I don't want to... get... infected."

Veraion looked at her then at everyone around them. She was the only person that wasn't dripping with sweat. "Shit."

As Zaiera called for a medic, Veraion grabbed a nearby bucket of water and flung it at Chester.

SPLOOSH.

She jumped, staring at him with wide eyes. He sent her an apologetic look as Zaiera and the newly summoned medic swarmed her. Over their heads he mouthed the words, *"You weren't sweating."*

Her wide eyes remained but she started laughing. As she wiped her face and flung water to the ground, he laughed too.

"I'm sorry," he mouthed. She merely nodded with an amused smile and a look of understanding.

"How are you feeling?" the medic asked. "Can you see clearly? Feeling faint?"

"Just tired," Chester said. She looked down to her soaked shirt, watching her blood turn the cloth red.

She cocked her head to the side. *Red.*

Chester smiled. "Anywhere I could get warpaint around here?"

Aven approached the opening of the holding area, scanning the crowd. Chester's opponent was now completely aflame, yelling at the referee, and fire azheek guards had to remove him by force. The audience didn't seem to care about anything but the name they chanted.

Mahriel! Mahriel! Mahriel!

Aven's single eye flicked up to the lord's podium. Athos. Watching him with a dark smirk.

Mahriel! Mahriel! Mahriel!

Even with the queen present, they were saying "Mahriel".

The name rang, repeating, chanting, echoing: a distant call vibrating across the earth, travelling for miles.

Mahriel.

Her name. Her presence.

Mahriel.

As hundreds of azheeks watched her, knew her, called to her, her presence grew.

Mahriel.

Thousands of miles away, in the city of fire, a woman heard the call.

The talk of her people echoed around the great dining hall, columns holding the ceiling in place above them. Fire danced on torches and sconces, burning in beacons and pyres, roaring up the city walls. Every man, woman, and child had hair like coal and eyes like embers. Their features were angular and sharp, as fierce as their element; their skin was radiant, ranging from tanned to brown, worshipped by the sun god.

Their food was served raw, on large platters, and as they ate with their hands aflame, by the time the food reached their mouths, it was cooked exactly how they wanted it to be.

At the far end of the hall, on a raised podium, was the lord's table. It was empty but for four azheeks. A woman in her prime, with blood-red hair, tanned skin, and yellow eyes. While her cheeks, nose, and lips were rounder, softer, the tension in her face and the intensity in her eyes were true to her element.

There were two men, identical twins, years past their prime. Their dark hair fell down their backs in waves and beards lined their jaws. Their brows were strong, noses large and hooked, and they had eyes of bright fire, contrasting with their brown skin.

And between them was a woman with fire-orange hair and angular eyes that shone like embers. Her skin was tanned, golden in the light. Her face was striking, intimidating, beautiful, her jaw strong and shoulders broader than most. Intricate gold jewellery hung from her earlobes and around her neck, two rings on the side of her nose and various more along the cartilage of her ears.

Her gaze was distant, glazed over. The talk of her Sirenveli people seemed so far away as she listened to the whisper in the wind.

Mahriel.

One of the twins looked at her.

"Yenea?" His voice was deep, hoarse.

Mahriel.

The woman with blood-red hair looked to Yenea, her brow furrowed. "*Yenea.*"

Yenea looked up, returning to her city. She gazed over the sea of her people, out through the open arches of the hall.

"I feel him," she said.

The other woman leaned forward, eyes wide, brow furrowed. "Where?"

Yenea cocked her head, eyes squinting as though fighting to understand the pull. The other woman stood, but one of the men grabbed her arm.

"Azhara," he warned. "Give her space."

But Azhara pulled her arm from his grasp. "Yenea," she pressed. "*Where?*"

Yenea rose to her feet and the men followed suit, watching as her eyes saw over the sea of heads, out the hall, and across the city, to a land far, far away.

Her gaze darkened. "Sontar Ivel."

CHAPTER 8
MOONLIGHT

Chester smeared red warpaint across her face and over her armour, clumping it into streaks of her hair, and when she entered the fighting pit, the crowd went wild. When fire licked at her hair and burned away dye, her blood red was already masked by painted strands.

After every match, as she walked into the holding cell, she was met by Veraion and a bucket of water. She embraced this with a laugh.

Again and again she rose victorious, Veraion just as successful.

As the games went on, more and more people were seen in the audience with streaks of paint across their faces in support. Others wore flowers in their hair as they gambled with the ever-winning Aven, and as always, Athos watched from his podium.

Paintings, tapestries, and murals appeared around the city as people chose their favourite champions: earth azheeks, fire azheeks, and air azheeks, hailed as the best fighters in the land. There were few humans this far into the tournament, and of them, Mahriel and Veraion were favoured most. On every painting, on every mural, she was depicted with her warpaint.

If there was one thing she loved, it was theatrics. And if there was one thing the city loved, it was *her* theatrics.

Any day the two weren't fighting, Aven was with Einmyria. And on many nights, he returned to see her in the woods. He found the city so beautiful but knew her favourite place was in the peaceful quiet of the southern forest.

He had stopped hunting, for he made more than enough gambling at the tournament to cover the costs of Five's Inn and his new addiction to collecting peace silk robes.

Chester and Veraion grew in recognition, to the point where they could no longer walk down the street without being stopped or at the very least stared at. Children pointed, for they had yet to learn how to be subtle, but subtlety would have been meaningless. The children that pointed had faces covered with warpaint.

* * *

Veraion, Chester, and Aven moved through the streets, and everywhere they went they were greeted and welcomed. Night had fallen but darkness did not take the city. Candles burned in glass jars and lanterns lined every street, along the floors by the city walls and hung in the air above them. Plants thrived and bloomed even in the dry summer.

Night vendors had stalls set up here and there, selling sweets and desserts to help lull people to sleep.

The three meandered through the city, so ripe with life, and the cool night's breeze ruffled their dyed hair and flowed through their peace silk robes. Robes that matched. Robes Aven had purchased.

Robes he had forced Veraion to wear.

"You will match, or you will die," was what he had said. It had been impossible for Chester to hide her smile as Veraion accepted the robes with a wide-eyed grimace.

As they moved, their clothes as vibrant as the flowers around them, Chester looked between the two men and smiled. They were still trying to uphold the mirage that they didn't like one another, but she knew otherwise. And though the three travelled with satchels full of coin, they never had to spend it.

"It's ironic how now that we have money, we don't need it," Chester said as someone offered her yet another free treat. She smiled and declined as nicely as possible. Aven took it instead.

"Fame," Veraion snorted softly. "What a strange thing."

Chester smiled as a group of children ran by, skidding to a halt when they spotted the giant Aven, and their stunned eyes only grew wider as they saw the two that were with him. The children had red paint smeared over the top halves of their faces, mimicking Chester's usual look, and Aven smiled and waved.

"Mahriel…" one of the children said, staring.

"Hi," she said with a laugh.

"*Veraion!*" another whispered. Then the children ran away, hiding behind a stall to watch from a distance.

The three meandered through the streets, and all the while Aven found himself glancing over the sea of heads, looking south, itching to race for the woods.

"You okay?" Chester said.

"Yeah." He smiled. "I, uhh… I'm just gonna… go. Hunt."

She raised an eyebrow at him as he smiled sheepishly and sidled away. Veraion watched him go.

"He hasn't brought anything back from his *hunts* in a long time," she murmured.

"He's seeing her, isn't he?"

"Probably."

"He's going to get himself killed," Veraion muttered. Chester watched him with a smile.

"Are you worried about Aven?"

"No."

He headed up a city wall and she followed, gazing over the brilliant capital. Lights as far as the eye could see: warm lanterns, bioluminescent rivers, and fireflies dappling the far woods. And when she turned to the skies, the brilliant colours of the night were just as beautiful, always blessed by the blood moon.

There was music, guitars strummed and plucked with ease. There wasn't a day that went by in Sontar Ivel that they did not hear music.

They sat on the wall and watched the water below, one of the canal rings of the city, and here and there floated gondola vendors. Veraion spotted one and smiled. The Vaian vendor noticed him and beamed, guiding his boat over to the wall.

"My brother!" the old earth azheek said, still smiling.

Chester glanced at him. "Our family grows every day."

Veraion hurried over to the rickety ladder and climbed down, looping an arm around the rope to secure his place.

"You're not selling taho, are you?" he asked.

"No, not at night. Sticky rice."

"Ohhh." Veraion laughed softly. "Give me some of that, *please.*"

The vendor reached for a pile of little parcels, sticky rice wrapped in banana leaves, and handed two to Veraion. Then he grabbed two more and shoved them into his hand.

"Oh, two is okay," Veraion said, reaching for coin, but the old man shook his head and pushed his boat away from the wall.

"No!" The man laughed. "You tell the city you are from Mahr Ivel, but we from Vaia know you represent us! Both of you!"

Chester pointed at herself with a questioning expression.

"We from Vaia know the two of you are from our islands!" the man called. "Long live!"

Veraion looked up at Chester with a smile, and he chuckled, waving a hand full of goodies before climbing back to where she sat. With green eyes, tanned skin, and dyed-black hair, she did indeed look as though she had come straight from Vaia.

He sat beside her, legs dangling over the edge, and gave her two of the treats.

"What's this?" she asked.

"Sticky rice," he said. "From our home islands."

She smiled. She had never felt at home in Foros and had never been to Vaia, but as she sat with Veraion and gazed over Sontar Ivel, she felt it.

Here. Home.

They watched the glimmering water, listening to music as they peeled back banana-leaf wrappings and ate.

"Be honest," she said. "You like the robes, don't you?"

He chewed, savouring the taste of rice boiled with coconut milk, and looked at the colourful peace silk flowing about his skin. He glanced at her with an amused smile.

"They're *really* comfy."

Her grin spread from ear to ear.

* * *

Aven's stallion trotted through the forest, its mood matching its rider's. Aven's robes flowed behind him, pants loose about his large legs, and he let out a pleasant sigh as he gazed around the woods.

Much of the city was asleep now; he knew Chester and Veraion were back in room fourteen. He had nothing to worry about but what his breath might smell like.

He reached the clearing where he and Einmyria always met, and though he could smell a trace of her, she wasn't there. There was fresh footfall in the dirt: her stallion's hooves. The ground had been upturned. She had been here not long before.

He smelled the air, inhaling her scent. He sniffed loudly, like a dog, every sniff growing stronger until he caught the smell. *Salt.* She had been crying.

His eye widened and he grabbed the reins, kicking in the stirrups. His stallion whinnied and turned, bolting back for the city, tearing through the trees of the southern woods until the thunder of hooves echoed around the streets.

Aven's face crunched as he took on a mutated form, smelling the air as they moved, guiding his stallion through Einmyria's trail.

They kept to the shadows, avoiding the streets still thriving with life, but here and there they tore past a person, leaving them stunned. A bolting stallion was a rare sight in the city.

They tore further and further into the capital, her scent guiding them closer and closer to the castle. From sand to dirt to cobblestones, the ground changed from laid brick to polished stone. Over bridges he rode, section by section of the city until they crossed over water to an island close to the castle. An island with mansions.

The stallion slowed and stared around, as awe-stricken as Aven.

Every house was huge and there were only a few on this private island. If it weren't for the direct view of the castle, towering overhead, Aven would have thought these villas were palaces themselves.

Private gates surrounded them, trees blooming all around, flowers bright even in the darkness, and as Aven guided his horse forward, smelling Einmyria's scent of expensive oils, they stared up at the largest house of all.

A mansion. It stood tall, some areas of the building square and others round. It was built of the same white stone as the city, with beams and columns to hold it tall, open archways allowing a breeze to flow through the estate.

Aven came from his saddle and stared up. He guided his stallion to a hidden area, giving the beast a fond pat.

"Stay here," he said. The horse snorted. "Please."

He pulled off his clothes, glancing at the stallion that was holding his gaze, and shifted his body to a mutated form, somewhere between man and beast.

"*Please.*"

The horse snorted again and started grazing.

Aven jumped up, climbing over the outer wall.

He moved in the shadows, creeping, staring around in awe. He snuck towards the house, smelling her. She was here.

He peeked through windows, careful to keep a distance. From where he crouched he could see a hall with bookshelves lining the walls, couches and tables, and a stone staircase leading away, inlaid with intricate tiles.

There was a balcony on a higher level, two or three stories up, with flower pots hanging along the railing, and he knew that on the other side of the mansion balconies overlooked the water, facing the castle.

He could smell her, but he could also smell someone else: a man, older. Her father was home.

Aven took a step away from the house and ducked into the shadows. He tilted his head back and let out a lilting howl. Nearby residents glanced out of their windows in confusion. Somewhere, a baby started crying.

His gaze was fixed on the top balcony, and it wasn't long before he saw her silhouette. Timidly, the beast stepped out from the shadows.

Upon seeing him she smiled sadly, her eyes bloodshot. She was in a peace silk nightgown, and in the open air, goosebumps crawled over her skin.

"You should go," she whispered. Her words were quiet, but Aven's sharp hearing didn't miss them. He shook his head. She watched him for a moment, knowing she couldn't invite him in but not having the strength to properly ask him to leave. So Aven took a step back, and another, and another. She watched, her brow furrowing, and her eyes widened as he ran towards her house.

Aven leapt up, body shifting as he needed, and swung onto the first balcony. Climbing up the carved arches and beams, he launched himself forward, swinging over her railing, landing directly in front of her. He landed lightly, but still, the balcony shook. Einmyria staggered backwards in alarm, staring to the street in a panic, and she grabbed him by the arm, yanking him into her room, away from the windows until his back was pressed against a wall.

"Aven!" she gasped. Slowly he turned into a man, staring around her room in awe.

"Holy shit," he murmured.

The windows sent pink moonlight cascading into her room, candles lit about the space to illuminate the chamber with warm light. A large bed was against the middle of the far wall, the headpiece a great mural carved from fine wood: intricate, winding, weaving.

Wooden beams lined the ceiling, a dark chandelier hanging in place. Many of the candles were still lit, and he knew for a fact that she hadn't taken the time to do that herself. The maids and house hands had gone home for the night, but he could still smell traces of them.

Her wardrobes, dressers, desk, mirrors, chairs, lounges, and tables were all built from rich wood. And on the other side of the room, her open windows overlooked the water. The castle.

For a moment he completely forgot why he was there and could only stand rooted to the spot, single eye wide, breath barely reaching his lungs. He could smell nothing but royalty. But when Einmyria sniffed, he was soon to remember what brought him there, and turned back to her with concern in his ice-blue gaze.

"You were crying," he said, searching her face. He could still smell the salt. She looked at him with a sad smile, biting back tears.

Aven pulled her into his arms.

Surrendering to his care, tears spilled from her eyes. He only held her tighter. When he let go, he gently pushed her hair from her salty cheeks, searching her face.

"What's wrong?" he asked.

"I miss him so much," she whispered. "My brother, he was my best friend. I still can't believe he's gone."

"I'm sorry. I wish there was something I could do."

"It's fine," she said. "I'm fine, I just… It just gets to me sometimes. Especially when…"

"What happened?"

She shook her head. "You wouldn't understand."

"I can try."

She took in a deep breath. "Baraduhr were in my house."

His eye widened. Hackles pushed through his skin, fur crawling over his body. His nose crunched sickeningly as it extended to become a beast's snout, and Einmyria backed away in alarm as he turned to the door in the far wall.

"Are they still here?" His voice was barely human.

"Aven!"

He looked at her with a snarl, but when he saw her fear, he withdrew. Clenching his jaw, he pushed a hand through his matted mane. Soon, his claws turned back to fingers and his mane to hair. "I'm sorry," he said.

"They aren't here anymore. Aven, how do you know of baraduhr?"

"I've been killing them my whole life. My master trained me to do so, as did hers before her. I know the baraduhr. I know what they do. I know what they deserve. What were they doing in your house?"

She took another step back. "Are you accusing me?"

"No! No, I'm sorry." He turned away, letting out a deep breath. Glancing back at her, he offered a hand. It took a moment, but she accepted it and he wrapped an arm around her, his height too great to let him rest his chin upon her head.

"They left when I came in," she said. "I don't know what they were doing. They were just standing there. I grabbed a torch, but one of them put out the fire with a wave of their hand. Then they left. Just like that."

He held her, unsure as to what to think.

"I don't know what's going on anymore," she said. "I don't know what's going on."

He said nothing.

"Thank you for being here," she whispered. "There is no one here for me but you."

He smiled and pushed her hair from her face. "It's not hard for me to be the best then, is it?"

She smiled, and this time it was real. She watched him, lips parting as she strived to find words, but words were not required.

Aven leaned in. He had to bend over, his back curved to lower his height two feet, and when his grizzled lips were barely an inch from hers, she let out a quiet gasp and kissed him.

Einmyria closed her eyes. Her fingers ran over his cheek, over the rough hair that covered his strong jaw. When the kiss came to an end, Aven pulled back a little and smiled, gently brushing a loose strand of hair behind her ear.

"Sorry," he said. "I probably shouldn't have."

"Don't apologize," she said, blushing. "I... I've been waiting for you to do that."

He smiled. "Really?"

She nodded and pulled him back in. Her grip was tighter on him now, and a low growl sounded from his throat as he felt her desire.

When she pushed her hands through his hair, he picked her up. Her legs wrapped around his waist and he carried her through the room, placing her on a dresser. She slipped her tongue into his mouth with a soft moan.

He let her lead, following her every movement, and it didn't take long before his apprehension went away.

Einmyria grabbed at him, his rough hands sliding over her silk dress. Her touch wandered down his body, feeling every valley of muscle in his abdomen, fingers moving down the bristly hair of his body that grew wilder the lower her touch got. Aven grabbed her breast and her hands took him between the legs.

A voice was heard outside the room.

"Einmyria?" her father called.

She gasped and pulled away from Aven, staring at him with wide eyes, clasping a hand over his mouth. He chuckled. He should have sensed the man coming, but he had been far too occupied to pay attention to what was happening outside. He should have smelled the man coming too, for now that he stood on the other side of the bedroom door, his scent was strong. His oils were mixed with myrrh, root of iris flower, and harsh cloves. But Aven had been too busy smelling the passion growing between Einmyria's legs.

"Yes?" she called, trying not to sound out of breath. Aven grinned beneath her hand, his own wandering to her legs. She gasped, fighting back a smile as she squirmed.

"I'm making some tea," her father said. "Would you like some?"

"No, thank you! I'm getting ready for bed." She grabbed Aven's arm, trying not to laugh, though she was trying just as hard not to moan. He watched her with a dark grin and moved his hands beneath her dress, softly trailing higher and higher up her legs.

"Are you sure?" came her father's voice again.

Einmyria looked at Aven with wide eyes, her hand tightening over his mouth, but it didn't stop the low rumble in his throat as he growled. His fingers touched her between the legs and she shuddered, head tipping back as her eyes fluttered closed, a soft moan upon her breath.

"Einmyria?" The doorknob turned.

"I'm sure!" she called, eyes snapping open. "I'm sure, I'm going to bed, thank you!"

The doorknob stopped. "Alright, sleep well."

Einmyria stared at Aven, listening to her father's footsteps as they got quieter and quieter.

"*Aven*," she gasped, finally removing her hand from his mouth. "He would have killed you."

He started rubbing between her legs and her breath hitched, words turning to a moan. She shivered, fingers gripping the edge of the dresser.

"*Aven*," she whispered, her eyes closing. As her body trembled, her head tipped forward to lean on his shoulder.

"Yes?" he asked lowly, still touching her.

"He'll… kill… you…" She was wet, and as her legs parted just a little bit more, he found her entrance and dipped a finger inside. She moaned, doing everything she could to stop it from being loud. Einmyria gasped, her forehead pressing into his shoulder.

"I'd like to see him try." Aven smiled. "Should I stop?"

Her fingers still tight on the dresser, her arms quivered. She shook her head.

"Are you sure?" he whispered into her ear, and goosebumps crawled over her skin. The giant took her leg with his other hand and spread it wider, shoving her dress out of the way, pushing another finger inside, and she had to bite his neck to muffle her moan.

"Fuck," she gasped. "Aven—"

"I've never heard you swear before." He smiled, slowly moving his fingers in and out. "Not very lady-like."

"Shut the fuck up," she whispered through her gasps. His grin only returned.

"*Fuck*," he groaned, feeling how wet she was.

"Curl your fingers," she gasped, and he did. Her gasp turned to a moan.

Finally she pulled away from his shoulder, looking up at him, and seeing her only made his blood pump faster. His free hand pushed through her wavy hair, cupping her jaw, and he pulled her back into a kiss, moving his fingers faster. Her high-pitched moan vibrated on his tongue.

Einmyria threw an arm around his neck, gripping for support, her other hand moving to his chest. Her fingers dug into his muscles as she tried to stop herself from falling off the dresser.

"Aven," she gasped, her eyes closed and brow furrowed.

"Mm?" He loved the way she sounded, gasping beneath him, coming undone on his fingers.

"Aven, I…"

"Touch yourself."

She looked up at him and he leaned in, brushing his lips against hers.

"Touch yourself," he whispered, and her hand dropped from his chest to where she was throbbing.

Their lips were brushing as she moved her fingers between her legs, rubbing as Aven pumped his in and out, massaging her walls. His low growls sent shivers down her spine, and with every one of her breaths came soft whimpers. He held one of her legs for support, his other fingers moving in and out, in and out, curved to hit her in all the right places, and as his pace quickened, so did hers. He could feel her tensing around him, breaths growing shorter and shorter.

"Do it," he murmured into her lips. He could feel her tightening, her core trembling. "*Do it.*"

She seized up and he pressed his lips against hers, tongue taking over her mouth. She gasped, moans spilling, one hand gripping his shoulder and nails digging into his skin. Her other hand remained between her legs, and though her rubbing slowed, he did not. He pumped his fingers inside her, again and again, revelling in the way she shook, squirming in his grip, her moans uncontrolled and pouring into his mouth.

Her hand pulled away and gripped his forearm as he kept going. Her lips came from the kiss, mouth hanging open as she fought back the urge to scream. Einmyria's toes curled, back arching, and Aven growled behind his smile, watching her. He kept going until it was too much, and when she gasped his name, her fingers digging into his forearm, he finally slowed. He slowed until he was still, though his fingers remained inside.

Einmyria's eyes opened, her chest heaving as she looked at him. He smirked, placing a soft kiss on her lips. He twitched his fingers and she spasmed, pulling away from him with a soft laugh.

Finally he stood back, and he watched as her dress fell down, covering her up once more, her hair a mess. Her cheeks were flushed, lips plump from his kisses.

She glanced at him, shy now. He sucked her juices from his fingers and she buried her face behind her hands.

"Aven," she mumbled.

"Mm?" He smiled, approaching once more, placing his hands on either side of her. He kissed her forehead. "Feel better?"

She looked at him, biting back her smile, and nodded.

"Good." He kissed her forehead once more. "My work here is done." He pulled back, heading towards her open windows.

"Wait," she said, still short of breath. She clambered from the dresser, landing on the floor with a thud, and hurried forward to take his hand. He turned back to her with a smile.

"Are you being greedy?"

"No, I—You—Your—I just…"

He pulled her back into a kiss, towering over her, their tongues still hungry for the other.

"Fuck," he groaned, and before he knew what he was doing, he was walking her backwards to the bed. Their kiss never stopped, hands roving hungrily, and he tucked his fingers beneath the straps of her dress. He pulled them aside and silk flowed to the floor, leaving her as naked as he.

Aven stood back, eye roving over her, and she bit her lip, cheeks only growing pinker. Then he grabbed one of her small breasts, squeezing her nipple, his lips returning to hers. She moaned into his mouth once more. Einmyria fell back onto the bed and he climbed on top of her.

Then came a knock at the door.

"Einmyria?" her father called. "Is everything okay? I keep hearing noises."

She gasped loudly, eyes snapping wide open. She had completely forgotten where she was.

"I'm fine!" she called. "I just dropped a book!"

"Okay. I'm going to bed now, try to keep it down."

Aven dropped his forehead against her chest as he stifled his laughter, shoulders shaking as he held himself up. Her fingers rested on his head, pushing through his hair as she let out a long, frustrated sigh.

"I guess that's my cue," he muttered, though with her breasts so close, he couldn't help but rove his tongue over a nipple, sucking it into his mouth. Her back arched as she gasped, but she was quick to clamber out from beneath him, trying to pat down her hair.

"I'm sorry," she said. He smiled, leaning forward, placing a peck on her lips.

"I'm not."

Then he rose to his feet, ignoring the rock-hard situation between his legs, and morphed into a mutant beast, disappearing from her room.

Einmyria fell back onto her bed, staring at the ceiling, her cheeks as pink as the flowers blooming upon her bedside table.

* * *

"They were in her house?" Chester exclaimed.

"She knows about your abilities?!" Veraion almost screamed. They were back in room fourteen, and his two friends look horrified.

"Did you not hear the part where we kissed?" Aven glowered.

Veraion grabbed a handful of Aven's chest hair and yanked. He yelled in alarm.

"You didn't honestly think I was going to stalk her as a wasfought forever, did you?" he snapped, rubbing his chest.

"I genuinely hoped so, yes," Veraion said.

"She's the one that figured it out." Aven grabbed back his stolen hair and slapped it to his red chest. "She's not dumb. She saw me as a human in the library and put it together."

"Has she told anyone about you?" Veraion reached for his dagger and Chester grabbed him by the arm. "If the baraduhr get so much as a *whiff* of what you can do—"

"Aww," Chester cooed. "Are you getting protective over Aven?" Veraion glared at her.

"She knows it's a secret," Aven said. "She hasn't told anyone, and she won't."

"Can you really trust her?" he pressed. "She's affiliated with the so-called queen. I don't trust her at all."

"I'm stunned," Chester said. "We've been here months now and I haven't seen so much as a hint that baraduhr walk within these walls, and now we find out that a group of them were having tea in a woman's kitchen?"

Aven glared. "I don't know if they were having *tea*."

"I *told* you that Siran, or Elaira, was working with the baraduhr," Veraion said darkly. "And we know that those two were once close. You said they were raised under the same roof?"

"Einmyria is not with the baraduhr."

"I never said she was. I'm saying that 'Siran the Third' is working with the baraduhr. Then there happened to be a group of them in Einmyria's house. Einmyria, who was raised with our queen. Not only that, but these baraduhr didn't care that she saw them. As Chester said, none of us have seen a glimpse of baraduhr in this city. If they're doing that much to stay hidden, why didn't they kill her?"

"She sounds dangerous, whether she knows it or not," Chester agreed.

"It's not her fault the baraduhr were there," Aven whined.

"Don't trust her," Veraion said. "Even if she doesn't know how, or why, she's involved."

He and Chester exchanged foreboding glances. Then Aven looked at Chester.

"I would like to mate with her."

She choked. "What?"

"We almost did."

"O… kay?" She watched him uncomfortably. Was he asking for permission?

"May I?"

Yes. He was asking for permission.

"Aven." She stared. "You don't need my permission to mate—or to do anything, for that matter. You can have sex with anyone you want to have sex with, as long as they want to as well."

"You sure?"

"Yes. You are the master of your own body, and life. You never need my permission to do anything."

This surprised him. Then he glanced at Veraion. "So can I kill him now?"

Chester looked at him dryly and laughed. Aven did so too, but when Chester looked away, he cast Veraion a threatening look.

The earth azheek rolled his eyes. "Do you even know how to mate?"

"Of course I do. I've had many a wasfought."

"Two-legs aren't the same."

"Kiss her with passion," Chester said. "Pay attention to her nipples—never forget the nipples—and be gentle. She'll indicate when she wants you to be rougher."

"I know what to do."

"Everyone says that," Veraion said.

"I was there every time Chester—"

"OKAY." She smiled. "This is a *great* conversation."

Veraion couldn't help but snort loudly. "People never think about that, do they? Pets watching them."

Aven nodded. "I'm very observant."

Chester pressed fingers into her temple.

"I gave Einmyria an orgasm," Aven said proudly. Veraion tried not to laugh, looking between the two in disbelief.

"From… kissing?" Chester stared.

"No, I pulled your trick."

"I... Which one?

"The one where you finger them and tell them to touch themselves."

Chester looked proud. "Oh yeah." She smiled. "Works like a charm."

She offered a hand and Aven high-fived it.

Veraion shook his head. "How did I get here?"

"If Einmyria is sexually active then she's probably fully stocked with contraceptive potions," Chester said. "But just in case, I'll buy you some." She glanced him up and down. "I'll buy you a lot. You'll probably have to drink five times as much for it to work."

"Or you could get snipped," Veraion said. "It's quite common here, completely reversible. When you decide you want to push out some puppies, you go for the second procedure and get it reversed."

"*Push out puppies,*" Chester wheezed.

"I'll take the potions," Aven said.

CHAPTER 9

FANG'EI

Veraion and Aven stood in the holding area, watching Chester. This would be her final match in the fighting pit. If she lost, she would be out of the tournament, and if she won, she would be one of the final twenty champions. If she won, she would fight in the arena.

Veraion had already made it and couldn't peel his eyes away from her as she fought. She had red paint smeared across her eyes, forehead, and cheeks, over her armour, and all through her hair.

She was deep in a fight with an earth azheek, and it was impossible to tell who would win.

Maina, Theideus, and Zaiera stood front row in the audience, their wide eyes fixed on the game. Around them, Chester's supporters wore warpaint of their own.

"When she was younger, she used to paint my markings around her eyes," Aven said.

"Why did she stop?" Veraion asked.

"She used up all the black paint in Foros. They didn't let her have any after that."

Veraion laughed. Aven smiled as he watched her.

"She seems to be doing well for someone who had her heart ripped out and torn into a million pieces," Aven said.

"You speak of Yrilim," Veraion said. Aven nodded. "I wouldn't know if this is someone taking heartache well."

They watched her beat the living shit out of her opponent.

Aven shrugged. "She's always done this. The audience is just bigger here."

Veraion smirked, though it turned to a solemn smile. "She hurts. I can feel it. She keeps it to herself, and she does it well."

"I wish killing him would help."

"Nothing will stop her from loving him," Veraion said. "Not even death. She will never feel that bond for anyone but him."

"But she can still love others?"

"Azheeks are capable of loving many, but the bind... is the bind."

"Even if she never sees him again?" Aven asked.

"She still sees him," he said sadly. "Every time he laughs, every time he cries, she sees him. In times of greatest peril, this seeing will become the strongest. At the times when he needs her most, she will be there with him."

Aven glanced at Veraion. He could feel regret and remorse flooding from him, and he knew he was speaking from experience.

"It hurts her," Veraion continued quietly. "Every moment she's away from him, it hurts. I think she's forgotten what it feels like, not to suffer with every breath. I know I have."

Aven watched him for a moment before looking to the ring. Chester was on her back, her opponent returning the pummelling from before.

Veraion glanced across the pit to where Athos was watching from his podium. Beside him stood the queen. He ground his teeth and forced his gaze back to the fight.

Chester threw her opponent off and grabbed her weapons. She dodged every strike, parrying any time the blade got near. Again and again. Over and over.

The two stood and stared at one another, chests heaving. Chester let out a loud huff, eyeing her opponent, calculating.

She threw her sword. It hurtled through the air and crashed into the other's weapon, sending it from her grasp. The earth azheek looked around for her sword in alarm and Chester ran. She tore forward, leaping into the air, grabbing her opponent by the head with her legs, and brought the woman to the ground. Leaping up, she swung her second sword to the woman's neck, stopping an inch away.

Finally her opponent raised a hand to the air, signifying defeat. The crowd erupted.

Mahriel. Mahriel. Mahriel.

Veraion looked back to Athos to see him smiling ever so slightly. He glowered and shook his head, forcing his gaze away.

Chester rose to her feet and threw her arms in the air, closing her eyes as her chest heaved, lungs gasping for air, heart racing. But she loved it. She loved all of it.

Mahriel. Mahriel. Mahriel.

* * *

Veraion, Aven, and a water-soaked Chester milled through the streets, fresh from her victory. She was still short of breath and accepted her compliments with a smile and a weary nod. Someone handed her a tankard of ale and she tipped it back, desperate for any drink to quench her thirst.

"Easy," Veraion said.

Aven laughed, and when he looked up, he saw Einmyria in the crowd. He let out a smitten sigh.

Einmyria's wavy hair pooled over her shoulders, her dress off-white and ruffled about the shoulders, neckline, and hems. Every layer swayed as she moved, and the way she moved was graceful. There was a leather belt around her waist, accentuating her form, and tucked into her hair was a bright pomegranate flower. He watched her with a taken smile.

She saw him and her cheeks filled with life, waving as she moved through the crowd.

Then he realized he still had yet to introduce her to his friends—one of whom was definitely not keen on the idea.

He panicked and tried to shield Chester and Veraion from view, using his giant silk sleeves to do so. Chester pushed a sleeve out of her face with a single finger and raised eyebrow.

"You okay?"

"I—just—fuck." He gave up.

Einmyria approached with a nervous smile. "Hi, I'm Einmyria." She offered a hand.

"Ohhh." Chester stared, shaking her hand. "You *are* pretty."

Chester's warpaint was streaked, clumped with bits of dirt and blood, leaking down her face from the weight of the water that drenched her. It was intimidating.

Einmyria blushed. "Thank you."

"Uh-huh." Chester nodded, still shaking her hand.

Aven coughed awkwardly and nudged her.

"Oh—yeah, hi. Mahriel." Chester finally let her go and Einmyria laughed. She offered a hand to Veraion but he didn't take it.

"Veraion." Einmyria nodded a greeting instead.

"You know my name." He glared at Aven.

"It's hard not to," she said. "What with everyone within a mile radius chanting it on a weekly basis."

He grunted.

"It's nice to meet you, *finally*." She smiled. "Had I waited for Aven to do the introducing, I fear he may have died of old age."

Chester clenched her jaw. She never wanted to be reminded that wasfoughts aged faster than humans.

"How old *are* you?" Veraion asked. Aven smiled.

"Twelve."

They all glanced up at the fully matured, bearded giant.

* * *

Aven and Einmyria sat at a separate table from Veraion and Chester, and Veraion glared at them from their usual booth. Maina first gave food to the couple before heading over to her friends.

"Who the hell is *that*?" She stared, putting down her tray. "She is beautiful."

"Aven's new wench," Veraion said.

"So cute," Chester cooed. "He's jealous Aven has a friend."

She had changed out of her fighting attire and bathed, now wearing clean, loose robes.

Maina was still staring at Einmyria. "I'm jealous of Aven."

"She's not right," Veraion muttered. "There's something about her. She isn't right."

"You think everyone doesn't feel right," Chester said. He gave her a dark look. Then his gaze moved past her and she followed, over her shoulder to a poster of Athos. They were plastered around the inn, all around the city, promoting the final rounds of the tournament.

"What's his story?" Chester asked. Maina looked at the poster and let out a long sigh. She took a seat at the table.

"Athos came to the city ten years ago," she said. "He was the first human to ever sign up for the tournament, the first human to dare face azheek champions. I was there. I can still remember watching him obliterate anyone that entered the ring. Most of them nearly died, and as you know, many did.

"I watched week after week as he rose victorious. Athos, the human. Everyone knew his name. None believed he'd make it, but he did. He beat every person he faced until he was one of the champions. One of the Twenty. And then one of the Ten.

"I was there that day, in the arena. The Battle of the Ten. One by one, the champions came, armoured from head to toe, armed with their weapons and powers. And then he entered, discarding his war-hammer. He removed his armour. First his helmet, then his pauldrons, his bracers, breastplate, greaves, boots—every piece of clothing until he stood before the city in naught but his skin. I watched as one man, one naked, unarmed human, destroyed nine armed and armoured azheeks.

"That is why we say he has the strength of a thousand men. That is why he is the undefeated champion of Sontar Ivel. Nobody beats him. Nobody *can* beat him." Maina's eyes rested on Chester, then Veraion. She finally gave him a small smile. "Think ill of him all you wish, but do not speak words of disrespect. Respect, he has earned."

Maina pat his hand before returning to the kitchens, leaving Chester and Veraion in silence. She looked over her shoulder, to the poster of Athos, his cold eyes ever watchful.

Chester turned away and downed her tankard of ale. Then another.

As the night drew on, both Chester and Veraion accepted free drinks for their victories, receiving praise any time someone walked by. Not far away, Aven and Einmyria were deep in conversation, and every time they laughed, Veraion glowered. He was beginning to look like Dog, who sat in the corner, watching Aven with distrusting eyes.

Tao moved by, heading for the kitchens, carrying with him trays of dirty dishes, and he spotted the two fighters deep in their drinks.

"You look like you need a break," the old air azheek said with a laugh, his gaze on the glowering Veraion. Then Tao leaned in and lowered his voice. "If you want opium, I have it."

Chester choked on her drink. Veraion's eyes widened and he stared at the man.

"I knew it," he gasped. "I *knew* that was what I smelled!"

"Shhhhh." Tao placed a finger to his own lips with a wink.

"Are you telling me…" Veraion lowered his voice. "That at the end of the hall… you have an opium den?"

Tao chuckled and gave an innocent shrug. Veraion smiled and shook his head.

"I thought I was going crazy." He laughed. "I kept smelling it. And I didn't want to make assumptions, but I mean…" He glanced at the elaborate robes Tao always wore. "You wear these because they're fun to look at when you're high, don't you?"

Tao smiled.

"You've done it?" Chester stared at Veraion with a smile of disbelief. "And you, Tao, where did you *get* it?"

"I have friends in Akana." The innkeeper winked. "Best opium in Zalfur—best opium on Ianar."

Veraion pointed at the man with a nod. "Correct."

"Ah, then you know! If you're feeling sore from the tournament, it'll help!"

"I'm alright," Chester laughed. "Raion?"

"Oh, I'm too old for that." He shook his head.

Tao smiled. "Never too old for that."

"Isn't it illegal here?"

"They made drugs illegal to protect humans." Tao shrugged. "I am not a human."

"The night we came," Veraion said. "The night Aven ripped the door off its hinges… were you on opium?"

"Probably."

Veraion laughed. "I wondered why you were so okay with a giant breaking your property."

"There are many things I don't worry about," Tao said. "Why live a life of worries when you can simply accept that everything is the way it is?"

Chester chuckled. "Maybe I should have some."

"You are always welcome in the room at the end of the hall." He winked. He smiled as he gazed around the tavern, resting his eyes on Aven and

Einmyria as they laughed. "Perhaps I should offer some to Aven and his new friend."

"No, please don't," Chester said with concern. "They're not azheeks— they could form addictions… and I feel like it would cost a *lot* to support an opium addiction the size of Aven."

"We aren't azheeks either," Veraion reminded her with a desperate smile. "Right."

"Are you from Akana?" Veraion asked Tao.

"My family was, yes." He nodded. "But they left after the Red Emperor threw all children from the walls. We had humans in our family. So they packed up and left. Turns out opium addictions can come in handy. The old owner of Five's Inn had a *very* strong one, so my family bought the place off him cheap, for trade."

Chester raised an eyebrow at him. "Your family left because they didn't like someone targeting humans, and then targeted and took advantage of human weakness?"

"Hey, wasn't me." Tao shrugged. "I just inherited the place." He lowered his voice once more. "And an opium connection."

Veraion snorted and shook his head. "I think we're good, thank you."

"If drugs are illegal here, how do you get away with it?" Chester asked.

"I don't parade it around town," Tao said simply. "And I only invite and sell to azheeks. Never humans. They'd get addicted and it would get… messy. I can't be bothered with all that human nonsense."

Chester nodded.

"So no opium for you?"

"No thanks," Chester laughed.

"Well, if you want more drinks, they're on me!" And with that he was off, taking dirty dishes to the kitchens. Dog followed with a wagging tail.

"It's… loud in here," Veraion said. "You want to head back?"

Chester nodded. "I'm grabbing those drinks first."

They swung by the bar, bringing bottles to room fourteen. Veraion laughed as he smelled the distant trace of opium, pungent and bitter, and closed the door as Chester plopped onto her bed with a groan.

"*Fuck*, I love beds." Her words were slurred. Veraion chuckled.

"You're drunk."

She looked at him. His face was flushed. "So are you."

"Do either of us have to fight tomorrow?"

"No."

"Then fuck it." He held out his bottle and she met his with hers, clinking the glass together over Aven's mess of a bed. They drank.

"Veraion, why do you hate people so much?"

"I don't hate people."

"You hated Aven, and Athos, and Siran, and Einmyria."

"Aven ripped my face off my face. And the other three… suck."

Chester chuckled. "Yeah, they probably do. Einmyria seems nice though."

He grimaced. "No."

"No?"

"No."

"Okay. Tell me about someone that *doesn't* suck."

He looked at her and smiled, stepping across Aven's destroyed nest. "Well, I saved this azheek in the woods once." She smiled. "And I haven't been able to get rid of her since."

"I'm a barnacle."

"I love that you don't even try to defend yourself."

"What's there to defend?" She shrugged. "You're right. Aven's tried to get rid of you continuously, and yet, I'm still here."

He smiled to himself. "Thank you. I… forgot what it was like to have friends."

"Loser."

He snorted into his drink and she laughed, raising her bottle.

"How do you say 'friend' in azheek?"

He looked at her and smiled. "*sahilahk.*"

"Well then, I am your *sahilahk.*"

He grinned, cheered to that, and then drank. But he laughed into his bottle and choked.

"What?" she glared. "*What.*"

"I just made you call yourself a shithead," he giggled. Chester threw a pillow at him.

"This is why you don't have friends."

He sat beside her, draping an arm around her shoulders. "Who needs friends when you can have shitheads?"

"*dahveh?*" She raised a fist, and he laughed, pulling away.

"You learn quickly."

"Damn straight I do."

He smiled and she took a drink, grimacing a little at the taste.

"Tell me about your life in Zalfur," she said. "You said you lived in Zeda, right? But you also... did opium in Akana? Surely you had friends in Zalfur."

"I did," he said, gazing at his bottle. "Nobaru, Vi'ra, Ilia. They were my closest friends."

"Ilia was a water azheek, right? How did she end up in Zalfur?"

"She was in the same situation I was: found, rescued, taken there."

"But I thought Zalfur was only air azheeks... Did you have to live in hiding? Surely the Red Emperor would have thrown you from the walls if he found you."

Veraion clenched his jaw, swallowing as though trying to avoid the question. Chester's stare only grew more intense. He drank, looking away. She followed him, impossible for him to ignore.

"What aren't you telling me?" she said.

He glanced at her. "I... may have been... rescued... by Ezaria."

Her face fell.

"I may... have lived in the castle."

Her eyes widened further.

"And I may… have been trained by Ezaria himself."

Chester stood up, staring at him, backing away as she took in a deep breath. "Holy *shit.*"

"Ilia too," he said. "And Nobaru, and Vi'ra. They were both his favoured apprentices. We all were, the four of us. There were others, but we were the closest. And the best."

"Are you… That would make you Fang'ei." She stared. "Educated in every single academic subject, access to all arts, music, and dance, and trained—"

"Technically those things don't make you Fang'ei," he said. "Everyone in Zalfur has access to proper education—"

"Veraion!"

"*What?* The education system in Zalfur is very good!"

"You just told me you were trained by Lord Ezaria himself, therefore, Fang'ei. It's no wonder you're a good fucking fighter—you're—you're fucking Fang'ei!" She took a step back and stared him up and down. She looked confused, as though knowing she should feel disgusted and fearful but unable to do those things.

"How do *you* know about this?" he asked.

"Everyone knows about Zalfur. Everyone knows about Lord Ezaria— the Red Emperor. Everyone knows about the Fang'ei. They're the…"

"Worst?" he finished. "Best? Scariest? Craziest?"

She swallowed the knot in her throat. "Yeah."

He looked at her for a moment and let out a sigh with a small smile. "This is the reason I never tell anyone."

She searched for words but didn't find any.

"Are you afraid of me now?" he asked.

She looked at him and sighed. "No." But she turned away, pushing a hand through her hair as she tried to let the information settle. "It's no wonder you know everything." She looked back at him almost irritably. "I cannot believe… you knew… you were *raised…* by the Red Emperor."

He smiled bitterly, biting back a snort. "Please stop calling him that."

"What, the Red Emperor?"

"Yeah. Nobody calls him that."

"Everybody calls him that!"

"Nobody in Zalfur calls him that."

"The rest of Ianar does!"

Veraion admitted defeat and drank more.

"Holy shit," she said. "And—oh my god, you don't even call him *Lord* Ezaria, you just call him *Ezaria*. Is he… is he like your *dad*? Is the Red Emperor your *dad*?!"

"No! Gods, no."

She paced for a while and then plopped onto the bed beside him, eyes wide and glazed over. "Okay… so… explain. Fang'ei. Please."

"The Fang'ei are people Ezaria chooses based off talent, skill, and drive. Kids that excel at school, in and out of the classroom, but excel the most on the training grounds. He trains them himself."

"So… so you're Fang'ei."

"Yes. Or… I was. Until I ran away."

"You ran away?"

He let out a long sigh. "Ilia and I both ran away when I was about nineteen. She was a few years older. It just never really felt right there, not for us. Like you said, Zalfur is a huge place, and we were the only ones that weren't air azheeks. Many of the Zalfuri, especially the Zedai, didn't like that we were being given special treatment, from a lord—an emperor—that had previously massacred non-air azheeks."

"Fuck, I can imagine," she sighed.

They sat in silence for a moment. They both drank.

"How many years has he been ruling now?" she asked.

"Officially, over a hundred and sixty or… seventy years? But non-officially, he had power before that. He was favoured by the people, so the lords had no choice but to listen to what he said and do as they were told—either that or have a coup and be removed."

"And you know this from history books? Stuff that he's told you?"

"I know what you're thinking," he said. "That he lies to make himself look better. But before him, Zalfur was an empire of war. Between clans, tribes, and gangs. Zeda, Akana, Usan—and especially Ground Country— rarely saw long periods of peace. They may have been 'united' as one empire, but the reality was, the cities still fought. Zalfur has only been a united empire since Ezaria took power. Before him, no one was safe. Before him, the poor were starving. Before him, only those born into high-class families were given opportunities. Before him, half of the empire was illiterate. I said the education system is good, and that was all Ezaria. Well… Ezaria and Zaoen."

"Who?"

Veraion let out a long sigh, gazing at his drink. "Zaoen was Ezaria's twin brother. Identical."

Her eyes widened. "He had a *twin?* And they didn't bind? Every twin I've ever known has been each other's ilis."

"That's the thing," he said. "They *were* each other's ilis—or they would have been had Zaoen lived long enough. I've heard all the stories, all the accounts and retellings. They were inseparable, the most loved brothers in all of Zalfur. Everyone admired them, and for good reason. They excelled in every subject at school, starting in the countryside of Akana until they were brought to Zeda to continue learning, surpassing the education levels offered where they grew up. They taught themselves how to read, write, and speak Sa'uri based off old scriptures, and at fifteen, they left Zalfur. People thought they had been killed, as the reigning emperor at the time had been trying to assassinate them, threatened by how quickly they were gaining fame and respect. But four years later they returned, completely fluent in Azheek. They had gone to Elizia, immersing themselves in the Old Ways, and when they returned to Zalfur, they brought with them kara'i. Elizi willing to teach Azheek to the Zalfuri. They solidified alliances with other cities, with Volehn, Paradiz, Sirenvel, Sakhala, and Okos. They ensured every single person in Zalfur, across Akana, Zeda, Usan, and Ground Country, had access to good education."

Veraion swallowed the knot in his throat, his gaze growing distant.

"Ezaria and Zaoen were so close, they could talk to one another even when they weren't near. They could speak to one another from great distances, pushing the skill further and further until they could contact the other from across Zalfur."

Chester stared in disbelief.

"*ulu*," Veraion said. "The ability—the art—of connecting with the gods or ancestors, or in their case, each other. They *were* each other's ilis. But before they reached their prime, before they could bind, Zaoen was murdered."

Chester's face fell. "No…"

"I'm sure you've heard about assassination attempts?"

She nodded.

"But the timeline you hear is wrong," he said. "There were no attempts after he became lord. After he became emperor. But up until then, from the time they were teenagers, they were targets. Ezaria never wanted to be lord. Zaoen never wanted to be lord. But they were so *good* at what they did, so *loved* by the people, that those who sought to stay in power were threatened by them most of all.

"Fear," Veraion said. "Fear makes humans do stupid things. And their fear turned Ezaria into what he is now. They feared what would happen if the twins gained power, so they tried to get rid of them. And they half succeeded." He smiled sadly, bitterly, gazing at his bottle. "*They* created Ezaria. They wanted to fear him so badly, eventually he gave them a real reason to. *They* created the Red Emperor."

Chester watched him as he downed the rest of his drink.

"But he *did* take the throne by force?" she said. He looked at her and nodded.

"He did."

"So… he *did* want to be lord. He *did* want to be emperor."

"Eventually he realized it was what was best for Zalfur. But *power* was never his goal. Never his intention."

"And Zaoen? Was Zaoen like him?"

"From what we hear, no. Obviously who Ezaria is now is very different from who he was then, but he was still… Ezaria. Zaoen was the nicer of the two, more outgoing, more friendly. Apparently he was really funny, funny enough to make Ezaria laugh."

Chester sat there in silence. "I've only ever heard horror stories."

"People tell the stories they want to tell."

"Yes or no," she said. "Ezaria murdered thousands of human children."

He glanced at her. "Yes."

"Ezaria seized the Zalfuri throne by force."

"Yes."

"Ezaria slaughtered the city of Amora, killing *everyone*, and took it by force."

He let out a sigh. "Well, not *everyone*."

She gave him a look.

"Ezaria also created schools across the empire," he reminded her. "And ensured that everyone, no matter who you were, where you were from, what life you lived—no matter your *age*—he ensured anyone and everyone could receive proper education."

"You already said that."

"Yes, but he didn't *need* to do those things," he pressed. "Ezaria was high-born. He was born privileged. But he and his brother ensured that *everyone* could learn how to read and write. Not one, but *two* languages. They ensured that wealth was properly distributed and not hoarded by those in power when they could have easily hoarded it themselves."

Chester closed her eyes and pressed her fingers into her temples, letting out a high-pitched sigh.

"This is hurting my head," she said. He nodded.

"Story of my life."

"How old was he? Zaoen. When he died."

"Twenty-five."

She stared at him with wide eyes. "They... they achieved all of that before the age of *twenty-five?*"

"Like I said, the people loved them, and they loved them for good reason. Ezaria was always efficient. He always knew what he was going for and he always got it done, but he wasn't always..." He sighed once more. "They say he was never the same after that day, the day his brother died. After that he started to feel... *cold.*"

Chester sat back, staring ahead with wide, glazed-over eyes. "To lose your own twin brother, your ilis..."

"Yeah." He nodded. "And keep in mind, the Zalfuri vote for their leaders. He may have taken the throne by force initially, but every five years they're allowed to vote in someone new. And every five years, the four cities choose Ezaria. The only place or system that has birthrights is Sontar Ivel. The queen. And, well, we know how that's going."

They both sighed, loudly. Chester grabbed two new bottles, passing one to Veraion, and they pulled out the corks, tipping their heads back to drink.

"Can anyone else... *ulu?*" Chester asked. "I've only heard of people *attempting* to achieve *ulu*, and even then, they try to speak to the gods."

"Ezaria trains every set of twins in the art of *ame'ulu*. Twin *ulu*. It proves incredibly useful. Send one twin with a scout party and keep the other in the castle and you can speak directly with those that are far away. Send one twin to the port of Yan'zi while the other is in Zeda, and both cities will have contact."

"Fuck..." she murmured. "Lord Ezaria is..."

"He's smart." Veraion nodded. "He's really. Fucking. Smart."

"Have you ever known him to not be cold?" Chester asked.

"No. The Ezaria I knew was already... what he is."

"I can't imagine," she murmured. "Alive for two hundred years, losing your ilis at twenty-five. One hundred and... seventy-five years. Alone." Her voice cracked, and she quickly started drinking to avoid succumbing to a drunken misery.

"Yeah," he agreed, throat tightening. "He has a reputation, and I know he's done bad things, and he continues to do them, and he's merciless, but I still… Everything he did for me, you know? Everything he did for Zalfur, for his people. He cares about his people *so* much. He might not have ever hugged me or comforted me when I cried or sung me to sleep… but he still…"

Chester looked at him, tears welling in her drunk eyes. "So he *is* like your dad."

"No, stop," he choked.

"God damn." She chugged the rest of her drink. "No. *No.* I did not come here to sympathize with a warlord." She leaned over and grabbed a new bottle, wiping her tears. Veraion sniffed.

"Clench your jaw," she said.

"What?"

"Clench your jaw."

He did, and she slapped him. He blinked, eyes wide.

"My turn."

So he slapped her. They sat there, looking at one another. The tears had stopped.

"Oh," he said. "Thank you."

"Thank you." She nodded. She took in a deep breath and reset her emotions. "Is it true he has… silver hair?"

"Technically it's just grey."

"Because he's old?"

"Yeah. It's the only part of him that shows any hint of ageing. It's… quite creepy, really. To have a face and body in its prime and the hair of an ancient."

She nodded, trying to imagine. She had seen many drawings, having learned about the warlord, but she was finding it hard to picture.

"So… how long were you in Zalfur?" she asked.

"About thirteen years," he said.

"Did you ever go back? After you ran away."

He shook his head. "I… They wouldn't want to see me. It was an insult, us running away. It was an insult that we were receiving special treatment in the first place, becoming Fang'ei, but it was even worse that we didn't appreciate it. All that, everything we learned, everything we were taught, the amount of time and effort and resources spent on us, and we just… ran away. I don't think anyone would want to see me."

"What about your friends? Nobaru and Vi'ra?"

"Nobaru might still like me, maybe. I don't know."

He gazed at his bottle, watching firelight reflected in the glass.

"Have you ever sent letters?" she asked.

"I used to send drawings." He smiled. "I'd draw the places Ilia and I went to, sending them to Noba. He was my best friend, always wanted to travel, but when you're one of Ezaria's best, he tends to keep you close."

"When did you stop drawing?"

He looked at her and then took a very long swig of his drink. She nodded. "Ilia."

"They loved her too," he murmured. "The last time I wrote was to tell them of her death. I couldn't bring myself to message after that. The last they heard from me was that the baraduhr got her. That she was dead."

Chester clenched her jaw and shook her head. "*kyale dehen uhr.*"

He smiled to himself.

"It's ironic, you know," she sighed. "The baraduhr hate azheeks so much they capture us, torture us, kill us, all so they can *try* and steal our powers. They hate what they're trying so hard to become."

"Humans are complex creatures. I think things are more simple when you're an azheek."

She let out a sigh. "What you said before, about fear… how it makes humans do stupid things. I've seen it. Most of Foros was human. In a few generations there probably won't be any azheeks left. I've seen humans try to mimic ilis relationships, convincing themselves that they can be with one person and one person only, and then cheat on their partner because they *feared* their partner was cheating on them. Even though most azheeks, even with an ilis, are not monogamous. I've seen humans sabotage friendships because they *feared* their friend was pulling away. I've seen humans kill each other because… fear."

He nodded.

"And yet." She smiled. "Here I am, miles and miles from my ilis. And here you are… trying to… kill the queen?"

He snorted. "Who am I kidding, nothing is simple."

She clinked her bottle against his and they drank again. She let out another long sigh. "Well, hopefully with a close group of friends, life in Zalfur wasn't too bad?"

"Oh, it was great at times."

"Hence… opium in Akana."

"Hence opium in Akana." He laughed. "That was Noba's favourite. Rice wine and opium at the hot springs."

Chester smiled. "Noba sounds fun."

"He was my best *sahilahk*."

"To Noba." She raised her bottle. "For being the best shithead there could be."

"To Noba." He smiled, clanking his drink to hers, and they drank some more.

"You should draw again," she said. "Send something back. You never know, maybe he's still as great as he used to be."

Veraion smiled. "Yeah, maybe." He paused. "You want to know something? The tattoo on my stomach, the compass."

"Yeah?"

"We all have it. Noba, Vi'ra—Ilia did too."

"You have matching tattoos?" Her eyes widened, voice cooing.

"Yeah."

"How old were you all?"

"Teenagers."

She sniggered. "*Cute*. Was there meaning?"

He sighed, ashamed of what he was about to admit. "We all got the compass... because we knew that no matter what happened... we'd find our way back to each other."

Chester looked at him. Expressionless. He held her gaze.

"And we all got it here... so it sits on our hearts."

"That..." she said. "Is... so... *stupid.*"

They burst out laughing.

"I know," he croaked. "*I know...*"

"And that's not even where your heart is!"

"I know." He laughed harder.

"Did they all have unfinished tigers too?"

He chuckled and shook his head. "Noba and Vi'ra had different pieces on their backs, and I'm sure by now they're covered. The compass was all Ilia ever had."

"Why a tiger?" she asked.

"Because Vaia has tigers." He shrugged. "It didn't feel right to get something specific to Zalfur, so I chose the one animal I'd also seen in my childhood."

"You've seen a tiger?" She stared, amazed. He looked at her with a raised eyebrow.

"Says the person that talks to wasfoughts and has one as a pet."

"He's not a pet."

"Okay. Says the person that talks to wasfoughts and has one as a *best friend.*"

She smiled proudly. "*Stupid compass,*" she whispered. "Young you was so dumb."

"I bet young you wasn't any better."

"Perhaps if I'd had friends, I'd have a stupid matching tattoo as well."

"You had no friends?"

"Okay, I had friends—I had a lot of friends, and they were great. Closest were probably Chukuma and Faraji, and of course, later on, Yrilim. But tattoos aren't really a thing in Foros. They're big on warpaint, but not so much tattoos."

"If you had such great friends, why did you leave?"

She let out a small sigh and smiled to herself. "I honestly don't know," she said simply. "I ran into you and then it just… You said Sontar Ivel and it felt right. And then Aven joined us, and that's all I need, really."

He shook his head. "Your best friend is a giant wolf-lion-bear."

"Giant *man*-wolf-lion-bear."

"With unbreakable bones."

"Speaking of *bone*, Einmyria looks so *small*, you know? I think she's even shorter than me—I'm genuinely worried."

Veraion choked on his drink. "*aishida.*"

"Maybe we *should* give her opium."

He was now laughing. "You know what, I think you'd love Noba. I think he'd love you too."

"Did you love him?"

"Of course I did. We all loved each other."

"The Core Four?"

He snorted. "The Core Four."

"Was Ilia your first?"

"Noba was my first. I am going to assume that Yrilim wasn't your only, unless you used to finger him and have him touch himself."

Chester's drink went flying from her nose, and as the two of them cackled, she barely noticed the sting.

"Gods, no," she choked, wiping tears from her eyes. "Yrilim and I were rarely physical, actually."

"But I like the mental image of you fingering—"

She punched him in the arm and he yelped.

"*dahveh?*" she yelled.

"Bruise!" He pouted.

"Sorry."

He punched her back and she yelled, rubbing her arm. "Hey!"

"Equal?"

"Equal."

They both sighed.

Chester rested her head on his shoulder. "Do you miss anything about Zalfur?"

He smiled. "The smell. The smell when you stand outside a noodle house, at night, in the countryside of Akana or Usan."

"That's... very specific. Does it have to be a noodle house?"

"Yes. Hot noodles. Preferably thick wheat noodles. And a countryside with plenty of foliage still, but cold. *Gods*, does the cold enhance the smell."

"And you have to be *outside* the noodle house? Not inside?"

"Got to be outside."

She smiled. "That's so specific. What does it smell like?"

"It's... It smells like countryside: crisp, sweet, cold, but... empty? The nothingness of the countryside. But then you add the smell of the food, *gods*, the food." He closed his eyes, slowly inhaling. "The smell of the bamboo steamers. And just... the wood, the smell of it, warm inside, cold outside."

"So what you're telling me is that in your next life you would like to be reincarnated as a dumpling."

He looked at her. Then ale flew out of his nose. Chester cackled and kicked her legs as Veraion clutched his face, shoulders shaking as his laughter turned silent. Eventually sound came in the form of wheezing.

When the giggling subsided she let out an amused sigh, gazing over to their pile of swords.

"Raion... you don't have to say, but what on Ianar is a Fang'ei doing with common weapons?"

He followed her gaze.

"Surely the Fang'ei have weapons," she said. "*Good* weapons—priceless weapons."

"They do," he said. "They have kara'i steel."

"And here you are, fighting with basic swords, killing with machetes. I have to say though, I do like the machetes. There's a certain flare to them."

He reached for another bottle and then shuffled further onto the bed, resting against the back wall. She watched him and then took her place at his side.

"You left them, didn't you?" she said. "You left the weapons behind when you left the Fang'ei behind."

He nodded.

"Because you wanted a new start?" She looked at him. "Or because you feel like you don't deserve them?"

He glanced at her. "Stop doing that. Stop... knowing me so well."

She smiled. "I don't know what they think, but I'm sure you're more than deserving. You earned it."

His smile was small.

"Are all Fang'ei trained from a young age?" she asked.

"No. Fang'ei basically is just... the best. Some of us are chosen as infants, but we can easily be denounced if we start failing. And we can quit at any time too. Likewise, if someone excels later in life, they can be just as likely to earn the title of Fang'ei. It's not always about fighting, too," he said, looking at her. "Fang'ei can be the best of anything. There are cooks given title of Fang'ei, musicians, dancers, painters, blacksmiths, potters. If you're good, you're good, and Ezaria recognizes that. He rewards hard work. Passion. Drive."

She chuckled. "I wouldn't be the Fang'ei of anything. Maybe... wasfought taming?"

He laughed, pointing at her. "A wasfought tamer and a horse whisperer walk into a bar."

She smirked. "Ouch."

Cackles ensued once more.

"What about you?" He wiped his tears. "Anything about Foros you miss?"

"Well, I have Aven," she said. "I don't know, Foros just... never felt quite like home. I spent my whole life there and yet it kind of feels like I was never there. I think, before Aven, I was closest with my trainer. I made friends later on—I made great friends later on—but as a kid... I lived in my own head. Waiting for my trainer to come by every month. The best part of my month was hearing him tell me how much I had improved. I think I scared everyone. Training, fighting. Learning to kill was my favourite thing. It isn't... normal... apparently."

Veraion smiled to himself. "Perhaps that is why he called you *Iron Heart.*"

She smirked, shaking her head. "He also called me... something similar, what was it? Nnnn... neem riel?"

"*nim riel?*"

"That's it."

Veraion looked at her and smiled. "*nim riel* means 'my heart'."

Chester's pale green eyes turned to him, widened, touched—saddened. Her lip trembled. "What?"

"*nim riel* means 'my heart'. Perhaps for him, seeing you every month was the best part of his month too."

Chester looked away, fighting tears. She took in a shaking a breath and let it out in an attempt to push away her drunken emotions.

"What was he like?" Veraion asked.

"I honestly don't know. He stopped coming when I found Aven, and everything I remember of him is hazy. And I know that I was young, imagining him to be something I wanted him to be. When I used to look forward to him coming, I guess I imagined him to be warm. Like the father I never had. But when he stopped coming and I finally started making friends, I guess I pushed it away. I'd like to say I wasn't bitter when he stopped coming, but the reality is... I cried. A lot. But I was a kid. And when I grew up, I realized that everything I thought he was, was just projections."

"Well, if it makes young, projecting you feel any better, he obviously cared. I don't think someone would call their apprentice *nim riel* unless they truly meant it."

She smiled to herself and sighed. "Look at us… we've left everything behind, whether we meant to or not. You willingly left Zeda and lost Ilia. I lost my mentor and willingly left Foros."

She sighed again. Then she began to cry.

"What…" He stared. "Wait, what, no—"

"I miss Yrilim," she managed between drunken sobs. He looked at her, his own face screwing up, and soon he was crying too.

"Do you miss Ilia?" she choked.

"I miss her so much," he sobbed. They clutched one another, both red in the face, both gasping between sobs—both an absolute mess.

"But I'm also so happy," she said. "I don't think I've ever been this happy in my life. I'm having so much fun." Snot was leaking from her nose to join the tears and Veraion nodded.

"This is the happiest I've been since Ilia died," he wailed. "I didn't think I'd have this much fun."

"*Right?*"

The door opened. Aven and Einmyria stood in the doorway.

"I'm so happy," Chester ugly-cried. "Why do I miss Yrilim?"

"Because we're fucking azheeks." Veraion's shoulders shook.

Aven backed out of the room and shut the door. "Nope."

Chester and Veraion sat there and sobbed, clutching their drinks, and as the night went on their words got more and more slurred, eyes more and more red. They drank until they screamed with laughter and whimpered with tears. They drank until Theideus knocked on the door and silently motioned for them to shut up. Veraion proceeded to say something very slurred in what Chester assumed was Ancient Azheek. Either that or he was too wasted to speak Common. Either that or she was too wasted to understand Common.

They locked the door, returning to their jokes and tears until they fell unconscious, battling over the same blanket.

Aven and Einmyria lay on the city wall Five's Inn was built into, watching the stars. They couldn't see what azheeks saw, but they still found it so beautiful. Perhaps it was the blanket of twinkling stars they enjoyed or perhaps it was simply being with each other. There was a carpet beneath them, creating at least a bit of padding on top of the city's white stone, but as Aven lay there with Einmyria in his arms, he had never felt more comfortable.

They could hear distant sounds of nightlife—soft music, chatter, and laughter—and from the inn below, they could hear the last of the night's patrons heading up the steps to the street, wandering home with bellies full of food, wine, and ale.

There were flowers in their hair, for Aven had plucked them from the wall, and with the blooms so close, they could almost taste the sweetness.

Aven let out a low, content sigh accompanied by a slight rumbling in his throat. Like the purr of a great lion. Einmyria smiled and glanced at him from her place. She was so tiny in his arms.

They could finally be together, in the city. He didn't have to hide anymore.

He closed his eye, slowly nodding off as the food and wine in his belly lulled him to sleep.

Einmyria watched him with a smile, gently tracing her fingers over his markings. He was so peaceful like this. So innocent.

There she lay, listening to the rumble in his chest that came with every breath. It was so relaxing, so comforting. But as he shifted in his sleep, she carefully came from his arms.

Einmyria smiled sadly as she looked at him. Then she turned away and headed down the wall, every footstep silent, moving quietly as to not wake the gentle giant.

She headed into Five's Inn, moving down the steps. It was dark now; everyone was asleep.

She followed the corridor. Candles lit the hallway here and there, but it was not the light that danced with her. Instead, darkness.

Past room two, four, eight, ten. She moved through the shadows until she stood before room fourteen.

There she stayed, breathing softly. She stared at the room number. She took in a deep breath and wrapped a hand around the doorknob.

Slowly she turned it, but the door didn't move. She tried again, less carefully this time, but it was locked.

Einmyria stood back, her hand falling away from the cold metal handle. She clenched her jaw, swallowing the knot in her throat. There was a sad look in her eyes, the same deep sadness that followed her everywhere she went.

Einmyria closed her eyes and took in a deep breath, filling her lungs with the underground air of Five's Inn. Then she headed back to where Aven lay.

CHAPTER 10
AZHARA

Twenty champions became nineteen. Nineteen became eighteen. And one by one, the champions fought until they could fight no more. Every day brought more and more people to the city, flocking to attend the tournament, desperate to see the Battle of the Ten. The final round. All ten champions in the arena at the same time, free to use whatever weapons and whatever powers they pleased. Free to pick each other off until Athos saw fit to enter the arena and destroy whoever was left. At least, that's how it had gone every year for the last decade.

Newcomers were setting up tents in forests and fields, unable to find space within the main city. Aven could no longer sneak off to the woods at night, choosing instead to simply pay for his stay at Five's Inn with gold.

On this day, Veraion and Aven sat on the parapets of a city wall, watching the busy streets below. Parades of foreigners were arriving, family and friends of the top champions. They watched as a legion of earth azheeks arrived, each with an animal by their side.

In the lead walked an elephant, clearing the streets with gentle sways of its great head, tusks adorned and decorated just like its people. A man was riding it, strong, past his prime. His skin was dark as night, hair braided and decorated with beads, bones, and feathers, brilliant gold-green eyes gazing around the streets. In his arms he carried a baby, both his and his child's skin decorated with paint.

Beside him, a heavy-set man rode a rhinoceros, grinning as others stared.

Among the herd were antelope, buffalo, gorillas, and even a giraffe. Aven's jaw dropped. Never before had he seen any of these creatures.

Chester hurried up the city wall, clutching something in her hands. She raced to where her friends sat, joining them, letting her legs dangle off the edge, and placed her items into Veraion's lap.

"Where are they from?" Chester asked.

"Okos," Veraion said, "the capital earth azheek city, and their animals are sikele, companions. Almost like ilis." He glanced to the gifts thrust into his hands.

Paper and pencils.

Chester smiled, nudging him, and then gazed back to the parade. "I'm sure Nobaru would love to see this."

Veraion wasn't looking at the parade anymore. He watched her, her excited eyes on the swarm of foreigners below, and he smiled.

"Where is Okos?" she asked.

"South," he said, looking at the supplies in his hands. "It's moved over the years—I think it's further east now. I've heard that their city is impenetrable."

"In the ground?"

"No, but I hear that the heads of their enemies hang from the city walls."

"I love them already."

He laughed.

The Kosi leader slid down his elephant and greeted a woman in the crowd—one of the final champions. Her skin was as dark as his, eyes a brilliant green, head shaved and body muscular. She was representing her city: the best from Okos. Chester had seen her fight and prayed she wouldn't have to face her until the very end.

Leader and champion embraced, and when the man held up the baby, she kissed her son on the head.

Azheeks and humans from all walks of life flocked to the city, but not one water azheek joined them.

The streets were packed, and as more and more people arrived, Chester and her friends headed back to the inn, never noticing as four fire azheeks entered the city.

The riders sat upon Sirenveli horses, every beast as radiant in the sun as the azheeks that rode them, their coats shimmering a metallic sheen in the light. The horses were the pride of Sirenvel, bigger, stronger, faster than all others. A ride that would take the average beast months would only take them a few weeks, and the pride of the city was clear in the way they were adorned. Every saddle blanket was intricate with patterns, and tassels hung from the edges. Coins jangled from neckpieces, every harness, rein, and bridle more jewellery than leather.

Moving through the streets, Yenea rode in the lead, pulling back her hood as she scanned the city walls. Her fire-orange hair shone in the sunlight, and behind her rode Azhara and the identical twins Fairo and Fehir.

Had they arrived any other season, they would have stood out. But here and now, Sontar Ivel was ripe with the festivities of the tournament, drawing azheeks and humans from all corners of the land, blending the four warriors of Sirenvel in with the crowd.

Yenea guided her stallion, her piercing eyes roving the city, and her gaze rested upon the place where Chester and her friends had just been.

* * *

Veraion, Aven, Zaiera, Maina, and Theideus stood in the front row of the arena stands. They were surrounded by people, hundreds, if not thousands, and the air was deafening. The grounds shook with stamping feet and clapping hands, and sweat dripped beneath the summer sun.

The audience was a sea of colour, different hair, skin, and eyes, every present azheek and human sharing one thing in common. They were here to watch Chester fight.

The arena was oval in shape, with awnings jutting from the top in an attempt to shade the stands, and with the sun at its zenith, it was mostly successful.

The fighting pit stretched far and wide and was naught but sand, dirt, and blood. There were scorch marks in the ground from where fire azheeks had been, and eerie patches of moss growing from where earth azheek blood had splattered. And above it all, watching in his tower, was the undefeated champion. Sunlight glistened off his burnt face, his eyes set on the grounds.

Chester stood in the shadows, waiting for the arena gates to open. Her black hair was braided back, red warpaint across her face, hair, and armour, weapons comfortable in her grasp. But something was different today. She could feel something. *Someone.*

She looked through the grating to the distant audience, scanning the crowd. Her brows were furrowed. Something was *calling* her.

A horn sounded and cheers erupted. The grating rose. Chester strode forward.

Mahriel! Mahriel! Mahriel!

She threw up her arms, yelling for the audience, and they responded. It was deafening.

Moving into the arena, she scanned the sea of faces. What it was she searched for, she didn't know, but something was calling her. She had never felt this before. The pull was so strong it was frightening. The sensation felt so foreign, yet the presence so familiar. It was becoming hard for her to breathe.

Then Chester saw her. A woman in the audience with wild flame-orange hair and piercing eyes. Jewellery decorated her, her ears, nose, and neck, and though she wore a hood of deep red, it did nothing to shadow her striking face.

Beside her were a woman with blood-red hair and two identical men, past their prime, with stares of embers. They were wrapped with cloth and gold jewels, attire that would cause any but fire azheeks to roast in the summer heat. As they pulled back their hoods, their skin radiated in the light, loved by their sun god.

Chester's brow furrowed. She had never met these people before, never seen them, and yet... she knew them. She knew that woman.

Yenea's eyes were fixed on Chester.

Then the horn sounded. Chester's opponent, an air azheek, charged at her. She hadn't even realized he was there. But she parried the attack, swift to defend herself.

Still, she was distracted.

As she fought, her eyes returned to the audience. Again and again to the woman with wild, flame-like hair. To Yenea.

Chester kicked her opponent away and he careened, sliding through dirt. She turned back to the stands, staring at Yenea. The air azheek kicked her in the back, throwing her to the ground, but she regained her footing and returned to battle. Her friends watched with wide eyes.

"She's distracted," Aven said.

"Yeah, no shit," Zaiera exclaimed. "But why now? I've got money on her!"

"It's someone in the audience," Veraion said. "She keeps looking at the same spot."

Aven followed his gaze.

"Her." Veraion's eyes fixed on Yenea. "Fire azheek."

Yenea's gaze never left Chester, watching her intently. But the audience gasped loudly and Veraion turned back to the fight to see Chester wheeling around and around, slamming her swords into her adversary again and again. He staggered and she leapt into the air, kicking him in the chest. He flew back, and instead of chasing him down and finishing it, she looked to Yenea.

Zaiera's eyes widened in confusion. Sweat covered her dark skin, soaking into her locks, and she yelled, fighting to be heard over the roaring audience, "What are you *doing?*"

In the stands, Yenea and her company were watching Chester closely. Azhara leaned in, her eyes still on the fight.

"That's who you feel?" she said. Yenea's brow furrowed, eyes still on Chester, and she nodded.

"You feel *him?*" Azhara pressed.

"Stronger than ever before." Yenea's words were low, foreboding, as though even she did not like what she was feeling. The pull. The call.

Across the arena, Veraion's brow furrowed. "*Shit,*" he muttered. "She's glowing."

Aven looked at Chester. It was subtle, barely noticeable, but he knew her like the back of his hand, and her skin looked different. More radiant. Like fire was flowing through her veins.

"What the fuck is going on?" He stared.

"That woman." Veraion looked between the two. "She shares some kind of bond with Chester."

"What?"

"Do you know her?"

"I've never seen her in my life!"

"If this gets any stronger…" Veraion hissed. "Everyone here will realize Chester is an azheek."

In the stands, Azhara rose to her feet. She threw back her cloak, drawing a sickle sword, long and hooked, shoving her way down the pews. Flames engulfed her weapon, causing people to leap back and yell in alarm.

Azhara moved faster, tearing for the arena. Her cloak went up in flames as she leapt over the railing, plummeting to the grounds. She rolled into the fall, swiftly back on her feet.

She ran.

Azhara wore fitted armour over her chest, built specifically for her. Bracers wrapped her forearms, leather about her waist, her knee-high boots plated for protection, and all over, she was adorned with gold. These were no cheap clothes. This woman was of importance.

Azhara tore towards Chester as horns blared. People around the arena shouted in panic as guards poured into the grounds.

Chester's opponent rose to his feet, staring around at the mayhem. Azhara raised a hand and sent a great blast of fire, fire so strong it threw him from his feet, repelling him so hard he only stopped when he collided with the arena walls. He did not rise.

Chester stared at her opponent, then at Azhara, but her eyes returned to Yenea in the stands.

Chester was fixed in place, feeling a pull so strong she couldn't fight it.

"Why isn't she moving?" Maina stared.

Aven's hackles rose beneath his robes, fur crawling over his hands as he gripped the railing, claws extending from his fingers. Veraion grabbed him by the arm, tight. Warning.

"Where is he?" Azhara yelled, charging straight for Chester.

She hadn't moved. She was just standing there.

"Where is he?"

Guards charged towards Azhara with their weapons drawn. Aven leapt into the arena, Veraion right behind him, racing towards Chester. Zaiera yelled loudly. Theideus was frozen with wide eyes, but Maina looked up, turning to the champion's balcony just in time to see Athos leap over the edge.

He plummeted for the ground. The earth shook upon impact.

"WHERE IS HE?" Azhara screamed, sending another blast of fire to engulf guards in flames. She raised a hand, aiming at Chester. Her skin began to glow.

Athos grabbed a shield from a guard and threw it. He was halfway across the arena, but the shield throttled through the air like a discus, pelting for the manic fire azheek.

It crashed into her legs, shattering them, bursting through skin, muscle, and bone.

Azhara fell to the ground with a blood-curdling scream.

Aven and Veraion stopped dead in their tracks, all eyes turning to Athos.

Azhara shrieked, her blood pouring onto the sands, legs destroyed.

Guards swarmed the arena, racing for her, for Chester, for her fallen opponent.

Yenea stared at the mess, at Azhara, at Athos. She started forward but her companions grabbed her by the arms.

"Yenea," Fairo said desperately. "We cannot lose you too."

Yenea's eyes were livid. Shocked. Her fiery stare went from Azhara to Chester to Athos, who was now looking right at her. His gaze was dark. Focused. A predator fixed on prey.

"*Yenea*," the twin pressed. "Azhara made her choice."

Yenea's jaw clenched and she finally pulled away, drawing forth her hood, and as Veraion watched from the sands, the fire azheeks disappeared into the fray.

* * *

Chester entered the Five's Inn dining hall to an immediate swarm of questions, bombarded the second she arrived. The entire inn had gathered.

"What on Ianar was that?" Maina exclaimed.

Chester walked through the throng, eyes glazed over. Theideus handed her a tankard of ale, and she sat down at the nearest available spot.

"Come on, give her space," Veraion said. "None of us know what that was about."

Chester took a long drink.

"Who *was* that?" Aven asked.

"I don't know," she said, eyes on her drink. "They wouldn't let me see her."

"Is she still *alive?*" Maina exclaimed. "Her legs... She... That..."

"She tried to *kill* you," Zaiera pressed. Chester didn't respond.

"You noticed them," Veraion said. "You were looking at them the entire match."

"Why didn't you *move?*" Zaiera yelled. "You just stood there!"

Veraion grabbed Zaiera's arm and pulled her away, giving her a stern look. Chester took in a deep breath, pressing fingers to her temples. She closed her eyes, fighting off a pounding headache. She didn't know how to answer any of these questions, for she was asking all of them herself.

"I knew her," she rasped. "I've never met her, never before in my life, but I knew her face. But the other one, the woman in the crowd, I didn't just know her face, I *knew* her. I could *feel* her there before I even entered the arena. I felt *her*, not the one that attacked me."

Looking at Veraion, she tried to contain her anger and frustration. He sat before her, concerned.

She grabbed another tankard and downed the entire thing. When she finished, she threw it across the room. People ducked, but Tao raised a hand and it veered off course, zipping into his grasp.

"You have a bond with her," Veraion said in a low tone.

"I've never met her in my life," she said, fighting the knot in her throat. "But I feel... I..." Chester clenched her jaw, taking in a slow, deep breath. She looked at Veraion. "Because of her, because of the whole thing, I didn't win the match."

The tavern gasped.

"You didn't make top ten?" Maina screamed.

"Oh, I still have a chance." Her eyes never left Veraion's. "I can make top ten... if I beat you."

The hall went silent. Aven dropped his bag of gold. Theideus sat down. Zaiera's eyes looked like they were going to pop out of her head.

Maina swallowed the knot in her throat and glanced around. "Alright, alright, everybody out. You heard me, everyone, off to bed!" She started shooing them away.

"This is an open tavern!" someone called.

"Okay! Fine! Just… give them some space, will you?"

With that, the crowd dispersed. People returned to their food and drink, though many still looked over to where Chester and Veraion were seated in silence.

"Remember why I'm in this," he said lowly.

"I know." She smiled. It was sad, and she took his hand. "You'll have your victory. But not before I give this city a kiss goodbye."

* * *

Azhara's yellow eyes rolled back in her head, legs the same colour as her blood-red hair. Bones protruded from her skin, gleaming in the eerie light of crystals. The night sky shone above her, but her company could not see the millions of stars and billowing colours she could.

Her head turned slightly, a weak moan coming from her lips. Her vision was blurry. All she could see was a distant sky and the vague pink glow of the blood moon.

She blinked slowly, gazing around, drawn to more light. Stronger. Glowing.

Large stones. Huge. Crystals.

They glimmered eerily in colours of orange, green, blue, and pale purple. They changed, fading in and out, lights wafting to a steady beat. Heartbeats.

Trapped heartbeats.

Azhara lay on the ground, on packed earth. Sand. It reminded her of home. But it was turning redder and redder as she bled.

A man approached, and though she tried to move, she couldn't. He was naught but a silhouette, the great crystals behind casting him to shadow.

A soft breath escaped her lips as she tried to plea, fingers twitching slightly, but no words came.

The man took her by the arm and dragged her towards the lights. Pain throbbed in her legs as her bones scraped across earth, feet lolling uselessly. He dragged her into the circle of crystals.

The ground changed to stone, ridges felt beneath her. Carvings, circles, holes. He left her there, moving away from sight.

Azhara lay still, chest rising and falling, every breath rasping and weak. All she could see was a haze. A bright, colourful haze. She could hear the stones, singing, shimmering, but within them, there were distant whispers—distant cries pleading for her to run.

She lay upon a stone circle. Shapes were carved into it, thin trenches leading deep into the ground. Circles, triangles: runes.

Azhara's head lolled to her left, and as she slowly blinked, the world somewhat came into focus. It was still a haze, a warped, pained haze, but she could make out the nearest forms.

Weapons. There were blades stuck in the ground. Before every crystal stood a weapon, before all but one.

Her gaze moved from the blades to the glowing stones behind them, and her eyes widened.

Azheeks. An azheek suspended in every crystal. Trapped.

The shimmering coffins grew brighter, lights flashing from within, heartbeats hammering. Fearful. Warning. Desperate for her to get up and run.

Then the stone beneath her changed. The openings began to glow and soon they sprang to life. The lights of the crystals shot into the open cracks, flowing through every shape and rune, creeping closer and closer to the centre where Azhara lay.

Light shot into the air, engulfing her. A gasp left her lips, her back arching from the force as a tear slid from her eye.

She was pulled from the ground. Azhara floated into the air, suspended in place.

Azhara's head rose, eyes opening, and her stare disappeared behind bright orange light, fire blazing from the sockets. Around her, the beam of light grew smaller, closing in.

Closer. *Closer.*

Beams of light solidified, encasing the woman, surrounding her with stone.

Then it was over. The surge of magic stopped and the bright lights dimmed. Azhara was frozen, encased—crystallized. Tiny lights of fire wafted from her stone, glowing with the beat of her heart.

Ropes were thrown around her coffin, tied tight, and she was dragged away from the stone floor.

Through rows of encased azheeks and displayed weapons, Azhara was dragged to the outskirts, shoved into place. Another body in a building ring of trapped azheeks.

The ropes came free, cast aside, and as the lights glowed with the beat of her heart, the man struck her sickle sword into the ground.

CHAPTER 11

MAHRIEL

The noise was deafening. Thousands were packed into the stands, filling the arena of Sontar Ivel with exultant roars. Yells, whistles, screams, applause, and the stamping of feet thundered in the air.

The ground shook.

Sunlight beat down on them, dried blood streaked across the sand.

Athos stood on his balcony, accompanied by the queen. Light beamed off her white gown, her hair, eyes, skin, and markings all glimmering, but nobody was looking at her. All eyes were fixed on the arena, flicking between the two gates at opposite ends, thirsting for their champions.

Chester and Veraion waited in the darkness of their holding cells, hearts pounding in their chests.

The queen stood. "My people!" she called, her voice carried by magic. Finally the crowd quietened. "Welcome to the final round of the Twenty!"

Roars erupted once more. Chester smiled.

"Today we are fortunate enough—nay, *blessed* to bear witness to one of the most exciting games we have ever anticipated in the history of this tournament. We are here to watch the renowned siblings of Mahr Ivel go head-to-head in a battle that will determine who will go on to become one of the Ten, who will go on to face the rest of the champions—who will go on to face the undefeated champion of the *world*, Athos!"

Stamping feet started a pulse, the sound travelling for miles through the city.

Boom. Boom. Boom.

"First, our beloved brother, Veraion of Mahr Ivel!"

Screams filled the air as the gate rose. Veraion walked into the arena, a machete in each hand. People called to him, reaching out to try and touch him, screaming his name.

Veraion! Veraion! Veraion!

Sweat dripped down his face, leaking into his eyes. His black hair was braided back, scars glistening in the sunlight, blades gleaming dangerously.

He raised his machetes into the air, opening his arms, finally embracing the thunder of the crowd. For once, he did not wear a helmet.

Veraion! Veraion! Veraion!

He couldn't help but smile. He was starting to understand what Chester loved so much.

"And his opponent!" Siran exclaimed. "Our beloved two-spirited sister, Mahriel of Mahr Ivel!"

The audience roared louder, the stamping of feet and clapping of hands shaking the arena.

The gate rose and Chester strode into the beaming sunlight. Her armour gleamed, her hair braided from her face. Warpaint covered her, red and gold streaked across her skin, armour, and through her hair, and around her eyes, painted in black, were Aven's menacing markings.

The arena was deafening.

Chester reached for the sheaths she had strapped in an X across her back, wrapping her hands around the hilts of her blades, and drew them.

Two machetes.

Veraion smirked.

Chester threw her arms into the air, a machete in each hand, a yell sounding from her throat, teeth bared.

The crowd erupted. They loved her. They worshipped her.

Aven stood in the front row with Einmyria, Zaiera, Maina, and Theideus. His face lit up the moment he saw her. He hadn't known about the warpaint.

Flowers were thrown onto the sand as Chester strode forward, and she laughed, a grin spreading from ear to ear. She caught a rose and turned towards the champion's podium, her eyes on the queen. She kissed the rose and held it up, casting Siran a wink, and the queen couldn't help but smile, her cheeks turning a little flush.

Chester threw the flower. Siran opened her hand and it flew across the arena, over the stands, zipping straight to her fingers.

The crowd went wild. Athos raised an eyebrow, looking at the queen as she blushed.

Chester turned to Veraion, pointing a blade at him, smiling darkly. He shook his head at her with a smirk.

Veraion lowered to a knee and struck his machetes into the ground, reaching into his pocket. When his hand came free, it was covered in black paint. He smeared it across his face, and from opposite ends of the sand, the so-called siblings of Mahr Ivel grinned.

Chester closed her eyes, listening to the thunder of the arena. She tipped her head back, weapons loose in her hands, and took in a long, deep breath. Only after Veraion rose to his feet and Chester opened her eyes did the queen speak once more.

"Let the games begin!"

The horn sounded.

Chester and Veraion jogged towards each other, picking up speed until they were running. Veraion wheeled around and swung his machetes but Chester slid to the ground, skidding past him. His blades hummed inches from her face as dust rose all about them. She leapt to her feet, spinning, her blades singing through the air.

CRASH. Her strike was parried.

With a machete in each hand, they fought. The sounds of their dual blades filled the air, accompanied by the shouting audience and low, beating war drums.

They fought like gods. It was a dance, so smooth and flowing.

Athos watched from the champion's podium, hands gripping the railing, his eyes fixed on the fighters below. The queen stood beside him, locked onto the battle. Chester and Veraion fought so similarly, so fast, it was almost hard to see what was going on.

Then the fight stopped. Veraion's blade was on Chester's neck. The crowd froze.

"So soon?" Siran gasped, but Athos smirked, a gleam in his dark gaze.

"Look closer."

Chester had the tip of her blade tucked beneath Veraion's breastplate, aimed straight for his heart. The crowd roared and the two backed away from one another, laughing lowly.

Chester smirked. "Nice try." She lunged.

No matter what Veraion did, she was prepared for it, and no matter what she did, he was just as ready. Dust billowed about them as their boots disturbed the earth, bodies wheeling and hair whipping. Their matching armour gleamed in the sunlight, muscles rippling.

Veraion dripped with sweat, Chester with not a drop.

Their machetes moved so fast it was almost impossible to see.

Veraion kicked her in the chest, sending her to the floor, and though he was quick to stand over her with a blade to her throat, she already had both of hers between his legs. He laughed and stepped away.

The crowd was going wild, Zaiera and Maina yelling profanities, gripping the railing with white knuckles. Aven was chanting with the people around him, Einmyria frozen, hands gripping the fabrics of her dress, and Theideus was banging his pots and pans together, slowly, too consumed by the match to pay attention to his rhythm.

Chester and Veraion circled one another, eyes never straying. Stalking, calculating, like predators about to feed.

She leapt through the air and kicked Veraion in the side of the head. He staggered back. He took a moment to spit blood. Chester swung her machetes by her sides, the blades gleaming, and smirked.

"Show me what you've got, Fang'ei."

She dove back in.

Again and again they attacked, swerving and ducking and lashing out, only to have their adversary dodge the move, every hit avoided or parried. Their chests heaved, muscles aching, but there was no end to the dance.

Then Chester pulled back. She walked away from Veraion and he watched her, panting in his place.

She closed her eyes once more, raising a machete into the air, and the audience cheered. Chester smiled, letting it down with a laugh.

She turned and charged. She raced for Veraion, and as he attempted to raise his weapons, she leapt into the air and drop-kicked him square in the chest. They both fell, both quickly regaining their footing. Veraion staggered, shaking his head to remove the sweat that dripped from his brow. One machete was embedded in his breastplate. With a groan, he yanked it from his armour.

Blood. His blood.

Above them, a smirk rested on Athos's lips. The queen was still watching in awe, genuine concern upon her face.

Veraion strode towards Chester and attacked. She blocked his move, swinging another blade, and he let her strike him with it. She got him in the arm, but he used his free hand to slice her leg. Blood flew from his blade, splattering the ground.

Smoke rose from the sand. Chester watched her blood burning the earth, nostrils flared, jaw clenched. She charged.

She struck at him, unforgiving. Veraion slashed at her but her swings cut deeper.

He staggered back, both cheeks bleeding. Chester knew just how far she could go before causing fatal damage, but she was beginning to draw more blood than he appreciated. They were locked in a dance of singing metal and dripping red.

Their hearts pounded in their chests.

The roar of the audience thundered like a chorus of war drums. Chester danced to the beat, her weapons mere extensions of her own body. She felt the vibrations from the hilt to the tip of her blades.

As she moved, her hair whipped behind her. As she moved, her muscles rippled. As she fought, Veraion struggled.

Again and again their blades met, but she could see it, she could feel it in the rhythm. She was beating him.

Again and again, metal on metal, blood on blood. He could see it. He could feel it. She was beating him.

Her chest heaved, her breaths rasping, eyes widening.

She was beating him.

The thunder of the audience beat like a chorus of war drums. She was too fast.

She was beating him.

Then she stopped.

Veraion kicked her.

His boot slammed into her armoured chest and she was sent careening backwards. As she soared, the world slowed.

Her chest rose and fell, hair whipping around her. As she flew, she let go. Her fingers eased and her weapons slipped from her grasp.

Chester crashed to the ground, skidding through sand. Veraion swung. His blade touched her throat.

Chester lay there, both of them gasping for air. The audience froze. The final fall seemed to last a lifetime.

There she lay, her eyes on her friend. And finally, after what felt like an eternity, she raised a hand, two fingers together to indicate defeat.

The audience erupted with deafening shouts and screams, and none sounded happy. Curses and insults rang in the stands.

"*What?*" Zaiera shrieked. "No. No—no, no, no, no, *no*! Bullshit! That's *bullshit!*"

Maina and Theideus exchanged wide-eyed glances. Aven let out the breath he had been holding.

The queen stood in her place, stunned. Then she managed a smile, a light gasp sounding from her lips. "People of Sontar Ivel, your victor and our final champion to join the top ten: Veraion of Mahr Ivel!"

The audience thundered.

Athos had not moved. His knuckles were pressed into the railing, his eyes fixed on the two below. His jaw was clenched so tightly, the veins in his temples were popping.

"Athos?" Siran said. He turned and strode away.

Back on the sands, Veraion dropped his weapons. He fell to his knees and pushed sweaty hair from his face, eyes closed. He felt sick.

Slowly Chester sat up, and he looked at her. She smiled, though there was sadness behind it.

"For Ilia," she said. She rose to her feet and pulled him up with her. Holding his gaze, she placed her hand on his chest. "*kyale dehen uhr.*"

* * *

Sontar Ivel had never been more busy or lively. Even at sunrise, the streets were bustling, and as Veraion moved through the throng, everyone stopped and stared. He smiled uncomfortably, nodding as people greeted him, but for the most part he knew what they were whispering.

He knew most people had been rooting for Chester, and if he were one of them, he'd have been rooting for her too.

He headed towards a messenger keep, where birds were taken care of and trained to fly across Ianar. Many of them were soaring above, stretching their wings and hunting in their down time. A few saw him, feeling his earthly presence, and called greeting. He smiled as he headed inside.

He nodded to the human behind the counter.

"Morning, Veraion," the woman said, and he smiled uncomfortably. He had never met her before.

"Sorry," she said, noting his expression. "I just… know who you are."

She was older, stout, weathered with age, but wore a friendly smile.

He nodded. "Sorry, I don't mean to be rude."

She waved him off. "Do you have something you would like sent?"

"I do. Can you send to Zeda?"

"Zeda!" She laughed. "I can, we definitely can. It's just rare anyone wants to send anything to Zalfur."

He nodded, placing a carrier on the counter. It was heavier than the average letter, much more so. The tube itself was made of light wood; it was the sheer amount of drawings he had stuffed inside that made it heavy.

"We'll send an eagle," she said, noting the weight, and he placed his coin on the counter.

"Thank you." Veraion nodded, heading for the door.

"Best of luck in the final battle," she called. "I hope you don't… break too many limbs."

He snorted uneasily. "Is that a common occurrence?"

"Athos will be in the ring," she said simply. "That's all you need to know."

They gave one another polite nods and he headed back onto the street, avoiding the looks everyone gave him.

He moved through the rising sun, heading to a familiar spot, and climbed a city wall overlooking the morning boat market. There he sat, legs dangling over the edge, waiting. He had gotten up early for this, before Chester or Aven rose, and walked the whole way. He needed the walk. He needed to at least try and clear his swarming head.

Veraion took in a deep breath and gazed over the water. Turquoise, crystal clear. He could see rocks jutting out below, and so many fish swimming here and there. Reefs, somehow surviving miles from the ocean, but he knew how they survived.

He gazed up at the castle ahead. He was still quite far, but he could feel the power. This was it, the umbilical cord connecting Ianar to their Mother god. He wondered if she knew. He wondered if she could see him right now. He wondered if she could hear his thoughts.

He wondered if the gods cared at all about what was happening here. And he wondered, most of all, how long Sontar Ivel would remain a place of magic now that the queen was an imposter.

Then came distant voices of vendors, calling in the morning air, and he pulled his gaze away from the shimmering castle. He smiled to himself, so fond of the life here. In another world, one where Ilia had survived, they'd have lived here. They'd have sat here every morning and tried food from all over the world. But that was not the world he lived in, and he could never stop feeling the guilt he carried.

Gondolas floated into view, every last one colourful and unique. The vendors decorated their boats to match what they sold or where their food came from, and Veraion watched them, waiting until he saw the old man from the Vaian Islands. He waved and the man beamed, steering his boat over with gentle pushes of his bamboo staff.

Veraion climbed down the rickety ladder and nodded a greeting. "Good morning."

"Good morning, brother. Congratulations on making it to the top ten!"

Veraion smiled, but it was unconvincing. "Yeah, thanks."

"I watched you—you're very, *very* good. Don't let anyone make you feel otherwise. It seems like common sense, but I'll remind you anyway. Thousands signed up for the tournament, and thousands have been eliminated. But you, you are still here."

Veraion's smile became more genuine, and he nodded. "Thank you."

"Taho? Two?"

"Please."

He watched fondly as the old man scooped silken tofu into two cups, adding sago palm pearls, pouring brown sugar syrup over it all. He mixed the ingredients and handed the cups over.

"Thank you, brother," Veraion said, shoving gold coins into the old man's hand, and before he could try and refuse, Veraion climbed the ladder.

"This is too much!" the vendor called.

"Never too much," Veraion said, smiling from his place. He gave the old man a kind nod and ushered him away.

"Long live!" The Vaian vendor put the coins in his pocket and waved a grateful goodbye, continuing down the canal to where the same little girl reached out of her window overlooking the market and gave him her giant jug to fill with taho.

* * *

Veraion entered Five's Inn, moving down the steps and into the dining hall. Chester and Aven were eating breakfast at their usual table, and she held up a scroll.

"A messenger brought this for you," she said as he sat down beside her, but he shook his head.

"This first." He handed her a cup of taho and smiled with a slight sigh. "Apology taho."

She glanced at it, then him. "What are you apologizing for?"

"Just... everything. The tournament. It should be you in the top ten, not me."

She smiled and shook her head. "Don't worry about it. I'm only here because of you, and I only joined the tournament for fun. But I will accept this offering."

She patted him on the head as if he were Aven and picked up a spoon, tucking into her new breakfast. Veraion held up the second cup for the giant, but the giant shook his head. So Veraion ate a good mouthful of taho before he put the cup down and picked up the scroll.

He let out another sigh. It was sealed with the queen's crest, a golden tree that signified life, roots as wild as the leaves.

"Is it from the queen?" Aven said.

"I doubt it's from her directly."

Veraion looked down as something poked his hand, and he smiled as Dog rested her chin on his lap. He petted her for a moment before returning to the scroll. He broke the seal, unrolling parchment, and raised an eyebrow at the letter. The invitation.

Dog moved to Chester for pats and she gladly obliged, much to Aven's dismay. He was sitting close to the wall and glared at Dog from his place. Dog looked at him with a satisfied gleam in her eye. Taunting.

"There's a banquet," Veraion said. "To celebrate the games thus far and congratulate the top champions." He smiled mischievously. "It's in the castle."

Chester looked at him, impressed.

"Told you." He beamed. "All I needed was to make top ten. Mahriel, oh great Mahriel, would you do me the honour of being my companion for the banquet? It should be you receiving this scroll, after all."

"I'm just happy you keep saying that," she said. She scratched Dog behind the ears, under her chin, and as she placed kisses upon Dog's head, Aven's jaw dropped. He watched with horrified disbelief. Veraion tried to bite back his very amused smile.

Chester re-emerged with excitement in her eyes. "Oooh, this is going to be fancy, isn't it?"

"Very."

"You better buy me a good fucking dress."

"The best."

"Einmyria invited me to the banquet," Aven said, trying to get Chester's attention back. "She asked if you'd like to have a gown made by her dressmaker. She knew you'd be attending."

Chester finally stopped petting Dog as she threw up victorious fists.

* * *

Colourful banners flowed in the wind, garlands and decorations littering the city as far as the eye could see. Music rang through the streets, ripe with talk and laughter, and in the air, the smell of food. Roast meat and vegetables, grilled fish, gravy, soup, bread, pastries, cakes, and fruit. But the best smells wafted from the castle's banquet hall, where the finest food had been brought to honour the champions.

The sun was setting, turning the sky into an array of dancing colours, basking Sontar Ivel in the golden hour.

It had been two weeks: two weeks of rest for the champions, and two weeks for the city to prepare for the festivities. Two weeks for the castle to decorate and build and cook, two weeks for musicians to practice and prepare to perform for the queen and the champions.

Six horses pulled a carriage through the city, bearing the crest of the queen. The coach rode towards the castle, towards the golden gates, and the guards stood aside, allowing them through. The horses rode through the castle gardens, making for the open doors that reached over six stories high.

When the horses slowed to a stop, guards rushed forward and opened the coach door.

Veraion stepped out first. His hair was slicked back, braided along the sides, looking clean and polished for the first time in a long time. He wore a dark coat with deep red trim and gold embroidery, a black shirt underneath that dipped into a low V, putting his strong chest on display. A blood-red sash was tied about his waist, with boots and bracers to match, his pants also black.

He offered a hand and helped Chester to the ground. She wore a deep red dress that was fitted about her waist and breasts, embellished with gold embroidery. From her hips, the gown pooled out in folds and layers. A black ribbon, decorated with gold, was wrapped around her waist. Her hair was done up, with jewels glistening among the locks, loose strands flowing about her face and neck, and matching earrings dangled in place.

When Aven stepped from the carriage, it rose a foot higher. He wore a fitted black vest over a deep blue shirt, with black pants and boots, embellished with silver and gold. His clothes fit him perfectly, finely tailored for his gargantuan build. He wasn't used to wearing clothes so fitted, and it took everything in him to not pick his wedgie.

Aven helped Einmyria down, unable to take his eyes off her. Her dress hugged her, the fabric somewhere between a dark purple and blue. Sitting off her shoulders, the sleeves were sheer and loose, ruffling in the evening breeze. The bodice was tight and embroidered with silver and gold, sparkling with her every move. From the waist down, tulle flowed, a long train gliding behind her, more embroidery glistening at the trim.

A thin silver-and-gold circlet rested upon her wavy black hair, pinned up and away from her shoulders, earrings sparkling with every movement.

She took Aven's hand, beaming up at him, and he couldn't help but smile. Veraion offered his arm and Chester took it, and as the carriage rode away, they headed towards the castle.

Flanked by guards, they approached the great open doors, and when Einmyria led them inside, they couldn't stop their jaws from hanging and their eyes from wandering.

Marble, as far as the eye could see. The walls, floor, ceiling, and every arch and statue was built from marble. The ceiling stretched high above them in arches, strengthened with beams. Gold sconces lined the walls and illuminated the entrance hall in golden light, colours of the sunset pouring in through giant windows. Curtains and paintings decorated the walls, every fabric twinkling in the light.

There was a group of castle hands gathered by the doors, all dressed in burgundy, the crest of the queen upon their chests, adorned with white and gold. One of the women came forward, bowing to the newcomers.

"Welcome to the palace!" she said, beaming. She glanced at Veraion and tried to hide her smile, but she was blushing. Chester smirked, casting him a look.

"My name is Eidis," she said, hands wringing in her nervousness. "I'll be your guide to the… banquet hall."

Eidis was human, a young woman, pretty, with wavy brown hair and large brown eyes. Her face was round and small dimples appeared when she smiled. Moles decorated her, like constellations across her olive skin.

She smiled every time she glanced at Veraion, despite how much she tried not to.

"Please, the banquet awaits!" Eidis beckoned them to follow, and that they did, absent-mindedly, as they stared around the whole way there.

"Holy shit," Chester murmured under her breath. Veraion simply nodded.

They were led through the castle, up a great flight of curving stairs, through more halls, until they could smell food—food that made their mouths water.

Through an open archway, they were led to the banquet hall. The ceiling stretched high above them, paintings covering almost every inch: paintings of their gods, the Five, and the creation of Ianar. That which wasn't painted was supported by stone arches, twinkling in the light of candlelit chandeliers.

Every torch and sconce was finely carved and inlaid with gold. Banners of deep reds, purples, and blues hung, detailed with gold and silver. They flowed in the evening breeze, wafting through a series of large open doors leading out to more gardens.

In the centre of the hall was a large dance floor, around which were raised podiums holding mahogany tables, stretching down both sides of the space, leading to the far wall where the highest podium sat. The queen's table. Every chair had huge backrests, intricately carved, but the chairs about the queen's table looked more like thrones. Bigger, better, and once again, inlaid with gold.

Across the tables were plates, bowls, goblets, and cutlery of all shapes and sizes, made of fine silver, engraved with intricate designs, plated with more gold. Giant platters of food were already being served, cooks and servers bustling about as they prepared the last of the feast.

Musicians played near the entrance, their songs resonating around the marble hall. Mandolins, guitars, harps, and flutes, and accordions and drums to create a rhythm. Vocalists sang, harmonizing with a hurdy gurdy, cellos and a double bass creating a low drone that flowed through the ballroom.

People were milling about: lords, ladies, queen's men and women, and the champions of Sontar Ivel, gazing around in awe, arm-in-arm with their partners.

In the middle of the hall stood the queen. Her gown glimmered, gold hugging her fit form, breasts jutting up from the pressure. Sea-blue velvet pooled from her waist, every panel and drape shimmering with elaborate gold embroidery. The velvet flowed to the floor in such a great train, no one could stand behind or beside her.

Hours had been spent on this dress—weeks, months, if not years.

The beaded bodice twinkled endlessly, almost blending into the queen's golden skin. Her snow-white hair was done up, away from her shoulders, and upon her head was a golden crown of painted flowers and thin spikes that protruded from her head like a halo. Or like perilous spikes to keep people away. Gold jewellery dangled from her ears, with small stones to match the sea blue of her dress.

And as always, her skin was radiant, her magical markings glimmering white.

"*Fuck*," Chester whispered. Siran was breathtaking.

People were talking to her, advisers, lords, and nobles, and though she smiled and nodded, her gaze rested upon the newcomers.

She look at Einmyria, longing to be by her side, longing to greet and embrace her sister, but she knew she couldn't. Her old life was behind her. She could only stand in her place and watch as Einmyria looked away, wrapping an arm around Aven's, guiding him towards a group of lords.

"Come, let me introduce you to my father." Einmyria smiled. Siran turned away.

Aven recognized the man's scent, and he looked every bit as royal as he smelled. His hair and beard were greying, the colour once black, his body wrapped in expensive leathers and velvet, and draped over his shoulders, pooling over his back, was fur. Jewellery glimmered all about his body, a heavy necklace lying over his chest, rings gleaming about his large fingers. His dark eyes turned to Aven and he smiled, extending an olive-skinned hand, taking Aven's into a strong grasp.

"You're *tall*." The man laughed, staring up at the giant. "Einmyria told me you were tall, but she didn't tell me *this* tall."

"I get that a lot." He smiled.

"My lord," one of the nearby men said. "I get that a lot, *my lord*."

Aven blinked at him. Einmyria leaned in, whispering, "You're supposed to say it."

"Oh!" he stammered. "Sorry, yes, *my lord*."

The lord laughed, ringed hands resting on his belly. "Lord Venhel," he said. "And if Einmyria truly likes you, just Venhel."

She smiled. "Looks like it's just Venhel then."

By the entrance, Eidis marvelled at Veraion a moment longer before she shuffled away, heading from the banquet hall and back to the castle doors.

Veraion let out a long sigh and Chester looked to him. This was all too much.

"Do you want to go outside?" she asked. He nodded, jaw clenched, and they headed for the gardens.

The moment they were outside, he took a deep breath. There were people milling about, talk ripe among the resonating music, and the two wandered until they found an area that was somewhat secluded. There they watched the sun slowly creep towards the horizon, the sky steadily turning its vast array of oranges, pinks, and purples to dark blue. Chester watched him knowingly.

"Ilia?" she asked. He nodded.

His eyes were bloodshot. There was pain conflicted upon his face, feelings of hatred and self-loathing. She placed a hand on his arm.

"Raion, whatever happened, it wasn't your fault."

A tear slid down his cheek and he smiled sadly. "*Almost.*"

His voice cracked. Something in the single word caused a lump to form in Chester's throat.

She pulled him into a hug. Veraion accepted the embrace and returned it, resting his chin upon her head, closing his eyes. When they parted, he brushed a hand over her hair and cheek, genuine fondness in his gaze.

"I'm going to go for a walk," he said kindly. "I just need a moment to be alone."

She nodded and he headed away, disappearing among the labyrinth of green. Then there came a low voice, sending a chill down Chester's spine.

"Why did you throw the match?"

She turned to see Athos watching her. Once more his thick hair was braided and cuffed with gold. His eyes held her, one a beautiful sea blue, the other clouded and blind, burned beyond repair. His scars from blade, beast, and fire were all the more intimidating as he stood before her.

She had only ever seen him from far away. As he watched her now, she felt so incredibly small.

Despite being the champion of Sontar Ivel, he was barely dressed up. A belt about his waist, pants, boots, and bracers were all he wore.

"Athos," she said, casting him a nod. She did what she could to hide her fear.

"Why did you throw the match?" he repeated. His voice wasn't kind.

"I didn't."

"You were going to win."

She held his gaze a moment longer before turning to the gardens. "Don't worry, Athos. I'll be back next year. You'll have your ass handed to you then."

She never saw the slight smile twitch onto his lips. It was dark, foreboding, but almost fond.

She looked back at him. "Why are you talking to me?"

"Why not?"

"I've seen you. You don't acknowledge anything or anyone, barely even the queen."

"She's not my queen."

He never broke eye contact. It was unnerving, but Chester did her best not to show fear.

He approached, slowly. She held her ground, but in her chest, her heart was pounding. Athos's piercing eyes held her, and they only moved from her face to look over her body. His gaze lingered over every inch. His fingers twitched, itching to touch her smooth skin. To see what she felt like.

She held his gaze, fighting the urge to run. There was something about him that made her skin crawl. It wasn't his scars or his unyielding eye contact, but a feeling deep in her bones that she had met him before.

When he spoke, his deep voice sounded like a distant memory.

"I will answer any question you ask," he said. "But do not ask a question you don't want to know the answer to."

Chester didn't say anything. He moved closer, and it took everything in her to hold her ground.

"Ask me anything."

She clenched her jaw. "Why do you watch me? Why have you been watching me?"

"It's my job," he said, almost taunting.

"Yeah. But why *me*? You barely watched any other contestants."

"The other contestants bore me. The other contestants have always bored me."

"Why?"

A slight smile crept back onto his lips. "They don't have what you have, Mahriel. Life. Personality. Bravery. Every man and woman I have ever fought was there to prove a point. To *win*. To bring home gold, to bring honour to their name. Either that or they were slaves, and they had no choice. But you, Mahriel, you have the choice. And you fight for fun."

He moved closer.

"You fight because you like it," he said. "You kill because you like it. There's an air to you, a spark." His gaze wandered over her face and he smirked. "*Fire.*"

She didn't move, despite how desperately she wanted to get away. His voice was so deep, like a growl. Every one of his words crawled over her skin and made her hairs rise.

"I answered a question," he said. "Now, humour me. What finally brought you to Sontar Ivel?"

"Finally?"

He smirked. "Someone like you should have been here, in the tournament, a long time ago."

"My brother." She forced a smile. "My brother decided he wanted to come. I came with him."

Athos grunted a little—almost a snort. He nodded. She held his gaze a moment longer and made a move to leave, but she stopped. She clenched her jaw and turned back.

"Where are you from?" she said. "I know Mahr Ivel isn't a real place. Where are you from and why do you hide it?"

He smiled slightly. "I lie because the place I am from, nobody knows exists. So there's no point in telling the truth."

"And where are you from?"

"Acolonia."

He was right—she had never heard of it. "And where is Acolonia?"

"East."

"How far east?"

He smirked. "The Dead Sea east."

She squinted slightly. Athos was a human, lying was second nature to them, and while he told her the name of a place she had never heard of, telling her he came from an ocean that left people dead, she couldn't shake the feeling that he was telling the truth.

"I assume you're going to ask me a question now?" she said. He took a step forward, closing the space she had created.

"Do you remember the faces of everyone you've ever killed?"

His words were cold, and yet, the worst part was that his slight smirk never went away.

"Do you remember what you say to them?" he asked. "What they say to you?"

He stood over a foot taller than her, eyes boring into her soul. Testing her. She smiled for a moment, bitterly.

"No."

She didn't move. She kept her pale green eyes on his. She held her ground until his sick smirk finally faded. And then she turned and walked away, heading for the banquet hall, heart hammering in her chest.

"Mahriel!" came a voice, and she almost leapt out of her skin. She turned to see a man with black hair, dark eyes, and gaunt skin. With him, a man with brown hair slicked back. They were dressed well, for the banquet, and both seemed familiar.

"I'm Thalamere," he said, noticing her confused expression. "We met a while back at a tavern. Rendel, too."

It took her a moment. They looked far more royal now than they did that morning, with flowing capes, long, fitted vests, and clean pants tucked into knee-high boots. Embroidered leather wrapped their forearms, belts embellished with gold, collar and shoulder trim to match.

"Twenty-inch cock," Rendel said, trying to refresh her memory. "Yours, not mine."

Then she laughed. "Thalamere! Rendel! Yes, sorry."

"That's alright, it was a brief meeting," Thalamere said. "Easy for me to remember you, though—you've become a celebrity. *Mahriel*, goddess of the arena."

"Oh gods, don't call me that." She grimaced.

"Sorry."

She tried to hide her trembling hands.

"Congratulations on almost making it to the top ten," Rendel said. The two men joined her on the walk back to the hall. "I'm sure if you compete again next year, you'll make it."

"Thanks." She smiled.

A bell rang from inside and they hurried their pace. The two men bowed to Chester before heading to their chairs near the queen's table.

Chester spotted Aven and Einmyria and quickly moved over. She took her place beside them, but Veraion was nowhere to be seen.

At the head of the hall, the queen had taken her seat, resting in the biggest throne of them all. On her one side sat Athos, and on the other, Einmyria's father, Lord Venhel. Around them were more advisers to the queen.

Lining other tables were lords, nobles, the top ten champions, and their companions. Earth azheeks, including the lady from Okos, fire azheeks, and air azheeks. No humans had made it to the Ten.

"Where's Veraion?" Aven asked. Chester shook her head.

Venhel rose to his feet and raised a goblet. "Ladies and gentlemen!" he called. "Welcome to the great banquet of Sontar Ivel! An annual celebration for the champions who have made it thus far into the games. Feast and drink knowing that you are in the presence of, if not one yourself, the *best* warriors from across the land. You are, all of you, skilled beyond imagination."

Veraion slid into his chair.

"Please," the lord continued. "We all know you're not here to listen to me." He chuckled, and the hall laughed with him. Then he offered a hand to Siran and helped her to her feet.

"Thank you." She smiled, subconsciously wiping her hand on her dress. "Thank you, everyone, for coming! I hope tonight will be an evening of feasting and drinking and dancing and celebration, a night to remember as we pay our respects to the top ten champions of Sontar Ivel—dare I say, the world?"

As she spoke, Veraion's hands balled to fists. They were under the table, hidden, but Chester placed her hand on his, giving a comforting squeeze as he shook.

"I would like to offer my personal congratulations to you all and wish you luck for your later trials," Siran continued. "I have watched all of you fight, and I am truly honoured to be among you tonight. I know that I would be terrified to face any of you."

Laughter rippled through the hall. Veraion remained as stone-faced as ever.

"I would also like to congratulate our reigning champion, the legend of Sontar Ivel, the undefeated god himself, Athos! I look forward to watching him in the arena with all of you." She turned to him. "Be gentle?"

He didn't feed into her joke at all. He continued staring ahead, bored out of his wits. Siran chuckled nervously and the rest of the hall did the same.

"Let us eat!"

The guests were served the best cuisine from across the land, food Chester had never before tasted, seen, or heard of in her life. Some of it was exquisite, sending her taste buds dancing, and some made her recoil and sneakily spit into a napkin. The goblets were emptied, filled, and emptied once more, all but for Athos's cup, which remained untouched. The new servers attempted to fill it and the old ones quickly pulled them away, warning them not to.

As the night went on, the guests wandered from their chairs and back to the floor. Aven and Einmyria were among the first to dance, moving joyously to the music. Aven had no idea how to and she laughed, doing what she could to teach him. Siran watched them from her place, a smile in her eyes. She missed seeing Einmyria laugh.

Lord Venhel stood near the musicians, listening to them play, watching his daughter and her tall companion. Rendel stood by him, speaking in low tones as he gazed around the hall.

Chester watched Aven, chuckling as she sipped her wine. Then Thalamere approached.

He bowed. "Would you do me the honour of granting me this dance?"

"Who the fuck are you?" Veraion raised an eyebrow. Chester snorted into her goblet.

"I'm a... friend?" Thalamere blinked.

"Don't mind my brother," Chester said, smirking. "He's over-protective. I'd love to have this dance."

She stood up and headed around the table to join the man, and all the while Veraion watched him with distrust.

Thalamere and Chester danced, swirling around the hall, and when they were almost knocked over by Aven, they laughed. The song ended and they pulled apart to applaud the musicians. When the band struck up another tune, Thalamere offered his hand once more. But Veraion slid in front of him with a smile.

"May I?" He offered his hand instead. Chester raised an eyebrow at him. "Really?"

He took her hand and whipped her away from Thalamere. "I don't like him."

She laughed. "You don't like anyone."

"That's not true."

"Name one person you don't dislike."

"You. Maina. Theideus. Zaiera. Tao. The guy that sells taho. Dog. Even Aven, on rare occasion."

She laughed again. "Well, whatever your motives, I'm glad you're dancing. I'm sure this won't last long, so I'm going to enjoy it."

He smiled. "You look beautiful, by the way."

"I know."

He laughed.

They danced, swaying and twirling with the music. He spun her around, dodging the train of her dress, and she couldn't help but laugh. She returned to his arms.

He pulled her close, one hand holding hers, the other on her waist. They closed their eyes, smiling as they listened to the music and enjoyed the food and drink in their bellies.

"You know…" Chester smirked. "People are going to think we're one of *those* families."

"That's fine. We're not from here."

She chuckled. "By the way, Athos told me where he's from."

"Really?"

"Acolonia."

He raised an eyebrow. "That doesn't exist either."

"You sure you know *every* place?"

"Fang'ei, my friend. Fang'ei. You said it yourself—I know everything."

She snorted, shaking her head, but her smile was genuine.

They danced and danced, drinking more and more. One song, then two, then three. The guests around them were starting to turn pink, flushed with alcohol and brimming with food. Veraion glanced around, noting the various doors leading away to the castle. He pulled Chester in close, murmuring lowly.

"I'm going to sneak off."

"Shall I cause a distraction?"

He pulled back to see she was smirking and raised an eyebrow. "You have something in mind?"

"That I do."

He nodded and they parted ways. Veraion made his way off the dance floor and Chester moved across it. Veraion sidled closer and closer to a door, away from standing guards, and Chester headed straight for the queen.

Guards wrapped their hands around hilts.

Chester walked up to where the queen's podium began. She stared up at the beauty, having to tip her head back to do so. Siran looked at her, surprised. Athos was beside her, but Chester ignored him.

"May I have this dance?" she asked. It took the queen a moment to realize she was actually talking to her.

"Me?"

"Of course."

Siran smiled and let out a soft laugh of disbelief. "Nobody has ever asked me to dance before."

"Really?"

"Nobody has ever had the guts."

"Well, I've got plenty of those." Chester smiled. "May I?"

Siran nodded, and Chester battled her way through her dress, onto the queen's podium. Guards started forward but Siran waved them away, and when Chester offered a hand, she took it.

Athos watched them as they made their way to the dance floor. Everyone stopped and stared. Einmyria smiled.

People cleared the area, leaving half the dance floor just for the two women. They had no choice—Siran's gown didn't leave room for anyone else.

Chester looked at her to ask for permission and she nodded. Then Chester placed a hand upon her waist and led the dance. Veraion watched them with a smirk, shaking his head before opening a door, disappearing from sight.

As the queen moved, her gown sparkled like the ocean, like white sand fading into turquoise waters.

She seemed shy, averting her gaze here and there.

Chester smiled. "I wish someone had told me how good the food was going to be. I wouldn't have worn this damn dress if I'd known."

Siran laughed. "Somehow I think yours allows more breathing room."

Her hand trailed the queen's waist. "Yeah, seems tight."

Siran watched her with a smile. Then, after a moment, she spoke. "Thank you. I haven't danced in years."

"No one's stopping you," Chester said lightly.

"This is true."

"But I will take it. You're welcome."

Siran laughed. "You're funny."

"I know."

"And an incredible warrior."

"I know."

"Beautiful too."

"I know."

"And so humble."

"Right?"

They laughed.

Chester watched her. No matter how much Veraion hated her, she couldn't help but feel as though this woman wasn't a part of the war, or at least, didn't want to be. There was an air of sadness about her, always.

They danced in silence and Siran closed her eyes, trusting Chester to lead, and that she did. Siran listened to the music, doing everything she could to block out the sounds of the castle around her. All she wanted was to dance, to forget where she was. To listen to the soulful singer and feel Chester's warm hands hold her.

Chester watched her. She was so used to seeing sadness suppressed. She saw it in herself every day, in Veraion, and as she looked at the queen, she knew that she too was suffering.

"You seem like a good person," Chester said. "It can't be easy, being in your position, however you ended up there. But I get the feeling that at the core of it all, you're a good person."

Siran opened her eyes, her sad gaze searching Chester's face. The words confused her, hurt her, but were also the nicest things anyone had said in years.

"People call you beautiful every day," Chester said. "I'm sure you're sick of hearing it. I wanted to tell you something that mattered."

Siran smiled sadly. "Well, now I feel bad for calling you beautiful."

"Oh, I loved it. From you? Loved it."

The queen blushed. She averted her gaze, looking instead to Chester's gown. And cleavage. Chester smirked.

"I like your dress," Siran said.

"Thank you. Einmyria took me to her dressmaker."

"It fits you well. Very well."

Chester smiled. "I know."

"Oh, stop that."

"Sorry."

They shared smiles as they moved about the hall, ignoring all the stares.

"I love your gown," Chester said. "And I'm not just saying that. It's amazing."

"Thank you." Siran's smile was genuine, spreading even to her pale blue eyes. "I just needed to not wear white for once."

Chester laughed. "You don't like all the white?"

"I hate it. Every piece in my wardrobe is white."

"Surely the queen gets to decide what to wear."

Siran averted her gaze, quickly doing what she could to deter the conversation. "I made this."

Chester blinked at her, then down at the masterpiece she wore. "*What?*"

"I made it," she repeated, hushed—shy.

"Are you fucking serious?"

"Yes." She smiled. "After last year's banquet, I decided I couldn't wear white. At least for *one* night. I started working on it immediately. Lord knows I have nothing else to do with my time, cooped up in the castle all day."

"Fucking Valduhr." Chester stared. "I take back what I said then. You're not just a good person but an insanely talented and hard-working one at that."

Siran only blushed harder.

"You hate white," Chester murmured. "Point noted. It's a good thing I didn't give you a white flower."

"Yes, I would have sent it right back."

"No, you wouldn't." She smirked. Siran smiled, averting her gaze yet again. Chester let go of her, taking a step back to truly ogle the dress. *"Seriously?"*

"Stop it," Siran laughed. Chester quickly swooped back in and took her hand, placing the other upon her waist.

"Don't tell me you made the crown, too."

Siran blushed.

"*Don't* tell me you made the crown too." Chester stared.

Siran nodded.

"*Fuck*, you're amazing."

"Stop it. You're going to make me cry."

"Oh, don't do that—the guards will chop my head off."

Siran laughed once more. Her cheeks hurt. They weren't accustomed to happiness.

"Perhaps I should make you a guard then," she said. "A private guard."

Chester looked at her in surprise. "Really?"

"Well, you won't be competing anymore." She smiled. "Mahriel, do you require employment?"

Chester stared. Then she laughed.

Veraion will never believe this.

CHAPTER 12

ELAIRA

Veraion snuck through the castle, keeping to the shadows. He had no idea where he was going or what he was searching for, but he followed his gut.

His instincts guided him through halls and hallways, down staircases, passing the kitchens. He could feel something. Magic. Overwhelming magic. The entire castle radiated it, but this, the trace he followed, was different. The castle's magic was old, ancient and deep, connected to the next world. What he felt here, growing stronger the more he followed, felt new. It felt wrong. It felt like death.

Down more steps. Perhaps he was just guiding himself to the dungeons.

Veraion closed his eyes, cocking his head. His brow furrowed. No. This was no ordinary sensation of death. It was magic.

Further and further into the darkness.

Every now and then he sensed people—maids, workers, cooks, guards—and always ducked out of the way to avoid being caught. He had to find out what this *thing* was. He could feel it calling him, a pull, drawing him in. It was frightening. Part of him knew he should fight the pull and run in the opposite direction, but with his pendant resting on his chest, providing him comfort, he followed the call.

He was underground now, deep underground. Torches lit the walls here and there, but it was still very dark. He swore he could almost *hear* something. Like a song of crystals, eerily shimmering, singing quietly. The castle had gone from smelling regal and pristine, to ordinary and musky, to dank and dirty, but the closer he got to whatever was calling him, the cleaner the air felt.

Torches faded away behind him, leaving him in darkness. But there was another light in the distance, a thin sliver peeking out from a crack of a doorway. White. Blue. Green? Orange? The light changed colours, shifting in strength, fading in and out like a calm heartbeat.

His brow furrowed. Veraion reached the wall, placing a hand on it, but there was no door. Only rock. This was just another stone wall.

He stood back, staring at the light peeking out at the floor. There had to be a doorway here. There was something on the other side. Something big. He could feel it.

Magic. The call of magic. Curious, innocent, and yet... tainted with death.

Veraion placed his hand against the stone wall, closing his eyes. He took in a deep breath, fighting to feel what was on the other side.

He flinched and yanked his hand away. His eyes were wide now.

Azheeks. Alive?

He took in slow breaths, finding it hard to do so. Veraion lowered to one knee, placing his hand on the floor, allowing the eerie light to caress his skin. The feeling was overwhelming. *Death.*

Then he sensed someone approaching and quickly stood, glancing around frantically. *Shit.* There was nowhere for him to hide.

A human, he could sense. A woman. Wait, this presence seemed oddly familiar.

"Veraion?" came a soft voice. He could barely see her, but he recognized her presence—the castle hand from earlier, the woman that had led them to the banquet hall. The one he had made blush. Eidis.

He immediately cracked a smile. A fake, drunk smile.

"Hey," he said, staggering a little. He leaned against the wall for support.

"What are you doing here?" Eidis said.

"Went for a pee, got lost," he laughed. "Fuck, this castle is huge."

"It is." She smiled, averting her eyes. He could already feel the blood rushing to her cheeks.

He came forward, draping an arm around her. Her heart hammered in her chest.

"What's that?" He pointed at the glow on the ground. She followed his gaze.

"Oh... I... I don't know, actually. It's always been there, at least, as long as I've been here. I haven't been here that long."

"Hm..."

She glanced at him, so close. "I—I think you're an incredible fighter."

He leaned in a little bit. "How many matches have you come to?"

"Um... most." She glanced at him again, and he stayed in his place. So close. "Sh-shall I guide you back to the hall? They've noticed your absence. I'm glad I found you before the guards."

He smiled, leaning in a little bit more. "I'm glad you found me, too."

Goosebumps crawled over her skin.

Then Veraion felt more people. With metal. Armour—weapons. *Guards.* He could hear them now, their footsteps growing louder as they made their way down the corridor.

"We should go," Eidis whispered. He nodded, allowing his nose to brush her hair. She quivered beneath his touch.

She guided him down the hallway, and they could see guards at the far end, illuminated by torches on the walls. The guards spotted them.

"Oi!" one of them yelled. "The fuck are you doing down here?"

The queen's men started running, drawing weapons. Veraion clenched his jaw, letting out a small, frustrated sigh. Then he pulled Eidis close.

"Can I kiss you?" he murmured into her skin. Her breath hitched, eyes searching his face in the darkness, and when she nodded, he placed his lips on hers. Soft, but when she moaned, closing her eyes, he deepened the kiss.

Veraion grabbed her, pressing her against the wall, tongue roving into her mouth. The guards were getting closer. She threw her arms around his neck, holding him tight.

Closer. *Closer.*

He picked her up and she wrapped her legs around his waist.

The guards skidded to a halt.

"Oh shit—sorry!" one of them exclaimed, ushering the rest to stop staring. "You should... maybe do that elsewhere?"

Veraion finally pulled his lips from hers and looked at them, feigning drunkenness yet again.

"Sorry?" he muttered.

"The banquet. You've strayed very far."

"Perhaps we were looking for privacy."

Eidis blushed, trying to hide her face, but she made no effort to remove herself from him. She revelled in the fact that he was still holding her, making no move to put her down.

"Yes, well... I guess you found it," a guard said.

"Apparently not private enough." Veraion smiled dryly.

"Apparently."

Eidis glanced at the guards, and while they were busy averting their eyes, she gave Veraion's junk a gentle squeeze. He made a slight, panicked noise, and as she giggled, hiding her face in his hair, he had to bite back an embarrassed smile. She was quite cute.

A guard cleared his throat, and they glanced at one another.

"Well uhh... private party's over," the man said. "We'll show you back to the banquet hall."

Veraion let out a long sigh. "If you must."

He stepped back, lowering the maid to the ground, and she tucked her hair behind her ears, avoiding eye contact yet again. But she glanced at his pants just to see what kind of an effect she had had. She was pleased to see a bulge forming.

Veraion smiled at the guards and didn't try to hide it. If anything, their clear discomfort would at least make up for this mission failed.

Guards flanked him and guided him back to the light, and he looked over his shoulder, sending Eidis a smile and a wave. He felt bad for having to use her, but the smile upon her blushing cheeks was genuine, and he was glad he could have at least given her that.

Siran let out a long sigh as she sat by a fountain. She and Chester were in one of the castle gardens furthest from the banquet hall, and they were far enough to hear the lapping of water louder than the distant chatter.

They were surrounded be green, surrounded by flowers, and above them, the mesmerizing night sky.

Chester moved some of the drapes of Siran's gown away from the fountain. "Don't want to ruin it," she murmured. "You put so much care into this dress."

Siran watched her with a smile. Chester stood back and looked at the queen, lost in the beauty of her glowing markings. Siran knew exactly what she was thinking.

"They're like stars, aren't they?"

Chester nodded. "Yeah. Sorry, I don't mean to stare."

"You can stare. I've spent more than enough time watching you."

"The tournament?"

She nodded. "If I'm being honest, the tournament has always been an escape for me. I can be out there, with people, and yet… no one looks at me. It's refreshing."

The queen sighed. She gazed at the garden around them, surrounded by perfectly pruned trees and bushes, flowers blooming everywhere, but her stare grew distant.

"Are you okay?" Chester asked. Siran forced a smile and looked back at her.

"Will you train me?"

"Me?"

"Yes. They can't know."

"You're not allowed to train?"

Siran smiled to herself. It was bitter. "I'm not allowed to do anything. They barely let me eat. They want me to be…"

"Weak."

The queen was unable to hide the fear in her eyes. She averted her gaze.

Chester moved forward, searching her face. "Tell me, would I be protecting you from people outside the castle? Or people within it."

The queen looked different now. She no longer held her strong persona together and grew smaller with every word. Chester wasn't looking at Siran anymore—it was Elaira sitting before her.

"Can I… tell you a secret?" Elaira whispered.

"Yeah."

"I… I shouldn't say."

"You don't have to. But I'm good at keeping secrets. You can trust me."

"I'm so stupid." She smiled to herself. "I just met you."

Chester smiled. "Well, I know you're not the real queen. I've been keeping that a secret."

Elaira's eyes went wide, a gasp sounding, but Chester stayed in her place, her face kind. Tears welled in the queen's eyes.

Someone knew. Finally, someone else knew.

"Elaira," Chester said softly.

Elaira gasped, relieved, and the tears came. "Well." She smiled, laughing to herself. "That was the secret."

"You were going to tell me that?"

She shook her head, shrugging. "I had to tell someone. Anyone."

"Einmyria knows, doesn't she?"

"She doesn't know the whole truth. And she can't. I have to protect her."

Chester nodded. She offered a hand and Elaira took it. Chester moved closer, their gowns heaping together.

"And what of Athos?" she asked. "You're frequently seen together—surely he could train you? Or is he one of them? Is he with you to prevent you from leaving?"

Elaira smiled slightly. "No, Athos isn't one of them. But he isn't here for me either. Athos is Athos. He does what he wants, when he wants. He comes and goes as he pleases. If he's here, it's because he wants to be here. If he leaves, it's because he wants to. There isn't a soul on Ianar that could control him."

"Should I be afraid of him?"

"We should all... be afraid... of Athos."

Chester clenched her jaw and nodded, a thumb gently tracing over the queen's hand. "I will be your private guard," she said. "And I will train you. And I will get you out of here."

Elaira wiped her tears. "I'm never getting out of here. But... at least if I know how to fight, it will feel like a choice."

"Why can't you leave?"

"You think I'd be here if they didn't have something against me?"

She nodded solemnly. "Someone?"

Elaira looked down, to their hands. "People would kill for this life, to be here, in the palace, to wear these clothes and have these jewels. To have these powers. But no matter how beautiful it is, no matter how pretty on the outside, it's a prison."

Chester watched her, and gently, slowly, giving the queen time to pull away if she wanted to, she reached up and pushed a wavy lock of snow-white hair from her face.

"White bird in a golden cage," Chester murmured. Elaira smiled sadly.

"Blue. All of these markings should be blue."

"Blue bird."

They looked at one another, and for a moment, Elaira felt safe.

Then Chester pulled the queen to her feet. Chester took a step back.

"Pretend I'm attacking you," she said, and she raised a fist. Elaira flinched, raising her hands, but Chester hadn't otherwise moved. Elaira's instinct was to fear a raised hand.

Chester's brow furrowed. Elaira was shaking. This was the behaviour of someone that had already been attacked.

"Elaira," she said. But the queen quickly stood straight and forced a smile.

"Sorry."

"*Elaira.*"

"Keep going."

Chester clenched her jaw and nodded. She raised her fist again, slowly, and then pretended to make a strike. "Grab my hand or wrist and yank me forward," she said. "In the direction I was already going. Use your attacker's momentum against them."

Elaira took her wrist.

"Hard," Chester said. "Yank me down as hard as you can."

Elaira did, forcing Chester to her knees. "Now what?"

"There's a few options. My go-to is breaking the arm."

"Oh."

"Slam your other arm down on the back of their elbow. Punch it, elbow, use your forearm. Or foot—you can stomp on them too."

Elaira swallowed the knot in her throat and nodded, releasing Chester.

"No," Chester said, staying in place. "I want you to act it out."

Elaira took her arm again, apprehensive, and acted out a motion as though to strike her forearm into the back of the elbow. Then she let her go.

"Good." Chester rose to her feet. "Again."

"Are you sure?"

"Yeah. And I want you to act out the entire thing. Don't break my arm, please, but pull me down as hard as you can, and fully act out the motion of breaking my arm. I want you to get used to that. Don't pause after you've done something—follow it through. Always."

She nodded. "Okay."

Chester raised her fist and moved to strike. Elaira grabbed her by the wrist and yanked her forward, using her momentum, and as she fell, Elaira struck down her other forearm, stopping only when it pressed into Chester's elbow. Chester smiled and nodded.

"Good."

Elaira let her go and stood back. "I'm sorry if I hurt you."

"You didn't." She dusted dirt off her dress. "Another very important thing you need to remember is to go for the knees. If you kick someone hard enough in the knee, at the correct angle, you can break their leg. If you have weapons, go for the tendons behind the knee and ankle."

Elaira grimaced.

"People often think, *Kick them in the balls*," Chester said. "But one, this only works if they *have* balls, and two, the rush of battle is a hell of a drug. People stop feeling pain. People stop feeling afraid. But if they are physically incapable of running, then you can get away. No matter how hard they try, even if they cannot feel pain, if they cannot get up, they can't chase you. And you can get away."

The queen gulped, nodding. Chester smiled encouragingly and held her hand again.

"Fun fact, it's surprisingly easy to rip off an ear."

Elaira made a noise that sounded both horrified and amused.

"Ripping someone's ear off won't incapacitate them in any way," Chester said. "But it hurts like a fucking bitch. And it's kind of satisfying. For the assailant."

"Even azheeks?" Elaira laughed.

"It's not *as* easy to rip off an azheek ear, but still pretty easy."

Elaira smiled, sitting on the edge of the fountain once more. She looked at her hands to realize they were trembling and quickly wiped them over her dress. Chester came forward.

"Are you okay?"

"Yeah," she murmured.

"Are you sure?"

Elaira looked at her and smiled. "Yeah. Thank you."

Chester looked at the halo of golden spikes upon the queen's head and curiously—and softly—poked one.

"That's sharp," she said with an amused smile.

Elaira blushed a little. "Yeah."

"Are these *nails*?"

"Maybe."

Chester laughed. "You don't need me—you're wearing a weapon on your head!"

The queen smiled. "It's quite heavy."

"Maybe wooden skewers next time?"

"No," she said lightly. "I like the nails."

Chester smirked. "Yeah, me too."

Elaira reached up and gingerly removed the crown from her head. Then she stood and moved as though to place it upon Chester's. "May I?"

Chester nodded, watching the queen as she carefully tucked it into place behind her ears.

Elaira stood back and smiled. "It suits you."

"Probably matches my dress."

"Yes, but it suits *you*."

Chester smirked. "Nails painted gold are still nails."

"I'll make you one."

"Oh, you don't have to."

"Would you like me to?"

"I mean…" Chester glanced at her reflection in the fountain. She looked powerful. Graceful, beautiful, and so powerful. "I do like this."

"Then I'll make you one," Elaira said. "You're wearing red tonight. You look beautiful in red. I'll make yours red and gold."

Chester smiled, watching the other woman. Elaira was so soft; everything about her was gentle. Vulnerable. Pure.

Chester put a leg up on the fountain, raising her dress, and the queen looked at her in alarm.

"Don't worry," Chester said. Higher and higher she pulled her dress out of the way, until the queen saw a harness around Chester's thigh, holding a sheathed dagger. Chester swore she saw Elaira's breathing hitch.

"I didn't know people actually did that," the queen murmured, swallowing once more. Chester glanced at her and smirked.

"Only when necessary. I'm not wearing boots, so there was nowhere else to put it."

Elaira smiled. Chester unbuckled the harness from her waist with great difficulty, battling her dress, and pulled down the sheath and its leg strap. Stepping out of it, she moved back in front of the queen.

"May I?" she asked. It took Elaira a moment to realize what she was saying.

"Oh—oh, sure, okay."

Chester tucked her hands under the queen's dress, finding her ankle, and Elaira gasped quietly upon the touch. Chester stopped for a moment. Then she pushed up the queen's gown, slowly. She looped the leather harness around her leg. Her fingers gently caressed Elaira's skin, higher and higher, glimmering white markings coming to view in the darkness. Chester looked up at Elaira. She was gripping the edge of the fountain.

"You okay?" Chester asked. But she couldn't hide the slight smile upon her lips and the gleam in her eyes. The queen swallowed as Chester moved the dagger to her thigh. She managed to nod. Chester smirked and then returned to her work, fastening the weapon in place.

Then she let the dress back down. Elaira let out the breath she'd been holding, and Chester smiled once more.

"You sure you're okay?" She moved forward. She took Elaira's hand, and the queen's grip was tighter this time. Chester's gaze roved over her face. "I'm not starting tonight, am I?"

Elaira looked at her curiously.

"If I'm on the job then… *this* would be unprofessional."

Elaira moved her legs, allowing Chester more room, and they grew even closer. "You're not on the job."

Gently, Chester brushed Elaira's hair from her face, caressing her jaw. Then she looked over her shoulder, glancing around the garden, to the castle. "Just making sure we're alone."

"Kiss me."

Chester looked at the queen and slowly moved in, pushing her fingers through locks of white hair, and placed her lips on the other's. Both closed their eyes as they savoured the soft touch.

Then touch became taste as their lips parted, tongues meeting. Chester held the queen's face with both hands, Elaira's moving to Chester's waist. Her touch was soft at first, but as the kiss deepened, her clutch grew more desperate.

Chester pulled her closer, moving her hips forward, pressing her thigh between the other's legs. Elaira moaned softly into the kiss. Chester pulled back, but only slightly. Her lips were brushing Elaira's as she whispered.

"When was the last time someone touched you?"

Elaira shuddered. "Too long."

"May I touch you?"

"Please."

Chester carefully removed the crown of golden nails from Elaira's head and placed it upon the fountain ledge. Then she grabbed Elaira back into a kiss, one hand holding her head, the other wandering down her neck, over her collarbone, and to her breasts. Her touch was soft, gently tracing, and when she trailed a finger over Elaira's jutting breasts, goosebumps rose.

Chester shoved her hand into the dress, having to be rough in order to do so, and the queen gasped, tipping her head back. Chester kissed her neck, licking, sucking, biting, gently pinching her nipple.

"Will anyone come out here?" Chester said against Elaira's skin. The queen let out a heavy gasp and waved a hand in the direction of the castle. The doors shut, locks snapping into place. Chester chuckled and bit her neck, eliciting another moan.

"Fuck, you sound good," Chester said. She pinched her nipple, twisting slightly, and Elaira's back arched. She was moving her hips now, grinding against Chester's thigh. But there was so much fucking fabric between them.

Chester looked down, watching how desperate she was for release.

"Mahriel," Elaira moaned softly, trying to contain her noises.

"Chester."

Elaira opened her eyes, and Chester took her face in her hands with a smile.

"You're not the only one with a fake name." She kissed her. "Mahriel is a name of mine, but my friends call me Chester."

Elaira smiled. "Who are you?"

"A criminal," she murmured against her lips. "Wanted by command of the queen."

Elaira pulled back and Chester smirked.

"Technically Veraion is the one that's wanted." She placed a hand between Elaira's legs, holding the fountain ledge beneath the gown, trapping her in place. "I'm just an accomplice. But everyone he killed was baraduhr, and everyone I've ever killed has been baraduhr, or a headhunter, or in my fucking way."

She kissed the queen again. Elaira was a little stiff now, but not from fear. Goosebumps rose over her skin, her breath hitched, and the tingling between her legs only grew stronger. Chester kissed her on the lips, jaw, neck, and breasts, and Elaira gasped, her hips moving to grind upon Chester's forearm.

"You like that, don't you?" Chester said, slowly lowering to a knee. She pulled her arm away and Elaira whimpered a little, so she grabbed her between the legs. The queen gasped, rubbing herself on Chester's hand, finding some release on the fabrics pressing between them.

Chester tucked a hand beneath her gown. She gently traced her fingers over Elaira's ankle, wandering up her calf. The woman shuddered with every touch.

Elaira released her grip on the fountain and Chester took her hand. The pressure between her legs was taken away once more, causing her to moan in frustration.

"The wanted posters," Elaira said. "It's you."

Chester nodded, licking Elaira's wrist right where it was most sensitive. She brought Elaira's hand down further, licking between her index and middle fingers, never breaking eye contact. The queen gulped, chest heaving, and Chester couldn't help but smile.

"Are you going to hand me in?" she murmured. Elaira shook her head. "You like that I kill baraduhr?"

She nodded. Chester raised Elaira's leg, shoving her dress out of the way, and bit her ankle. The queen grasped the ledge desperately.

"Stop playing," Elaira rasped, and Chester bit her leg once more, softly, but enough to make the queen gasp, desperately trying to squeeze her legs together and release some of the tension between them.

Chester stood up, placing a rough kiss on her mouth. "Get up. Lie down."

"What?"

"On the floor. You'll fall into the fountain if we don't move."

Chester took her by the hand, pulling her up, in for another kiss, and then motioned at the ground. Cobblestones and grass. Elaira kissed her, then her neck, and Chester craned her head to the side, letting out a breathy sigh. But she pulled away.

"This isn't about me right now," she said. "And there's only so much time before the guards start looking for you. So. Get on the ground."

Elaira did as she was told. The moment she was down, Chester grabbed her gown, shoving the expensive fabrics aside. She kissed her ankle, calf, knee, following the glimmering markings. She kissed up Elaira's thighs, past the harnessed dagger, closer and closer until she licked between her legs. One. Long. Stroke.

The queen gasped, clasping a hand to her mouth. Her moans were so soft, so desperate.

Chester kissed her, licking, sucking, and as Elaira moved her hips, Chester trailed her fingers up her legs. Elaira's back arched, a contained gasp falling from her lips. Chester gently caressed Elaira's entrance, slipping a finger in easily, and the woman moaned. A second finger, and then a third, massaging her on the inside at a steady pace as her tongue moved quickly.

The queen trembled, her legs shaking as she clutched at her gown, fingers tensing, nails scraping against the embroidery. Her moans were soft, high pitched, and fell from her lips as quietly as she could possibly make them, lost behind heavy breaths.

Elaira stared at the night sky, surrounded by millions of stars and billowing colours, but that wasn't what she looked for. Guards. Air azheek guards that could appear at any minute. But her eyes shut tight when Chester closed her mouth around her, giving a harsh suck. She let her tongue return to licking, quickly, tipping her head to get a better angle. Her fingers moved faster now, pumping in and out.

There came a rattling at the far doors. Someone shaking the handles. Elaira gasped, her eyes snapping open, and Chester growled into her heat. *Not. Yet.*

Chester pulled out one finger and rubbed it against Elaira's other hole, and as she gasped loudly, hips bucking, she slipped it in. Licking. Pumping. In and out.

The doors shook.

Elaira gasped and threw up a hand, fingers tensed as she sent her powers for the castle. Her arm was shaking, doing everything she could to keep the doors bolted. Her chest heaved, moans growing heavier and heavier, eyes shut tight as her hair caught on the cobblestones, and as her hips bucked wildly, she felt the build.

Chester pushed her tongue harder against Elaira, moving just as quickly, fingers in and out, curved and massaging.

Elaira gasped, loud, her call echoing through the gardens. Her head flew back and her body seized up, legs shaking as she struggled not to scream.

Her hand was still raised, fingers tensed and shaking wildly as she fought to keep the guards at bay.

Chester softened her movements but she didn't stop, allowing the queen to ride out her high, and as her orgasm came to an end, Chester placed a kiss between her legs and pulled out.

She sat back, watching Elaira with a satisfied smile. She crawled forward, on top of her, and looked at Elaira's outstretched hand.

"You did good," Chester said. Elaira laughed softly.

"Thank you."

Chester bit her lip, gazing over Elaira's flushed form, her cheeks so pink and her markings glowing stronger, pulsing with the beat of her racing heart. Chester smiled and then kissed her. Hard.

Elaira sat up, her free hand holding Chester close, tongues roving wildly.

There came bangs at the castle doors.

Elaira sighed. "Fuck the guards."

"I'd rather not."

Elaira laughed, hitting her on the arm. Chester kissed her once more, but when she leaned back, her brow furrowed. Blood dripped from Elaira's nose.

"You're bleeding," she said, and the queen wiped it away with the back of her hand.

"If they gave me powers that didn't have consequences, I could leave."

Chester's brow furrowed more, genuine concern upon her face, and in her eyes, anger. "Baraduhr."

Elaira smiled sadly. "Baraduhr."

Chester took in a deep breath, clenching her jaw, letting out a sigh with flared nostrils. "I'll kill them. I'll kill them all."

"One day."

They looked at one another, and Chester offered a hand, helping the queen to her feet. She pulled her in for another kiss, murmuring against her lips.

"It's time."

The queen let out a heavy sigh and nodded. She released her powers, her arm finally relaxing, and instantly the castle doors burst open. They could hear guards racing towards them.

Chester picked up the crown of golden nails and placed it back upon Elaira's head, pulling her into another kiss. Deep, passionate.

She pulled away seconds before the guards burst into view.

"My queen!" one of them called. "We've been looking for you!"

"I'm right here." She smiled.

"Your presence was greatly missed."

"But I'm with a guest," she said simply.

"Yes, well... the banquet is over. The guests must leave now."

Chester cast the queen a smile. Then she bowed respectfully. "I'll see you tomorrow, my queen."

Elaira blushed, nodding, watching as the guards led her away, and she couldn't help but smile.

CHAPTER 13
THE TRUTH

By the time the guards led Chester to the castle doors, all the other guests were climbing into their carriages or had already gone home. Veraion was waiting with a smug smile on his lips but a hint of disappointment in his eyes. Aven and Einmyria were by their carriage, speaking to Lord Venhel.

"Will you be... coming home tonight?" he asked. Einmyria smiled shyly, holding Aven by the arm.

"No."

Venhel nodded, glancing at the giant man with his daughter. "You treat her well, you hear me?"

"Always, my lord." Aven smiled. The lord glanced between his five-foot-one daughter and the seven-foot giant.

"She likes you," Venhel said. "No need for the formalities."

Aven nodded, but as the lord headed away he still bowed. Einmyria smiled, hitting his arm lightly.

Aven let out a huge sigh of relief as Venhel disappeared into his carriage. He turned to see Chester and smiled.

"Where were you?" he asked.

"Oh, I was with the queen." She climbed into their carriage.

Veraion and Aven glanced at one another. They climbed in after her.

The ride to Five's Inn was pleasant, for Einmyria had bottles of wine hidden in compartments of the coach. The four were happy to keep drinking, and Veraion finally gave up on his brooding normalcy and didn't glower at her once.

By the time they reached the inn they were well and truly buzzed. Perhaps it was the alcohol, perhaps it was the amount of food crammed into their stomachs, or perhaps it was different for each of them.

Aven and Einmyria waited in the tavern as Maina and Theideus prepared a room for them. Chester bid her Little One good night before clomping to room fourteen. The moment she and Veraion were inside, she let out a loud groan.

"Free me from this trap," she said, waving him over, and he laughed, helping untie her dress.

Chester belched as he did, and as the ropes came looser and looser, she took in a deep, *deep* breath. The first one she had managed all night.

"*Fuuuck,*" she groaned. "Dresses are pretty but not very comfortable."

"Nobody said you had to wear it that tight," Veraion said, laughing.

"But the *waiiiiist,*" she said, shaking a hand with clenched fingers.

She clambered out of the fabrics, belching some more, and her friend only kept laughing. He pulled off his formal attire and chucked it on the floor. As both of them returned to comfortable, loose tunics, they climbed into their beds on opposite sides of the room and nuzzled into the sheets.

"Mmmmm." Chester smiled. Veraion watched her from his place.

"So… how's the queen?"

Chester's smile turned very, *very* triumphant. "I'd say she's feeling quite satisfied."

He raised an eyebrow at her. "You didn't."

"Oh, I did."

He laughed and shook his head, lying on his back. He let out a sigh, holding his crystal pendant, and gazed at it. "I'm glad one of us came out of the castle satisfied."

"No luck?"

"I… don't know?" He turned to look at her again. "I definitely feel something in there, something big. But I couldn't get in."

"I'm surprised you gave up."

"Well… I got caught."

Her eyes widened. "What? How are you not dead?"

"You remember that castle hand? Eidis?"

"The one with the crush?"

He nodded. "Luckily she's the one that caught me. At least, she got there before the guards did. So…"

It was her turn to raise an eyebrow at him. "*You didn't.*"

"Just a little," he said. "Just a kiss."

Chester gasped with the smile of a teenage schoolgirl that had just heard the juiciest piece of gossip. "Dost mine ears deceive me?"

He snorted and waved her off. "It was just a kiss. Well, a tongue-y kiss. And she grabbed my…"

Chester nodded with a look of pride. "Fuck yeah, Eidis. Get it."

Veraion laughed and shook his head. "Go to sleep, Chester."

She chuckled. "We should both get to sleep or we'll never be able to. Aven and Einmyria will probably keep us up all night."

His eyes were closed now, but he shook his head at her.

She cooed. "My little boy is all grown up."

He snorted.

"Hey, Veraion. You reckon Eidis thinks about you when she mast—"

Veraion threw his pillow across the room.

Maina finally returned to the tavern, tossing a key at Aven. He caught it with one hand.

"Room twenty-three," she said. "It's one *big* bed."

Einmyria blushed, avoiding eye contact. As the couple shuffled from the empty dining hall, Maina called after them.

"Try not to break the furniture!"

Einmyria changed course and veered back to the bar, grabbing a bottle. She nodded at Maina and then disappeared from sight.

The couple hurried into the entrance area only to be faced by Dog. As she growled, Aven finally had enough.

He morphed, his face crunching into that of a beast, and gave a warning snap. Dog yelped and tore away, bolting down the corridor to where she scratched at Tao's door, only stopping once he let her in.

Aven returned to his human form in a heartbeat and strode down to room twenty-three with a very proud pep in his step.

Maina was right. Room twenty-three had one big bed.

"We can just sleep," Aven said, lighting a torch. "Don't feel uncomfortable or anything—it'll be just like the woods, but… with no risk of dying."

"But that's the best part," Einmyria said, laughing. Then she uncorked the bottle and drank.

"Whoa." He started forward. "You okay?"

"I'm good." She smiled, confident, and offered him the bottle.

"Are you… What's going on?"

"Just needed to keep up the buzz."

"Why?"

"Because I want to fuck you tonight."

He looked at her. He blinked. "Okay."

He took the bottle and chugged the rest of it. Einmyria laughed. It sounded like music to his ears.

"Daddy won't show up at the door?" he asked.

She glared. "*No.*"

He reached behind her, opening the door, and peered into the hallway. She smacked him on the arm. He barely felt it.

"Just making sure." He smirked and locked the door behind her. Einmyria stood with her back against it, closed in by the giant, and she took the bottle from his hand, placing it on the table beside her.

"You don't have to if you don't want to," she murmured. He took her hand and placed it between his legs, upon the bulge already forming in his perfectly pleated pants.

"Oh." She smiled. "I…"

"You said you wanted to fuck me," he said simply. "I am aroused."

She laughed. "Come here."

He leaned in, bending down, and kissed her, deeply, passionately, and she moaned into the kiss. He picked her up, pressing her back to the door, and she wrapped her legs around his waist, fingers pushing through his wild hair. He lowered her for a moment, just enough to grind his bulge between her legs, and she gasped, looking up at him desperately.

"Now," she said. "Please."

He carried her to the bed and she landed with a soft gasp, watching as he yanked off his vest, followed by his shirt. She couldn't help but bite her lip as she watched every one of his gargantuan muscles rippling in the firelight. He struggled as he tried to take off his boots, yanking at them, and he let out an irritated growl. She laughed as he finally managed to get them off, throwing them across the room.

Aven climbed onto the bed, towering over her. She pulled him into a kiss. Aven kissed her neck, moving to her chest. Then he leaned back and took her bodice into his hands, ripping it open. Gasping, she stared down with wide eyes. She looked back at him, his single eye fixed on her breasts, and couldn't help but laugh.

"You have no idea how expensive this was!" she said.

He smiled. "I'll pay for it."

"With what coin?"

"Does your tailor accept dead animals?"

She laughed, their gazes meandering over the other. Einmyria seemed shy now, and he slid his hands into her gown, removing it from her. She sat up, allowing him to push it down her arms, her breaths growing heavy as her lips rested inches from his. She could feel his warm breath on her skin, the low growl from his throat sending a shiver down her spine.

"Also," he murmured, "I'm kind of rich now."

She smirked. "Really?"

"Really." He nodded, lips brushing hers. "Turns out betting on your friends can make a man heavy with coin."

He kissed her as she laughed.

"What are your plans as a rich man?" she asked.

He sat back and thought about it. "I'm going to commission a statue. Of a giant... gold... bunny."

Einmyria laughed, burying her face in her hands. He kissed her hand with a chuckle, then her jaw, and as he kissed down her neck, he revelled in the way she moaned.

She lay back, lifting up her hips as he pulled the dress down her legs. Slowly. He kissed her stomach, her hips, another between her legs as the fabric came away. She let out a soft gasp, her legs quivering as she craved more.

He threw the gown away, bending over her. Aven took her bare breast into his mouth, kissing and licking her nipples. She moaned, closing her eyes, tipping her head back, and he kissed his way down her body once more. Lower and lower until he was between her legs, licking her.

Einmyria's breaths grew heavier and heavier. Her moans echoed through the room. Aven spread her legs wide, earning a loud mewl from her lips.

"I want you," she gasped. "I want you inside me."

Aven pulled back, looking at her. Slowly he rose to his feet, removing the rest of his clothes. Not once did he take his gaze from her naked body, and she couldn't look away from him either.

He stood tall, gargantuan. Firelight danced over his muscles, over every ridiculous hunk of power, and when he pushed down his pants, he came free.

Aven slowly climbed back onto the bed, crawling over her.

The difference between them was vast. She was a noblewoman, her skin soft and supple with not a scratch to mark her. Aven was the opposite. A beast. Discoloured, burned, scarred, with coarse hair covering his body.

He kissed her and she melted beneath his touch. His hand moved between her legs. Gently he rubbed her, causing her to moan into the kiss, and when he felt how wet she was, he couldn't help but groan. She moved her hips, desperate for more. Aven dipped a finger inside her, gently pushing it all the way in, and her mouth fell open. He inserted another.

Einmyria opened her eyes and looked at him, breathing heavily. He started moving them in and out, slowly, and a high-pitched moan fell from her lips. He kissed her, forcing her to whimper into his mouth as he moved his fingers inside, massaging. Then she pulled back and looked at him. She nodded.

He withdrew his fingers, spreading her wetness onto himself, and positioned between her legs.

"I can't believe I'm about to fuck a wasfought," she whispered.

"Do you want me to turn?"

"What?"

"I can turn—"

"No! No, gods no. You're good like this—you're great like this. Please don't turn."

He laughed, kissing her neck, biting, and she spasmed desperately, grabbing at him.

"Is this your first time?" he asked. She snorted.

"No," Einmyria laughed. "Contrary to how cute and innocent I may look, I am a sexual woman. And I have needs. And right now, I need you."

He kissed her, slowly, deeply, tongue roving in her mouth until he finally leaned back and slowly began to push inside. Einmyria let out a loud gasp, her nails digging into his skin.

"Einmyria."

"Keep going," she breathed. "I want you inside me."

He continued, slowly, allowing her body to accommodate him. He went until he bottomed out, staying still once he did. Not until she nodded did he gingerly move.

Einmyria moaned, closing her eyes, tipping her head back. "*Aven.*"

He stopped. Her eyes opened in confusion to find him staring at her in fear.

"Does it hurt?" he asked. "Do you want me to stop?"

She laughed softly. "No, Aven, I was moaning your name—it's a good thing."

"Oh."

She smiled and pulled him into a kiss. "Keep going."

He did. Slowly the rhythm built, gradually picking up pace. He was careful not to hurt her, and she looked at him, smiling, kissing his hand as he caressed her cheek. She moved with him, causing him to groan.

Faster they went, deeper.

She was so small beneath him, her legs around his waist barely registering in his mind.

Einmyria pushed him over until she was on top, and when she was, she moved on him. Dancing with him in the firelight, she gyrated her hips with him inside her. She threw her head back and moaned. Aven placed his hands upon her legs, trailing his fingers up her thighs until he held her waist, moving with the rhythm. He watched her in awe.

Sitting up, he pushed his fingers through her hair. Then he took a fistful and pulled her head back. She gasped and he took her exposed neck into his mouth, licking, biting, and sucking. Loud moans fell from her lips, shivers travelling down her spine. He bucked his hips, pushing himself up and into her, and when he let go of her hair, her head dropped down, pressing into his shoulder as she clung to him. He wrapped his arms around her as he continued thrusting.

Her moans were growing shorter, higher pitched and more desperate. One of his arms held her close to him, the other trailing down her back, softly caressing her skin. It travelled lower and lower until his fingers slid between her cheeks, caressing her there. She swore into her gasps, her moans loud and uncontrolled.

"Do it," she moaned. "*Do it.*"

He answered her pleas and slipped a finger inside. Her head threw back, eyes shut tight as her body seized up. She shook as he held her close to him, continuing his pace inside her.

His name spilled from her lips like a mantra among curses and gasps, and as she started to struggle, her legs shaking uncontrollably, he finally slowed his pace.

Slowly her head came forward, her gaze meeting his. He couldn't help but smile.

"Gods, you're beautiful."

She smiled, shy, and he kissed her. Wrapping her arms around his neck, her tongue explored his mouth.

"Can you keep going?" he asked. She nodded. "We don't have to."

Now it was her turn to grab him by the hair, forcing him to look at her. She placed a soft kiss on his lips and held his gaze.

"I want you to fuck me like an animal."

His eye darkened. Another beastly sound rumbled from within him. "Say one word," he growled, "and I'll stop."

She nodded and released her grip on his hair. Then he tossed her onto the bed, her breasts pressing into the sheets as he climbed on top of her. She was almost crushed by the weight as he pushed his length against her cheeks, grinding against her a few times before positioning himself to slide back in.

Einmyria moaned loudly, gripping the sheets. Her legs shook, body quivering from the shockwaves travelling through her.

Aven propped himself up on his arms, his long black hair hanging messily about his face.

He thrust, groaning as he did. His shoulders were tensed, every muscle in his back dancing in the firelight.

With every buck of his hips, air left her lungs, drawing gasps and moans. Faster and faster he went, his pace becoming sloppy and inconsistent, and as he finally reached his climax, a loud groan left his throat, accompanied by a growl resonating deep in his lungs. Aven continued thrusting through his high, his eye shut tight and claws digging into the mattress beneath him.

His movements slowed as his body shuddered, and eventually he came to a halt. He stayed in place, breathing deeply, growling with every exhale. Then he pulled out and flopped onto his back.

The bedframe collapsed.

Their eyes widened as the mattress fell, wood breaking and snapping beneath them. They stared at each other.

"Oops," Aven said.

Einmyria buried her face in her hands as she laughed, and he rolled over, pulling her into his arms, nuzzling his face into her chest. A low growl came with every breath, like a content purr, and as they lay there, he slowly nodded off.

* * *

Einmyria lay with Aven, nestled into his arms. She didn't know how long they'd been there. Minutes. Hours. But no matter how much time passed, she couldn't fall asleep.

The fires around them had died. Only one remained, a single candle, illuminating his face so softly. She watched him, gently running her fingers through his black hair, tracing his features. Her touch followed the scars along his face, caressing his markings. A sad smile rested upon her lips, tears welling in her eyes.

Einmyria placed a soft kiss upon his head.

Gently she pulled from his arms, coming from the broken bed. She picked up his giant shirt and pulled it on, turning to her gown heaped on the floor. Rummaging through the mountain of fabric, her fingers wrapped around the hilt of a dagger.

Her eyes rested on Aven.

Taking in a slow, deep breath, she rose to her feet and moved to the door. Gently she unlocked it, turning the knob as quietly as possible. Her hazel eyes turned to the sleeping giant.

"I'm sorry," she whispered. She left the room.

Down the hallway, her gaze roved over the doors. Twenty. Eighteen. Sixteen. Fourteen. Her hand wrapped around the doorknob and she turned it. *Click*. Unlocked.

Chester was almost invisible beneath her heap of blankets at the far end of the room. Veraion was asleep on his back, one hand loosely holding his pendant. Soft light glimmered through his fingers.

Einmyria moved to his bedside, clutching her dagger. She drew in a long and shuddering breath, never seeing the pendant flash.

Veraion snapped awake, eyes wide as he grabbed her by the arm, but she yelled and yanked free, plunging the blade into his shoulder. Veraion shouted in pain and Chester woke, pupils blazing as she fought to understand what was happening. Her thundering heart slammed in her ears.

Einmyria pulled the dagger from Veraion, about to stab him once more, aiming for his chest, but Chester threw up an arm and the hilt burst with flames. Einmyria staggered back with a gasp, dropping the weapon, and Chester tore across the room, throwing the blade aside.

A loud bang sounded as the door burst open, and Aven stared around the fray with wide eyes. Veraion, bleeding, Einmyria, his blood on her hands.

"What the fuck is going on?"

Einmyria tore towards the dagger but he raced forward and grabbed her, holding her back as she kicked, fighting to break free. Tears streamed down her cheeks.

Chester pressed her hands firmly against Veraion's wound, but his shirt was already soaked. He grimaced, yelling through clenched teeth. Chester stared at Einmyria. "What the *fuck*?"

But the woman looked past her, bloodshot eyes set on the bleeding man.

"You killed my brother," Einmyria rasped. "You killed my brother!"

Veraion sat up, wincing as he clutched his wound. He glared at her, but as he did, his expression changed. Realization. Frustration. His face fell.

"I remember you now," he said. "I remember your screams."

"Well, that's a dismal thing to remember," Chester said.

"You admit it," Einmyria hissed. "You killed my brother."

"Your brother was fucking baraduhr."

She froze. Her eyes were wide, body shaking in disbelief. "How dare you. How *dare* you say that to me!"

"You didn't know?"

"Wait." Chester glanced between the two. "She... Her brother was one of the baraduhr that took Ilia?"

"Ehl, wasn't it?" he said. "He and every one of your friends were baraduhr."

"You murdered her brother in front of her?"

Veraion glanced at Chester. "I asked her to leave."

Chester sat back, her face fallen. *Angry.* "You slaughtered a man, in front of a family member, and left her breathing? Are you fucking stupid? *Never* leave loved ones alive, Raion. Collateral fucking damage!"

He stared at her. "Wow, Chester, you're heartless."

"Yeah, and I also don't have people hunting me down and seeking revenge, putting holes in my chest."

He cast her an uneasy glance before turning back to Einmyria. "You issued the wanted posters."

"Does your father know you're here?" Chester said.

"Of course he does," Einmyria rasped through her tears.

"Well, fuck. We can't kill her—they'll be after us."

"We can't keep her here either," Veraion said.

"And I assume if we let you go, you're not going to stop trying to kill him?"

Einmyria kept her bloodshot eyes on Veraion.

Chester took in a slow, deep breath, running a hand through her hair. She came to her feet only to pace the room, eyes wide, livid. She kicked over a bedside table.

"Fuck!" Chester yelled. "You just fucked *everything* up!" She was yelling at Veraion. He stared at her.

"*Me?*"

"Yes! Why didn't you kill her? Of *course* she was going to try and avenge her brother. Look at what *you're* doing! That's why *you're* here, right? Revenge? For Ilia? What she's doing is completely understandable and fucking *expected*. What's fucking stupid was that you let her *walk*."

"My god, you've been doing this too long."

"How could you be so *stupid?*" She stared. "You, raised by Lord *Ezaria*. The Red *fucking* Emperor. You of *all* people have seen what the loss of a sibling can do to a person. How murderous it can make them."

Chester shook her head, fighting to hold in her anger. It came out as a frustrated laugh.

"You realize this fucks *everything*, right? God *damn* it, Veraion! I let you fucking beat me! I let you get into the top ten, and for what?" Tears were welling in her eyes, her voice shaking. "Oh, and guess what else? The queen offered me a job. A fucking *job*. In the castle. By her side. We all know you'd get destroyed in the final battle, but after last night, we had a place secured in the castle *regardless* of what happened in the tournament. But now what? *Now what?*" She laughed again, shaking her head in disbelief. "*You fucking idiot. You fucking*—FUCK!"

She slammed a flaming fist into the wall, and Veraion watched her with wide eyes.

"What?" His voice was hushed.

"Yeah," she snapped. "I was going to be a personal guard to the queen. But now that's ruined. All of it. If we let Einmyria go, what? The guards will be here in seconds because she'll call them. And if we don't let her go? The guards will be here in a day because her father will send them."

All colour had left his face. Tears fell from Chester's eyes.

"I was happy here. I was *so* happy here."

Maina burst into the room, Theideus hot on her heels. With a wave of her hand, every torch and sconce bloomed with flames.

"What the fuck is going on in here?" She stared. "You're waking everyone up!"

Her eyes landed on Einmyria and then Veraion, his shirt growing progressively redder and redder. Her face fell.

Chester looked at Aven, his face lifeless. He was pale, his eye glazed over.

"Aven?" she said. "Are you okay?"

He released his grip on Einmyria and she staggered forward. His voice was barely a whisper. "You were using me."

"Aven," Einmyria gasped.

"You were *using me.*"

"I didn't know you were with him," she cried. "I promise, I didn't know you were with him, not until I saw you with him at the tournament."

"The tournament began *months* ago."

"I didn't know. *I didn't know.*"

"How could you not know?" Chester snapped. "How—*baraduhr*? A brother capturing, torturing, and killing, and you *didn't know*?"

"In her defence, the baraduhr are good at hiding it," Veraion muttered darkly. "I've seen it. No one wants their family to know they're monsters."

Einmyria looked at him, tears spilling from her eyes, and collapsed to her knees.

* * *

Chester walked through the streets, eyes glazed over. She had been walking for hours, thoughts swarming. She barely noticed anyone around her. Einmyria was still being held in room fourteen, watched by Aven, who had gone completely silent—completely emotionless and cold. Chester had cauterized Veraion's wound, and finally he had taken up Tao's offer of opium, however small the dose, just to help him through it. But they were running out of time. The longer they held Einmyria, the more likely her father would send guards looking for her.

Walking past a wanted poster, she tore it down. Crumbling the parchment into a ball, her fist glowed red. When she let go, all that fell to the ground was ash.

Finally she stopped walking and gazed at the castle towering miles above her.

"We can fix this," she said, trying to convince herself. "We can fix... *Fuck.*"

Chester leaned against a city wall and closed her eyes. The sun was warm on her skin and it was the only thing comforting her. Nausea waved through her body.

She yelled in frustration, slamming a fist into the wall behind her.

A doorway opened and she fell back, plummeting into darkness.

Chester yelped as she fell down a flight of stone stairs, exclaiming in pain with every collision. She hit the ground and stayed there, too sore to move.

Surrounded by black, her doorway was sealed. Flames bloomed in her pupils.

She was in a dark tunnel, a secret passageway. Chester rose to her feet and stared around.

"No fucking way," she murmured. A hidden passage of Sontar Ivel.

She took in a deep breath and gazed around before heading up the stairs. Her fingers roved over the wall but there was no handle or knob. So she clenched a fist and thumped it against stone. There came a low rumble and the way opened once more.

Sunlight cascaded onto Chester's face. She peered onto the street. There were a few people here and there, but nobody was looking her way. The door closed once more.

She stood still, pondering her options. Then she descended the steps.

Flames bloomed up her arms, and she trailed a finger along the wall as she went, leaving a charred line to mark her path.

Left, left, right, left, right, left, right, right. She could feel the floor sloping, guiding her deeper and deeper underground.

She let her flames disappear and gazed around. The tunnels were pitch black. A labyrinth impossible to navigate.

Fire bloomed in her eyes and upon her arms once more. She couldn't hear anything. The world above was so far away now. She couldn't even hear a scurry of rats. She glanced around, feeling as though she'd find a couple of skeletons down here.

Double-checking she'd left a trail to guide her back to the light, she placed her finger where the trail left off and kept going.

She had no idea where she was going or why, but she continued into the maze.

Right, left, left, right, right, left.

She reached another fork, and when she raised her arm, she could see one passage stopped not far away. But her brow furrowed and she cocked her head. She swore she could almost hear something. Shimmering eerily, like a distant song of crystals.

Chester snuffed out her flames to see a thin sliver of light peeking out from the end of the tunnel, on the ground, as though through the crack of a doorway.

White, green… blue. Purple. Orange. The light changed colours, fading in and out like a heartbeat.

Chester moved forward, watching the eerie glow. She ran her hands over the stone wall to find no door, so she clenched a fist and softly thumped it against stone.

Nothing.

She changed positions and thumped again.

Nothing.

She let out a frustrated sigh. Then she moved to the other side of the wall and tried again. With a low rumble, an opening appeared. Light pooled into the tunnel, and she inched forward, gazing through the crack.

Stone floor curved into walls, curving to a ceiling. The rock was dark, black, but the cave was lit by crystals—huge crystals. Eight of them. They stood in a circle in the middle of the cavern, glowing brightly. They shone different colours, with soft lights wafting from them. Along the floor, lights glimmered in cracks.

Chester's eyes were wide. She was no earth azheek, but even she could feel the amount of power radiating from the crystals. There was something inside them. Figures.

Chester glanced around the cave. There was nobody there, so she pushed the opening further and squeezed through.

The air was cold and dank. Wet. Water dripped from the ceiling and trickled down the curving walls. Slivers of light glowed beneath her boots and she moved towards the circle of giant crystals. Her face fell.

Azheeks.

Chester stood between two of them, between two of the glimmering coffins. To her left, a fire azheek, and to her right, an air azheek. Both were naked, suspended in their magical casings. Their eyes were open, glowing.

Around the ring, Chester saw two of every kind. A man and woman of each element, every one of them naked, suspended, their eyes open and glowing. Lights came from them, glimmering as though to soft heartbeats. Their heartbeats.

Her own quickened in her chest, thumping, her body swaying from the force.

Chester walked into the circle of encased azheeks. In the middle was a stone basin atop a pedestal. Magic glimmered from the coffins, flowing across the floor, leading up the sides of the table, gathering there. There was white light inside, liquid light, dancing calmly. The various colours of the azheeks led to the basin, gathering to combine all lights to white.

Chester stared at the trapped people, and her brow furrowed further when she laid her eyes on the man and woman of water. Their markings glimmered blue, winding over their sun-kissed skin, but it wasn't their bodies she looked at. Chester looked at the woman's face. She was so familiar.

"Elaira?" she whispered. No, not Elaira. Her features weren't the same, her markings even less so, but there was no denying the similarity.

Then came footsteps.

Chester's wide eyes turned to the far end of the tunnel, hearing people approaching, and she gasped, racing back to where she had come from. The door had closed but she clenched her fist and thumped it against the wall, glancing back over her shoulder as the rumbling sounded.

People entered the cave, their cloaks billowing about their heels, and in their hands, they carried masks.

Baraduhr.

The colour flushed from Chester's face. Her stomach dropped. Among the group of humans were two people she knew.

Thalamere. Rendel.

Chester squeezed through the crack, desperately trying to shut the way behind her with shaking arms. Then she ran.

Chester ran as fast as her legs could take her, pupils blazing to guide her way through the darkness. She followed the charred trail left on the walls, never looking back.

Her breaths were dry and shaking in her throat, blood pounding in her ears, but she never stopped running.

CHAPTER 14
THE LORD

Chester ran through the city. Her eyes were wide, heart racing, breaths shallow and frantic. She tore through the streets, under arches, and through alleys, sprinting for the inn as fast as her legs could take her. Turning a corner, moments away from the inn doors, she skidded to a halt.

Castle guards surrounded the inn, on foot and on horses. Lord Venhel was sitting upon a proud stallion, Einmyria on her own palomino horse. But she wasn't there, not really. Her gaze was far away, face gaunt.

Aven, Veraion, Maina, and Theideus were bound and gagged, on their knees.

Chester took a step back, straight into another guard, and Venhel hissed through gritted teeth.

"Seize her."

* * *

Bags were swiped off the captives' heads. They knelt in a row, in a marble hall. They were in the castle.

Five statues rose to the ceiling, at least three stories high. Statues of the first lords of earth, fire, water, and air, and their first queen, Natura.

The Five stood tall, reaching to the domed ceiling that had been carved to depict the gods. Mother Nature, with woven hair like wild roots, rivers flowing from her breasts, and the world in her pregnant belly. The Sun and the Moon with their hands touching her stomach, providing light in the darkness of her womb.

Sunlight streamed through the stone carvings to pool over the marble floor.

A throne sat before each statue, and between these were more seats that had been built in an attempt to replicate the originals. Council members sat around the hall, men and women of every race. But there were far more humans than azheeks, one of whom was Einmyria's father.

The captives knelt in the centre of it all, bound and gagged. They were in a lowered area, forced to look up at those surrounding them, and Veraion kept his loathing stare on Venhel.

A man stood before the main throne with his back to them. His long purple robes pooled over the stone steps, hair long and grey, tied back with a navy ribbon. When he spoke, his quiet voice echoed with a sneer.

"Welcome to the Council of the Five." He turned to face them. He was old, gaunt, cheekbones protruding and nose long and thin. His fingers pressed together, wrinkled, the rest of him hidden beneath long, rich robes.

"You have been cast upon the mercy of this council for reasons I am sure you are well aware." He looked to the councilmembers, disgust seething in his stare. "This man is a felon, guilty of the murder of twenty-seven innocents across the mainland." The council gasped in cued horror. "And these *friends* of his have been keeping his whereabouts secret, going so far as to help disguise his appearance."

Veraion finally removed his glare from Venhel and directed it at the councilman. Maina looked frightened to the bone, but it was Theideus that was the most petrified. He stared at the floor, trembling, unable to look up. Unable to live through this. Again.

A tear leaked from Maina's eye, staring around at the councilmembers, pleading silently.

"Black dye was found in your room," the councilman said, his eyes on her. "Dye used to disguise these people. People you clearly knew were wanted. You are as guilty as they are."

She closed her eyes and hung her head, fighting to swallow the knot in her throat.

"Twenty-seven noblemen and women died at the hands of this… this *Veraion*," he hissed.

"He has been competing in the tournament," another council member said. "Has he not?"

"He has. And he made it to the top ten."

Shocked gasps echoed through the hall.

"Welcomed into the castle," the lead councilman said. "That was your plan, wasn't it?"

Veraion's glare never faltered. Had he not been gagged, he'd have given this man a piece of his mind. The councilman smiled.

"All in favour of sentencing this man to death?"

Chester's eyes widened, and as she looked around, one by one, every hand rose into the air, condemning Veraion to public execution.

"Throw them in the dungeons," the man said. "Brand them. We'll decide what to do with the rest later."

* * *

The five captives were brought to the dungeons and locked in individual cells, their bonds and gags removed. Chester sat on her bench, eyes glazed over, staring at nothing at all. Maina was hyperventilating. Theideus looked like he was going to be sick.

Nearby was a furnace where guards were stoking coals, preparing a branding iron. The dungeon doors opened and the guards stood up straight. Venhel descended the steps, flanked by his men. They pulled back their hoods and colour flushed from Chester's face. Thalamere. She moved further from her cell door.

The guards bowed. "Lord Venhel."

"You are dismissed," he commanded.

Veraion hissed, his glare fixed on the man as the guards made their leave. When the door shut, Venhel looked at his captives with a gleam in his dark eyes. He stepped towards Veraion.

"The murderer of my son. I finally have you in my grasp."

Veraion spat through the bars. Venhel held his ground and sneered, wiping his face as he turned to look at Aven.

"It's a shame you're with *him*. You're a modest man, yet you clearly possess more strength than anyone in this room. You could have been useful."

Aven snarled. Venhel smiled bitterly before turning away.

"Brand them."

His men nodded. Venhel ascended the steps and left the dungeons, and when the doors closed, Thalamere rested his eyes on Chester.

"Well, isn't this a shame?" he said. "I actually liked you."

She clenched her jaw, nostrils flared as she held his stare.

"What are you mad at me for?" He laughed. "I'm not the one that's done anything wrong."

Her lips curled to a snarl, hand balling to a fist. *Baraduhr.*

The dungeon doors opened once more. All eyes turned to watch as Athos strode in. Venhel's men glowered, as did Veraion and Aven.

"What do *you* want?" Thalamere snapped. Athos rested his eyes on the man as he descended the steps.

"Know your place," he said. "Do as you're told."

"Watch me." Thalamere unlocked Chester's door, and the instant he moved in he struck her across the face. Chester staggered back and Veraion grabbed the metal grating between them. Aven snarled, hackles rising beneath his shirt.

Thalamere drew a dagger and pushed Chester against the wall with his blade to her throat. His other hand moved over her leg.

"You know, I liked you." He breathed down her neck. "Until I found out what you are. Murdering scum."

She glared. "In my defence, I'm just the friend of the murdering scum."

He struck her again, the back of her head hitting stone.

"You are in no position to talk to me like that," he snapped.

"Would you prefer me sitting?"

He raised the dagger.

"Watch yourself, Thalamere," Athos said. "If you value your life."

Thalamere gritted his teeth, lowering the blade. Veraion glanced at Athos.

"Don't tell me you're here to rescue her," Thalamere snarled.

"She doesn't need my help. Now do as you're told and brand her."

Veraion squinted, watching the champion.

Thalamere shoved Chester from the cell. He snapped his fingers and his henchmen grabbed her, hauling her to the furnace.

Thalamere took the branding iron. Embers flicked behind the glowing red metal: an *M* for murderer. His eyes gleamed.

"This might hurt," he said with a sneer.

The first henchman grabbed Chester by the hair and yanked her head to the side. Thalamere raised the iron. With hunger in his eyes, he pressed the burning metal to her neck.

Chester's skin glowed where the scalding brand touched her. She gritted her teeth from the amount of pressure he was forcing against her neck.

Thalamere pulled the iron away, eyes wide and grin spreading from ear to ear. The mark glowed bright red on her skin.

Then it faded.

His face fell.

"Yeah," she said. "About that."

She kicked him square in the chest, throwing him from his feet. Fire shot down her arms, sending the henchmen back as they yelled in pain. The furnace sprang to life in her presence.

Chester grabbed one of the men and shoved him face-first into the fire, his screams echoing around the dungeon. She seized the other, yanking him back towards her, slamming her knee into his spine. Then she took his head in her flaming hands and snapped his neck.

Aven grabbed his cell door and heaved it from the hinges. He threw it aside and grabbed Veraion's.

Chester turned around, her pupils blazing. The first henchman was collapsed, screaming in agony, clutching at his burning face. She grabbed a dagger from his belt and slit his throat. As blood showered, she continued towards Thalamere. He was on the floor, eyes wide as he tried to back away. Chester picked up the branding iron, and as he tried to stand, fighting to flee, she slammed her foot onto his chest.

"No no. I don't think so."

Fire shot down her arm as she shoved the iron onto his chest, flames spreading down the rod to burn through his clothes. Thalamere screamed as metal seared into his skin.

Aven heaved Theideus's cell door away, freeing the last of his comrades. Veraion grabbed their weapons from a pile nearby, having to take Maina by the arm, desperate to shake her from her frozen state. But her eyes were on Chester.

Chester was on top of Thalamere, slamming her flaming fist into his face again and again and again. He was already unconscious. What was once his pale skin was now melted, disfigured, and scorched flesh.

Veraion tore forward and yanked her back, but her skin burned and he released her with a yell, shaking his hands to try and rid them of her heat. Chester stepped back from the mutilated man, pushing her hair from her face. She spat on his body.

"We have to go," Veraion said. They moved for the stairs, but Athos stood in their way. Aven raised a fist.

"Get the fuck out of my way," he snarled.

Athos held his glare and nodded towards a wall nearby. Chester moved to it and thumped a fist against the stone, and a low rumble led to a slight opening. She heaved it open.

"How…" Veraion started.

"I'll tell you on the way."

She stepped aside, ushering Maina and Theideus in first, looking back at Athos as the others headed through. He retained his ever-watchful gaze. Chester gave him a nod before disappearing into the darkness.

$$* * *$$

A low rumble was followed by an opening emerging in a city wall. Chester poked her head out, glancing around, only to duck back inside and press into the darkness, holding her breath. A group of guards marched by. She winced at the sound of their boots stomping the cobblestones, waiting, waiting, until they were gone. When the coast was clear, Chester pushed the opening wider.

"Leave the city, all of you," Veraion said.

"Where are *you* going?" Chester stared.

"I have to go back."

"Are you *mad?*"

"They took my necklace."

Maina looked at him with wide eyes, as though he were insane, but Chester sighed through flared nostrils.

"Fine. I'll go with you."

He shook his head. "No. They know you're an azheek now. That's not a risk I'm willing to take. I'll handle this."

"Raion—"

"*No.* It's too dangerous for you now."

"They know *you're* an azheek," she reminded him.

"If I don't get that necklace, I'm already as good as dead."

Chester clenched her jaw, letting out a sharp sigh. Finally she nodded, and when he turned away, she took him by the arm.

"Veraion," she said. "I saw... azheeks. Trapped in crystal."

His brow furrowed. "What? Where? When?"

"Earlier today. The secret passages. I ended up... I think I ended up somewhere in the castle. Underground. There was a light, I found a way in, and I found them. There were two azheeks of every element, naked, suspended in crystal. Veraion, I think they're still alive in there. They're being used. I think that's how the baraduhr made Siran."

He clenched his jaw and swallowed the knot in his throat. "I felt it too, in the castle."

"Last night?"

He nodded.

"Be careful," she said. "Please."

He nodded once more, pulling her in, and placed a long kiss on her forehead. After, he touched his forehead to hers, closing his eyes. They shared a breath.

"Go to the forest," he said. "And not the ones within the walls. Leave the city. Southern forest *outside* of Sontar Ivel." He turned to Aven. "If I don't meet you there by nightfall, sneak back into the city and find out what's going on. I pray that won't be necessary."

"How on Ianar is he going to do that?" Maina shook. "We're all wanted now."

"He has his ways," Veraion said. He shared a look with Aven before turning away, but Aven grabbed him by the shirt and pulled him back.

"Don't... get yourself killed," Aven muttered. "That's my job, remember?"

Veraion smiled, patting the giant's hand. Then he moved into the darkness.

Veraion headed back through the tunnels, feeling the trace his own friends had left, but when he came to a fork, he turned away from the path that led to the dungeons. He swallowed the knot in his throat and did what he could to clear his mind, taking in deep breaths as he walked.

He couldn't see anything. The tunnels were black as a moonless night, but he could feel his surroundings. He could sense stone, the same stone that built the city, and marble. He could sense what was on the other side. And when he reached a dead end, he ran a hand over the wall. Clenching his fist, he hit it. Nothing. He tried again, in a different spot, and this time there came a low rumble.

Golden light pooled into the opening and he peeked his head in, carefully glancing around. Marble floors, marble walls, marble ceiling. Sconces of gold and banners coloured with expensive dyes.

Veraion took in a deep breath and hurried forward, moving through the corridor. He turned a corner, then another, and when he heard footsteps, sensing the approach of guards, he dove under a nearby table. Curling up, he hid behind the hanging tablecloth, shaking his head at himself.

"*aishida*," he murmured. Veraion waited for the guards to pass, disappearing around another corner.

He lifted the tablecloth and peered around.

The castle was too big. He had no idea where he was or where he was intending on going. He swore at himself for even letting someone take the necklace from his person in the first place.

Then he felt someone, someone familiar. Einmyria appeared around a corner, wiping tears from her cheeks. He clenched his jaw and watched her as she moved down the hall, and as she passed, he came from his hiding place. Veraion grabbed her by the arm and yanked her into a nearby room, clasping a hand over her mouth as she gasped. He stared around the space to ensure it was empty before he removed his hand.

"What are you doing here?" she rasped.

"Got arrested, remember?"

"I told you my father knew where I was staying. It's your fault you didn't leave last night."

He smiled bitterly, still looming over her, and she held his glare. Her eyes were bloodshot, nose red, and though she tried to stand tall, he could feel the grief in her.

Einmyria poked him in the shoulder wound, and he backed away with a pained yelp.

"I don't appreciate being loomed over," she said, wiping another tear. She looked at him and her words came quietly. "Are they safe?"

He nodded.

"Why are you still here?"

"I'm looking for my necklace."

"A necklace," she repeated in disbelief.

"It belonged to Ilia, the woman I loved. The woman your father sent a group of baraduhr after."

Einmyria clenched her jaw and turned her gaze to the floor.

"You really didn't know," he said lowly. She looked back at him, eyes bloodshot. Her next words came as a rasp.

"If I had known, I would have killed Ehl myself."

He nodded. She averted her eyes again, sniffing harshly, wiping her tears as though ashamed they were coming.

"Did you know?" he asked. "That Aven was with me?"

"No." She shook her head. "I didn't. I promise you, I didn't. Not until it was too late." Her tears came once more. Veraion let out a soft sigh and nodded.

"I'm sorry."

"What does your necklace look like?"

"Gold chain, crystal pendant. It glows. White."

"Magic?"

He nodded.

"My father's study," she said. "Eighth floor, double doors, mahogany. There's a carving on them, a woman. My mother."

"You expect me to trust you?"

She smiled sadly. "I don't know if your necklace is there, but if it has power, he would have taken it. If it's not in his study, it's still on him."

Veraion clenched his jaw and nodded. "Thank you."

"I shouldn't be here either," she said. "I'm not allowed in the castle. But they brought me when they brought you, and I couldn't leave until I knew Aven was safe."

"You sent Athos?"

"Athos?"

"He was the one…"

Her brow furrowed, and he shook his head, fighting to understand the mysterious champion. He couldn't.

Einmyria wiped her tears. "If you see my father…"

"Are you asking me to kill him?"

Her eyes met his. The pain was so clear in her stare. Heartbreak. Betrayal.

"Or are you asking me not to?"

She swallowed the knot in her throat and took in a deep breath. "Eighth floor. Double doors. Mahogany. My mother."

Veraion nodded, heading for the door, but Einmyria whispered in her place.

"She was an azheek."

He stopped and looked back at her. She met his gaze and smiled sadly, tears streaming down her cheeks.

"It makes me wonder."

* * *

Chester, Maina, and Theideus were huddled in the south woods, unable to risk making a fire and exposing their whereabouts. The sun had set, and before long, Aven headed back for the white walls.

Now, they waited for him. It felt like it had been hours.

Aven appeared through the trees and Chester raced forward, grabbing him into a hug. He closed his eyes, wrapping his arms around her.

He had snuck to the inn and got their horses, retrieving Chester's kara'i weapon. She was lucky she had hidden it well or it would have been lost to the baraduhr. He had also retrieved a few trinkets for Maina and Theideus and had shoved as many of his silken robes into a rucksack as possible.

Chester finally let go of Aven, and he tried to smile, but from the look in his eye it was clear what he had found.

He threw down a poster. On it was an illustration of Veraion, as he looked now.

Execution.

"The entire city is talking about it," Aven said. "His execution is tomorrow."

Chester clenched her jaw and the poster went up in flames.

"What are we going to do?" Maina choked. "There's too many of them. I know you're good fighters, but there's no way we can go back into that city and make it out alive."

"I'm going to kill them," Chester rasped.

"I'm sure you want to, but you can't go back there. The city is swarming with guards."

"And baraduhr," Aven said.

"What? No way... not here."

Chester and Aven gave her a sharp look, and she stood corrected.

"Your queen is one of them," Aven said.

Chester started pacing and soon she let out a yell, slamming a glowing fist into a tree. Her body shook with rage, and as she let out a long breath, she rested her trembling, bloody hand on the charred bark.

"We can't do this alone."

* * *

Chester moved through the trees, fighting to stay calm. She had been walking for what felt like hours, searching for solitude—searching for some kind of peace. But she found none.

She pushed hair from her face, glaring at the forest canopy with bloodshot eyes. Sunlight streamed through rustling leaves, caressing her tanned skin, but it gave her no comfort.

A twig snapped behind her.

Chester grabbed her weapon, wheeling around, but a blast sent her away. The force threw her through the trees, crashing down to skid through dirt and leaves. She scrambled to her feet, searching for her weapon, but her eyes widened and her blood went cold.

Baraduhr.

They strode towards her, ten of them. Their cloaks billowed at their heels, faces hidden beneath masks. The man in the lead carried a staff, the crystal head glowing, stolen azheek powers billowing from it.

The baraduhr swung his staff and Chester froze. Paralyzed from head to toe.

The humans formed a circle around her and the leader moved forward, stopping only inches from her petrified face. The mask gleamed in the sunlight, rays glistening eerily off the blank visage. Then he reached up with a gloved hand and pulled the mask away.

"Hello, *Mahriel.*"

Thalamere, or what was left of him. Melted. Mangled. Mutilated. His lips were peeling away, nose missing, exposing cartilage and bone. But he was healing already—too quickly for a human to heal. His face was stuck in places, mobility lost, skin hardened and scarred, but rare few of the wounds looked fresh.

He picked up her kara'i weapon and gazed over it. "Who did you take this from?"

His words sounded pained, forced through melted lips, spoken as though his jaw were permanently clenched.

She said nothing. She couldn't move. He smiled at her, casting the blade aside.

"You've made a monster of me," he said. He leaned in, whispering in her ear, "I think I'll add you to my staff. I could use more fire."

He struck her across the face, releasing her paralysis, sending her to the ground with a gasp.

Chester sent a blast of fire at him, but he raised his staff and her flames disappeared into the swarm of magic billowing at the crystal head. He smiled sickeningly, as best he could with his melted face.

"That's cute."

He raised his staff and she was sucked into the air. When he swung, she was thrown to the ground. Chester gasped for breath, but before she could move, he did it again. Into the air, slammed to the ground.

"You may be better than me in the ring, Mahriel," he said, "but out here, in the real world, you'll find that you are nothing."

He swung his staff once more and she flew through the woods, crashing into a tree before collapsing to the ground. Thalamere laughed and strode forward, grabbing her by the neck, dragging her to her feet.

She punched him in the face. Sparks cracked against his flesh when her fist met his skull, a pained yell leaving his deformed lips. She tried to run, but he grabbed her by the hair and slammed her against a tree.

Thalamere waved his hand. His staff flashed and Chester was paralyzed. She quivered in place, fighting desperately to move. Tears welled in her eyes.

The man struck his staff into the ground beside them and began to undo her bodice.

"You may get out of this alive, Mahriel. As long as you do as you're told."

He shoved her to her knees. Holding her head with one hand, he pushed down his pants with the other.

"You know what to do."

He released her paralysis and she spat. She spat boiling-hot saliva on him, searing like acid. Thalamere screamed and she ran.

Chester tore through the trees, gasping for breath, but she was thrown to the ground, dragged across the forest floor, back to the baraduhr.

"Aven!" she shrieked. "*Aven!*"

Her screams turned to a cry as Thalamere struck her head against a rock, punching her a second later.

"You fucking bitch!" he snarled, his body shaking violently. He waved his hand, freezing her once more, and beckoned at one of the others.

"Give it to me," he gasped, trembling. His body was going into shock. "Give them—*give them to me!*"

One of his followers handed him two bottles, each with eerie, glowing liquid, and he grabbed one filled with a milky white substance. He yanked off the cork, frantically drinking the whole thing.

Thalamere clenched his jaw, screaming through his teeth as he waited for the potion to kick in. As it flowed through his veins, his pain was dulled.

He grabbed the next, glowing green. He glared at Chester in her frozen state and smiled sickly, dangling the bottle in front of her face.

"How many earth azheeks do you think it took to make this?"

He chuckled. Then he uncorked it and drank the whole thing.

Thalamere leaned over Chester, staring her in the eyes, and as she lay frozen she had no choice but to watch as his burns began to glow. It was slight, beneath the skin, but it was there.

The burns began to heal, only a little, but her frozen gaze was fixed on him as he smiled.

Saliva dripped through his teeth with barely any lips to hold it back.

"You want to feel something burn?" he snarled. "*I'll make you fucking burn.*"

Aven stood up. Maina and Theideus looked at him. His single eye was wide and fearful. His heart hammered in his chest.

"Did you hear that?" he said. The other two glanced around but they heard nothing.

Aven craned his ears, moving forward as he listened to the woods. He squinted, fighting to hear through the trees. There was a haunting scream in the wind, a distant cry that only he could hear.

His face fell.

"*Chester!*"

Aven charged through the trees, leaping into the air, his body morphing, muscles and fur tearing through clothes.

Chester's screams were silenced. Tears streamed down her face as she shook. Thalamere was on top of her, forcing himself inside. She couldn't move.

The baraduhr stood in a circle around them, watching.

Watching.

Thalamere was on top of her. Inside her.

Everything was numb but for the burning in her arms and legs, hands and feet incapable of feeling anything but pins and needles. But between her legs, deep in her stomach: *pain.*

Excruciating.

It burned. Tearing her up from the inside out. Ripping her apart with every angered thrust of his hips.

She couldn't move. Paralyzed. Unable to do anything but *feel.*

To feel what was happening.

Unable to scream. Unable to fight.

Torture.

Then Thalamere was sucked away. Chester was splattered with blood.

She shook in her place, broken from her paralysis, and instantly she curled up, unable to contain her rasping breaths. Shaking. Convulsing.

All she could smell was blood. The metallic reek was so strong, she could taste it. Blood dripped down her face, and as she looked up, shaking through the red, her eyes widened in fear.

The baraduhr were floating, turned inside out. Their entrails were on the outside, hearts beating in clear view, pumping blood through their mutilated bodies.

Their hearts were beating fast. Too fast.

They were still alive.

Somehow the baraduhr were still alive, feeling every second of this. Unable to move. Unable to scream. Unable to fight.

Something was keeping them alive.

Rocks, twigs, and leaves floated in the air, the clearing held in suspended animation.

Thalamere floated in the centre of it all, seemingly untouched. But he clutched at his throat, mouth opening and closing as he struggled to breathe. He stared around at the massacre, at the horrid carcasses of his henchmen. His legs kicked uselessly as he fought to escape the invisible force holding him.

A man emerged from the trees. An arm was raised, fingers outstretched and tensed, the veins popping under his deathly pale skin. There was a tattoo on his hand, mimicking Old magic, and the ink marked his face, neck, and forehead, to extend his widow's peak.

His eyes were gone, lost behind a pale grey light that looked almost purple. The light blazed in his stare, his empty gaze fixed on the baraduhr held at his mercy.

He was dressed in black from head to toe, robes billowing about his boots as he strode forward. Bracers were bound about his forearms, a belt firm around his waist, cloak flowing from his shoulders. And from his head, growing down to his waist, was pale silver hair.

Lord Ezaria.

Eerie, glowing smoke surrounded the lord as he moved, lights rising from his body as he called on his powers to torture the baraduhr, and in his presence, Chester felt cold.

Ezaria looked at her. She trembled, unable to move from her place. There was a change in his glowing eyes, slight, but it was there. He struck his bladed bow into the ground and used his free hand to remove the cloak from his shoulders. With a flick of his wrist it flew to Chester and covered her shaking body.

Then he turned back to Thalamere. The baraduhr was staring around at what had become of his brethren, their hearts still beating, lungs still breathing.

"Please," Thalamere gasped. "Please!"

Ezaria's teeth ground as he snarled, hatred seething from his body, and slowly, he began to close his hand.

First moved the fifth finger. It brought the sounds of breaking bones.

Thalamere screamed. His cries were blood-curdling and they did not stop.

Starting at his feet, his bones splintered. His bones shattered, tendons snapping, muscle tearing.

Thalamere's legs shattered slowly.

From the ankles, horrifying cracks sounded one after the other, travelling up his shins as his legs bent and contorted with every break. From his knees to his hips, bone protruded from skin, through his clothes, blood splattering in every direction. His pelvis broke with deafening snaps. Spine fractured and split. Ribcage imploded.

Thalamere's mouth gaped as he screamed.

Screaming.

Screaming.

Then his jaw broke, his mouth spreading even wider, face peeling open.

His face turned inside out. Blood bubbled in his throat, rising from his mouth, and so did his heart. Beating as fast as the others.

Ezaria's billowing gaze was fixed on Thalamere. His concentration was on the baraduhr and the baraduhr alone, doing everything he could to prolong their suffering.

He was the one filling their lungs with air. He was the one forcing their hearts to beat. He was the one forcing blood to pump through their brains. To keep them conscious. To prolong the torture.

He was making sure they felt every second of this.

Pale light billowed from the eyes of the lord. But in this state, so focused on his task, he was blind, deaf, and dumb. He was so concentrated, so focused on the baraduhr before him, he did not see nor hear the roaring wasfought tearing at him through the woods.

Aven erupted from the trees and slammed into the lord, taking him down, skidding across the dirt.

In an instant the destroyed baraduhr fell to the ground. The rocks, twigs, and leaves all fell. A breeze swept through the clearing once more. The hearts stopped beating.

Aven took the man crashing through the woods. It didn't take much for the azheek to shove him off, using his powers to send the beast away, throwing him into a tree.

Ezaria's stare was no longer glowing, but his eyes were no less frightening. His irises were pale grey, so pale they looked almost white.

His skin was porcelain, his features just as doll-like. His nose was perfectly straight, cheekbones and chin strong, his jaw chiselled. He didn't look a day over his prime. The only sign of age was his long straight silver hair. It was half tied up, a fringe hanging to one side, and as he stood, he angrily flicked his head to get it out of his face.

The lord looked over to where the baraduhr remains were splattered across the ground. He snarled. "They should have suffered longer."

Aven pulled himself up with a groan, shaking his mane, about to make another attempt.

"Stop." Chester's voice was barely a rasp. "He saved me."

Some of Ezaria's ribs were broken—it was clear from the indent in his side. The azheek looked down at this, and with an irritated snarl, used his powers to snap his ribs back into place.

"That's going to take months to heal," he hissed.

Aven ignored him, hurrying to Chester, turning into a human as he went. Ezaria watched in shock.

"Chester." Aven was about to take her into his arms, but she pulled away.

"I'm fine," she whispered.

"*Chester.*"

"She will survive," Ezaria said. Aven looked at him with a snarl.

"Who do you think you—" But his words were cut off as he looked at the man.

Silver hair. The Red Emperor.

Aven's eye widened. He stared at the lord, looking back to the mess of blood and bones. The forest was red, strewn with intestines, muscle, and skin. Teeth littered the earth, shards of bone protruding from the ground like stone.

Aven couldn't breathe. The colour flushed from his face. Not a single word rested on his tongue. He had never seen a massacre like this.

He looked back to the lord, to the man with silver hair.

"I am Lord Ezaria of Zalfur," he said.

Aven was frozen, like he'd seen a ghost.

Maina and Theideus burst through the trees, clinging to the reins as their horses reared and whinnied. Maina was thrown back, landing on the ground with a painful thud, and Theideus leapt from his saddle. He ran to her side.

"Since when—the *fuck*—have you been a wasfought?!" she screamed.

They stared at Aven but were soon frozen, horrified eyes on the mess of blood and bones. Maina staggered behind a tree and threw up.

Theideus's eyes were wide, unable to look away from the carnage, but when he finally did, he saw Ezaria. The colour left his face and his stomach only dropped further. He took a step back, trembling, and instinctually stood between the lord and his once-human ilis.

Ezaria raised a hand and Thalamere's staff flew into his grasp. He looked at the glowing crystal head, stolen azheek powers billowing about it, reflecting off his pale face.

Hatred seethed in his stare. Teeth grinding, his lips turned to a snarl.

He smashed the crystal on the ground and lights flashed in every direction, colours of every power, culminating in bright white. Colourful smoke lingered upon the ground, the beauty of every colour a horrid juxtaposition of what had happened to the original azheeks.

Lights flickered about the forest floor, remnants of the people that had died. Earth, air, fire, and water.

Chester spoke quietly, still shaking. "Veraion…"

Ezaria's brow furrowed, interest sparking in his cold gaze. "You know Veraion?"

"He needs your help," she rasped. "They have him. In the city. He's going to be executed. Please."

Ezaria watched her, his gaze roving over her bloody face. Then he raised a hand and his bladed bow flew into his grasp.

* * *

Thousands of people were packed into the city square to watch the execution. Chester moved through the throng, a black hood pulled low over her face, revealing only strands of dark hair clumped together with dried blood. Her weapon was slung across her back, hidden by the baraduhr cloak she wore.

Slowly she moved, surrounded by voices. So many voices. And yet, they sounded so far away.

Further and further, weaving through the crowd until she stood before the platform.

An executioner stood tall, sweat glistening off his large stomach, dripping from beneath his hood and over his breasts.

Chester's gaze moved over the buzzing crowd to the city walls. Guards roamed above, armour glistening in the beating sun. Air azheeks patrolled the skies, weapons held in their grasps.

There stood a great man on the walls, his sea-blue eye already watching her. Athos nodded. It was slight, unseen by all but Chester.

Then the crowd parted as a swarm of guards stomped forward. Veraion was lost between them, his bare feet dragging across the ground. His head hung, hair dangling before his battered face. He was wearing only his pants and shirt, now ripped and torn. Veraion's skin was bruised and bloodied, wrists and ankles raw from bonds. On his neck, freshly burned, was the brand of a murderer.

The crowd hissed and booed as the guards hauled him onto the platform. They shoved him to his knees and he blinked weakly through his hair.

The lead councilman stepped onto the podium, addressing the crowd. "People of Sontar Ivel!"

The noise quieted to a murmur.

"You are gathered here today to witness the execution of the mass murderer Veraion."

A hiss sounded through the crowd, and he turned to the battered azheek.

"You are sentenced to death for the murder of twenty-seven men and women across the mainland."

Gasps of horror rippled through the square. People yelled and threw rotten vegetables at Veraion, and the lead councilman unrolled a scroll, reading the names of the twenty-seven victims.

Chester's gaze turned to the queen's guard around the parapets. It was clear that they knew some of these people, and when the name Ehl was read, many were visibly angry. She spotted Lord Venhel seated at another platform. He was missing half of his right leg. His bandage was already bloodied, eyes fixed on Veraion with deranged loathing.

Chester looked back at Veraion, then at the amputee lord. She smirked.

A buzz sounded as more people emerged on a city wall, and she looked up to see Elaira, flanked by guards. Elaira's eyes were wide and filled with tears, lip trembling. She didn't want to be here. The guards weren't keeping her safe—they were controlling her.

"In addition to these horrid crimes," the councilman continued, "he slaughtered fourteen of our city guards just yesterday in an attempt to escape the castle."

"Oh, but I did," Veraion said. "I just decided to sneak back in for shits and giggles."

"Silence!" the old man snapped. Veraion clenched his jaw and closed his eyes, letting out a sigh as the fourteen names were read. People yelled in shock and anger, throwing more rotten vegetables. He gritted his teeth, trying not to react when they hit his already battered body.

"Any last words?" the councilman asked.

"I thought you just told me to be quiet."

"Why, you insolent—"

"I do have some last words." Veraion rose to his feet, slowly, painfully, and he swayed in his place. "I would try and explain myself, but I don't have time for the whole story. For the few of you that are willing to listen, you need to leave the city. Get as far away as you can. Do not associate with any of the queen's guard or lords of the castle. They are baraduhr." The guards grabbed him. "The queen is a fraud! She's not the real queen!"

A guard punched him across the face, striking him repeatedly as he yelled through the assault.

"The real queen was murdered by the baraduhr, replaced by a fraud! Siran the Second never named her daughter Siran! Her name isn't—"

He was gagged, shoved back to his knees, and the executioner came forward.

Elaira trembled where she stood. She swallowed the knot in her throat, wishing more than anything that she could run. That she could run before Veraion and shield him from the beating. That she could stand before him and tell everyone the truth.

Veraion swayed in place, gazing up at the sky. He blinked slowly, the sun caressing his broken skin. It was comforting.

Then his head hung, unable to hold up any longer.

The executioner raised his colossal axe. With a heavy swing, he brought it down.

It stopped an inch from Veraion's neck. The audience gasped.

Lord Venhel sat up. The councilman looked on in confusion.

The executioner's arms were shaking, the man trying as hard as he could, but the axe wouldn't move. Then it was yanked from his grip and floated into the air.

The square was dead silent, eyes wide and fearful.

The axe shot sideways, splitting the executioner. His body fell to the ground in two pieces, blood, guts, and yellow chunks of fat splaying across the podium, slipping to the street below.

Mayhem.

Chester charged for the stage. She swung onto the platform and severed Veraion's bonds with a dagger, shoving it into his hands once he was free. The guards ran at her, but she drew her kara'i blade, extending the hilt to make it a polearm.

Chester sent blood and guts across the stage. She moved through the guards, splattering Veraion with their fluids. He was still trying to stand.

Lord Venhel was screaming but none of his commands were heard over the shrieking crowd. People pushed and shoved as they fought to flee the scene.

The queen's guard swarmed Elaira and ushered her to the castle, dragging her as she stared back with wide eyes. Lord Venhel was screaming to attack, but his own guard hauled him from the scene.

Air azheek guards tore towards the commotion, but Ezaria was standing upon the parapets, and with a harsh flick of his wrist they were repelled. His hood was pulled low, every strand of his hair hidden from view.

Chester let out a blood-curdling cry. Her call sounded so loud above the fray, people stopped and stared. Chester threw back her cloak, and as she yelled, fire rose.

Flames crawled over her skin, igniting the cloak as it fell. Fire surrounded her, eating through her hair, burning away the blood and dye, and once again, her red hair billowed like flames.

Chester shrieked, hellfire blazing in her pupils.

Muscles rippled as she swung her blades, metal singing, painting red. The crystal flashed as she spun, blue lights wafting around her.

Athos never once looked away, eyes gleaming as she slaughtered across the stage. And for the first time in decades, he felt an emotion.

Pride.

More guards flooded into the square, racing towards the chaos. Civilians rushed to escape the scene, but as they ran, they were thrown from their feet. A wasfought tore through the crowd, his great body an unstoppable battering ram, sending swarms to the ground.

Aven charged towards the incoming guards, ramming into the first row. He sank his teeth into them, raking his claws through armour, skin, and bone.

Ezaria leapt into the air, drawing three arrows. They shot from his bow with ungodly speed, propelled and aimed with powers, striking through the skulls of three different guards before a single one could blink an eye. He landed on the podium, grabbing Veraion. The earth azheek looked at him, vision blurry, mind not entirely there. All he saw was a familiar face beneath a black hood.

"Dad?" he croaked.

Ezaria grimaced and slapped him across the face. He blinked widely.

"*Ezaria?*"

The lord wrapped an arm around him and shot back into the sky. In an instant, they were gone.

Chester watched them go and was about to call for Aven when she saw the lead councilman gaping at the carnage. He staggered back, fear ripe in his eyes.

"Please," he gasped. "Please! I didn't do anything wrong!"

With a twitch of her fingers, flames started at the hems of his robes, climbing higher and higher until they roared all around him. Fire engulfed the old man, melting his skin, and as he shrieked, Chester strode forward. She slammed her foot into his chest, sending him from the podium.

She stood there, looking down at him, watching as he writhed and screamed. She watched as his clothes burned, rings and jewellery melting into his wrinkled skin, peeling away to expose flesh. Only when he stopped moving did she turn and walk away.

Chester whistled for Aven as she strode across the podium, yanking a dagger from a quivering guard. She swung her polearm and dismembered another.

Aven charged towards the stage, and as he leapt onto it, she grabbed his mane and swung onto his back.

Veraion fell to the ground. He lay there, gazing at the grass. Streams of sunlight caressed his withered body, and he rolled onto his back, blinking at the forest canopy. He smiled weakly.

Ezaria touched to the ground nearby, bow slung across his body, and pulled back his hood. His long silver hair pooled behind him, flowing with every step. In one hand he carried a bundle of clothes, and he thrust it at Veraion.

"*shazeu,*" he spat, calling him a fool.

Veraion chuckled, replying in the old tongue. "*I'd apologize, but we both know the words won't change anything.*"

He put the bundle of clothes on the grass beside him, lifting up his bloody shirt, and dug his fingers into one of the gaping wounds on his stomach.

Yelling through clenched teeth, he only pushed his fingers in deeper. He found what he was looking for and pulled out his necklace. He held it in his shaking hand for a moment, clenching his fist while his eyes rolled back in his head. He fought the instinct to go into shock.

Ezaria watched him coldly. "*You have made interesting friends.*"

"*Yeah,*" he rasped.

"*The beast broke my ribs.*"

Veraion chuckled through his shudders. "*He does that.*"

Slowly he rose to his feet, staggering as he did. Ezaria didn't help him and merely stood there, watching as he struggled. Eventually he found his footing, though he swayed, and draped the necklace over his head. He let out a tired sigh and glanced at his old mentor.

Ezaria came forward and took the bloody pendant into his hand, his cold eyes livid as he looked back to Veraion's face. *"You let them take it?"*

"Didn't really have a choice. I went back for it though."

Ezaria smiled slightly—bitterly.

"You know I would protect this with my life," Veraion said.

"You said that about Ilia."

Now it was Veraion's turn to smile bitterly, attempting to hide the pain behind it. He held Ezaria's gaze.

"Don't make me take it from you," the lord said.

"I won't."

Ezaria nodded. Then he grabbed Veraion's bloody hand and put it on his broken ribs, gritting his teeth through the pain. Veraion tried to pull his hand away, but Ezaria's grip was stronger.

"Heal me," he ordered.

"What?"

"Heal. Me."

"I can't—"

"Your powers have been getting stronger, have they not?"

"How do you—What—I don't—"

Ezaria's grip tightened, crushing as he took a step closer, his cold gaze boring a hole into Veraion's face. *"Heal me."*

"Ezaria—"

"Try."

"I'm not that kind of earth azheek!" He finally managed to yank his hand away, stumbling back as he did. He fell to the ground and let out a loud gasp as pain shot through his body.

"Then what kind of earth azheek are you?" Ezaria said, using the common tongue with spiteful intonation.

"I... *I sense things.*" Veraion finally managed to switch back. *"People. Objects. The earth."*

"*Do you hear them? Animals? Trees?*"

"*Yes. But not like how I know other earth azheeks can. Animals just like me more, that's all.*"

"*Train your powers,*" Ezaria commanded. "*They were subdued for so long. Perhaps that was my doing, keeping you in Zeda, but they have awoken. Use them.*"

Veraion was gingerly rubbing his wrist and looked at Ezaria fearfully. Still, he nodded.

"*What are you doing here?*" Veraion asked, wincing as he slowly rose to his feet.

"*The same reason I assume you are here. The false queen. The missing champions.*"

Veraion nodded.

"*I've attended the final games of the tournament for the last few years, unannounced,*" Ezaria said.

"*Have you found anything?*"

"*What do you think?*"

Veraion snorted. "*Right. Why… why are you here alone?*"

"*Company draws attention. Nobody notices me when I'm alone.*"

Veraion glanced at him, looking up as he sensed people approaching. Maina and Theideus raced through the trees, rushing to his side.

"Thank the gods you're okay," Maina gasped. Theideus looked at Ezaria and gave him a respectful nod to say thank you, though it was clear he was still just as afraid.

"You know," Veraion said, "you could have just grabbed me and left. That was quite the spectacle back there."

Ezaria's words were cold. "*Mahriel required blood.*"

Theideus looked at him, hearing the warlord speak his mother tongue, but those were not words he welcomed hearing, and this was not a man he wanted to hear them from.

Worry flooded Veraion. He knew what that meant.

"*What happened?*" He stared.

"*She will survive,*" Ezaria said. Veraion was about to ask more questions when his horse came through the trees, hurrying towards him. He decided not to press the matter and greeted his mare, kissing her nose, resting his forehead against hers as she snorted, pushing into his stomach. He flinched, gritting his teeth, but welcomed her affection.

Maina and Theideus helped him into new clothes, glancing at one another and at Ezaria.

Chester and Aven broke into the clearing. When the beast came to a halt, she came from his back. She looked at Veraion but quickly turned away, heading for her mare.

"We have to go," she said. "They'll be here soon."

"Go to Zalfur," Ezaria commanded. "I will send a message to Ziang. She will have refuge prepared for your arrival."

Finally Veraion was clothed and they readied themselves for the ride, mounting their steeds.

"Head for the mountains," Ezaria said. "They will find you. It will be a long journey. You will need thicker clothing. Do not rely on your powers to stay warm—you will only tire yourselves out."

Veraion nodded. "Thank you."

"Be wary of headhunters. The north is crawling with them."

"Headhunters?" Maina said.

"They wait in the woods for travelling azheeks. They'll capture you and sell you to the baraduhr."

She clenched her jaw, gulping nervously.

"But headhunters in the woods are the least of your problems," Ezaria said to Veraion. "The hunters in the icelands have started using the mammoths."

Maina stared. "*What?*"

Ezaria merely held his cold gaze.

"They're using the *mammoths?*"

"There are still woolly mammoths in the north," Ezaria said. "It was only time before the humans turned them into slaves too." He looked back to Veraion. "Make haste for the mountains."

Veraion nodded. He looked at Ezaria, at his old mentor, and beneath the lord's icy gaze he remembered what it was like to feel small.

"*Train your powers,*" Ezaria said. "*They have awoken. Answer the call.*"

Ezaria clapped his hand against Veraion's mare and the five horses sprang to a gallop. Veraion looked back at the lord, and Ezaria watched them for only a moment before taking to the skies.

CHAPTER 15
THE CARRIERS

North-east the five fugitives rode, taking rest when they could—when necessary. Food and sleep, and when far enough from civilization, a fire for warmth.

Weeks passed, the weather matching their spirits. Colder. Wetter.

Aven's dyed-black hair faded to grey. Veraion's beard grew back in. Maina was weary, Theideus weak, and Chester a shell of who she once was. Her gaze was ever distant, face gaunt, and she barely spoke. She slept away from the others, away from Aven.

The howl at the moon sounded cold now, no longer bringing a smile to her lips. But she knew, from hearing him and the other beasts in the woods, just how much time had passed since the last time she'd felt okay.

Aven was quiet, too. He knew something had happened to Chester, but she hadn't spoken since they left the capital and he was too afraid to ask. Unable to comfort the woman he loved most, unable to grieve the one that had come second, the seven-foot beast was finally learning what it was like to feel small.

They now rode through a thick wood. Veraion was in the lead, and as he sensed something, a strong energy, he slowed his mare. The others followed suit. He slipped from his saddle, his brow furrowed. He raised a hand for the others to halt.

"Do you feel that?"

They came from their horses.

The night was lit by soft streams of moonlight, but through the trees there was a dim, fiery glow. Aven sniffed the air.

"I don't smell anything burning," he said.

Veraion lowered to one knee, placing a hand to the ground. "Gangul."

Aven glanced at the others. "What?"

"Gangul," Maina whispered. "The gods' second children."

She quickly headed forward and the others followed.

"Morden were the first," Veraion told the giant. "We don't know much about them. Mother Nature created them before the Sun and the Moon, and she put them deep within Ianar to rest, as they couldn't survive in the light of the new gods. Some people say the land moves because morden are walking deep below. Some people think they're dead. Some think they're sleeping. Waiting.

"Gangul came second. They, too, possess elemental powers, guarding and nurturing the land. Should a river run dry, water gangul will fill it. Should land become barren, earth gangul will fertilize it once more. Storms are created by air and water gangul, volcano eruptions and forest fires by fire gangul, but without the fire gangul, our world would be naught but ice and snow. They are the balance."

"I think there was one in Foros," Aven said. "Just the skeleton though. It had already turned to crystal." He looked to Chester, but she remained quiet, her eyes set ahead. He swallowed the knot in his throat, so desperately wanting to hold her and ask her what was wrong, but he couldn't. He clenched his jaw and looked down.

Veraion watched them, knowing exactly what Aven was feeling, but most of all, he knew what Chester was feeling. He felt it too. So much pain came from her, radiating in waves, beating, relentless, impossible for him to ignore, but he had to. She avoided every gaze, evading every question, and he knew the worst thing he could do was pressure her. Maina had told him what Ezaria did to the baraduhr, and he knew that only the worst abuse garnered that sort of torture from the lord. Chester hadn't told anyone what happened, but he knew. He could see it on her face every time she woke from a nightmare. He could see it every time she pulled away from any form of physical contact. Even Aven couldn't touch her. She hadn't petted him in weeks.

They moved through the trees, and Veraion pulled his gaze away from Chester. He didn't want to make her feel uncomfortable. So he took in a deep breath and focused on what was ahead.

"Gangul remains hold incredible power," he murmured. "If there was one in Foros, perhaps that is what kept your underground city alive." He looked ahead to where Maina was getting closer and closer to the light, but when he didn't feel the presence of power getting any stronger, he sighed. "This one has passed, too."

The five friends moved towards the light, their horses faithfully following. Trees shone brighter and brighter until they gave way to the fallen beast.

The creature was enormous, its body stretching through the woods. It was monstrous and great, a mutation between reptile and bat, scaled, horned, and winged. The beast shone in the darkness. Its flesh was hard and cracked, ancient magic shining from within. Where its scaled skin had begun to chip away, crystal bones were visible. The creature's great wings had turned the ground to coal and embers, twinkling through the woods.

Lights wafted from the beast, colours of red, orange, and yellow, rising from its crystallized flesh. Maina swayed before the fire gangul, staring up at it.

"Did someone kill it?"

"I don't think you can kill gangul," Veraion said. "Humans figured that out a long time ago… the hard way."

"Are they like azheeks?" Aven asked. "All… connected to the gods? Next-life stuff?"

"Yes and no. Connected to the gods, yes. Next life, no. Their magic remains on Ianar and births another gangul. I've... never seen a fire gangul up close before."

"You've been close to others?"

"Not close, necessarily, but there is the air gangul of Zalfur, always circling in the skies." Veraion reached forward but could feel how hot the fallen creature was, so he took a step back and marvelled from a safe distance.

Then he and Aven turned, looking over to the gangul's ribs.

"Someone's inside," the giant snarled. They drew their weapons and moved over to where they sensed company.

Where the gangul's crystal ribs were showing, some of the hard skin had been chipped away to make a hole large enough for someone to walk through.

As they approached, they saw a man. A human. He had weathered skin, his black hair greying, messy, and long. His facial hair was unkempt, skin riddled with scars. He wore a loose shirt under an aged leather vest, tucked into bracers. Strange tattoos marked his skin, scribbles across his chest, but they were old, blurred, and hidden beneath wild, greying chest hair.

His black eyes watched the others, distant madness in his calm stare. An old sword hung from his waist, and as he saw the newcomers with their weapons drawn, his hand twitched towards the hilt.

Then came a voice from inside the chest cavity, the voice of an old woman with an accent of Okos on her tongue.

"They won't hurt you, Jarrik," she said. "Leave your weapon be. The gods would not appreciate you threatening their Carriers."

Jarrik obeyed, folding his arms over his chest. "Blood will not be shed this night." The accent of the Highlands was thick upon his tongue.

"Let them in, my dear."

Jarrik stepped aside and nodded to the five. There came the sound of someone shuffling forward, and soon the old woman came into view. She was wrinkled like bark, skin deep brown and glowing in the gangul's light, and over her face was white paint. It was cracked, a few days since application, but it mimicked a human skull. She wore a wrap about her head, hiding what would be pale grey hair from view. There were gloves about her hands, resting on a large walking stick. The cane was so decorated and adorned it was almost impossible to tell that beneath all the accessories, it was a wasfought bone.

The woman was wrapped in shawls, decorated with jewellery. Bones, beads, feathers, and wooden trinkets dangled about her body, tinkling with every movement. Old scarification marked her skin, giving her ridges like a crocodile's, but no age would stop the brightness in her golden-green eyes.

"Come then," she said. "Help me collect firestones."

Aven cocked his head. "Ayaba?"

Ayaba smiled and nodded. "Come, come." She waved them in and disappeared inside the gangul once more.

"That's her." Aven turned to the others. "The woman that gave me the blood." Then he followed, ducking through the hole. He burned himself a few times as he clambered through.

Slowly the others followed, putting away their weapons.

Inside the gangul the walls were dark, lined with glowing firestones. The stones swirled with lights, twinkling like a sky of red stars. The gangul's bones were bright, flaming crystal.

Ayaba wore a pair of leather gloves, protecting her from the heat, and used a dagger to pry firestones from their places.

Being inside the gangul was a clear reminder that the great beasts were never truly alive. No organs. No stomach, lungs, or a heart. If they were to look into the gangul's great skull, they would find no brain. Instead, all the gangul had were glowing crystal bones and firestones lining the inside of its hard skin.

It seemed Ayaba and Jarrik had been here for some time, for there were already several buckets filled with glowing crystals.

The friends gazed around in awe.

Then Maina screamed. Veraion caught her as she fell into him, all eyes turning to see what had scared her.

A ten-foot-long crocodile.

They all stared—all but Aven, who had already met the beast. He smiled and waved.

"That thing kind of looks like a gangul," he observed.

"Don't mind Ife," the old lady said, tossing firestones into a nearby bucket. "He won't hurt you. Unless you hurt him."

Maina and Theideus sidled away from the crocodile, glancing at it every now and then. It slowly moved forward and they shuffled further away.

Veraion held his ground, however uneasily, but when Ife approached him, waiting for something, he timidly reached forward and petted it. The crocodile looked pleased.

"Earth azheeks," Aven muttered.

"Is Ife… sikele?" Veraion asked. Ayaba smiled and nodded.

"Come," she said. "Help us collect firestones."

Jarrik pulled on a pair of gloves and continued his work.

"Are you taking *all* of them?" Maina glanced around.

"Would you prefer we leave them for humans to find?" Ayaba looked at her. "We all know the humans would never let the element return to Ianar. They would keep it. Exploit it."

Maina gulped and nodded, accepting a dagger from Veraion, and she helped the old woman in her quest. Chester did too, but she watched Ayaba. Veraion, Aven, and Theideus did what they could, but they burned themselves more than a few times.

"How did you find Aven?" Chester asked, her voice hoarse, unused in weeks.

"The gods," Ayaba replied simply.

"The gods told you to find him?"

"It was time."

"It was prophesized?"

"He Who Walks with Wasfoughts needs the Blood of the Brother to be. And He needed to be, to carry the King."

Veraion looked up, eyes wide. "What?"

"Aven has a brother?" Chester said. "Where? Has he drunk the blood?"

"Aven has a brother," Ayaba said. "He has not drunk the blood."

"But you had his blood."

"You ask too many questions."

Veraion spoke up. "You said king. What do you mean by king?"

Ayaba stood back from her work and looked at them, her gaze resting between Veraion, Chester, and Aven. "You are the Carriers of the King."

"There is no king," Veraion said. "The bloodline is passed through daughters, whether two-spirited or one. The queens do not bear sons."

Ayaba looked at him, her gaze steady and unfaltering. "A queen will not bear the King. For the queens are dead."

"*What?*" Maina stared. All eyes were wide.

"The queens are dead?" Chester said.

Ayaba gazed at them. "Yes. The bloodline has ended."

The friends looked at one another, fearful—foreboding.

"The world is changing," Ayaba said. "I see the rising of darkness. And the King is the one who will take us to the light. The King will not be born. But he will be made. And when he is made, all of Ianar will know."

"Made," Chester repeated.

Veraion watched the old woman, frozen in place. "When?"

Ayaba took a deep breath and gazed over the five of them. They were all staring at her. "You ask too many questions. You must have faith in the gods and their plan."

"But—"

"One. The gods have granted you the answer to one question each. No more, no less."

Veraion clenched his jaw in frustration and almost fear. Ayaba knew this, so she turned away from him, addressing Maina.

"My child?"

"Sorry?" she stammered.

"One question, any question, and I will know the answer."

Maina blinked. She was flustered for a moment, and when she spoke, she was quiet. "Will I ever return to Sontar Ivel?"

It took a moment.

"Yes," Ayaba said. "You will return very soon, for only a moment. After that, you will never see the city again."

Maina looked down and nodded, swallowing the knot in her throat.

Ayaba turned back to Veraion. "Have you decided?"

"Is Ilia at rest?"

"You know the answer to that question."

"Then how can I help her be at rest?"

Ayaba looked at him, listening as the gods whispered to her. "You must release her soul. She is trapped. Bound between worlds. She cannot reach Savai."

Aven leaned over to Maina. "Savai?"

"The spirit world," she whispered. "Valira, where you feast with the gods and your loved ones, and Valduhr, where you suffer for your crimes, an eternity alone, away from your ilis."

"Right... but only azheeks have to worry about that."

"Perhaps that's why baraduhr are so terrible."

Veraion was about to ask another question, but Ayaba turned to Chester. The fire azheek was quiet, but eventually she spoke.

"How can we release Ilia's soul?"

Veraion looked at her in surprise, her one question used on him.

"You must find her," Ayaba said. "And summon the In Between. The City of the Dead. Only there can she be freed."

She turned to Aven. The giant shrugged, having no questions. She turned away, but he glanced at Chester and quickly changed his mind.

"Where will we find Ilia?" he asked. Ayaba looked back at him, taking a moment. Her brow furrowed, head cocking. She was having difficulty knowing the answer.

"I hear only whispers," she said. "A muffled scream. *Aion.*"

Aven looked to Chester for praise, but her gaze was on the ground. The old lady turned to Theideus.

"My child?"

Theideus glanced at her. He motioned at his throat and shook his head.

"The gods have granted you a question." Ayaba said. She pulled off her gloves and held out her hand. There was an intricate symbol upon each palm, glowing green with Old magic—a symbol that could only be gained through achieving *ulu*. A gift from the gods.

Veraion's brow furrowed upon seeing it. He opened his mouth, about to question, but Ayaba's eyes were fixed on Theideus. Theideus was afraid, confused, but he took her hand and lowered to one knee. Ayaba placed her other hand upon his cheek.

Theideus's markings bloomed to life. Brilliant blue lights glimmered across his body, shining along every pattern on his skin. His breaths were heavy as the magic of his people returned—breaths that the others could hear.

He took in a long, shuddering inhale, hearing himself for the first time in years. Tears welled in his eyes as he stared at her, swaying in place. Maina had a hand over her mouth, biting back tears.

"Speak," Ayaba said kindly. It took him a long moment before he could, and when he did, he spoke in his native tongue, speaking words only Ayaba and Veraion could understand.

"*How are my people?*" he asked. "*Are my people safe? Is my home safe?*"

He spoke softly, the old language rolling off his tongue like song, spoken with a Volehni accent. Every *R* was pronounced in the back of his throat, almost like a purr.

Ayaba smiled. "*Your people, and your home, are safe. They are happy. They thrive.*"

He smiled with relief, tears sliding from his bright eyes. "*Thank you.*"

She leaned in a bit closer. "*You will see home again.*"

Theideus took her hand, holding it against his cheek. He closed his eyes, overwhelmed by the magic of his people flowing through him for the first time in a decade. It caused him to tremble.

Slowly Ayaba moved away, and as her touch left him, so did the Old magic.

She pulled on her gloves and turned to pluck firestones, leaving Theideus to slowly rise to his feet. Maina held his hand, giving a gentle squeeze.

Then Ayaba froze. An eerie green glow appeared on the wall before her, and as she slowly turned around, her eyes billowed with bright green light.

The others took a step back.

"There was a lonely woman," she said, her voice echoing and otherworldly. Everyone stood transfixed, watching her with wide eyes, listening as her voice echoed through the hollow body of the gangul.

"There was a lonely woman,
Who had an empty womb,
So day did come, the kingdom from,
She chose to end her gloom.

"She felt a child within her,
To join eternity,
But while it grew, no light shone through,
Was dark eternally.

"Gave Ianar more children,
The morden roamed the world,
But land was dark, within their hearts,
The woman felt the hurt.

"So walk and search she did for years,
To find what could give life,
And met a man who felt he can,

Give light to endless night.

"The lonely woman fell in love,
And felt it deep inside,
Sent morden deep to rest in peace,
Sent Ianar new life.

"She placed on earth her second,
To nurture the world to thrive,
The gangul did, but all they did,
They lived to serve and die.

"So placed on earth a new rebirth,
Her children many and small,
And with them there were more to bear,
To serve azheek for all.

"But anger grew within them,
The Fen began to fight,
So Mother Nature sent her kin,
She sent to earth her Five.

"She placed on earth the mighty lords,
Of water, of air, of fire,
To keep in line, refused resign,
Of earth and their entire.

"And ruled for years a many,
The lords did keep the world,
But under heart, a dark did start,
And sent them back to her.

"So disappeared from daylight,
The Five were never seen,
As moons passed by, their children thrived,
But fell apart in dreams.

"A darkness stirs before us,
A darkness they can't see,
A rise of hurt and suffering,
A flood of agony.

"The Fen were first to bring it,
But will not be the last,
Foreseen a future enemy,
Darker than the past.

"But do not fear an ending,
For in the gods we trust,
When the hours of darkness come,
A King will rise for us.

"A King of light and power,
Of fire, of earth, of air,
Of rivers, oceans, land, and sky,
Reborn, the Five will bear.

"Who knows what future holds us,
Through daughter, son, or both,
Shall follow them, or so condemned,
Forever hold our oath.

"Our Mother of Nature watches,
Sees everything we do,

Every step and every breath,
She watches over you.

"Until that day you join her,
Do choose your actions well,
Save your power for darkest hour,
Be rested where you dwell.

"Until the day the Five return,
To lead the war of end,
The children of the gods must wait,
And put your trust in them.

"Who knows what future holds us,
We pray for brighter day,
And when the King has risen,
Will fight until we lay."

The green light flashed in Ayaba's eyes, and Jarrik raced forward, catching her as she collapsed. The magic disappeared from her stare.

Veraion came forward, looking to the elder in concern. Maina exchanged wide-eyed glances with Theideus and Aven. Chester was still. She'd barely been there to begin with.

"Was that... a prophecy?" Aven asked.

Jarrik searched Ayaba's face, checking the pulse in her neck and wrist. The old woman took in shuddering breaths. Ife hurried forward, and Maina shuffled out of the way.

"That hasn't happened in a long time," Jarrik said, giving the crocodile space to check on its azheek.

"But it... happens?" Veraion asked. Jarrik nodded.

"Why are prophecies always poems?" Aven muttered. "How is anyone supposed to remember that?"

"So there's a king?" Maina said. "Or there will be? Is it... one of us? One of you? The king?"

"You," Ayaba said weakly, taking Veraion's hand. "And you." She looked to Aven and Chester. "You are Carriers of the King."

Maina stared at them, at Chester, who seemed completely unmoved. If anything, she looked bitter.

"When is he coming?" Chester said, her words low, sceptical. "Your prophecy spoke of darkness. A *saviour* to bring us back to the light. Is the world dark enough yet? Or is it going to get worse?"

Maina's stare returned to the elder. Ayaba said nothing. Her eyes fluttered closed, leaving the others in silence.

* * *

Chester jolted awake. She sat up, closing her eyes, taking in slow, trembling breaths. It was warm inside the gangul, yet she had felt cold all night. Nearby, her friends were still asleep, all but Aven, watching her from his place. He desperately wanted to comfort her, to curl up with her and lick away her tears, but every time he got close, she moved away.

Chester clenched her jaw, fighting to find calm. She could feel him watching her.

Rising to her feet, she climbed from the gangul, into the lightening wood. Jarrik was seated at the base of a nearby tree, strumming a lute, singing lowly. He was wearing only pants and a loose shirt, enjoying the cool morning air. She approached the man.

"How did you become Ayaba's protector?" Chester asked. "You seem to come from very different worlds."

He looked at her and smiled. "I don't know."

"You don't know?"

He put the lute aside and came to his feet, stretching. "There is a lot I don't know. I cannae remember my life before Ayaba."

"You don't ask? Surely she could answer that question."

"I don't want to know," Jarrik said. "Something in my mind severed those memories, and I think it's for a good reason."

She nodded, understanding. "Some things we're better off forgetting. I'm glad you found her—you seem to be happy, or at least… content."

"Safety in exchange for sanity. I haven't lopped off a head in a while."

Chester smiled a little. He watched her.

"I see it in you," he said. "There's madness in your eyes."

She smiled once more.

Chester gazed back to the fire gangul, monstrous and great, stretching through the woods.

"Does she know everything?" she asked. "Ayaba."

"Ayaba knows nothing. She knows only the answers to questions people ask. She cannae ask them herself, and I think once she has spoken, she forgets."

Chester nodded. "A strange life."

"We're all strange."

She smiled a little. "How long have you been here? How long will you stay?"

"We've been here a few days, maybe a week. And once we've collected all the firestones we'll be on our way. It's what we do."

She looked at him curiously.

"Every day I ask her," he said, "as she cannot ask herself. I ask where the next gangul will fall, and we go. I ask every day, as sometimes the gangul next to fall will move and we'll have to change directions. Air gangul are the worst for that."

"To collect the stones?"

He nodded.

"What do you do with them?"

"We return them to Ianar. Firestones we burn, earthstones we bury, airstones we take to the highest mountains, to where it's windiest. They deteriorate on their own."

"Why? They'll return to their element regardless."

He gave her a look. She nodded knowingly.

"Humans," she said.

"Mhm."

Chester gazed at the fallen gangul—great, otherworldly. An immense beast of power and purity, untainted by free will.

"I wonder..." she said. "If we left the firestones for the baraduhr, if they would stop trying to steal power from azheeks."

"You know they wouldn't."

She smiled bitterly—it was slight, but it was there.

"The symbols on Ayaba's hands," she said. "Do they mean anything?"

"Ayaba is a guardian. Of the gangul. Or at least, of the elements they leave behind. It is why we do what we do."

"Did she choose this life?"

He looked at her, curious. "It is an honour to be a guardian. To be chosen by the gods."

"Yeah, but did she choose it? Who was she before she was a guardian?"

Jarrik blinked, clenching his jaw for a moment as he pondered the question.

"Does *she* even know who she was before?" Chester asked. "Did she want this? Or did the gods choose this?"

He chuckled. "You ask very good questions. The kinds of questions that could piss off a god."

She smiled a little.

They stood together, gazing at the gangul. They could hear that her friends were awake now, their voices muffled as they rested inside.

"You don't remember anything?" she asked quietly. "About who you were?"

Jarrik looked at her a moment and then pushed up his sleeves. Tattoos marked his arms. Old tallies that were messy and blurred, more so on one side than the other. They were more organized and parallel on his left arm, untidy and chaotic on the right.

"These," he said, "cover me entirely."

Chester looked at him, then back to his arms. "You did them to yourself."

"You think?"

"Are you right-handed?"

"I am."

She nodded. "You did them to yourself."

He smiled a little. "And why do you think I did that?"

Chester thought for a moment. She glanced at him, curious. "Why do *you* think you did that?"

"Well... perhaps I was counting kills."

She nodded a little, but the smile on her lips told him she didn't agree.

"And what do you think, Chester?"

She let out a soft sigh, unsure as to whether or not she should say. "I think you were captive somewhere. I think you had a window. You could see when the sun rose and set. And you marked yourself to count the days. To try and remember. To stay sane. And when you ran out of space on your left arm, and stomach, and legs, you had to use your left hand."

Jarrik was silent. Then he pulled up his shirt, pushing down his belt just a little. The tallies covered his stomach and disappeared into his pants. He turned slightly to show her that they didn't reach his back.

Chester looked at him, at his black eyes, at the distant madness in his stare.

"I think you're right," he said. "And that... that is not a life I want to remember."

She nodded. "You've thought about it before, haven't you?"

"I have. And Ayaba tells me that when I think about it too much, I remember. And I lose my mind. And she has to make me forget."

Chester clenched her jaw and nodded. Quiet. Solemn.

"There is something you want to forget, isn't there?" he said.

Chester said nothing. She took in a quiet breath and then looked at him. She smiled sadly. But the smile faded away and her eyes were cold. Her voice came low. "I don't want to forget."

The Highlander watched her. He smiled. "I pity the fool that gets in your way."

She smiled. It was slight and would have been unnerving if the man she shared it with wasn't already half mad.

There came a distant tinkling through the woods, and they looked over to see Ayaba approaching through the trees, the great crocodile Ife by her side. She had a basket with her, carrying herbs, and behind them followed two draught horses, pulling a heavily adorned caravan. Tapestries and blankets draped the carriage, so covered that barely any wood was exposed. The caravan tinkled and chimed as much as Ayaba did. Once more she was wearing gloves, hiding the symbols upon her hands.

"Good morning, my children," she said. It seemed as though she had already forgotten what happened the night before.

"Who are the Fen?" Chester asked. Ayaba stopped what she was doing and looked at the redhead sharply.

"What?"

"The Fen. From the prophecy last night."

"We do not speak of the Fen," she hissed. Chester scanned her face.

"You're afraid. The Fen frighten you."

Ayaba almost snarled at her, turning away, but Chester followed.

"They killed the Five, didn't they?" she pressed. "Who were they? How did they do it? Surely the Five—"

"We do not speak of the Fen." Ayaba rounded on her. "For what they did was unforgivable. For what they did, they are gone from history. Do not ask me about the Fen again."

Chester scanned her face, reading the fear in her golden-green eyes. "You're terrified."

Ayaba tried to stand her ground.

"And that kind of fear…" Chester said. "That means they're still here."

Ayaba didn't react, refusing to, but Chester smiled a little, in disbelief. "The Fen are still here."

"We do not speak of the Fen," Ayaba hissed. "Do *not* speak of the Fen."

"Okay. Where is Aion?"

"What?"

"Aion. Where we will find Ilia."

Ayaba squinted at her, taking in a deep breath as though searching. "The answer you seek lies within the Heart of Sontar Ivel. That is all I hear."

"Sontar Ivel," Chester repeated. "We have to go back. To Sontar Ivel."

"The Heart of Sontar Ivel."

Chester sighed, looking to the woods with a bitter smile. Ayaba's piercing gaze didn't leave her. The old woman watched her, eyes scanning her face.

"There is a power within you," Ayaba said. "An unstoppable force. You are capable of so much good. And so much bad."

Chester held her gaze, a distant look of madness in her eyes. When she replied, the words were soft, simple. "I know."

Ayaba's jaw clenched. Chester held her gaze and then cast Jarrik one last look, with a slight smile, and headed back for the opening in the gangul.

"We have to go back to Sontar Ivel."

Maina's face fell. "*What?*"

CHAPTER 16
SISTERS

By the time the travellers laid their eyes on the great walls of Sontar Ivel, Aven's hair had returned to white. Veraion's wounds from his stabbing, capture, and subsequent branding had almost healed, but the only healing had been physical. Maina's and Theideus's spirits were only more bleak, and all the while, Chester barely spoke. Ayaba had given them a firestone each, and while Veraion clutched his for warmth, it couldn't help the chill he felt whenever he looked at Chester.

They waited for the dead of night before sneaking through the southern entries, through the sleeping gate city, into fields of green. They made camp in the woods, and as Chester sat by a small fire, blinking slowly at the flames, the two former innkeepers gazed at the familiar city. They watched bioluminescent rivers and dancing fireflies, the sight so beautiful it brought tears to Maina's eyes. If Ayaba was right, she would never see this again.

"I guess this is it," she murmured. "The last time I'll see the city."

Theideus wrapped his arms around her and she smiled sadly, resting her head on him.

Back at the fire, the wasfought sat across from Chester. He wanted to be beside her, but every time he tried, she moved. Veraion was tending to the horses, and he glanced at the two of them. He too didn't know what to do.

Maina and Theideus returned to the fire, taking their places. Eventually they huddled near the flames. Maina and Theideus fell asleep, soon followed by Veraion. As the night crept on, Chester managed to nod off, curled up in a ball as though she were freezing.

Aven watched her from where he lay. He wanted to be with her so badly.

He got up and headed away, padding through the trees. The breeze flowed through his mane, swaying thick fur about his body, and as he walked, moving further and further away from where his friends were sleeping, he felt a tingle in his paws. When he took in a deep breath, he smelled it.

Flowers. Expensive oils.

Einmyria.

Aven inched forward. There she was, asleep in their old clearing. She was wrapped in furs to keep warm in the steadily changing winds.

Aven stayed where he was. Watching. She was so beautiful, so frail. So sad. He could feel the sadness wafting from her sleeping form, so vulnerable in the woods. By now the beasts of Sontar Ivel would know he no longer claimed the clearing his territory.

He didn't know what to do. So he sat there, watching her. Sadly.

Then he was nudged by a nose and nearly leapt out of his skin. Einmyria's horse.

He stared at the stallion in shock. He had never known a horse that didn't bolt upon first sight of a wasfought, let alone be brave enough to nudge one. But he pushed away his surprise and returned the greeting, sharing a moment with the stallion.

Then the horse snorted nervously, eyes wide. Aven smelled it too. Another wasfought.

Immediately he stood in front of the stallion, looking to the clearing. A she-wasfought, creeping towards Einmyria. The she-wasfought had light brown fur and pale markings, and she snarled at Aven, claiming her prey. He growled, hackles rising.

The two wasfoughts glared at each other from opposite sides of the clearing. The other beast stepped forward, letting out a sharp growl. She was just as big as him.

Aven reared onto his hind legs and morphed. His muscles stretched and bones crunched, arms and legs extending. As he took on a form somewhere between man and beast, the she-wasfought took a step back. But the growling in her stomach consumed her. She had to feed.

She took another step towards Einmyria.

Aven leapt forward and collided with the beast, throwing her from the clearing. Einmyria woke immediately, heart thundering in her chest, but the wasfoughts had disappeared from sight.

Beast and mutant were sent howling, roaring, biting, and clawing at each other, crashing through the woods. Aven was trying to get the fight as far away from Einmyria as possible.

By the time the two wasfoughts pulled apart, both were bleeding heavily. The she-wasfought growled, hackles on end. She charged, roaring as they collided once more. Aven's body morphed as he battled, arms and legs changing as he warred with the creature. He grabbed her and threw her off.

"Go," he snarled. "Please."

But she refused to admit defeat and charged.

Aven grabbed her by the neck and slammed her to the ground, sinking his teeth into her throat, tearing.

He stood in the night, the crisp wind ruffling his thick fur. All that could be heard was the rustle of leaves, his low growls, and the she-wasfought beneath him as she drowned in her own blood.

Aven lowered to his knees, morphing into a human.

"I'm sorry," he rasped. He took her head into his hands and snapped her neck.

Aven remained in place, his great chest rising and falling. Placing a bloody hand on her body, he ran his touch over her matted fur, from her head down her gaping neck. But when it reached her stomach, he froze. His eye widened.

"No… no, please, *no!*" He tore her gut open. Blood and guts spilled from her, and so did a cub.

He staggered back in horror. The puppy moved ever so slightly in its umbilical sack, its heart slowing in the cold air. It was too small.

Aven shook as he reached forward and picked it up. It was barely as big as one of his hands. Tears streamed down his cheek, throat tightening and stomach churning. He cut through the slimy sack and looked at the cub's tiny face.

Life left the baby. Its soft stirring ceased, leaving it still in his hands.

Aven shook uncontrollably. He pulled the puppy close, holding it to his chest, fighting the urge to scream. But he couldn't hold it in. He let out a blood-curdling cry.

His grief cracked like a whip through the night, the roar travelling for miles. As his call came to an unsteady end, he raised the pup, touching its forehead to his as he cried.

* * *

Sunrise came and the others waited for Aven, not knowing where he had gone. They rose to their feet as they saw him through the trees.

His movements were slow. He was covered in blood, new gashes gaping across his body, hair streaked and stiff in reddened clumps. His legs trembled. In his hands he carried a bundle of bloody leaves.

The others watched him in alarm. He was still crying, unable to look away from the burden he carried.

Slowly he walked to Chester, and when he reached her, dropped to his knees. He swayed in place, holding out the bundle, unable to look her in the eyes. Fearfully she took it, pushing a leaf aside.

Her grief was instant. Tears filled her gaze, stabbing her heart.

Aven finally looked at her. She raised a trembling hand and slowly placed it upon his head, touching him for the first time in weeks.

He broke under her touch. He clutched her, shaking. Chester closed her eyes and finally held him back, resting her forehead upon his.

"I didn't know," he rasped. "I didn't know."

* * *

Aven and Chester buried the cub and its mother while the others snuck into the main city. She tended to his wounds, stitching them shut, applying a healing paste and wrapping them with what cloth they could spare.

By the time the others returned, the sun was inching for the horizon, turning the sky to a dancing myriad of colours. Chester was cradling Aven.

"Any luck?" she asked weakly. He was still trembling.

Veraion let out a dark sigh. "What did Ayaba say again?"

"Aion. The Heart of Sontar Ivel. She said she couldn't see any answers, but she saw, or heard, something about the Heart of Sontar Ivel."

"Well, I highly doubt we can break into the castle and not die."

"We have no idea if Aion is a person," Maina said with a sigh. "Or a place, or… a phrase. What if it's just a word?"

"You didn't find anything at all?" Chester said.

"Well, we found out that Athos won the tournament. Again." Veraion's words were bitter. "Good news is, nobody died, and only two of the contestants are still in hospital."

Maina gave him a look as though to say *I told you so*. But Chester and Veraion were exchanging a foreboding look.

"Aven, we have to ask Einmyria."

* * *

Aven moved through the woods, slowly, with a dark and distant look in his eye. He didn't want to do this. But he headed to Einmyria's clearing, and when he got there, she was waiting for him. Einmyria was seated in the grass, her blue cloak tinged slightly purple in the moonlight. Furs ruffled in the breeze, her nose pink.

Einmyria rose to her feet and he followed suit, transforming into a human.

A tear rolled down her cheek. He held his ground for a moment, fighting back his own pain, and when he moved forward, she trembled. Closer and closer, both upon shaking legs. He took her into his arms and she let go, giving in to her tears. Aven closed his eye, doing everything he could to fight back his own.

"I thought you'd never come back," she whispered. She pulled away to look at him, but he averted his stare. "What happened last night?"

"Nothing." His voice cracked.

"Aven."

He looked at her, tears slipping down his cheek. "I protected you. Again. And I killed for you. A mother and her child. I killed a mother and her child."

Einmyria tried to hold back her tears, but she couldn't. "You shouldn't have."

"Why do you keep coming here?" he said. "It's dangerous out here."

"I can't be in there anymore. I can't be… I can't be near him."

"What would have happened if I hadn't been here last night?"

"I would have died," she said simply.

"Is that why you come here? Are you trying to get yourself killed?"

She said nothing. He clenched his jaw, swallowing the knot in his throat, and looked away. He could feel how broken she was.

Einmyria reached into her cloak and pulled out a pomegranate flower, blooming even in the changing season. She smiled sadly and gave it to him.

"Thank you," she said softly. "For giving my life some light, even if it was for only a moment."

He took it, a tear sliding from his cheek to land on a petal.

"I need to ask you something," he said.

"Anything."

"Who is Aion? Or… where. Or what."

"I'm sorry, I've never heard of them. Or it. I'm sorry."

"You must."

"I haven't. Aven, I'm sorry."

"Don't lie to me." He snarled into his words, but the fear and desperation in his voice were stronger than the anger.

"What makes you think I would know?"

"You're a part of it," he rasped. "Whether you like it or not, whether you accept it or not, you're a part of it. The baraduhr. Venhel. Ehl. You're a part of it."

Tears slid down her cheeks, but she otherwise didn't react. She had accepted the truth, she just couldn't say it.

"I'm sorry," she said. "But I have never heard of Aion. My father never tells me anything. I'm his *little girl.*" Her last words were spiteful.

Aven clenched his jaw and sighed, turning away as he gruffly wiped his tears.

"Is that what you're here for?" she asked. He nodded. "And you'll leave when you're done?" He nodded once more.

Einmyria wiped her tears and took his hand, managing a smile. It was so sad, the saddest smile he had ever seen, but there was also light to it. She meant what she said. He had given her light, even if it had lasted only a moment.

"Goodbye, Aven." She smiled sadly. "Thank you for being there for me when you were."

"Don't," he choked.

"Let me say goodbye." She held his hand tighter, her fingers so small compared to his, and yet, beneath her touch, he had never felt more weak.

"Please," she whispered. "Let me say goodbye."

Aven leaned in, lower and lower until his lips were inches from hers.

"Thank you," she cried.

He placed his lips on hers, closing his eye. Her hands moved to his hair, clinging to him, longing, and he could taste the tears upon her lips as strongly as he felt the ache in her heart.

Aven let the flower fall to the floor and picked her up, wrapping his arms around her. Tears slid down his cheek, wetting her fingers as she caressed his face.

Aven lowered to his knees, her legs on either side of his own, his fingers pushing through her black hair. Einmyria pulled back, gently tracing the markings on his face.

"I loved you, you know," she said quietly.

"I loved you too."

He kissed her, grabbing her close, and she moved the fabrics of her dress until she was positioned on top of him. Slowly she lowered, her fingers digging into his shoulders, his own grasping her hair as he growled.

Einmyria wrapped her arms around him, her cheek brushing against his, and he buried his face into the crook of her neck, breathing in her scent for the last time.

* * *

The others waited in the rising sun, and when he approached, he looked dead. Broken.

"Any luck?" Maina asked.

"She doesn't know."

"She could be lying," Veraion pressed.

"She. Doesn't. Know," he snarled. "But her father might."

* * *

They waited until nightfall, and when the sun set and darkness spread, they headed for the main city. Maina and Theideus stayed in the woods, watching the horses, the other three travelling by foot to move as quietly as possible.

Hours passed as they walked, closer and closer to the castle. No horses, no running—no drawing attention. Their feet ached, but still they didn't stop, following Aven as he walked in the lead, hunched over, hood pulled low.

Further and further into the capital, closer and closer to the castle. From sand to dirt to cobblestones, the ground changed from lain brick to polished stone. They crossed bridges until they reached an island of mansions.

Veraion stared around the private island, following as Aven led them to the largest house of all.

"*natura's ma'ale, natur*," he murmured.

They moved into the darkness, standing near the outer stone walls.

"I can swing you over," Aven said. "Easiest way in."

Veraion nodded, and they peered around to ensure no one was there. Then Aven morphed into his mutant form and wrapped his arm around the man. He kicked off the floor and swung up, grabbing on to the wall, and tossed Veraion over the ledge. The man rolled into the fall, making almost no sound as he landed. Then Aven took Chester, bringing her with him as he jumped up and leapt over the wall. But when he let her go, she rolled back her shoulders, averting her gaze. Her body was reacting to his touch— to being touched at all. It made her skin crawl.

Veraion had his back pressed against a pillar, and moved in the shadows towards the mansion. Chester and Aven followed until they reached a set of large glass doors. Veraion dropped to his knees, slipping pins into the door locks. Click. Click. *Click.*

Carefully he opened the way, and one by one, they slipped inside.

They gazed around the vast hall. Even in the dead of night, with no fires lit, the space glimmered. There was no denying that Lord Venhel was one of the most wealthy men in all of Sontar Ivel.

Aven followed his nose, up the great stairs and to the second level. He could barely smell Einmyria anymore. She hadn't come here in weeks.

He ignored the distant scent of her flowers and instead followed the trace of her father, his oils mixed with myrrh, root of iris flower, and harsh cloves.

The smell led to a set of double doors, and Aven nodded to the others. He wrapped his hands around the handles, and slowly, quietly, he opened them. Veraion and Chester drew their weapons, their footfall silent as they slunk into the bedroom.

Venhel's chamber was twice the size of Einmyria's and just as lavish. His bed was gigantic, the carved headpiece bold and strong. Wasfought furs were draped over the foot of the bed, more stretching across the floors. Aven snarled.

The man was asleep in his bed, and the three took their places. Chester to one side, her back to the great windows, Veraion on the other, Aven looming at the foot.

Veraion grabbed Venhel by the cuff of his shirt and yanked him up, a sword pressed to his throat. The lord woke with a harsh grunt, eyes darting around in alarm.

"Morning, Venhel," Veraion hissed.

"*You.*"

Veraion pulled the sheets back and gruffly patted down the lord, checking for weapons. He was a fool to sleep so vulnerably.

Chester climbed onto the bed, sitting cross-legged beside the lord. Her weapon glowed eerily beside her, soft blue lights illuminating her skin.

"We have a few questions for you," Veraion said.

"I would rather die."

"You will. First, tell us about Aion."

Venhel's dark eyes squinted slightly. Then he laughed. "Aion died three years ago."

Veraion hadn't once looked away from Venhel, and his jaw was clenched, veins popping in his temples.

"You're lying," he snarled.

"Why would I lie when the truth is so sweet?" Chuckles sounded deep in Venhel's belly, and he leaned back, arms crossed behind his head.

Then he raised a hand, slamming a fist against the carved headboard. A piece of stone jutted into the wall. A horn blared.

Chester jumped, looking to the others with wide eyes.

"*Shit,*" Veraion snapped, and grabbed the man, raising his sword. But a window shattered and an arrow flew into his shoulder, causing him to drop the weapon. Before the others could blink, another flew into Chester's back.

Aven dove between her and the windows, five arrows spearing him down the torso.

The three yelled in pain and Veraion reached for his other sword, but as he grabbed it, he was sent back by more arrows.

Footsteps thundered through the house as guards charged towards the chamber.

"Fuck this," Chester snarled through bloody teeth, and grabbed her blades, plunging them into Venhel's gut. The lord shrieked.

In an instant the room swarmed with guards, their white-and-gold armour gleaming eerily in the light of the blood moon streaming in through shattered windows. As the queen's guard grabbed the intruders, Chester yanked her double-bladed sword from Venhel's stomach.

* * *

The sunrise flowed into Elaira's bedroom through a domed ceiling and open windows. Light cascaded in heavenly rays, particles of dust glimmering in the golden beams. Drapes and curtains flowed in the breeze, chandeliers twinkling as they swayed. Her bed was stationed on a raised platform, with furs and carpets pooling about the marble floor, her sheets and pillows haphazard.

Everything was white and gold. White. And gold.

Chairs and lounges were spread all through the chamber, but the queen never had company—none she desired. Tall bookshelves rose to the ceiling, but she already knew every book inside and out.

A tree rose through the room, winding roots breaking into the stone, branches reaching for the skylight, every leaf sighing in the morning sun. The tree was her favourite part of the room. For one, it wasn't white, nor gold. Even *brown* was a sight to see.

Elaira gazed out of a large window, blinking slowly as she watched the sun caress her city. She didn't want to step onto the balcony, for she would be seen and would have to put on a smile.

Her tanned skin looked golden in the morning light, illuminated by glimmering markings. White hair fluttered about her shoulders, white nightgown silky upon her skin, flowing about her legs.

Then came a knock at the door. The doors were large, heavy, and intricately designed, and whenever someone knocked, the low sound would echo around the chamber. Elaira loved the sound. It was one of the few things she could find comfort in.

She smiled to herself. "Come in."

The door opened. She loved that sound too. She loved how she could tell just how big the doors were without even looking over. Then the doors closed and she listened to the echo, not speaking until the moment passed.

"What is it?" she asked, turning around. Her eyes widened. "Einmyria!" She ran forward, pulling the woman into a hug. "How are you here?"

"Secret passageways." Einmyria smiled sadly. "Do you ever use them?"

"That's how I met you in the forest," she said. "But they've closed the ones I know. They figured out I was leaving."

"I'm sorry," Einmyria whispered. "I'm so sorry."

Elaira shook her head and pulled her back into a hug. "*I'm* sorry."

There they stood, holding each other, unable to make up for the years spent hidden behind lies and deceit. When they pulled apart, Einmyria smiled sadly, heartbroken.

"It was him, wasn't it?" she said. "My father."

Elaira's grief was instant. She tried to hold back her tears, fighting the knot in her throat, but Einmyria could see it clear as day. The terror in her sister's eyes. She nodded.

"I need your help."

The council hall was filled with guards. Chester, Veraion, and Aven were on their knees, arrows still protruding from their bodies. Their jaws were clenched, nostrils flared and glares seething as blood oozed from the wounds. Not a council member was in sight.

Then came footsteps approaching from outside.

Thump *clunk*. Thump *clunk*. Thump *clunk*.

The tall doors burst open and Lord Venhel limped in, his peg leg made of fine mahogany. He shook with every step.

Thump *clunk*.

His stomach was wrapped in gauze, already red.

Thump *clunk*.

He stared over the captives with madness in his eyes, residue upon his lips from the potions he had taken just to be able to stand.

"I'm going to make an example out of you," he snarled. "The whole city is going to watch as I have you gutted and quartered. Your heads will hang on spikes outside the castle gates."

The doors opened again and he turned to face the intruders. His face fell.

Einmyria, followed by the queen. They were flanked by maids and servers. By witnesses.

Elaira's gaze landed on Chester, eyes wide, flicking between the arrows protruding from the prisoners. Chester smiled sadly, as though to apologize.

"Einmyria." Venhel stared. "What are you doing—"

"Let them go," she said. All eyes turned to her.

"Einmyria, you have no place in the castle," her father warned.

"But I'm here. And I have brought the queen." She spoke quietly, calmly—contained. "She's in charge, is she not?"

The maids behind her looked at one another in confusion and fear. There was a familiar face there, the human Eidis.

Venhel's temples looked like they were about to burst. "*Einmyria.*"

"Siran is queen, is she not?" Einmyria held his gaze. She was speaking so softly, so devoid of any emotion.

Elaira stared between father and daughter, at his bleeding gut—at the bleeding prisoners.

"Einmyria," Venhel warned again, but she turned to Elaira.

"You are queen," Einmyria said. "It is your decision. Above all others. Above the lords and nobles. Above the council. I am asking you to let them go."

Elaira glanced at Venhel, who was turning purple.

"You say you once loved me as a sister," Einmyria said.

"I still do," she pressed. Einmyria smiled sadly.

"Then I beg of you, let them go." Einmyria returned her lifeless gaze to her father once more. "You killed her, didn't you? You killed my mother."

Venhel's face fell.

"You told me she was sick," Einmyria whispered. "But azheeks can't get sick. It was you, wasn't it?"

He was silent, frozen, and she smiled sadly. Her gaze was cold but upon her lips was a hint of satisfaction. As though to tell him that what was about to happen was his fault. His punishment.

"As my dying wish. Let them go."

Elaira's face fell. Before she could react, Einmyria drew a dagger—the dagger that had been meant for Veraion.

She plunged it into her own stomach.

All eyes widened, every heart stopping.

Einmyria tore the blade left, then right. Her organs came from her body. Lord Venhel screamed.

Elaira caught Einmyria as she fell, tears spilling from her eyes as she lowered her to the ground with shaking arms. Elaira's gasps echoed around the chamber, her cries ringing.

Venhel fell to his knees, eyes wide in horror.

Aven's single eye was fixed on Einmyria. Wide. Frozen. Unable to move. Unable to think. Unable to see anything but her. All he could smell was her blood and bile. Her intestines moved with every pained breath, the casings pink and slimy, riddled with dark veins. They slid from her gaping stomach to the marble floor. Her hands were lost among the mess, red, bloodied, too weak to move. With every rasping breath, her skin opened. With every rasping breath, he could see her diaphragm. Expanding and contracting in her stomach. Blood burst from her mouth as she coughed, trying to speak, but no words could come. Her breaths were loud, pained, wet as she choked. Her once olive skin looked grey and pallid, her hazel eyes glazing over, and as she drew in one last, shaking breath, he felt her life leave.

The queen shook in her place. Her white nightgown had turned red, hands slippery with blood.

"No!" Venhel screamed. "No! *Einmyria!*"

But she was gone.

Elaira knelt in blood. There was a long moment of haunting silence before Venhel's voice ruptured through the marble hall.

"Guards! Seize them! Brand them! *I want them dead!*"

His guards drew their weapons. Elaira rose to her feet.

Her eyes turned white. Light filled her gaze, billowing from the sockets. Her once glimmering markings filled with a white blaze, pulsing over her body with the slamming beat of her heart. She threw her hand forward, fingers outstretched, and yelled.

Everyone flew back. The guards blasted from the prisoners, crashing to the ground—into the statues of the Five. The maids careened from their places, striking against walls, falling to the ground unconscious. And the prisoners flew, colliding with stone thrones.

Chester gasped, shaking her head in pain, but looked to where the guards were lying. They had been holding their weapons, and her polearm now lay dejected on the ground, Veraion's swords nearby.

Elaira turned her stare to Venhel, and he gasped, clutching at his neck.

"They are free to go," she said. Her voice was distant and eerie, echoing through the marble hall. Chester slowly reached for her blade, wrapping her hand around the hilt. Veraion took his swords back into possession.

"Siran," Venhel choked. "These criminals—"

A tear slid down her cheek, illuminated by the lights on her skin.

"Einmyria was my only friend," she said. "And because of you, I lost her. Because of you, she was alone. Because of you, I will never see her again."

"Siran—"

"*My name is Elaira,*" she hissed, rounding on him. "And I will honour my sister's dying wish."

Elaira released Venhel from her magic and he fell to his knees, gasping for breath. He winced from the pain stabbing his gut, his own blood oozing from the gauze, saliva dripping from his lips as his breaths drew in like screams. Guards were rising from the ground, staggering towards their weapons.

"Get them!" Venhel rasped. "*Get them!*"

Elaira leapt over Einmyria's corpse, running towards the prisoners. "Hold hands! *Now!*"

Chester grabbed the men beside her as the guards rushed forward, but Elaira was faster, throwing herself at the three.

In a burst of white light, they were gone.

Light flashed through the woods. Chester, Veraion, and Aven fell to the ground, Elaira collapsing to her knees. Blood spilled from her nose, bursting from her mouth as she coughed.

"Elaira!" Chester gasped, rushing forward, but Elaira raised a hand to keep her away.

"Go," she rasped, shaking. "Leave!"

Tears spilled from her eyes. Pain shot through her body, her chest heaving as she fought to control it.

Veraion ran to the edge of the woods. They were outside the city, Maina, Theideus, and their horses still within the walls. He placed his fingers to his mouth and whistled, loud, knowing the horses would answer the call.

"Go!" Elaira pleaded. Goosebumps crawled over her skin, her arms shaking as she keeled over on the ground.

"I will come back for you," Chester said. "Elaira." The queen looked at her, gasping in pain. "I will come back for you."

Elaira smiled through her cries and shook her head.

Light shot through her body, uncontrolled—uncontrolled by her. She screamed, her face screwed up in agony, and in a burst of white light, she disappeared. All that remained were tiny lights and her blood on the ground.

* * *

Athos's eyes rested on the south, on the woods beyond the wall. He stood on his balcony, naked, knuckles pressing into the stone banister. His nostrils flared, a snarl upon his lips. Strands of his hair flowed in the breeze, the rest too thick to move.

A woman, a fire azheek, came from his room, leaning against the balcony doorway. She was naked too, her long orange hair flowing in the breeze. The drapes cascaded around her, sheer fabric tickling her radiant skin. She had been there since the night before, seemingly unable to leave.

"My champion," she sighed. He glanced at her over his shoulder, and the harshness in his stare did not falter.

The woman came forward, running her fingers over the valleys of his back. Her other hand moved to his front, caressing his chest. She kissed his shoulder. His gaze returned to the woods.

The woman looked to the city across the water. There were people there. "They're watching." She smiled. He ignored her.

She started kissing his arm, pushing his hair over his shoulder, freeing the way to his neck. She kissed that too.

Then another pair of hands were on him, another woman. Another fire azheek. This woman had dark red hair, and her touch roved over him hungrily. She too looked at the people below, a smile crawling over her lips.

"Come back to bed," she fawned.

He didn't respond, nor did he move or react even slightly. Their hands caressed him, worshipping every exaggerated muscle, dancing over his chest hair to follow the trail down his stomach, lower and lower, until they started stroking him.

The women looked at each other, glancing to the city people with a smirk. They were proud that they had slept with the champion, taking the time to boast.

The woman with dark hair lowered to her knees, positioning herself in front of him, and she kissed him between the legs, licking, sucking. The first woman continued her kisses over his muscles.

Athos didn't move. His dark gaze remained on the trees. The sounds of the woman sucking him off barely made it to his ears.

Then one of his hands moved to her hair. She smiled, moaning as he finally paid her a semblance of attention. He grabbed a fistful of her hair and shoved her lower onto his cock, and when she choked, he pulled out and walked back to his room.

The chamber was huge, made from marble, but it wasn't nearly as decorated as the queen's room. Far more bare. In fact, it didn't look lived in. His large bed was on a raised platform, and the messy sheets were the only sign that he had spent time in the room at all. Another fire azheek was lying on it, watching him with a hungry smile as he entered.

He walked past her, through a large doorway to the bathroom. Columns lined the walls, and through the middle of the chamber was a large bath, sunken into the floor. Sunlight reflected off the water to send dancing colours across the marble. There was a sink against the wall, and he leaned on the edge, running the tap. Partly to get water, partly to drown out the women's voices in the next room.

Athos splashed water over his face, running a hand over the back of his neck. It trickled down his skin, and he watched in the mirror as the droplets ventured down his body, over every scar and burn, stopping at the largest mar that scored across his stomach. His dark gaze flicked up to meet his eyes. One as beautiful as the sea, the other pale and milky. He looked at the burns that covered his face. The sight had once made him angry, unbelievably so. It had driven him mad for so many years, but now, looking at them, he almost smiled.

Athos splashed more water onto his back before returning to the bedroom. He didn't care to notice where any of the women were, and he sat at the edge of his bed, craning his neck to the left, then the right. The bed sank with the weight of more people climbing onto it, and soon hands were on him again. Touching. Always. Touching.

Some massaged his shoulders. That was fine. Some stroked his muscles. That was fine. And some moved back between his legs.

Kisses were placed across his body, and as a pair of lips moved their way up his neck, they trailed to his jaw. Athos pulled his head away, finally looking at whoever it was that tried to kiss him on the mouth. The look he gave her was not kind. But he was the undefeated champion of Sontar Ivel, and she didn't care. He hadn't kissed a single one of them.

She started kissing him elsewhere.

Athos sat there, hands all over him.

He heard a scream. It was muffled, from somewhere else in the castle. It wasn't loud, very quiet in fact, but he had heard it many times. The cries continued.

One woman was kissing his back, another with her lips upon his shoulder, the third between his legs, head bobbing up and down.

This was it. This was all they wanted. All they ever wanted.

He clenched his jaw, glaring down at the one between his legs. "Don't touch me."

The women stopped. The one he looked at pulled back. The one behind him did too. But the one to his right did not.

"Athos," she cooed. "Let us please you."

The muscles in his jaw popped as his teeth ground. The other two backed off. The redhead beside him smiled, kissing his shoulder, and her hand moved to caress his face.

He grabbed her by the arm, hand shaking. "Don't. Touch—"

Her bones snapped. She screamed.

"Ah, shit."

The woman shrieked, falling back as she clutched her broken arm, eyes wide as she cried.

"You bastard!" She stared. "You—you—" But her voice was silenced as she went into shock, her eyes rolling back in her head.

Athos left the room.

He moved through the castle with water and saliva dripping down his body. He walked past guards—no maids working on these floors. They had all been ordered to leave. They couldn't overhear her screaming.

He moved towards the distant cries, away from the ones in his chamber, towards the screams he had heard so many times.

Athos walked up winding stairs until he reached the queen's doors, and with a shove, they opened.

A group of guards were towering around her, kicking, beating with the pommels of their swords, one man with a whip. Elaira was on the floor, in a bloody nightgown, her own red soaking into the fabric.

"That's enough," Athos said. The guards glanced at him.

"We were told to beat her," one said.

"And you beat her."

"Venhel—"

"There are three women in my chambers. Get rid of them."

They stood up straight, nodding quickly. "Yes, my lord."

His dark gaze followed them until they were gone and the door was shut. He looked at the woman on the ground. She stayed there, quivering. She looked at him through her bloody hair, bordering on a glare.

"I hope you don't expect me to say thank you," Elaira hissed. He merely held her gaze.

Slowly she rose to her feet, swaying, staggering, and had to brace herself on a footstool. Then she sat on it, closing her eyes. She was doing everything she could to stop herself from crying. But the tears came.

"I don't want to be here," she whispered. "I hate this place."

"You can't go anywhere else, you know that."

"Then take me… to a different… fucking room. At least."

Athos moved forward and picked her up, carrying her battered form from her quarters. He walked through the castle, burdened by the bloody queen. Guards averted their stares, saying nothing.

The walk was silent. She closed her eyes, imagining she was somewhere else. Anywhere else.

When Athos reached his chambers, the three fire azheeks were gone.

Shutting the door behind him, he yanked the barricade in place and carried the queen to the bathroom. He lowered her to her feet, and she leaned against the marble sink for support. Disappearing into the other room for a moment, he returned with a dagger and began cutting the blood-soaked dress from her body. She stood still, letting him.

The fabric clung to her, and when he peeled it away, it made her shudder. She trembled as the sodden silk was removed, and he tossed the bloody rags aside. He looked up at her from where he was crouched.

Elaira gazed past him. He stood up. She still didn't look at him.

"You're not in your room anymore," Athos said. "Your bloody dress is gone. Shall I finish?"

She looked dead, blinking slowly, but nodded.

Athos picked her up once more and carried her to the bath, walking down the stone steps until water reached his stomach. He lowered her, and her breath hitched when water touched her wounds.

Blood trailed from her, spreading into the bath. Gradually she took a seat on the steps.

Reaching for a basket nearby, Athos retrieved a washcloth and offered it to her. She sat there, still not looking at him. He let out a short sigh and started washing her himself. She winced when he brushed her cuts and bruises but otherwise didn't react.

Slowly blood came from her body, washing away until the only red that remained on her skin was her own. Athos was gentle when he wiped the blood from her face, from her nose and lips.

"I am a slave," Elaira whispered. Athos nodded.

"Yes."

Finally she looked at him. "You feel sympathy for slaves."

"Yes."

She held his gaze. He always looked at her so coldly, and yet, here in this moment, he was the only semblance of a friend she had.

"Why are you still here, Athos? Normally you leave as soon as the tournament ends."

He took a moment. Then he sat on the steps and leaned back, a slight smile residing on his lips as he gazed at the far wall. "I found what I was looking for."

She looked at him for a moment before returning her eyes to the water, watching as the red from her flesh mingled away. "Will I ever be free?"

He watched sunlight dancing upon the surface, upon the columns that lined the walls. It reminded him of a place he had once called home.

"You could free yourself," he said. "If you were willing to kill anyone in your way. If you were willing to let those you love die. If you were willing to never see home again. If you were willing to let your city burn."

She smiled sadly, and a tear slid down her cheek. "Then I will never be free."

CHAPTER 17
NORTH-EAST

The fugitives rode from Sontar Ivel, heading back in the direction whence they had just come. Aven was as unresponsive as Chester now.

North-east, towards the mountains. Towards the empire of Zalfur. The weather only got worse and worse the closer they inched to the icelands.

They reached the fallen fire gangul, but Ayaba, Jarrik, and the great crocodile Ife were long gone. All but a few firestones had been taken. The few that remained were stuck in the topmost areas, impossible to reach.

The travellers took refuge in the gangul's warmth for only a night.

On they rode, through wind, rain, and hail. When they neared towns, they rode past, camping in the woods. Maina and Theideus stared longingly at the firelight coming from inside homes but never said anything, following the others on their journey.

This night was the same, camped in the woods by a town, unable to make a fire, unable to draw attention to themselves. If the air wasn't cold enough, the rain certainly made it so.

Theideus leaned against a tree, watching the village, watching firelight glow from the windows.

"I could really use some hot food right now," Maina murmured at his side. Theideus nodded. She looked at him. He was shivering.

Maina wrapped her arms around him and he smiled, closing his eyes. Her warmth spread through his body, and for a moment he stopped quaking.

"What's it like?" she asked. "Feeling cold. It's been so long for me, I've forgotten."

He gave her a look. *Not good.*

She gazed over her shoulder to where Veraion was huddled in a ball at the base of a tree, clutching a firestone for warmth. Aven and Chester were nearby, though both were silent.

"Veraion," Maina called. "Do you think we're far enough from Sontar Ivel? I have some money—I'll pay for a room at an inn."

"It's risky," he said. "They may have already sent wanted posters."

"I'm not on them."

"You might be now. But it's your call. We'll be here in the morning."

She looked at Theideus. "Maybe just food? Ducking in for dinner should be fine."

He nodded, and she looked back at Veraion, but he had already returned to his ball of misery, clutching the firestone to his chest.

Maina and Theideus headed into town, following signposts until they found the local tavern, ducking into the warmth. They stood by the door, soaking in things they had once taken for granted. Wood floors, walls, a ceiling. Shelter. Torches. Paintings. They could hear talk from within the tavern, but with nobody in the entrance area, Theideus quickly waved his hand over Maina and pulled all the rain from her sodden hair and clothes. He cast the water aside, then dried himself off.

They headed into the tavern, breathing deeply, inhaling the smell of hot food. Roast meat and vegetables.

Theideus took a seat at a far table while Maina headed to the bar, ordering tankards of ale and food for two. She spoke with the barmaid, pointing to their table at the back. A man at the bar glanced at her, and as she headed back to Theideus with their drinks, he nudged his friend. The two men watched her go.

Maina sat opposite Theideus, and as they drank, their eyes closed in glee. Soon their food arrived and they inhaled it.

"Is it just me, or is this the best food you've ever tasted?" Maina sighed. Theideus smiled. "I'm not fit for this," she said. "Life on the road. Running. Hiding. Camping in the woods. I'm not cut out for it." She let out a sigh. "I miss it. I miss Sontar Ivel. I miss *home*."

Theideus reached across the table and took her hand. He did too, and she could tell from the look on his face. They had to leave everything behind; all they had of their old lives was the clothes upon their backs, weathered and torn from their travels.

"We have to live in Zalfur now," she murmured. "What… what are we going to do? I mean, they have inns… right?"

He gave her an unsure look.

"Do you think all Zalfuri are like Lord Ezaria? He's very…" She made an uncomfortable face. Theideus only returned the look. "Of all the places," she said, "we're going to the floating hunk of ice."

He grimaced. They ate the rest of their food in silence.

"I'm going to use their bathroom," Maina eventually said. "I've missed bathrooms."

She moved away as Theideus snorted silently, and he collected their dishes and cutlery before heading to the bar. He returned the items to the barmaid, gazing around the tavern one last time.

The two men that had been seated at the bar were gone. But he swore they had just been there. They had to have left when he was collecting the dishes. When Maina left.

His eyes widened. He turned to the barmaid, waving to get her attention, and mouthed the word *bathroom*.

"Through the entrance area," she said. "To the left, down the hall."

Quickly he followed her instructions, heart hammering in his chest. He moved down the hallway and froze.

Wanted posters. Veraion. Chester. Aven. Himself. *Maina*.

He ran, kicking open the bathroom door to see the two men grabbing her. One of them had his hand over her mouth, the other trying to tie her hands behind her back. She was crying, one arm bent in a way it shouldn't be bent, her shoulder dislocated, yanked out of the socket. Flames flickered over her skin, but one of the men was a fire azheek and he was snuffing her out. They froze when they saw Theideus.

"Look, mate, we don't want no trouble," one said.

"Hold on—isn't he on the posters too?"

Theideus's gaze moved between the two, and calmly, he closed the door behind him. The men let go of Maina, drawing daggers, and she fell to her knees, shaking.

"Watch it," one of the men snarled. "There's two of us and one of you."

Theideus locked the door.

They charged.

Theideus stepped to the side, swerving the first attack, weaving past another. A dagger came pelting at him but he blocked the man's forearm with his own, knocking the knife from his grip, sending it flying with an effortless swipe of his hand.

Theideus fought swiftly, calmly, every movement graceful like a flowing river. He never attacked, only defended, and didn't attempt to hurt either of the men. He barely moved, his smaller, more contained actions so different from the way the two men lunged and swung.

He parried them both back until they fell to the walls. The fire azheek raised his hand, sending a blast of flames, but Theideus returned the attack with a downpour of water, showering him so hard it felt like a bitch-slap.

Theideus moved over to Maina, but one of the men lunged at him from behind, planting a dagger in his back.

Theideus yelled, but no sound emitted from his lips.

He spun around, demeanour returning to calm as he looked at the attacker. His expression was retained, but behind his blue eyes was a new emotion. Up until now he had only been defending. But with a blade in his back, he was done.

Theideus wheeled around, ramming his elbow into the azheek, and he grabbed the man's arm, raising it, slamming an open palm against his ribcage. The man staggered backwards, clutching at his chest, and collapsed against a wall, gasping for breath. His heart had stopped beating.

Then Theideus turned around and grabbed the other by the neck, raising him off the ground. The human choked, coughing.

The coughing was wet.

As he wheezed, his face turning purple, water rose from his throat. Theideus's eyes were livid, his stare fixed on the man he held at his mercy. Water welled in the human's lungs, rising up his trachea, spilling from his mouth. His eyes were popping, veins bursting.

Theideus held him there, watching as he drowned. Eventually he stopped moving.

Slowly the water azheek lowered him. Then he let go and the corpse landed with a wet thud.

He turned to Maina. She was frozen, watching him fearfully. He scanned her face timidly.

"*I'm sorry*," he mouthed.

"Have you always… You can… fight…"

He nodded. "*Are you okay?*"

She nodded, however slight. Theideus pointed to her dislocated shoulder. She let out a pained sigh and nodded again.

Taking her by the arm, he looked at her once more, and she clenched her jaw, closing her eyes. He shoved her arm back into place. Maina cried loudly, gasping in pain, and clutched her shoulder. Trembling, she tried to calm herself.

Slowly she came to her feet, and when Theideus offered a hand, she took it. They left the bathroom, leaving behind the corpses, and solemnly headed back for the freezing rain.

* * *

On they rode, every one of them with dampened spirits. Veraion was looking like his old self, dishevelled and unkempt. The sky changed from blue to grey, and as they grew closer and closer to the mountains, they could hear the distant whistle of wind—the whispers of winter.

They rode until Veraion slowed his mare, and the others followed suit. The sky was filled with grey clouds, and they knew they would be in for another night of rain. At least they had a few hours until then.

"Are we going to the Cradle?" Maina asked. "Can you feel it?"

"Luckily we're not," Veraion said. "The Cradle is still directly north of Sontar Ivel. Zeda used to be above it, in the sky, but Zeda has moved east since then. I've been near to the Cradle only once before, and my powers were weak back then, but I could still feel the overwhelming death. It's... not a place anyone would want to go."

Their horses walked now, slowly through the cold.

"Is it called the Cradle because of all the... dead children?" Maina asked.

"Originally it earned the name because of the vast crater in the land where the city of Zeda was uprooted and brought to the sky, looking like a cradle in mountains, but now..."

Maina nodded. Veraion pulled a firestone from his pocket and rubbed it in his hands, fighting to feel a hint of warmth.

There came the soft flutter of wings, and he looked up just in time to see a barn owl land in a nearby tree. It turned its gaze to Veraion. Then it took off.

Aven's hackles rose just as Veraion's brow furrowed and he turned towards the trees, reaching for a sword.

"God fucking damn it," he muttered. Maina's face fell.

"What? *What?*"

He passed Theideus one of his swords, and she stared at them with wide eyes.

People came through the trees, surrounding them. Humans. Twenty, thirty, maybe more, dressed in furs of browns, greys, and blacks, holding swords, axes, and crossbows. Chester clenched her jaw, her expression cold, and drew her weapon.

"Headhunters," Veraion snarled. Chester came from her horse.

"You're surrounded," a woman called. "We know how this ends. No point in drawing it out."

Chester tore forward. She ran, not even drawing a weapon, and the headhunters fired their arrows. She dove down, rolling across the ground. Her arrow wound from Sontar Ivel ached in her back, but she snarled into the agony, allowing shockwaves to shoot through her body, using the pain as an excuse for the tingling in her hands.

She leapt up, drawing her polearm, and sliced a head from its neck.

Aven leapt from his stallion and hurtled towards the nearest headhunters, his body morphing as he went.

Mayhem flooded the trees. Veraion yelled, commanding the horses to get away from the fight, and when he jumped to the ground, Theideus followed. The horses bolted, taking Maina with them. She screamed, throwing fire where she could, but her shoulder was still healing and her mobility was restricted.

Aven ripped humans to shreds, Veraion and Theideus slicing off heads and limbs, moving swiftly. But Chester was hacking people apart.

Blood covered her already, and though she mowed through her attackers as easily as she once did, her breathing was different. Her breaths were shallow, fast, her heart thundering in her chest.

A man grabbed her, spearing her to the floor, and she yelled, grappling across the earth. Their weapons tumbled away and he landed on top of her, hands around her neck. He was between her legs. She could feel him between her legs.

Chester shrieked. Fire burst from her body, and he fell back. She leapt onto him, slamming her fist into his face again and again. He yelled, sitting up, grabbing at her, but she sank her teeth into his neck.

The man screamed. Blood showered from his throat, bursting from his skin, flooding up her nose and into her mouth. The taste was rancid and bitter, the liquid thick and warm. As she tore away, she brought his flesh with her.

He fell to the ground screaming, clutching his neck. Chester spat, chunks of flesh splattering his body, and she grabbed his ear, tearing it from his head. He shrieked.

Her hands were shaking, her vision almost blurry. But she saw the glowing lights of her steel and tore forward, grabbing it back into possession.

Veraion slammed his head into a hunter's, swinging his sword as they staggered back, and when their entrails showered the earth, he moved to the next. He ran forward, dropping to the ground, sliding through a swarm of headhunters to slice the legs of multiple men and women, kicking another in the knee to bend their leg backwards.

Theideus spun through the trees, his hair whipping behind him as he went, every move graceful. He ducked and parried every swing, movements a clean, calculated dance. His kills were neat and precise, skin slit just deep enough to sever arteries, and he'd move on to the next.

Aven left a bloodbath in his wake. He tore limbs from bodies and heads from necks, ripping out entrails with a single swipe of his great claws. Everyone around him was fighting, doing what they could, and though they were making a massacre, they were surrounded. The headhunters were prepared.

Veraion yelled, stamping his foot down on a woman again and again, crying out as an arrow planted in his back. He was still recovering from the wounds of Sontar Ivel, and as he staggered forward, pain shot through him.

He found his footing just in time to stare into a pair of pale grey eyes that looked almost purple. A menacing mask of black and gold covered the woman's mouth, the nose hooked and snarling, teeth between man and fanged beast.

Fang'ei.

She was dressed in black from head to toe, adorned with gold embroidery. Furs and feathers ruffled about her shoulders, a balaclava beneath the mask to protect her neck. All that could be seen was her black hair, long and straight, a fringe covering her forehead. All that could be seen were her piercing almond-shaped eyes.

"*Move.*"

Veraion ducked as she threw a sword and it shot through the air, faster than a normal person could throw, landing with a loud crack in a man's skull. The human flew back from the force, brain splattering. She threw her second sword to fell another.

More figures zoomed down from the skies, dressed in black, moving so quickly they were barely visible. They fought with swords, scimitars, and polearms. One man, another Fang'ei, wielded bladed tonfas.

The Zalfuri moved through the air with such speed and precision, they were naught but shadows in the night. All that was seen was the moonlight reflecting off their blades, illuminating the furs and feathers draped over their bodies. Only their piercing eyes could be seen, every pair a shade of grey.

Of the Zalfuri, there were only two Fang'ei—only two adorned with gold, two that moved faster than the others, every hit a precise kill, every hit landing stronger.

Human after human fell to the ground, blood soaking the earth.

The last thing the headhunters would see was naught but shadows. That, or the haunting masks of the Fang'ei, designed to instil fear, designed so any who fell before the feet of Ezaria's finest would fall in terror.

The headhunters stood no chance against the Zalfuri, against the two masked Fang'ei that moved through headhunters with ungodly speed.

The woman wielded her dual blades and the man his tonfas, kicking off trees and flying through the air, and in seconds, it was over.

The Zalfuri zoomed back into the skies, gone in an instant, all but for the Fang'ei.

The woman raised her hands and her swords yanked from corpses, zooming into her grasp. She threw her arms down, blood flying from the blades, cleaned in one swift motion. She returned them to the sheaths strapped in an X across her back.

She drew away her mask and pulled down her balaclava.

The azheek was in her prime, face round, nose, mouth, and chin fairly small. Her face had a naturally kind build to it, but the black tattoos on her cheeks, chin, and neck changed that. Tattoos to mimic the markings of Old.

"Vi'ra," Veraion said.

"Veraion." Her tone was as cold as her gaze.

Chester watched them, blood dripping down her chin and neck. She was trembling and had to turn away, clenching her jaw with her eyes shut tight.

Leaning against a tree for support, she forced her breaths in through her nose and out through her mouth. She could barely hold on to her weapon, her hands and feet tingling.

Vi'ra walked past Veraion, crouching by a corpse, going through the human's clothes.

The second Fang'ei put away his weapons and leaned against a tree, arms crossed, head cocked slightly. He pulled off his mask but the balaclava remained. His shoulder-length wavy black hair was half tied up, strands falling about his blue-grey eyes, which rested on Veraion. He too did not have a kind look in his gaze.

"You're late," Vi'ra said as she worked, not looking at the earth azheek.

"We had to go back," he said.

"I told them you would be late. You never did take to obeying orders, let alone a favour."

She rose to her feet and returned her icy gaze to Veraion. The barn owl soared through the trees and landed on her shoulder. Both air azheek and owl watched him, and it made him fidget in his place. He glanced at the man still watching him with crossed arms.

"I'm sorry," Veraion said. "I would have sent a message but I had no means."

Then the other Zalfuri returned, zooming through the forest canopy, one after the other.

"*Clear to the east,*" one said in Azheek.

"*Clear to the west.*"

"*Clear to the south.*"

"*Clear to the north.*"

Vi'ra nodded. "*At ease.*"

Once the squadron finished reporting, the man watching Veraion finally peeled himself from the tree, uncrossed his arms, and pulled down his balaclava.

He was in his prime, his face striking. Moonlight glistened upon his sharp cheekbones, and starting at the edge of his forehead, a tattoo lined the side of his face, encircling an eye and continuing down his cheek. Beneath his other eye was Azheek Sa'uri, stacked in two syllables, designed to look like a stamp upon his skin. *Fang'ei.*

He scanned Veraion up and down, his expression cold. "Veraion," he said.

"Nobaru."

Nobaru watched him, jaw clenching, but after a moment a smile crept onto his lips. The cold façade shattered as he started to laugh, a grin spreading from ear to ear.

"I can't," he cackled. "I fucking can't. Don't give me that shit."

Nobaru spread his arms wide and Veraion let out a laugh of relief, grabbing him into a hug. They held each other tight, and though they hadn't seen one another in over a decade, it was clear it didn't matter.

When they pulled back, they placed their foreheads together, eyes closed, drawing in deep breaths.

The others watched them. Vi'ra's jaw was clenched and she turned away, speaking to one of her soldiers in the old tongue.

When Nobaru opened his eyes, he clasped Veraion's face into his hands. He scoured over his features, studying every blemish, every scar, and every sign of ageing from having once had an ilis.

Nobaru kissed him on the cheek before muttering curses. "*mida'ar baba aishida.*" A kiss on the other cheek. "I ought to kill you." He planted one last, firm kiss on the forehead. Then he leaned back and smirked. "*natura's ma'ale, natur!* Age looks good on you."

Nobaru made a growling sound to express just how good he thought Veraion looked, and the man in question laughed.

"You haven't aged a day."

"Of course I haven't." Nobaru smirked. "Nobody is good enough."

Veraion smiled. There was a warmth in his heart he'd forgotten he could feel.

Some of the other Zalfuri greeted Veraion with waves or friendly nods, but most remained cold and distant. Still, they couldn't help but be amused by Nobaru's behaviour.

"Gods, it's so much easier to breathe down here," he murmured. "I feel as light as a feather." Nobaru raised an eyebrow, inspecting the scars on Veraion's face. "Let me guess. You got your ass handed to you by a wasfought?"

"He did," Aven said through the trees. Veraion snorted.

An air azheek came through the woods, guiding Maina's horse by the reins, followed by the other steeds. The poor fire azheek was still in place, clutching her sore arm.

"You sent me *away?*" She stared.

"Would you rather have stayed and fought?" Veraion asked. She glared.

Nobaru turned to the rest of the travellers with a smile. "So which one of you has taken up the mantle of Raion's best friend?"

Nobody said anything. Nobaru burst out laughing, leaning on Veraion for support.

"Oh god," he wheezed. "Too good, too good. Still as prickly as ever, I see. You were always so outgoing." Sarcasm dripped from his words.

"Are you done?" Vi'ra said.

"No," Nobaru replied. He circled Veraion, looking him up and down, and the man laughed. Nobaru smiled and nodded. "Okay, now I'm done."

"I bear a message from Lord Ziang," Vi'ra said, her cold gaze upon Veraion. "Lord Ezaria spoke with her again last night."

"He has returned?" Veraion asked.

"They spoke through *ulu*," she said. "Ziang received word from the city of fire and contacted him. There is an important matter he would like to discuss. He has been requesting your presence there for weeks."

"What?"

"As I said, you're late. You should have been heading in that direction long ago. He left Sontar Ivel not long after you did and has been waiting for you since."

Veraion let out a long, restrained sigh. Maina shared a glance with Theideus.

"The city of fire?" she repeated.

"Sirenvel," Vi'ra said. "Ride south-east, past Endwood Forest. Through the tundra. You'll know it."

One of the Zalfuri stepped forward, speaking to her in a low tone, and she stood aside. Veraion turned to Nobaru.

"Any idea what this is about?"

Nobaru looked unsure but hopeful. "From what I've heard, years ago the lord's son went missing, taken by baraduhr. They thought him dead or... worse. Then, a few weeks ago, he turned up at the city gates. Rumour has it, he still has his powers."

Veraion stared. "Nobody has ever survived the baraduhr. Nobody has ever escaped and lived to tell the tale."

Nobaru's look stated that he was equally as interested in the case. "Which is why Ezaria went there immediately. This is the first survivor we know of." He placed a hand on Veraion's shoulder. "Perhaps the lord's son will have information that will help you get one step closer to Ilia."

Vi'ra overheard his last words and looked away.

"I miss her too," Nobaru said, giving Veraion a comforting smile. "We all do. I hope you find peace."

"I'm doing alright." He smiled.

"I got your drawings. I missed them. I honestly thought I'd never hear from you again. I spent so many nights *weeping* in my bedroom."

Veraion laughed. He looked over to Chester, who was busying herself with cleaning her weapon.

"She encouraged me to do it," he said.

Nobaru followed his gaze. Blood surrounded her mouth, dripping down her neck.

"Holy shit," he laughed. "You're an animal. I love it."

She snorted slightly. Then he cocked his head.

"Chester?"

She nodded.

"I recognize you. Raion drew you, too."

She smiled, and though it was very slight, the fact that it was there gave Veraion a spark of hope.

"Make haste for Sirenvel," Vi'ra said, pulling her balaclava over her face. "Try not to make any detours this time."

She pulled on her mask and her owl took off. She gave Veraion a departing nod before disappearing into the sky. The other Zalfuri followed suit but Nobaru remained, opening his arms for another hug, and Veraion gladly obliged. They held one another tight, and when they pulled back, kissed each other on the cheek. Their foreheads touched together, eyes closed, sharing a breath.

"Good to know at least this is still the same." Nobaru smiled.

"Always."

They pulled back. Their gazes were fond, deeply so. If not for Ilia, Nobaru would have been Veraion's ilis.

"I've missed you," he said. Nobaru looked at him. Then he whacked him on the side of the face.

"You were the one that left."

Veraion laughed, nodding, though he gingerly rubbed his cheek.

"You should come home sometime," Nobaru said, taking steps back.

"You should come see the world sometime."

"You know I'm not allowed to do that." He smiled. "Besides, the view is better up here."

"But how will you ever find your island?"

Nobaru's smile only grew more fond as he reached for his mask. "Keep an eye out for me."

"Always."

"Keep sending me drawings," he said, pulling up his balaclava. "Maybe I'll take one look and know."

Veraion smiled. "I will."

Nobaru tied his mask in place, and after one last nod, shot into the sky, disappearing into the night.

Veraion lingered. He hadn't realized how much he had missed his friend, and now, standing alone again, he almost felt homesick for a place he had never called home.

He let out a long sigh and turned to his friends. "I'm sorry. For all of this."

But Maina was already holding her reins, waiting for the others to mount their steeds. "City of fire sounds good to me."

* * *

By the time the five reached the tundra surrounding the city of fire, winter had come. Veraion, Theideus, and Aven were freezing, and Chester and Maina were quick to grow tired as their bodies fought to retain their warmth.

The tundra surrounding Sirenvel was naught but igneous rock as far as the eye could see. Foliage had grown through the black stone, regaining life where lava had once killed all, but still, the flatland was predominantly barren. On the horizon stood a volcano, glowing from within.

"Is that a volcano?" Maina asked. They were atop their horses, stopped at the edge of Endwood Forest, gazing over the tundra.

Veraion nodded. "It's extinct."

"Are you sure about that?"

He smiled, but it was small. "That isn't lava you see, it's fire."

He clicked his tongue and the horses started walking.

"I don't know if that's much better," Maina murmured, listening to the crunching of igneous rock beneath hooves.

"If you want an active volcano, head to the Eloan Islands," Veraion said. "Or Vaia. But the most deadly of them all is in Vora."

"Has the volcano of Sirenvel ever exploded?"

"The day the Five were killed," Veraion said.

"Right," she said, nodding.

"What happened?" Aven asked.

"The Five were murdered within the walls of Sontar Ivel, within the walls that had been built to protect them, and all across Ianar... tragedy. Every volcano erupted, fire gangul bursting from the depths. Water gangul came from the oceans and flooded entire cities, air gangul formed hurricanes and tornadoes, and earth gangul split the ground. Many of the islands we have now were created that day, separated from the mainland."

"Fuck," Aven murmured. "I thought gangul don't have feelings or thoughts. I thought... they live to serve and die."

"I think the day the Five were killed was the only time in history the gangul have reacted to anything."

"And this volcano erupted?" Maina asked.

"Yes."

"The city still stands?"

"It was rebuilt many years later. The volcano of Sirenvel went extinct after that. The city of Vora also stood within a volcano, but no one will ever be able to rebuild Vora. It was destroyed. Completely. And that volcano is still active. Nobody goes to Vora anymore. Nobody lives there."

"Mm..." She sounded fearful.

"You have nothing to worry about, Maina—you're a fire azheek now. Even if the volcano of Sirenvel was active, you'd be fine." Veraion lightly kicked in his stirrups and the horses picked up speed.

Faster and faster they went, galloping over igneous rock.

As they rode, Chester's brow grew more and more furrowed. There was something about this place that felt eerily familiar. The distant city called to her.

The volcano grew bigger and bigger until they could see flaming city walls. As the horses climbed the mountain, the riders pulled off their warm layers, sweating beneath the heat of Sirenvel. Streams of fire trailed across the ground, and from a distance, they looked like cracks of lava.

By the time they reached the city the sun had begun to set. The walls rose high, made of a sand-coloured stone, flames dancing upon the parapets, and the travellers followed the wall until they found a gate. They slowed the horses to a halt, coming from their saddles.

Desert birds circled in the sky, calling here and there, and Veraion gazed up to see a lesser spotted eagle. If it weren't for the city of fire this bird would never be out here. Sirenvel created its own climate, creating its own ecosystem of plants and animals that would otherwise not survive in these areas.

"Well, it certainly doesn't feel like winter anymore," Aven said, sweating profusely.

Veraion smiled, glancing back at Chester. That's when he noticed her wide, glazed-over eyes and furrowed brows. She looked up at the billowing flames, nausea waving through her.

"Chester, are you okay?" Veraion asked. She looked at him and managed a smile, nodding. It didn't look very convincing.

Maina moved to the gate and ran her fingers over the thick bars. "I guess they don't get visitors very often."

Chester gazed through the metal grating. She could see buildings up ahead, built from the same sandy rock. The ground was packed earth, and every tree and plant in sight was one of warmer climates.

Aven moved forward and grabbed on to the bars. His face screwed up as he pulled with all his strength, and soon there was a horrid screech as he lifted the grating from the ground.

"Hey!" came a voice, and Aven let down the barrier with a grunt as two fire azheeks came into view. The man and woman were many years past their prime, with dark reddish hair and eyes like embers. Their skin was tanned, brown in the setting sun. Both had thick, angular eyebrows and noses that were hooked. They wore barely any clothing, naught but loose robes. It was warm in the fire capital, very much so, but they barely felt it. Not a drop of sweat beaded upon their radiant skin.

Aven's hand was still resting on the bars, so the woman raised hers. His fingers burst into flames. With a yelp, he yanked his hand away, frantically shaking it out. He turned back to her with a snarl.

"Who are you?" she scoffed. Aven stepped forward angrily, but Veraion hurried in front of him.

"We were summoned by Lord Ezaria," Veraion explained. "He is here by invitation of your own Lord Ekhrem. They are expecting us. I'm sorry, we should have been here weeks ago."

The man and woman of Sirenvel exchanged glances before nodding to someone the others couldn't see.

The gate rose and the two stepped aside. The gatekeepers retrieved their horses, Sirenveli beasts with radiant coats that shone in the setting sun, and swung into their saddles, watching the newcomers as they entered the city.

"It's a long ride," the woman said. The friends mounted their steeds once more.

When they were in their saddles, the woman let out a commanding yell and her horse took off. The others followed.

They galloped through the city of fire, further and further in, forgetting how cold it was outside the great walls. The air was thick, hot, and unforgivingly dry. Veraion, Aven, and Theideus struggled to moisten their throats, sweating profusely. A breeze wafted through the city, rustling leaves of trees around them, but it did not do much to cool the air.

Bay laurel grew around them, cypress, judas, lime, pistachio, sycamore, hazel, yew, and as far as the eye could see, date palm trees. The sights and smells were so different to what they were used to, yet there were familiar hints in the cypress, reminding Maina and Theideus of their lost home.

Veraion gazed around knowing that there was no way these would grow in the outside climate.

They passed farms and fields growing tomatoes, cucumbers, potatoes, and eggplants. Trees grew cherries, figs, quinces, and grapes, and on almost every corner they could see apricots.

There were gazelles, wild goats, and closer to the rocky walls, mountain sheep. Wild horses grazed lazily, some running alongside them for a time, and the newcomers marvelled at their radiant coats, shining beneath the setting sun.

Every building was made of the same sandy-coloured stone, some carved from cliffs and rock formations. Fire danced along walls and on rooftops, burning in beacons to illuminate the night. It was never dark in the city of fire.

Above them were hot air balloons, floating lazily, adding warm light even to the skies. The newcomers stared up in awe.

Every man, woman, and child was a fire azheek. Their faces were piercing, features as dangerous as their element. The Sirenveli had skin ranging from tanned to brown, hair from fire orange to red, to deep browns and blacks that shone like blood in the light. Every pair of eyes was as piercing as their flames.

Clothes weren't popular here. Many wore barely anything at all, choosing loose robes when they did, but jewellery of gold and brass, of necklaces, bracelets, anklets, and chiming coins, was everywhere—on people and on horses.

As they rode, Chester's nausea only grew stronger and stronger. There was a pull, a pull so strong she was breathing slowly, with difficulty.

She had been here before. She had felt the breeze and smelled the air. She had distant memories of stealing hazelnuts from trees. Memories of scratches and cuts from climbing date palm trees. She knew the people she passed. But she had never been here.

They rode by water holes, fire azheeks lounging, talking, and laughing, but whenever the locals saw them, they stopped and stared. The presence of foreigners was rare in Sirenvel, extremely rare.

The closer they got to the main hub of the city, the more cats they saw. Cats everywhere, living in the streets. Many looked dusty from the dry air and sandy ground, but none were hungry. In fact, some looked like they could benefit from a diet. The Sirenveli people kept them well fed.

The sun had dipped below the horizon by the time their guide slowed her horse, leading them to a large building lined with columns supporting an overhanging roof. Open archways let the smell of food waft into the night. Raw food and cooked food. Aven was already drooling.

The air was ripe with talk and laughter, voices ringing through the hall and out into the city.

They came from their saddles. Veraion looked back at Chester, feeling energy coming from her in waves. She stared up at the great hall, every breath a difficult task as she felt heavy, weighed down. Small. In the city of fire, a place she had never before been, she felt a life so full of memories.

"Are you sure you're okay?" he pressed. She swallowed the knot in her throat and looked at him fearfully.

"I know this place," she said softly. "But I've never been here before. I feel something. Someone. I feel everyone, but… how do I know this place? How do I know these people?"

Her eyes rested on the building before them, tears welling in her gaze.

There was something about her that looked different. Her skin looked eerily bright in the firelight, as though she were about to start glowing.

"It hurts," she rasped. "Standing here hurts. I… I have to go inside."

The guide glanced at the others. "Follow me."

The gatekeeper led them up the stairs and into the building.

Sirenvel's dining hall was massive. The ceiling rose high and was littered with chandeliers and candles. Rows upon rows of tables flooded the space, every bench filled. There were platters of raw food: fruits, vegetables, and meats, with sauces, dips, and marinades. The Sirenveli ate with their hands aflame, and by the time the food reached their mouths, it was cooked just the way they wanted it.

Paintings and tapestries lined the walls, with illustrations of Atesh, the first lord of fire, and many warriors that had followed.

The moment the newcomers entered, the Sirenveli looked at them. The loud chatter quietened, talk and laughter disappearing in seconds. Some children stood on their chairs to look at Aven with wide eyes, pointing in awe.

At the far end of the hall was a raised platform where Lord Ekhrem was seated. He was old, his tanned skin wrinkled, hair grey, but his tired eyes still held life, bright with orange fire. His beard was thick and sections were braided and cuffed with gold. Ekhrem's hairline had receded, his brow strong and nose hooked, but about his eyes were many wrinkles to show that he had lived a good and happy life.

Ekhrem wore thick robes, unable to sweat or feel discomfort in the heat of his city: robes of deep red, decorated with gold embroidery.

To his right sat a woman with fire-orange hair, her angular eyes shining like embers. Her skin was tanned, golden in the light, her face striking, intimidating, beautiful, her jaw strong and shoulders broader than most.

Yenea. His daughter.

Near her sat the twins that had travelled with her, years past their prime: Fairo and Fehir.

Veraion saw them and his brow furrowed, eyes widening, and he looked to Chester in shock. But she didn't seem to notice Yenea's familiar presence.

Chester's eyes were fixed on the man standing on the other side of the old lord. He was just past his prime, with long reddish-brown hair in waves, his skin tanned, stubble lining his sharp jaw. His eyebrows were strong and angular, nose pointed, a little hooked. His eyes were a bright orange, darker around the edges, flecks of golden yellow dappling his stare. His stare that had fixed on Chester the instant she walked in.

"Yrilim," Chester whispered.

At the far end of the lord's table sat Ezaria. His pale hair was draped down his back, his body dressed in looser robes for the climate, but as always, he wore black. Tattoos peeked from beneath his clothes, on his face, neck, and hands, and he watched the newcomers as cold and unfeeling as always.

The Sirenveli stared between Yrilim and Chester—between the lord's son and the stranger. Aven's single eye was just as wide, just as surprised to see the man.

Chester walked forward, as did Yrilim. They couldn't control it. The pull was too strong. Both of them were glowing, their skin too radiant even in the firelight.

"What's going on?" Maina stared between the two.

"That… would be Yrilim," Aven muttered.

"Yrilim, as in the person Chester is bound to, Yrilim?"

The giant nodded, just as confused.

"Were you aware he's a lord of the city of fire?" Veraion asked. Aven shook his head.

As Chester and Yrilim got closer, lights rose from their skin. Lights of red, orange, and yellow. The magic grew brighter the closer they got.

They grabbed each other into a desperate embrace. Fire licked over their glowing skin, the strength of their bond too powerful to control.

There was no one around them now. It was just them.

Lights rose from the two, shining beautifully, flickering brighter and dimmer with every thundering beat of their hearts.

The pain stopped. The agony of being apart finally went away. They had forgotten what it was like to not suffer with every breath.

Yrilim held her tighter, his arms shaking.

Veraion smiled. He could feel it. Her pain was gone.

Yenea and her father exchanged a glance, the woman displeased. She shared a look with the twins beside her.

"They look familiar," Aven muttered under his breath, nodding towards the people in question.

"They were in the arena," Veraion said. "The day Chester was distracted. The day she was attacked. They were there."

Yrilim pulled back from the longing hug only to place his lips upon Chester's forehead, kissing her gingerly. Then he pulled her back into his arms, holding her as though he never wanted to let go.

Maina glanced around. Everyone was staring.

Yrilim's father coughed awkwardly. Finally he opened his eyes, only then remembering where he was.

Ezaria rose to his feet, speaking to Lord Ekhrem in a hushed tone. He nodded and stood up.

"My people!" Ekhrem called. "These newcomers are welcome here under invitation by Lord Ezaria, thus by invitation of my own. We have many matters we wish to discuss."

Someone in the audience raised their hand, pointing at Yrilim and Chester in confusion, but Ekhrem gave them a look as though to say *not now*. They put their arm down.

"Wasn't he bound to someone else or something?" Maina asked lowly. Aven shared a look with her, once again just as confused.

Ezaria beckoned Veraion with a twitch of his hand, and Veraion obeyed. Yrilim and Chester finally looked at one another.

"Can we talk?" he asked. "Somewhere less... busy."

She nodded, and he led her from the dining hall. All eyes followed.

The moment they were out of sight the hall erupted. The Sirenveli gossiped loudly, yelling at one another as they speculated as to what on Ianar was going on.

As Veraion approached the lord's table, he looked at Yenea. "You were at the tournament."

"I was looking for my brother," she said curtly, rising to her feet. "I felt his presence there, but all I found was her."

"You felt him in her."

She nodded, a bitter smile upon her lips. "Yes. It seems her presence grew with her fame, and in doing so, Yrilim was felt there too."

"The amount of people watching her... The more people knew, the stronger her presence."

Yenea smiled yet again, but it wasn't very friendly. Behind her, Fairo and Fehir were watching Veraion carefully. Warily.

"Your friend attacked her," Veraion said. "Was that under your command?"

"Azhara acted upon her own wishes," Yenea replied. "She was always a little brash. Always a little impulsive."

"Her legs were destroyed."

"Yes." She smiled bitterly. "I was hoping you may have answers in regard to that. Who that man was, how he did what he did, and where Azhara went?"

Veraion's brow furrowed. "You don't know where she is?"

"We never saw her again," Fairo said. His voice was deep and gruff.

There was a sadness in his and his brother's eyes, despite the naturally harsh features of their faces.

Veraion clenched his jaw, fearful as he thought of the missing azheek, and he couldn't help but feel guilt. He shared a foreboding look with Aven over his shoulder.

CHAPTER 18
THE CITY OF FIRE

The sun set and the sky turned dark blue, and for all azheek eyes the galaxy shone bright above, twinkling with millions of stars. The air was warm, always warm in the city of fire.

A breeze wafted through the open streets, moving Yrilim's and Chester's hair about their shoulders.

"She lied," he said. "Zahura lied. We're not bound. We never were."

"I figured that out." She laughed softly. "Just now."

He smiled. "May I touch you?"

"Yes."

Yrilim gently took her head in his hands, his gaze flicking between her eyes. "I am yours," he said. "Always."

She smiled, wiping a tear from her cheek. "Thank the gods."

He laughed. Yrilim gently pushed her wild hair from her face. "May I kiss you?"

She smiled and nodded.

He placed his lips on hers. Their kiss was soft at first, but it didn't take long for it to deepen. He pulled her into his arms and her hands pushed through his hair, their kiss ripe with longing. Even when it ended, their eyes stayed closed. Their foreheads touched together, each breathing the other in. Then Chester pulled back.

"Are you a lord?"

He smiled sheepishly.

"Are you the lord's son?" She stared. "The one taken by baraduhr?"

He nodded. There was a long moment of silence.

"The fuck?" she said. "You never told me that."

"It was behind me," he said simply. "I didn't want anyone to know who I was. I liked that in Foros. Everyone treated me like I was normal, like I was just some guy. Like I was... just *me*."

"When I found you, you said you had been attacked by baraduhr but you didn't say you had been *taken*. Where did they take you?"

"That's the thing," he sighed. "I don't remember... and I don't think I want to."

Chester nodded. She looked at him and smiled, gently tracing a finger over his jaw. "I like your beard."

"It grew thicker after I started ageing." He chuckled. "I like it too."

Then she smirked, giving him a look. "Do you live in a castle?"

"It's not... a *castle*."

* * *

Maybe not a castle, but a palace nonetheless. The keep overlooked the city with a great set of steps leading to the stronghold. The lords and their companions led the newcomers up the stairs and to the palace, but the friends stared back at the city in awe.

They could see everything. The dining hall, the training grounds, the farms and marketplaces, and at the centre of the extinct volcano was a sparkling lake. Reflections of the night sky rippled calmly on the surface, pink moonlight dancing upon water.

Up the palace steps, they moved through an open courtyard. Guards were sitting here and there, and they rose to their feet, but Ekhrem waved his hand with a smile and they returned to their relaxed positions.

The palace was built from the same sandy-hued stone as the rest of the city. Columns and archways let air travel through the halls, thin hangings flowing through open windows and doors.

A palace hand approached and Yrilim pulled her aside, whispering into her ear. She nodded and hurried away.

Yenea held her father's arm, helping him walk. Fairo was close behind, and as a woman appeared with a child holding her hand, Fehir smiled and came forward.

"My son." He beamed. The boy was young, a toddler, and he ran to his father, laughing as Fehir swiped him off the ground. Fehir picked him up as though he weighed nothing, miniscule in his father's strong arms.

"It's past your bed time," Fehir said lowly, though his eyes glanced to the woman. She gave him a knowing smile.

"He *was* asleep," she said. "Until he felt you coming."

She had a square face with strong cheekbones, her nose and mouth appearing quite small in the middle of it all. Her eyebrows were thick and bushy, skin tanned and eyes golden yellow. Her hair looked black in the night. She was in her prime.

"Aiyat, I'm sorry," Fehir murmured with a laugh. "I know how hard it is to get him to sleep."

"I'm right here," the boy said. Aiyat smiled.

The child had thick dark red hair and bushy eyebrows, and though he was young and still carried all his baby fat, it was clear, looking at his parents, that one day his features would be strong.

"Come," Fehir said, taking Aiyat by the hand, and he headed away, down an open corridor, guiding his family back to their chambers.

Yenea and Fairo bid Lord Ekhrem good night, and she looked at her brother one last time before they too headed into the palace and for their resting places.

"I'll take care of our guests," Yrilim said to his father, and the old man nodded, bidding the newcomers farewell before he and Ezaria moved off, robes billowing at their heels and grey hair flowing behind them.

Yrilim let out a deep sigh as he stood with the newcomers, freed of expectations now that the rest of the lords were gone.

"Come." He smiled, and guided them into the palace.

Yrilim took them through the fortress, up a set of stairs and to a balcony that overlooked another courtyard. The courtyard was lined with pygmy date palm trees, reaching into the sky, overlooking a long stretch of grass that led to a large fountain. Decorated tiles surrounded the fixture, glimmering in the light of the blood moon. Chester gazed over the railing and smiled.

Doors lined the wall, tiled intricately, and Yrilim nodded to them.

"You can each take a room to yourself—we have plenty of space."

Maina and Theideus exchanged an excited glance and opened a door, peering in.

"Holy shit," Maina gasped.

A great chamber with a massive bed at one end and a large bath at the other. Columns lined the walls, decorative tiles stretching down the hall and ceiling.

"I've sent a message to our healers," Yrilim said. "They'll check all of you tomorrow, just to make sure your wounds are healing well."

"I'd love to stay and chat," Maina said. "But I'm going to bathe and sleep. For three days."

The others laughed, and quickly she and Theideus ducked into the room, staring around in awe. The door closed.

"You can... have a room each," Yrilim said.

Two earth azheeks appeared around a corner, with dark skin, dark hair, and smiles from ear to ear. The man stood just over five feet tall and was built of muscle and hair, his dreadlocks tied back and eyes bright green. His earlobes had been stretched, turquoise stone in the holes, gold hoops decorating the cartilage. But the most prominent thing he wore was his smile, lighting his whole face, his teeth sparkling like pearls.

The woman was taller, made even more so by her huge head of thick curly hair. Gold and turquoise earrings dangled about her face, her eyes a golden green. Her cheekbones were filled with life, nose widened further by her smile that shone even brighter than her companion's. She too had the muscles of a warrior.

Chester's eyes widened, shock ripe in her stare.

"Chukuma?" she gasped. "Faraji?"

She ran towards them and they only tore at her faster, yelling. They grabbed each other into a tight embrace, and Yrilim smiled to himself.

Chukuma and Faraji squeezed Chester between them, arms wrapped around her to almost disappear her from view. All she could feel was their skin. All she could smell was their sweat. But she wouldn't have had it any other way.

When they pulled apart, Chester stared at them in shock, a smile upon her lips and tears in her eyes. She hadn't thought much of Foros, but as she looked at her closest friends, it was like she'd never left.

She grabbed Chukuma by the stubbled cheeks, turning to Faraji. When she spoke, she put on a Forosi accent.

"You're as beautiful as I remember." She smiled. The two laughed.

"I'm only getting more beautiful with age, you know that." Chukuma grinned. Chester laughed and finally let him go.

"You look different," she said, eyes moving between them. "The same, but different. Did you—did you bind? Did you two bind?" They smiled and nodded. "*Fuck*, I can't believe I missed that!"

Faraji shrugged. "You knew we were going to anyway."

"Yeah," she laughed. "Oh, the amount of fighting there must have been."

"What?" Chukuma scoffed with fake insult. "We never fight."

"He's so annoying," Faraji muttered.

"You know what I can't believe I missed?" he said. His next words were delivered with an exaggerated Forosi accent, one the current generations had lost. "You, Mahriel, our fiery lioness, fighting in the tournament of Sontar Ivel!"

Chester laughed and looked over to Yrilim. "You saw it?"

"Of course he did!" Chukuma scoffed. They headed back over to where the others were.

"He is bound to you," Faraji reminded her. "All your highs and lows, he saw. He got glimpses of the tournament, and we made him retell it again and again and again."

Chester laughed.

"So of course," Chukuma said, "be prepared. We will make you tell us everything."

"Veraion," Chester managed around a chuckle. "This is Chukuma and Faraji. We went to school together and they were both with me in the Forosi guard." She turned back to her old friends. "When did you get here?"

"We came with Yrilim," Faraji said. "We knew he couldn't make the journey alone. It's not like he ended up in Foros on purpose."

"Hey." The lord gave her a glare, though it was fond.

"This is Veraion," Chester continued. "Maina and Theideus just went into their room, and of course you know Aven."

Chukuma and Faraji stared up at the giant in shock. They *had* known him, but they had known him as a wasfought. Chester realized this and laughed.

"Sorry, I forgot to say! Look at what he can do now!"

Aven smiled, and with a series of horrid crunches and snaps, he turned into the beast they all knew.

Chukuma screamed.

* * *

Yrilim's quarters were massive. His bed was so large Chester was having a hard time believing it was a bed, and around the space were closets, dressers, tables, chairs, and a great desk. There were lounges along the walls, colourful floor sofas littered in every corner, and plants Chester had never before seen, standing tall in decorated pots.

The hall was dappled with dancing light, bouncing off the surface of the bath, stretching across the other half of the chamber. Light came from the moon, cascading through open windows, and from tiled lamps, mosaiced with coloured glass. Some lamps hung from the walls, others from the ceiling in spirals, and every one of them brought life and colour to the room.

To the right side of the bed were windows overlooking the garden courtyard; behind it and along the left wall, they overlooked the city.

Chester wore a long, sheer nightgown, washed, cleaned, and dried. She stood by an open window, gazing over Sirenvel with a soft smile upon her lips. A breeze wafted through the room, causing the drapes to flow gracefully, the nightgown caressing her skin.

Fire flickered all around the city and music flowed quietly through the streets, instruments she had never heard before. She could hear strings, plucked and strummed, and soft drums to accompany them. The musicians played for the time of night: a calming tune, a lullaby.

There came a soft knock on the double doors, and she looked over to see Yrilim poke his head in. She smiled.

"This is your room," she said. "You don't have to knock."

He entered, closing the door behind him, and approached as she turned back to the city. He wrapped his arms around her and placed a soft kiss on her cheek before resting his chin upon her head, following her gaze.

"This is all yours," he said.

"Hm?"

"Sirenvel. It's yours if you want it. You're bound to a lord."

She laughed softly and shook her head. "Did you tell *anyone* about this? Back at Foros? You were with us for some time."

"I had a new start there," he said simply. "A chance to be normal. People in Foros liked me for who I was and nothing more. Growing up here, I had so many people befriend me, and more, purely because of my status. I was adopted when I was a kid and the ass-kissing didn't start until *after* I was made the lords' child. People who once bullied me suddenly wanted to be my friend." He smiled to himself, snorting softly. "But I did tell someone. I told Zahura. I confided in her, told her I was binding to you, and I didn't know how to tell you about all of this. The next thing I knew, she told everyone that she and I were bound."

Chester looked at him in shock. "That's what happened?"

He nodded.

"Why would she say that? That's... that's a big lie."

"Yeah," he murmured. "So was the other lie she was telling. Turns out, she's human."

Chester blinked. "*What?*"

He nodded again. "Her whole life she told people she was an azheek. I guess... out of jealousy. Maybe hoping she might be?"

"Well, now I feel like an idiot," she muttered. "I didn't really know her— we didn't talk much—but she had the eyes of an earth azheek. I never questioned it. But now that you mention it, I never saw her use her powers either."

He murmured an agreement. "I was going to tell you, but you... ran away."

She let out a chuckle of disbelief. "I didn't mean to—I just went for a walk, to clear my head above ground. Then the baraduhr popped up and chased me away from Foros. Away from Foros and right into Veraion. It's been a bit of an adventure since then."

"I'm glad Aven found you," he said. "He needs you more than you know."

She smiled sadly, thinking of the weeks she had spent unable to speak to him. "I need him too."

He placed a kiss upon her forehead.

"You didn't react," she said. "Seeing his ability."

"I already saw it… through you."

She nodded.

"Is it different now?" he asked. "Now that you can have proper conversations with him? Now that he's… a man?"

"It was weird at first, but now… I don't know what I'd do if he lost the ability."

Yrilim nodded. They held one another in silence, and Chester rested her head on him, closing her eyes. But he didn't move, he didn't hold her tighter. He was holding back.

"You know what happened, don't you?" she said softly. "What the baraduhr did."

He swallowed the knot in his throat and nodded. "I was with you when it happened. And I saw what Lord Ezaria did to them. I will forever be in his debt."

She nodded, and neither of them moved from their place.

"If you need to be with Aven tonight, I understand," he said. She smiled.

"You're such a good man, Yrilim."

He placed a kiss upon her hair. "Yes, I am."

Chester laughed.

* * *

Chester and a great wasfought lay on a bed, Veraion asleep on a nearby lounge chair, which was still large enough to be a bed in itself. He had taken the opportunity to properly bathe, taming his hair, trimming his beard to stubble, and he had drunk more water than he'd ever drunk before. The air was ungodly. Hot, he could handle. The Vaian Islands were hot, but the Vaian Islands were humid. Sirenvel was not. Sirenvel was dry. And it made him feel like a prune.

Softly Chester traced Aven's markings, and a chuffing noise came from his throat. Eventually he opened his eye and looked at her.

"I'm sorry I've been distant," she whispered. He let out a soft, sad sigh. "I just…"

The beast leaned in and licked her cheek, and she gasped, grimacing, wiping his spit from her face.

"Aven!" she laughed. She could tell he was too.

He moved in closer, resting his head upon her stomach, and she gently pushed her fingers through his thick fur.

"How are you?" Her words were soft.

He let out a sad breath, a distant whimper heard beneath it.

"If you ever need to talk," she said, "I'm here."

He nodded; it was slight, but she could feel it upon her stomach.

Chester closed her eyes, listening to a distant song as musicians played somewhere in the streets. She smiled to herself, gently petting Aven, and for the first time in what felt like months, she relaxed.

She opened her eyes and looked down to see that the beast was still watching her. He was afraid of going to sleep. She gave him a comforting smile.

"Go to sleep, Little One. I'll be here when you wake up."

He watched her for a moment before nuzzling in, closing his eye.

* * *

Chester's eyelids fluttered as she came around, feeling a soft breeze upon her skin, listening to distant voices. Familiar voices, laughing in the morning sun. She opened her eyes and gazed at the ceiling, admiring intricate tiles before glancing over to her companions. Aven was asleep on his back, his paws sticking into the air. Veraion was slouched against the backrest of his lounge chair, but he was awake.

"Morning," he croaked. He reached for a nearby jug of water and chugged, attempting to moisten his throat.

"Mm," she rasped, rubbing her eyes. "That is, by far, the best sleep I have had in weeks. If not months."

"I slept on a damn chair and I agree."

"First of all, that chair is huge, and second of all, nobody was stopping you from joining us. Or getting your own room."

He waved her off, and she smiled.

"It's comforting, isn't it? Knowing that we're here."

He tried to give her a glare but it wasn't convincing. "I'm a creature of habit. I'm just used to having you two around."

"Sure." She rose to her feet, taking in a deep breath, stretching her arms and legs, and Aven let out a deep grumble, stretching his own giant limbs.

Chester moved over to a window and looked to the garden courtyard below. Beneath the thicket of plants she could see people gathered on a blanket with a spread of food and drink. Chukuma, Faraji, Yrilim, Maina, Theideus, and two men she didn't know.

There came a series of unsettling crunches, and soon a giant was standing behind Chester, following her gaze. It didn't take long before Yrilim felt her watching him, and he looked up, beckoning for them to join them.

"Fuck yeah." Aven smiled. "Food."

He pulled on a pair of his peace silk pants and its matching robe, finally in a place warm enough to wear them again. Chester watched him with a smile as he hurried from the room.

In the courtyard, Faraji looked over her shoulder to see the giant heading across the balcony. His colourful silk robe billowed behind him as he moved, loose pants gliding elegantly about his massive legs.

"I still can't believe Aven is a human-thing now," Faraji murmured. "Is it wrong that I find him… attractive? I mean… he was a wasfought for so long…"

"He still is," Maina reminded her.

Faraji raised an eyebrow at her fig before busying herself with it.

"You know," Chukuma said, "I was thinking of adopting a dog, but that might not be a good idea if that's how you'll view my baby."

She threw her fig at him.

Back in the room, Chester headed for the door.

"Hold on," Veraion said. He approached, pushing his messy hair from his face. He was wearing a loose shirt, his pants just as much so, freed from layers of clothing and heavy weapons for the first time in a long time.

He looked at her and seemed to be trying to find specific words.

"Are you okay?" she asked. He smiled to himself.

"I... was going to ask you that."

She looked at him and moved over to the bed, sitting on the edge. He took his place beside her.

"How are you feeling?" he asked.

"Better. A lot better. I'm still not... *better*, but... you know."

"I'm sorry that I haven't known what to say. Or do."

She smiled a little. "You have no need to apologize. It's nobody's fault. I haven't known either."

He nodded. "I don't know what happened, and I'm not going to ask, but if you ever need to talk to someone, I'm here."

She smiled sadly, her words quiet. A whisper. "You know what happened."

He clenched his jaw, fighting off the building knot in his throat.

"I can't say it," she said.

"You don't have to. You never have to. Not unless you want to."

She nodded. They sat in silence for a moment. He wanted to hold her hand but he knew he couldn't. She still couldn't be touched.

"Thank you," she said. "I haven't known what to say or do either... but at least I got to not know what to say or do... with you. And the others."

"Do you feel safe here?"

"We just got here, but... I guess I do."

"Then I'm glad we're here. Even if it's hot as balls."

Chester laughed, only then realizing he had sweat upon his forehead, soaking into his once fresh pair of clothes.

"Sweating sucks," he said.

"I don't doubt that."

They smiled. He glanced at his hands, swallowing the knot in his throat.

"I never got to say thank you," he said. "For using your question on me. With Ayaba. Both you and Aven. You didn't have to do that, but you did."

She gave him a small smile. She wanted to place her hand on his, to comfort him, but the thought of feeling anyone's skin made hers crawl.

"Nothing to thank," she said. "You would have done it for me."

He looked at her and nodded.

"And I'm sorry," he said. "About how everything fell apart in Sontar Ivel. I know how much it felt like home to you. All of that was taken away because of me."

She smiled sadly. "We were both wanted, our faces were on posters all around the city—there was only so long it could have gone on. And... we all made it out... mostly in one piece. It could have ended a lot worse."

He nodded, but his jaw was clenched and he sighed.

"If you apologize any more you're going to have to give me taho—you know that, right?" Chester said. He snorted and finally smiled.

"It would be hard for me to find apology taho around here."

Then a voice came from the garden outside.

"Chester! Veraion! You coming?" It was Chukuma.

Chester shared another smile with her friend before they rose to their feet and headed from the room.

By the time they reached the morning picnic, Aven had already eaten five spicy sausages and was crying into his tea. Chester laughed, ruffling his hair, and though he huffed through the pain, he grabbed another serving. There were cheeses made from sheep and goat milk, butter, olives, eggs, tomatoes, cucumbers, and bread served with jam and honey.

At the other end of the garden, Fehir, Aiyat, and their son sat in the shade of a tree, eating breakfast. Aiyat was trying to get the child to read, but he was too busy playing with his father's double-handed battle-axe.

"Fehir." Aiyat cast him a glare. "Why did you bring this to breakfast?"

"He asked me to," he said, chuckling, and picked up the weapon, holding it above his head. His son reached for it, jumping up and down, and he laughed.

Then he struck it into the tree behind him, out of reach, and the toddler finally gave up. Still, the boy refused to eat and instead started playing with honey.

A palace hand moved through the courtyard, carrying a small tray with two bowls of soup. She hurried over to the large group of friends, giving the soup to Chester and Veraion, glancing at Aven and his spice-induced tears.

Yrilim smiled. "Thank you, Meha."

One of the men Chester didn't know waved a hand for Meha, laughing at Aven as he struggled to eat.

"Perhaps some milk for our giant friend." The man smiled, and Meha laughed, nodding, quickly heading away.

"Chester, Veraion, this is Kazim and Talen," Yrilim said, introducing his friends.

Kazim was in his prime, with brown skin and long dark hair that fell down his back in waves. His eyes were bright orange, almost yellow, contrasting his darker skin. His nose was pointed and hooked, lips thin, and brow strong.

Talen had been the one to ask for milk. He was in his prime, with tanned skin, wavy brown-red hair to his shoulders, and orange eyes. He had a stronger jaw and thicker nose, and like his friends and many others in Sirenvel, his nose was hooked a little. His stubble was shaved short while Kazim's was longer.

Both men were trained to fight, Kazim of a stockier build and Talen taller. Kazim wore naught but pants while Talen sat in just his underwear.

While Talen wasn't wearing much cloth, what he did wear in abundance was jewellery. Gold hung about his ears and was draped about his body in chains, pendants, and coins. He jingled with every moment, shimmering in the sunlight, but still, his wide smile shone brighter. He had quite a few scars, several of which were on his face.

Talen eagerly shook hands with the newcomers, though he spent a longer time on Chester.

"It's nice to finally meet you all—especially you, you who is bound to one of my best friends." He jingled as he shook her hand.

"*Atesh*," Kazim sighed, though he chuckled. "Don't freak them out."

"I'm bound to freak them out sometime." Talen grinned. "Might as well just be honest from the get-go."

Yrilim smiled. They tucked into their food, drinking freshly squeezed juice from brass goblets.

"You have a lot of scars," Aven said to Talen around a mouthful of cheese.

The man nodded. "I get stabbed a lot." The others snorted, Chukuma choking on his sausage. Seeing everyone's amused and expectant faces, Talen laughed and shrugged, smiling sheepishly. "I'm bad with money—we'll just leave it at that."

"Says the man covered in gold," Yrilim said with a smirk.

Kazim snorted, shaking his head. "You'd think you would have learned after the first time."

"See, that's the problem." Talen smiled. "I never learn."

Yrilim chuckled at his friends.

"It's smart." Kazim shrugged. "The last time Talen was chased for his debts they cut off and took his jewellery, and not a body part."

Talen grimaced and placed a protective hand over his loins.

"How do you all know each other?" Maina said, laughing.

"I grew up in the palace because my mother is a healer," Talen said. "Kazim was a stable boy, and I mean, so was Yrilim until the lords adopted him."

"You're adopted?" Maina asked.

"Yenea and I both." Yrilim nodded. "My fathers adopted her when she was nine, and about five years later, when I was six, they adopted me."

"You're not blood related?" Veraion asked. Yrilim shook his head. "You don't share a blood bond, and yet she felt your presence in Sontar Ivel because of Chester. That's… that's a powerful bond."

"She's swapped spirit," Yrilim said, and with a knowing look, Veraion nodded. Theideus smiled.

"Swapped spirit?" Aven asked.

"Spirit of a woman," Yrilim told him. "In a body otherwise. It is said that swapped-spirit azheeks are closer to the gods, closer to the next world as they left their bodies and passed through Savai before birth. Yenea has always been more connected. It was one of the reasons our fathers chose her."

"Are you?" Maina asked Theideus. "More connected?"

He gave her a look as though to say yes and no.

"All water azheeks are more connected, right?" Faraji said. "Are swapped-spirit water azheeks even… *more?*"

Theideus shrugged as though to say *sometimes.* He pointed at himself and shook his head. *Not me.*

"Were you before?" Maina asked. "Before the curse?"

He shrugged a little.

"Yenea has always been gifted," Yrilim said. "She was the best sister one could have had. Protective, hence her going all the way to the capital when she felt me. But that's it—she loves her people, she loves me and my father, and of course, our late father. She was adopted because she was demolishing everyone on the training grounds, excelling in school. Bright mind, great potential."

"Yrilim was also doing those things," Kazim said. "He just doesn't like to brag. The lords chose their future successors wisely."

"Ehhhhh," Talen interjected. "They adopted a future lord that would rather run away and not be lord. Don't know if that was wise."

Yrilim ate his food sheepishly, and Chester cast him a smile.

"And yet, upon his return, everyone still voted to keep him lord," Talen said. "Sometimes the best lords are the ones that don't want to be."

"To be fair," Yrilim said, "I didn't intentionally leave Sirenvel. I was taken."

"And then decided not to come back when you survived," Kazim reminded him. "Or... send a letter."

Yrilim accepted this with a guilty nod. "I'm sorry. You should have voted me out."

"Why would I do that?" Talen scoffed, raising his hands. He looked around the courtyard, soaking in the sights, smells, and sounds: the intricate tiles, mouth-watering food, and lapping fountain. "If you're in, I am too. I'm not about to give up this privilege."

The others laughed.

"It's fine." Kazim waved him off. "Yenea could still feel you were alive, and not in pain, or afraid. Made the rest of us feel like shit though. Everyone speculated if you'd gotten hit in the head real hard and forgot who you were, or if you just... didn't want to come back. Turns out it was the latter."

Yrilim averted his gaze.

"What would you be doing if you weren't lord?" Chester asked.

"Technically I'm not lord yet," he said. "My father is still lord of Sirenvel."

"Yenea and Yrilim will be anointed soon," Kazim said. Yrilim smiled a little, apprehensive.

"Look at him." Talen grinned, draping an arm around Yrilim's shoulders. "A humble lord already."

Yrilim cast him an amused glare.

"Let's say you never got adopted to be lord," Chukuma said. "What would you be doing?"

Yrilim thought about it for a moment and smiled. "Farming apricots."

The others laughed.

"You'd want to be a farmer?" Faraji stared.

"I like apricots."

Chester smiled and placed a hand on his arm, gently tracing her thumb over his skin. He looked at her and his face softened.

"Would you farm apricots with him?" Talen asked.

"I'd be his bodyguard," she said. The others laughed.

Yrilim smiled to himself and ate a dried apricot. After a moment, he looked to Veraion, who had remained quiet thus far.

"Veraion," he said. "I know that Lord Ezaria summoned you here because of what happened with the baraduhr, and I know you must have questions. I've told him everything I remember, and I'm sorry to say… I don't remember much."

Veraion nodded. "I'm sorry, I don't mean to go prying into your unpleasant past."

"It's about time I faced it—I've been avoiding it for so long." Yrilim took in a deep breath and put down his goblet. "About two years ago, I was with the hunt in the Hallow forest. Every few months we camp for a day or two and bring back whatever we can get. It's an old tradition. We had been there for about a day. Kazim's brother and I were tracking a deer when we were ambushed."

Kazim busied himself with his drink.

"And then everything else is a blur," Yrilim said. "Some of us were taken; the rest died in the fight. I remember stone—black, wet, *cold* stone. It takes a lot for a fire azheek to feel cold. I could hear my people crying. Screaming. I remember the smell like it was yesterday… the reek of death and decay. They drugged us. We were too weak to fight back, too weak to even stand. They beat us. They broke us.

"I remember the sound of keys in my cell door. I couldn't see anything. I barely had strength, but I used what little I had left and just… fought. I remember falling against a door. I opened it and fell down a flight of stairs. I ran. I don't think I could even see. Next thing I knew, I was in freezing water. And then… I woke up in Foros."

The others were silent.

"Did you ever have visions about it?" Veraion asked. "Dreams?"

"Plenty of nightmares, yeah, but only of what I just told you—things I already remembered. Although… sometimes… sometimes I see a pile of weapons. I don't remember where I saw that—I have no recollection of seeing that. But sometimes when I dream, all I see is a mountain of weapons. A mountain of swords, axes, maces, polearms, spears, hammers. Other people's weapons…" His voice trailed off quietly. "They scare me. Sometimes it's all I see. And it feels like I'm staring at corpses. Hundreds of thousands of corpses."

"Did you ever hear the word 'Aion'?" Chester asked. He shook his head.

"No, I'm sorry. What is it?"

"We don't know," Veraion said. "The baraduhr took my ilis. The only clue I have as to where they are keeping her body is the word 'Aion'."

"Is she alive?"

"No. But the baraduhr are still somehow preventing her soul from reaching Savai."

"Veraion," Chester said. "Do you think… crystal." Her dark, fearful gaze rested on his, and when he clenched his jaw, it was clear they were thinking the same thing.

"The Heart of Sontar Ivel," she said. "The castle is in the middle of Sontar Ivel. What did Ilia look like? Maybe she was there."

The others were glancing between the two in confusion.

"She…" Veraion's brow furrowed, and he swallowed the knot in his throat. Then he turned to Yrilim. "Is there anywhere I could get parchment? And a pencil?"

Yrilim nodded and quickly hurried off. Talen watched him go with a raised eyebrow.

"Has he forgotten he's a lord and has other people to run errands for him?" he muttered.

"Yrilim always did things himself—you know that," Kazim said.

The palace hand Meha returned with the milk Talen had asked for. She passed the jug to Aven and the giant tipped his head back, drinking the whole thing in one go. The others watched and laughed when he belched. He smiled and nodded, handing the jug back to the woman, and she took it away, disappearing behind a thicket of plants. Yrilim returned, giving Veraion the items he had asked for.

Veraion sat back, closing his eyes. His jaw was tight as he took in a deep breath, and with one hand holding his glowing pendant, with the other he began to draw.

Yrilim looked up as Yenea entered the courtyard, Fairo by her side. She wasn't wearing her usual amount of jewellery, just simple earrings, and flowing about her body were loose robes. Fairo headed over to his brother, laughing at the axe protruding from the tree, for he knew exactly why it was there.

"Behraz!" Fairo laughed, picking up the boy as he raced over. He then grimaced wildly. "*Atesh*—why are you *sticky?*"

Fehir chuckled into his tea. "He's a child. Children are always sticky."

Aiyat sighed, finally admitting defeat, and put the book away.

"Are you going to hunt?" Behraz asked.

"Of course," Fairo answered, craning his neck as he tried to avoid being touched in the face. Aiyat looked at Fehir with concern.

"Fehir," she said. "Tell me you're not going."

He gave her a look. "Of course I'm going."

She sighed deeply, and he leaned in, kissing her on the cheek as she gazed off with a glare.

"I will bring back food just for you," he said.

"We have food here." She looked at him sharply. He didn't pull back and only smiled, inches from her face. She shook her head at him, though she softened.

"Come." Fairo smiled, bouncing sticky Behraz in his arms. "Let's meet your uncle's friends!"

He headed over to Yrilim and the others, Yenea at his side.

"Morning." Yrilim smiled.

"Good morning," Yenea said. "We leave for the hunt tomorrow—would you like to join us?"

"Hallows!" Behraz giggled.

"The Hallows?" Chester repeated. "Isn't that where you were ambushed?"

"Yes," Yenea said.

"Is it wise for you to return?"

"Humans cannot and will not deter us from upholding traditions," she said curtly.

"There have been many hunts since the attack," Talen said around a mouthful of food. "I'm in."

Kazim also raised a hand, nodding.

"Can we come?" Faraji asked. "It's beautiful here and all, but I'd happily take a break from the heat. Even if it means freezing for a day."

Fairo nodded. He'd lost the war with Behraz and now had a sticky face.

"Yrilim?" Yenea asked. He glanced at Chester. He didn't want to leave her.

"I'll go," she said. "Don't let the baraduhr ruin this for you."

Aven raised a hand to join, and Yrilim smiled. Aven was always so loyal.

Yenea nodded. "Then it is done. The carriages will be here tomorrow after breakfast."

Behraz's sticky hand reached for her and she glanced at him. He wanted her earring. So she took it off and handed it to him. Yrilim smiled.

"We'll be ready," he said, and she nodded. Then she and Fairo headed back to his parents. Fairo flung the boy into the air, eliciting a loud laugh, and caught him swiftly.

"How did they become friends?" Maina asked, watching them go.

"Yenea, Fairo, and Fehir went to school together," Yrilim said.

"But they're so much older than her—*Ohhh*..."

"They're all the same age." He nodded. "But Fairo and Fehir bound, as most twins do, whereas Yenea hasn't yet, so they've aged while she hasn't."

"That's confusing," Aven murmured.

"Aiyat was a castle hand," Yrilim said. "Still is, but she's in charge now."

"So she has a baby with Fehir, but he's bound to Fairo, and she's still in her prime," Maina said. The Sirenveli nodded. "And Yenea is the same age as Fairo and Fehir, but is in her prime." They nodded. "Is Aiyat the same age?"

"Aiyat is younger, maybe ten years."

"I don't blame her at all," Faraji said, watching the twins from a distance. "I also like my men older and rugged."

Chukuma snorted into his juice.

"And you two," Talen said. "You're bound, friends?"

They nodded.

"It is my job to find Faraji a rugged, older man." Chukuma smiled painfully, and the others laughed.

Veraion finally stopped drawing and handed his parchment to Chester. Her eyes widened.

Veraion was an exceptional artist. The picture was quick and sketchy, yet stunning. Chester had no frame of reference, for she had no idea what Ilia looked like, but from what Veraion had drawn, she could see Ilia had carried herself with grace. Her eyes were almond-shaped, nose slender, eyebrows and lips thicker. Despite the drawing being black and white, Chester could tell her eyes had been bright and mesmerizing.

Aven leaned over to look at the drawing and dropped his latest sausage. "Holy... You sure you're not exaggerating?" He glanced at Veraion.

"She was more beautiful than I could ever draw," Veraion murmured.

"More beautiful than this?" Aven pointed. Chester yanked the parchment away from his grubby finger.

"Don't ruin it," she said, still staring.

"She dyed her hair black," Veraion said, explaining the dark locks. "To try and fit in. It... never did much. She took potions too, to remove the colour from her markings."

Maina leaned over to look at the drawing and nodded. "Can confirm Ilia looked like that, if not more beautiful in real life."

Now everyone was trying to get a look.

"Holy fucking Atesh," Talen muttered. "That was your ilis?"

Veraion nodded, though he seemed withdrawn from the bustle.

"Well, I don't know if this is good news," Chester said, "but she wasn't one of the water azheeks they had in that cave. I didn't see her there. In fact, the woman, the water azheek, she looked... like Elaira."

Veraion's brow furrowed.

"Elaira once told me they had something on her," Chester said. "Someone. It could have been her sister, or... given that Elaira was raised by Venhel, I think... I think it was her mother."

The man sighed, closing his eyes. "I feel bad, you know. I spent so much time hating her. I should have known it wasn't her fault."

Chester smiled, though it was small. "You did what you could. So did I." She handed the parchment back to him. "I didn't know you were such a good artist."

He blinked at her. "You knew I used to draw for Nobaru. You bought me supplies!"

She smiled sheepishly. "I mean, part of me thought—part of me *hoped*— you were sending stick figures back to Zalfur."

He laughed.

"You know what?" Talen piped up. "We have a whole day and a night before heading out to the Hallows. How about we show you around the city?"

* * *

Talen was a very avid tour guide, waiting impatiently as a healer checked the newcomers' wounds before he swept them away and showed them his favourite spots in the city. From his little house on the outskirts of the palace, built into a rock face, to the pastry shop he frequented. He took them to the training grounds, the city square, and to the busiest bazaar. They spent hours there, and Talen guided them through, pointing out his favourite merchants and craftsmen, trying to shower the newcomers with gifts of silk and tapestries, of floor cushions and spices, and it took both Kazim and Yrilim to get him to stop.

Any time someone stared at the foreigners, Talen pointed at Chester and loudly informed the entire market that she was Yrilim's ilis. The lord blushed every time, hiding behind his hand.

Aven's extravagant robes blended perfectly into the colours of the bazaar, and when he saw a vendor selling peace silk clothes he rushed over and commissioned the man to make a set large enough for him—pants and a robe to commemorate the city of fire.

And matching sets for Chester and Veraion.

Aven seemed to forget he wasn't rich anymore, but as he wandered off to stare at a distracting pipe, Yrilim slipped the vendor all the coin he needed.

Talen had a name for every cat they passed. At first the names seemed genuine, but after a while it was clear he was making them up on the spot. After the sixth time he called a cat Habib, Kazim made him shut up.

Talen guided them through markets of cloth and clothes until he brought them to a sea of Sirenveli lamps. The newcomers stared around at the twinkling colours in awe. Aven wanted to poke them, play with them, but he was afraid of shattering the glass.

They hung from the ceiling in clusters and spirals. Some boasted various shades of blue, others green, while some had tiles of fire and some held every colour under the sun. Faraji, Maina, and Theideus all bought a lamp each. Chukuma bought one of the floor-lamp spirals, needing seven of the mosaiced lanterns to satisfy his taste.

He then regretted it as his five-foot form had to carry it around the rest of the day.

Talen dragged them around the city, but it was his last stop that he was the most excited about.

The lake.

Turquoise water twinkled in the sun, growing darker and darker the deeper it got. Greenery lined the surroundings, rocky ledges overhanging one side, dirt turning to fine sand closer to the crystal-clear water.

Theideus's eyes lit up and Maina smiled, leaning over from her horse to nudge him.

The lake was busy, many Sirenveli lounging about in the sun, swimming in the cool water. Some had built small rafts and floated peacefully away from the busier areas.

Talen came from his stallion, tossing a stable girl a coin, and she beamed, rushing about their horses. She bowed for each of them. At first the newcomers thought it was because of the lord, but as they slipped from the saddles and she continued bowing at their horses, they discovered it was the beasts she showed her respect to.

"Is that normal?" Aven asked, voice low. Talen glanced at him and then looked at the girl.

"Of course," he said. "Our horses are beautiful, majestic—powerful. We respect them as much as they respect us. We only ride—we only *touch*—with permission."

Aven nodded, appreciating the respect for beasts. Then he glanced at the lake. "Is nudity allowed?"

"Welcomed."

Aven ripped off his clothes, throwing them aside, and ran. He leapt off a rocky ledge and soared into the air, curling into a ball, landing with a splash that showered everyone around him.

"If he turns into a wasfought, don't be alarmed!" Yrilim called to his people. "He's a... mutant. A big... friendly... mutant."

His people looked at him in confusion.

Aven broke the surface, still a giant man, with a grin from ear to ear. He beckoned the others to join him. They were already halfway out of their clothes, leaving it all in a great heap, and they ran for the lake, kicking off the ledge.

The water was crisp and cool, a relief for all that weren't fire azheeks. The Sirenveli watched them in awe, at Aven's sheer stature and shocking abilities, Veraion's, Faraji's, and Chukuma's darker skin, but mostly, they watched Theideus. Who had not yet surfaced.

The water azheek shot around the bottom of the lake. His pale hair and lighter skin twinkled in the depths, moving so quickly and gracefully he looked like a fish. Maina smiled.

"Drinks!" Talen called. The stable girl hurried forward. "Could you pop into Ferhat's and tell him Talen is at the lake? And that I want to show the newbies a good time? My pants are over there—take some money."

She smiled and nodded, hurrying off once more.

Chester floated on her back, eyes closed, a smile upon her lips. Cool water muffled the world around her, lapping against her skin. The sun worshipped her skin.

She felt good. She felt safe.

As Yrilim neared she smiled and opened her eyes, looking over to find him floating on his back.

"This is nice," she said. He nodded, as blissful as she. "I can't believe you left this behind."

"I mean, I didn't plan on staying away *forever*."

Chukuma and Faraji swam over, and Chester watched them with a smile.

"I bet you're glad we taught you how to swim," she said. Chukuma laughed.

"Yes, okay, you were right. Swimming is fun."

The stable girl returned. A middle-aged man followed, carrying a crate full of colourful drinks.

"Ferhat!" Talen beamed. "Thank you!"

"Always a pleasure." He smiled, crouching to pass Talen a drink. Talen was sitting upon a ledge, deep enough to remain in the water but shallow enough to enjoy his booze. He took the offering from Ferhat, and as the others swam over, taking their places along the ledge, they were given a drink each.

"Come by sometime," Ferhat said, caressing Talen's cheek, and the man grinned.

"You know I can never stay away too long."

"Did you take them on a tour?"

"I did."

"He took us to a different brothel today," Kazim said. Ferhat scoffed.

"You're going to have to make up for that," he warned, and though he turned with a huff he still sent a coy smile over his shoulder as he went.

"This is why you get stabbed." Kazim smirked over his drink.

"Hey, I have never owed Ferhat money," Talen scoffed. "For... too long."

The others laughed.

Theideus finally emerged from the water, tossing his head back, pushing away his hair with a smile.

"Feels good?" Maina asked. The man nodded, ecstasy in his gaze. He sat on the ledge, accepting a drink.

Azheek markings decorated his entire body in points and swirls like winding rivers. He had only a few scars from fighting, the two beneath his chest from old surgery.

"Is there any chance I could ask for paper and pencils again?" Veraion said. Chester smiled, and quickly Talen beckoned over the stable girl.

"Paper and pencils! Or parchment and charcoal, whatever you can find."

She bowed, hurrying off once more.

"She's going to be so tired tonight," Yrilim said, chuckling.

"Rich too," Talen said.

"Yeah, be careful." Kazim smiled. "You don't want that one coming after you."

Veraion climbed from the water, sitting cross-legged on the rocks, drying off in the sunlight.

By the time the girl returned he had finished his drink and the others had returned to lounging in the pool. He sat back, gazing over the twinkling lake with a smile, and began to draw.

* * *

Colours flooded the sky as the group of friends watched the sun set. The roof of the palace was swamped with carpets and cushions, every one decorated and sewn with warm patterns and motifs. Large pillows and floor sofas lined the sides of the roof's railings, allowing comfort no matter where one would lie or lean.

Low tables boasted food and drink, the meals pre-cooked by palace workers as many of the guests were not fire azheeks themselves. There were plates of fried vegetables—eggplant, peppers, and potatoes—served with yoghurt and sauce. Once more they were given sheep cheese, cucumbers, and tomatoes, and on every table was a plate of pita bread, surrounded by bowls of dips: dips made of ground hulled sesame, chickpeas, lemon juice, and garlic; dips of cooked eggplant, olive oil, and seasonings, mixed with the seeds of pomegranates. There were bowls of fruit—plums, apricots, pears, apples, grapes, and figs, some fresh, some dried—and beside these, pastries and cakes made with nuts.

The air smelled of tobacco, molasses, and fruit, for there stood hookah pipes around the space. Each pipe was decorated, the stems carved with patterns, the bases painted or intricately crafted. Most had one or two hoses to smoke, though some of the larger hookahs had three or four. The largest was plated with gold, the base in the shape of a sitting camel.

In the city they could hear music—drums beating, rababs and sarangis ringing—flowing through the streets and to the palace.

Chester was with Yrilim, resting upon a colourful floor sofa as they ate, and around them the air was ripe with laughter. Chukuma, Faraji, and Talen were the loudest, coughing every time they smoked, not due to discomfort but to the onslaught of jokes that were impossible to ignore. Chester watched her old friends with a smile.

Veraion was beside Aven as Kazim took apart a hookah and showed them how it worked, and seated upon a ledge with a plate of pita bread and a bowl of hummus, Maina and Theideus watched the sunset. Buildings glowed with warm light: torches, beacons, and towers of fire illuminating the great city. There were fewer hot air balloons in the sky now, as most went up in the day, and they gazed up in awe.

Aven shoved eggplant and cheese into his mouth before pointing to the base of the pipe Kazim held, the golden camel.

"What is that?" he asked.

"A camel," Kazim said as he reassembled the piece. "We don't have them here. This was gifted to Lord Ekhrem and his ilis, Mazhar, at their binding celebration, by Lord Hamsa of Sakhala, a desert city to the south-west. Sakhala and Sirenvel are sister cities, technically, but due to the shifting earth, we are very, very far away now. When Hamsa travelled here for the ceremony, it was the first time our cities came together in centuries."

"Why the travel?" Veraion asked. "Sakhala is very far away."

Kazim glanced at him, then around the roof to double-check who was there—more importantly, who wasn't.

"Well… when the three air azheek cities came together and formed an empire… it made many of the others feel a little… uneasy."

"Ah."

"I think they just wanted to make sure old alliances still stood."

"But Zalfur was founded generations ago," Veraion said knowingly. "And yet the fear only kicked in within the last century."

"Look, the Red Emperor has a reputation."

Veraion smiled and nodded. "There it is."

"Zalfur may have been united physically before him, but it was still at war. And an empire at war with itself is nowhere near as powerful, or terrifying, as an empire united."

Aven ate more food, munching slowly as he watched the blood moon making her way into the night's sky.

Maina and Theideus came from the ledge, taking seats around the Sakhalan hookah as Kazim added the last of the tobacco, flavoured with apple and mint.

"I still can't believe you're a human now," Chukuma said, watching Aven.

"I still can't believe you're a fucking wasfought," Maina said.

"It never occurred to you that I was a wasfought?" Aven laughed. "I mean, every hunt had holes in it."

"Oh, I'm sorry," she said loudly. "Is it common knowledge that wasfoughts can turn into men? Was I *supposed* to assume something I had never before heard about ever? Also, in my defence, it's not like I ever saw you in your wasfought form. And even when you are a wasfought, you're not a common wasfought, are you?!"

She got louder and more theatrical as she went, and the others laughed. Theideus looked like he couldn't breathe.

"Look at you!" Maina motioned at him. "When was the last time you saw a white-and-grey-and-black wasfought? Every wasfought I've ever seen has been brown!"

"Okay, sorry," Aven laughed.

"He's a northern wasfought," Veraion said. "They only look like that in the icelands."

"So every time I told you I was from the north, I wasn't lying." Aven smiled to display all of his teeth—teeth he had continued to brush.

Into the night the friends talked, laughed, and smoked. They ate until they could eat no more, drinking juice, tea, and wine. They smoked apple and mint tobacco, orange and peach, and Talen insisted that two-apple was even better than one.

The sky was filled with a blanket of stars when Lord Ekhrem came up the steps, and Yrilim hurried forward, taking his father's hand.

"Would you like to join us?" he asked.

"Actually, I was going to see if any of you wanted to join me," Ekhrem said. "It's a beautiful night—I'll be taking a balloon up."

Maina's eyes widened. "Yes please."

Ekhrem smiled. "You can get the best view of the city up there. You can even see the east ocean."

Veraion, Aven, Maina, and Theideus moved forward, joined by Talen and Kazim, and though Chester rose to her feet and smiled respectfully to the old lord, she declined.

"I'm really tired," she said. Aven immediately came back, but she smiled and placed a hand on his arm. "Go. I bet it'll be beautiful. Veraion can draw it for me."

Veraion smiled. Aven nodded, and Chester watched the group head away, down the steps, disappearing from view.

Chester and Yrilim sat back down with Chukuma and Faraji, listening to the distant music. Chukuma seemed to be falling into a food-induced coma, resting his head in Faraji's lap, smoking the Sakhalan pipe.

"How long have you all been here?" Chester asked. "It looks like you've been here your whole life."

Chukuma smiled. "I'm bringing so much stuff when I go home." He gasped and sat up. "That's it! I'll start trading Sirenveli goods in Foros—I'll sell pipes and lamps and—and Habib cats! I'll be rich!"

Chester snorted into her drink. Faraji cackled and hit him, and he laughed his way back to her lap.

"I left Foros when I saw Yenea at Sontar Ivel," Yrilim said. "I saw what you saw, her there, and Azhara attacking you. I knew I had to come back, let everyone know I was okay. I should have left earlier—I should have left the moment you did—but I just… I don't know. I wasn't ready."

"What's the story with Azhara?" Chester asked. "Why did she attack me? Why didn't they just approach me to talk?"

He sighed. "I think they were going to. That was Yenea's plan. But Azhara was always brash. She was prone to using her fists and not her words, and she…" His voice trailed off and he swallowed the knot in his throat. "Azhara was with us in the Hallows when we were attacked. She was one of the only ones that managed to get away, and I think… I know… she lived with that guilt. The guilt of losing her friends. The guilt of losing her lord. So when Yenea felt me and there was a glimpse of hope, they went as fast as they could to where Yenea felt the call."

"But all they found was me," Chester said. He nodded and smiled sadly.

"Guilt," he said. "It does things. Makes you lose your mind a little bit."

Chester thought of Veraion, the pain he felt over losing Ilia, and she thought of Ezaria and everything she knew he had done after losing his brother. She nodded.

"Nobody knows what happened to Azhara?" she asked. Yrilim shook his head. He sighed.

"When I disappeared, Yenea could still feel that I was alive, and okay, but I… I didn't contact them. Or anyone. I was a fool."

"Nah." Chukuma shook his head. "It's nobody's fault but ours. Foros was too good, we were too good—you didn't want to leave."

Yrilim smiled. "You're right. It's your fault entirely."

They watched the blanket of stars above them, and in the distance, a new hot air balloon rose into the sky.

"Are you going to go back?" Chester asked her friends.

"At some point, I think so," Faraji said. "But I'm in no rush. It's hot here, very hot, but beautiful."

"I feel like my head is in a bowl of water," Chukuma said, head still in her lap, and she flicked him roughly on the forehead. He laughed, sitting up, rubbing his skin. "Ow!"

"You." Faraji pointed. "Curse the gods for giving me you."

Chester smiled. "I always knew you two would bind."

"Tell me about Sontar Ivel," Faraji said. "Is it true, what they say about the eternal bloom? The City of Flowers?"

Chester nodded. "Aven developed a bit of an addiction for plucking them," she said fondly. "He always had flowers in his hair and got so excited when we'd find the buds growing back."

"So there's an endless supply of food," Chukuma said.

"That's what it was built for, right? To protect the Five and all azheeks from the Fen. From what was trying to kill them. Even if you closed every gate to Sontar Ivel, the city would never run out of food or water."

"The Fen?" Yrilim said.

"Oh, the Fen… They were the people, or the things, that killed the Five."

"How do you know this?"

"An elder," Chester said. "A guardian. The one that gave Aven his ability. She… she had some prophecies."

"Holy shit." Chukuma stared. "What were they?"

"A king."

"A *king*?"

"Apparently a king will rise and save the world." Chester spoke dismissively, almost mockingly. "Made, not born."

"Made," Chukuma murmured. "Fuck it, make me king—I'll save the world!"

They laughed. Ekhrem's air balloon was floating in the distance, and as Chester watched it, her smile slowly faded. She thought of Aven, how distant she had been, how unable she had been to tell him why.

She looked down, to the pillows around her, and swallowed the knot in her throat. She knew she had to tell someone or it would eat her alive.

"I… I think I have to tell you something," she said. Yrilim looked at her. He could already feel how scared she was, his throat growing as tight as her own.

"You don't have to," he said. Chukuma and Faraji looked at one another, and then Chester.

"You don't have to," Faraji said.

"You know, right?" Chester murmured, eyes still on the ground. She held the fabric of her pants, wringing it as her hands began to tremble.

"I'm sorry," Yrilim said. "I didn't say it, but when I saw what happened, I reacted, and…"

"Nothing happened," Chester whispered, trying to lie. "Nothing happened. Nothing happened." Her voice cracked, throat tight, tears welling in her eyes. And with every repetition, the words became less and less believable.

"Nothing happened," she said. "Nothing happened. *Nothing happened.*"

She broke. Tears spilled from her eyes as she shook, hands and feet tingling, and the air became impossible to breathe. Every breath was shallow and rasping.

Yrilim watched her from where he sat, knowing he couldn't touch her. Not now. Chester closed her eyes tight, wiping the tears from her cheeks, pulling her legs close to her body as she trembled. Chukuma and Faraji remained still, fighting to hold back their own tears.

"Chester," Faraji rasped, but Chester shook her head, eyes shut tight. She raised a hand, as though to ask them to wait, but soon it balled to a fist and returned to her body.

Chester cried, every breath a dry rasp, her body numb but for the haunting pins and needles in her hands and feet. The pins and needles that came every time she was reminded of what happened.

"Four seconds," Yrilim said. "Breathe in through your nose, slowly, for four seconds."

She did.

"Hold it for four seconds, and then breathe out slowly, through your mouth. Four seconds."

Chester followed his instructions. Four seconds. Four seconds. Four seconds.

"Hold your breath," he said. "And then repeat."

Chukuma took Faraji's hand and squeezed it tight, his own trembling. Seeing Chester like this—one of their oldest friends, one of the strongest people they knew—was difficult to bear.

Four seconds in, four seconds held, four seconds out, four seconds held.

The distant music was all they could hear but for her controlled breathing, and as they listened, it grew more stable. More and more until her breathing wasn't forced, until feeling had returned to her limbs.

Chester sniffed loudly, wiping away the snot from her nose and tears from her eyes, and she finally opened them. She kept her gaze on the ground for a moment.

"Ah, fuck," she sighed. "I still can't say it."

Yrilim smiled encouragingly. "You don't have to, and never have to. Not if you don't want to."

Chester looked at him and smiled. "Thank you." She offered a hand. "You can touch me now."

Yrilim took her hand and moved close, wrapping his arms around her, and she closed her eyes, resting her head upon his shoulder. He was so warm, so familiar: a part of her. Then she held out a hand for her two oldest friends, and in an instant, Chukuma and Faraji were with her, arms wrapped around her, shielding her from the world.

Chester cried, doing what she could to swallow the knot in her throat.

"I can't tell them," she whispered. "I can't tell Aven. I can't do that to him." She looked at Yrilim. "It would destroy him. I can't tell him."

He nodded. "Then don't."

"He's been through so much—I can't do that to him."

Chukuma held her tighter.

"Take care of yourself." Faraji nodded, smiling as best as she could. "If you can't tell Aven then that's okay. Just make sure you do what's right for you."

Chester nodded, wiping the tears from her cheeks before closing her eyes once more, disappearing into the embrace of her friends.

CHAPTER 19

THE HALLOWS

Five carriages and a swarm of Sirenveli horses poured from the city gates, heading across igneous tundra, riding for the Hallows. Among the hunters were Chester, Yrilim, Aven, Chukuma, Faraji, Talen, Kazim, Yenea, Fairo, and Fehir. Many more fire azheeks had gone with them.

Every horse was adorned with intricate saddle blankets. Tassels flowed from the edges as they galloped, coins jangling about the beasts' necks, the horses as jewelled as the people themselves.

Every rider was wrapped with cloth—even the fire azheeks. While they could not feel the cold, their bodies would be working harder to stay warm. So every man and woman of Sirenvel wrapped their heads and bodies in thick cloth, decorated and beaded like their horses.

The beasts rode fast and hard with little need to rest, reaching the Hallow forest by sundown. The hunters made camp, setting up tents and building a fire. It didn't take long for them to start eating and drinking, and soon enough, Talen was singing a drinking song as he encouraged Kazim to swallow his entire bottle.

Chester was seated between Yrilim's legs, leaning back on his chest as he sat against a tree. Aven lay as a wasfought beside them, his head in her lap. Chester's fingers gently roved through his thick fur.

"Aven!" Talen called. "What is the alcohol tolerance of a wasfought?"

Aven transformed, though he remained in place. It made some people uncomfortable, but Chester was so used to it she didn't react.

"I have to drink a lot," he said simply. Kazim held out a bottle, and he finally picked himself up, accepting the offering. He flicked the cork aside and tipped his head back, swallowing the whole thing in three large gulps.

He handed the empty bottle back to Kazim, who stared at it with wide eyes. The group laughed loudly, and Fairo chucked another bottle at Aven. The giant caught it and took a seat, taking his time with this one.

"Alright," Talen said. "It's about time we asked the big question. Tell us the story, the great love story of Yrilim, lord of Sirenvel, and Mahriel, champion of Sontar Ivel."

Chester laughed. "Everyone knows about that."

"We were there, remember?" Fehir smirked.

"Right."

Yrilim was shy now, growing progressively smaller and smaller behind her.

"Chester and I were at the river," Aven said. "And then we saw him at the waterfall. Pulled him out. My senses are strong, but even I thought he was dead."

"I'd never met another fire azheek at that point," Chester continued. "But I had a feeling, just by looking at him, that he was one. So... I went for it."

"You... kissed him?" someone asked.

"I set him on fire."

They looked surprised. Talen laughed.

"I started small first," she said. "Just in case he *wasn't* a fire azheek, but it worked. It brought him back from whatever world he was passing into."

"Valduhr," Kazim said. "Definitely Valduhr." Yrilim snorted.

Talen started a slow clap. Chester now looked just as shy as her ilis. He rested his head on hers, kissing her hair, though he also did it to hide some of his face from the people looking at him.

"It's not like I healed him," Chester said. "It still took many weeks with the healers for him to be at full strength."

"But you probably saved him from death," Talen finished. It was what he wanted to believe.

"How strong are you, Yrilim?" Chukuma asked. "We know you can fight, but you never really showed us your powers. Are you hiding that too? Are you ridiculously powerful?"

Yrilim glanced at him from where he was still using Chester as a shield. He tried to hide behind her even more. She pulled away and looked at him with a smile of disbelief.

"How strong *are* you?" she asked.

"Strong?" he said sheepishly.

"Blue flames, strong?"

"Sometimes…"

Aven looked impressed. Chester shook her head with a smile.

"Anything else I should know about? A second penis you keep tucked away?"

The others laughed.

"Hey, Aven," Chukuma piped up. "Have you mated with a wasfought?" Aven nodded. "A human or azheek?" He nodded. "Which one is better?"

"I mean, either way my dick is in something warm."

Kazim choked on his drink.

"So it doesn't matter?"

"They both have perks," Aven said. "I've mated with several wasfoughts and only one human. The wasfoughts aren't as passionate, but they never tried to kill my friends in their sleep or themselves later on, so…"

The group went quiet, and they glanced at one another, unsure as to what to say. Chester placed a hand on Aven's arm. Talen laughed awkwardly and moved the conversation on

"How far did you get in the tournament?" he asked.

"I almost made top ten," Chester said. "I would have, had I not thrown the match and let Veraion win."

They laughed, taunting him despite his lack of presence.

"Did you ever hear of Azhara?" Yenea asked. The group went quiet once more.

"No, I'm sorry."

"Her mother says she can't feel her anymore."

Chester's brow furrowed. "As in…"

"Turned human, died human, or trapped."

"Are you going to go back and try to find out what happened?"

"She exposed herself to an entire city of people, a city she knew had humans. She knew the risks. She made her choice."

"Take it easy, Yenea," Kazim said. "Don't express your grief so hard."

"And who was the man that shattered her legs from halfway across the arena?"

Aven growled. The others leaned forward with interest, having heard the story. Fairo and Fehir were listening intently.

"Athos," Chester said. "Undefeated champion."

"For how long?" Chukuma asked.

"Ten years. Eleven now."

"What is he?" Fairo asked.

"Human. Apparently."

"You don't believe it?"

Chester was silent for a moment. "I don't know what to think of Athos."

* * *

The sun rose and the hunt began. They spread out in groups with no less than four members in each, bringing back their kill to the main camp, where a few Sirenveli were tending to the haul.

Aven placed a deer into a carriage, Chester laying down a string of rabbits in another. When they stood back, Aven's nostrils flared.

"There's a wasfought in there."

"I'm sorry," she murmured.

"We're not creatures of prey. We are the hunters, not the hunted. We don't eat azheeks, especially not fire azheeks—you would burn us alive from the inside out. They should leave us alone."

Yrilim approached, hauling a boar to the load. Aven clenched his jaw and clicked his neck, heading back for the woods. Yrilim noticed his mood and glanced at Chester, but she was already following the man back to the hunt.

They moved through the woods and saw the rest of the hunters crouched in bushes up ahead, so they dropped down and carefully inched forward. Yenea was in the lead, her eyes fixed on something through the trees.

Slowly she raised a hand and two hunters raised their bows, drawing back arrows. Aven sniffed the air and his eye widened.

Wasfoughts.

Aven charged forward, his body transforming as he tore through the group, throwing them aside with a roar. Two arrows landed in his back, but he hurtled towards the beasts.

Every one of them had a body of warm fur, tan to brown and even black, with markings like warpaint. The beasts turned to him with hackles raised, baring their teeth, but upon hearing his warnings, they turned and bolted.

Aven rounded on the azheeks with a snarl.

"What the hell was that?" Yenea snapped, coming to her feet.

"Did you see how many of them there were?" Talen exclaimed. "That could have fed so many people!"

"Those are my people," Aven snapped, his body turning somewhat human.

"You aren't one of them—you know that," a Sirenveli woman said.

"Those wasfoughts were with child. They were mothers. Would you kill a pregnant woman?"

Chester came forward and placed a hand on Aven's back. His hackles rose and fell as he fought to control his anger. Heavy breaths fogged the air before him as he glared at the azheeks. They were still arguing, throwing insults at him, but as he looked at Chester, he couldn't hear the others.

Tears welled in his single eye. He focused on her, fighting to find calm in her light green gaze, and she took his hand, squeezing it tight. Something had changed in him the night he killed the pregnant wasfought, and she knew it.

Aven closed his eye, a tear sliding down his cheek.

"What were you thinking?" a Sirenveli man spat.

"They would have killed you," Chester said.

"We could have taken them. Wasfoughts are no match for fire."

"Those were *mothers*," Aven hissed.

"Oh please," Yenea scoffed. "It's not like you haven't killed a wasfought before. I guarantee you, you've killed mothers."

The giant started forward, his colossal hand balled in a fist. Fehir and Fairo stood before Yenea, but it was only Chester's touch, grabbing his hand, that made him stop.

Aven stood in his place, holding Yenea's cold gaze. The others were beginning to think they should drop the matter.

"I have killed wasfoughts before," he snarled. "But I gave them warning. I told them what they were up against. They knew I was there to fight, or to protect. I don't *sneak-attack* them. You know you would stand no chance in a real fight."

"And what about the deer you sneak-attack?" Yenea said. "Or the rabbits? The boar? Don't pretend you care. We all know how many carcasses you eat in a day. There isn't a single wasfought that isn't a serial killer."

Aven turned away from her with a growl, running a clawed hand through his hair. He was so close to caving her skull in.

"You hypocrites," he snapped. "You love your horses. You show them respect. You *bow* to them. But every other animal can go fuck itself? Why?

Because you don't need anything from them? Only the animals you want to *mount* are worthy of respect?"

Yenea laughed. "You want to talk about hypocrisy? You only care about wasfoughts because you happen to be one. You will kill and eat every other animal that lives. Wasfoughts kill for *fun*. Just because you can stand on two legs now doesn't mean you're any less of an animal. You can't pick and choose what meat people eat. Here we eat wasfoughts. And you? You've probably eaten humans."

Aven clenched his jaw, grinding his teeth, nostrils flared.

"Guys, leave it," Chester said. "You have more than enough."

Yenea let out a snort, turning to Yrilim. "I hope you knew you were signing up for a three-way relationship with a woman and her dog."

She spoke lowly, but everyone heard it.

"*Yenea.*" He stared.

"I'm about to fucking kick your ass," Chester hissed.

"Have at it, Mahriel," Yenea said. "Or will you have your dog fight the battle for you?"

Chester took a step forward. She had to look up at the woman, but there wasn't a hint of intimidation in her eyes. "He's a wasfought, you dumb bitch."

Yenea's hand wrapped around the hilt of her scimitar.

"*Yenea,*" Yrilim said darkly, but his sister kept her piercing gaze on Chester.

"What is your problem?" Chester snarled, her face inches from the other's. "You've had an issue with me since *before* we met. You made up your mind before you even knew who I was. *Why?*"

"What kind of a person leaves their ilis behind?"

The air was silent. Even Chester couldn't respond, and Yenea knew it.

"What kind of a person leaves and chooses a *stranger* over the one they are bound to?" Yenea hissed. "What kind of a person travels with a *stranger*, further and further away, to a tournament? What kind of a person leaves their ilis to gloat in *gold and glory?*"

Yenea's voice was low and shaking, every word a justified insult.

"You may love him," she said. "And he may love you, and you may share a bond that even I can feel. But I will never call you my brother's ilis. I will never call you a daughter of Sirenvel. Because you had the ability to leave him behind. I have never known an azheek that could willingly leave their ilis, and I curse the gods for making you the first. I don't know what you are, but deserving of my brother, you are not. Deserving of a place in Sirenvel, *you are not.*"

Yrilim swallowed the knot in his throat, taking a step back. He could feel his sister's anger, and from the woman he loved, guilt. Chester understood every word Yenea said, and she had nothing to say in return. Because she too did not understand how she had left him in Foros.

Aven's brow furrowed, and he turned to the trees. The hackles rose through his skin. He cocked his head, listening.

"Something's coming," he said lowly. "I hear footfall. A *lot.*"

Yrilim's eyes widened and he grabbed his weapon, staring around fearfully.

"Baraduhr!" Aven yelled.

A masked rider charged through the wood. Yenea didn't waste a second before she grabbed the horse's reins and was dragged through the trees. The stallion's neck twisted from her weight but it kept galloping. The rider drew their sword and swung, but she dodged it and planted a dagger in their leg, drawing a loud yell from beneath the mask. Yenea grabbed them and yanked as hard as she could, both rider and azheek falling from the horse.

Back in the clearing, war had broken loose. Baraduhr poured in through the trees, the air filled with shouts, screams, and the clash of metal on metal. There were muffled cries from beneath metal masks, but the loudest calls of all were Aven's roars. His bones crunched and muscles shifted, his body changing from man to beast as he fought.

Chester yelled, slamming her hilt into a mask again and again and again until it cracked and the hilt met skin. And she kept going. She didn't stop until skin peeled from bone. Blood sprayed her face, but she never looked away from the mess before her.

She leapt back as a sword swung for her face. She rolled over the ground, swiftly on her feet, and with a harsh jerk, her hilt extended. She swung her polearm, splattering trees with blood. Red dripped down her face and she yelled, her pupils glowing.

Kazim and Talen were fighting through the trees, swinging their sickle swords, hacking off heads. Talen leapt off a tree and pummelled a man in the face, dismembering another as Kazim separated arms from bodies.

He stared through the trees with wide eyes, seeing no end to the swarming baraduhr.

"There's too many," Kazim gasped. "There's too many!"

"They were waiting for us!" Chester called to him. "I knew it was a stupid idea coming here!"

She ran for an approaching group of baraduhr and dropped to the ground, skidding through them, swinging her blade. Legs split in half, showering the ground with blood.

Aven roared, ripping a man in two. He threw the halves at another, grabbing the nearest, ramming the baraduhr face-first into a tree. By the time it fell, its skull was in pieces.

Aven's single eye was wide as he stared around. There was no end to the masked men.

He turned to look at Chester, her pupils glowing as she wheeled around, slicing limbs from bodies, but soon she was surrounded and a baraduhr took her down. Aven charged towards them, ripping the attacker from her, engulfing another in his jaws. He threw the baraduhr away.

His wide eye looked to her, to the masks swarming.

He turned and ran.

Chester's face fell.

She ducked to the side, dodging a blade that only just missed her face, but her eyes were still searching the trees where Aven had disappeared.

Her attacker came close once more and she grabbed him, slamming her forehead into his mask. He staggered back in alarm. The baraduhr swung his blade and she parried the attack, raising his weapon, kicking him in the gut. With a swing from her blades, she slit his throat open. Red sprayed as he fell, flesh peeling from his gaping oesophagus.

Veraion was asleep in the palace gardens, listening to the fountain, but there came a disturbance in his dreams, in his visions. His brow furrowed, sweat beading on his forehead, and soon Maina looked at him from where she and Theideus sat.

Veraion woke with a loud gasp, eyes snapping open and body rigid as he sat straight up.

"Baraduhr," he rasped. "*Baraduhr!* They're being attacked! *They're being attacked!*"

Maids raced to tell Ekhrem, and Ezaria shot into the courtyard, landing heavily before the earth azheek.

"They're being attacked," Veraion said. "In the Hallows. South-west of the city."

Ezaria shot back into the sky, and they watched as his armour and weapons zoomed after him through open windows, wrapping around his body, bladed longbow soaring into his grasp.

A chilling horn sounded through the city as Veraion tore for the stables.

Yrilim raised a hand and a blast of fire sent three baraduhr from their feet. Fire ignited their robes, surrounding their bodies, and he wheeled around, parrying an attack with his scimitar. He ducked another swing, raising his hand to send forth an explosion of flames.

Nearby, Faraji slammed her warclub against a baraduhr's head. The obsidian stones embedded into skull and she kicked the man away, wrenching her weapon free. Chunks of flesh clung to the stones.

She ran, leaping into the air, kicking off a tree, and planted her club into another baraduhr. As she moved, the trees whispered.

With a yell, Faraji threw forward an open hand, summoning her powers. The trees answered and vines fell from the skies. As a baraduhr ran into their midst, they grabbed him. Faraji closed her fist, throwing her arms apart, and the vines tightened around his limbs, tearing them from his body.

Another baraduhr ran for her, and she slammed her elbow into their mask. She swung her warclub, planting obsidian into their ribs.

Chukuma threw his axe and it landed in a baraduhr's chest, sending the man backwards. He had a shield strapped to one arm, a great mask with horns along the sides and top, painted and lined with furs on the inside, padding every blow. Arrowheads protruded from the bottom, and as a baraduhr ran for him, he raised his shield and pelted towards his attacker.

Faster and faster he moved, and though Chukuma was small in stature, the impact of his muscle, throwing all of his body weight into the shield, blasted the baraduhr from her feet. Her arms fractured in the blow.

Azheek and human tumbled through the trees and he was quick to scramble on top of her, bringing down his shield. The arrowheads punctured her throat, blood spurting from arteries as he yanked it away.

Chukuma came to his feet, and as more baraduhr ran for him, he stood his ground.

Chukuma opened his hands, every muscle tensed as he pulled at the earth. A low rumbling caused the forest to shake. He shouted, throwing his arms forward, and roots split the ground. The earth cracked and crumbled, breaking as roots charged up from beneath, shooting forward like whips, grabbing the baraduhr, yanking them into the ground. The baraduhr screamed as they were pulled in, legs disappearing into the dirt. Chukuma closed his fists and pulled his arms back, and the earth wrenched the baraduhr down in forceful jolts.

Their legs were taken first, then their torsos.

They screamed, grabbing on to whatever they could reach, but it was hopeless. They disappeared, buried alive.

Chukuma ran forward, yanking his axe back into his possession.

Fire licked up the trees. Every azheek was using their powers.

Yrilim swung his flaming scimitar and separated a head from its body. No blood was shed, the wound cauterized upon impact. He saw Chukuma through the woods.

"Get out of here!" he yelled. "Get Faraji! Get out of here!"

Yrilim dropped to one knee and closed his eyes, burning bright beneath the lids. Veins around the sockets glowed like molten lava.

"Oh shit." Chukuma stared. He turned and ran, grabbing Faraji by the arm as he went.

Yrilim knelt, hands on the hilt of his weapon. His muscles shook, flames licking his skin, which was starting to glow. Lights flickered from him, but before he could finish, a blade plunged through his side.

Yrilim yelled, eyes snapping open. The fire disappeared from his stare.

The sword was pulled from him and he fell to the ground, rolling over to slice through the back of his attacker's heels. The human fell, screaming, and Yrilim plunged his scimitar through their throat.

With a groan, he returned to one knee, closing his eyes, gasping in pain.

Yrilim summoned his powers once more. His eyes shone beneath the lids, veins molten, skin glowing. His hands clutched the hilt of his weapon, blood spurting from the throat it was embedded in.

Fires around him flickered out, sucked from the air, the element transferring to him instead.

Power surged inside him, more and more, swelling within his veins like a volcano ready to burst, and as he felt the fire churning, he let go.

Flames burst in every direction, the baraduhr before him charred in seconds.

Fire blasted through the woods, catching every baraduhr in its way. The flames raced through the trees, getting weaker the further they went, but they didn't stop.

Chukuma and Faraji ran for the tundra as fast as their legs could take them, tearing for the horses that were still tied in place. Many had broken free and were bolting in a panic, and they cut the others from their bonds.

"Go!" Chukuma yelled. "*Go!*"

They could hear the roar of fire through the trees.

Chukuma and Faraji yelled with desperation, running for the open plain, commanding the horses to follow, and as they reached the tundra, fire blasted behind them.

Chukuma and Faraji fell to the ground, sent from their feet by the force of the explosion.

Chester yelled as pain shot through her side, as she felt Yrilim's wound. She raced for a flaming baraduhr, severing head from body, and charged for another. She moved through the woods, searching for her ilis, but couldn't see through the swarm of masks.

Fehir body-slammed a baraduhr and swung his axe at another, sending the human from his feet. He cracked open ribcages and sliced through guts, spilling intestines over the forest floor, and as he saw more masked men running at him, he yelled and charged. He swung his blade, glowing with heat, cauterizing wounds, the metal singing as it moved. He worked his way through the numbers, every muscle rippling beneath his armour.

The man kicked a baraduhr away, embedding his axe in another, and grabbed an attacking human. He raised the man above his head, throwing him down. A spear throttled through his chest.

Fairo froze. His eyes snapped wide open as he felt it, a phantom blade in his heart.

Fairo wheeled around, tearing through the trees.

Fehir dropped to his knees, looking at the spear in his chest. Fairo raced to him, catching him as he fell, but it was too late.

Fairo screamed, eyes bloodshot and tears spilling down his cheeks. Staring around, he saw the assailant.

He charged.

He grabbed the baraduhr, spearing him to the ground, striking the human's head against a large rock. He grabbed the man and slammed the back of his head against the boulder again and again and again until his skull split, leaving hair, scalp, bone, blood, and brains over the stone.

His voice cracked as he shrieked, and though a blade plunged into his side, nothing hurt more than the pain of losing his brother.

He turned around with glowing pupils. He snarled through blood and grabbed the attacker, slamming his skull into their mask, and as they staggered, he ripped the metal from their face.

Fairo dug his thumbs into their sockets, screaming, yelling, bursting eyeballs, and as another baraduhr came for him, he threw the first down and left them to burn. He ran, grabbing Fehir's battle-axe, and decapitated the second.

Ezaria pelted through the sky, towards the burning trees. Over igneous rock, he saw a skirmish up ahead: Chukuma and Faraji fighting off five baraduhr.

Ezaria drew three arrows and released them. Each arrow landed through an eye-hole, taking down three of the baraduhr. Chukuma and Faraji stared up in alarm, but the silver-haired lord continued into the burning woods, leaving them with an opponent each.

His arrows pulled from the corpses and shot after him. Ezaria broke through the flaming canopy, and when the arrows returned to his grasp, one with an eye sliding along the shaft, he pulled back on his bow and fired them again, felling more attackers.

Landing beside a fallen fire azheek, he sliced off a baraduhr's head with his bladed bow. Then he threw it. The bow throttled through the trees like a boomerang, decapitating five men before it zipped into his grasp, and the moment it was in his hand, he threw again, sending it straight into the chest of another. The human flew backwards.

Ezaria knelt, placing fingers upon the fire azheek's neck. No pulse.

He rose to his feet, eyes livid. A group of baraduhr charged towards him so he threw up a hand, sending them from their feet, blasting them into trees. Their spines shattered on impact.

His bladed bow ripped out of a corpse, flying into his grasp, and he kicked off the ground, shooting into the sky.

Through the woods he could see bodies everywhere, baraduhr and azheek. Then he saw Yenea, her flaming scimitar separating limbs from bodies. Ezaria tore for her, brandishing his bow, drawing three arrows to fell three men.

He landed beside her, kicking away an oncoming baraduhr, and she looked at him in confusion as she sliced off a head.

"There's more coming," he said, raising a hand, imploding an attacker with a close of his fist.

She swung her scimitar and dismembered a man, cutting off head and limbs. "How did you know?"

"Veraion."

She slammed her foot into a baraduhr, sending them careening back, and swung her blade through another's gut.

The lords fought side by side, and one after the other, baraduhr fell to the ground.

Chester moved through the trees with no remorse, swinging her polearm. She worked fast, severing limbs from bodies and heads from necks, but where there was a moment to slow the killing, she took it.

She grabbed a baraduhr and slammed the woman into a tree, pushing her blades into the human's gut. She stared into the eyeholes, pushing her weapon higher and higher, cutting through flesh, muscle, fat, and organs, into the woman's diaphragm. The baraduhr's screams rang.

Chester ducked as another attacker swung at her. Then she shoved her hand into the first human's gut and grabbed her intestines. Chester swung around the second, wrapping the first's innards around the human's neck, choking the man with organs.

Yrilim grabbed a baraduhr sword, his own nowhere to be seen. He kicked the man to the ground, slicing his head off.

"*Come on!*" he yelled.

Two baraduhr charged. He ducked, casting a fireball, but it wasn't strong enough. Blood dripped from his torso, pooling down his stomach and back.

A baraduhr kicked him in the chest and he was sent staggering, but he caught his footing, glaring with bared teeth.

Yrilim lunged, swinging his sword at the nearest opponent. With a crunch it sliced through the man's neck, stopping halfway. He grabbed the hilt with two hands and yanked the sword back, and as the baraduhr fell to his knees, Yrilim kicked him in the head, knocking it loose from his body.

Another baraduhr charged at him and the two went tumbling over the ground. When they stopped, the human grabbed a dagger and plunged it into Yrilim's chest.

Yrilim yelled, his eyes blazing. Flames glowed inside his throat.

He clenched his teeth and spat scalding saliva, sizzling the mask, melting eyeballs. The baraduhr fell back, screaming, clawing at their own face.

Yrilim stood, his chest heaving.

He was thrown off his feet. The blow came so suddenly and with such force, he flew through the air and crashed into a tree, so winded he couldn't even gasp.

As the world wheeled around him, he pushed off the ground, blinking widely. When he stared around, fighting to bring the forest into focus, he saw figures—giant figures.

Wasfoughts.

Wasfoughts charged through the flaming woods. They leapt over fallen logs, hackles raised and claws bared, teeth dripping with manic drool. They were already covered in blood.

Among fur of black, brown, and tan was a beast of white.

Aven stood, his body shifting, and let out a deafening roar. The mutant saw Yrilim through the chaos and held his gaze for only a moment before charging into the flames.

The pack tore through the woods, ripping baraduhr apart. Blood splattered in every direction as they slashed their claws, spraying organs across the earth, breaking bones as easily as though they were twigs.

Yrilim saw a sword and painfully dragged himself forward, reaching with a groan. Just as he had the hilt in his hand, someone stepped on the blade. A baraduhr stood over him. The woman raised her sword, chuckling beneath the mask.

A wasfought threw her from her feet. One of the pregnant beasts from earlier that day.

The mother wasfought stood over the baraduhr. She bared her teeth, engulfing the baraduhr's head in her jaws, and tore face from skull. Yrilim stared in horror as the woman screamed, left with naught but muscle and veins. The wasfought reached forth with her claws and slowly raked the remaining flesh from her skull. Yrilim choked in horror.

The beast looked over her shoulder and he shook, trying to pull himself away. She growled, baring her teeth, and turned to face him.

Step after step, she advanced. Her muscles rippled in the firelight, every scar and burn on her body glimmering in the flames. She snarled, challenging him.

Then she stopped, almost as though she were smirking.

The beast turned and charged into the fray.

Through the forest, naught could be heard but the burning of trees and the growls of wasfoughts. The fight was over.

Hackles flattened against beastly backs. The pack scanned the trees with piercing eyes, sniffing the air. Aven rose to his mutant form as a few Sirenveli approached. The pack snarled at them.

"I... How?" Kazim croaked.

"Under one condition," Aven snarled, his voice halfway between beast and man. "You never hunt wasfoughts again."

"What?" A woman stared.

"You heard me. These wasfoughts agreed to help you, to *save* you, on the condition that you and your people must swear an oath that you will never hunt wasfoughts in the Hallows again."

A she-wasfought snarled, understanding every word they said. The fire azheeks gulped.

"You may still hunt," Aven continued. "You may return, as you have always done. You may hunt for your people. The wasfoughts will not touch you, and you will not touch them. This is their land. From now on, when you are here, you are their guests. Disobey their rules and you and every surrounding village will be exterminated."

The Sirenveli stared at him, turning their wide eyes to the beasts.

"I promise," the woman said.

"As do I." Kazim nodded. "I'll tell the lords. I'll tell the city. We promise. And please, tell them we're sorry. And thank them. Please."

Aven's cold glare remained on the azheeks a moment longer before he returned to his wasfought form and spoke to the pack. The azheeks exchanged shocked glances.

Then the pack leader stepped forward, a huge beast of black. His mane and hackles were tipped with gold, more markings of the same colour adorning his face and body. He was missing an eye, the remaining one a piercing yellow. The pack leader gave Aven a nod of respect.

"Give them their dead," the mutant said, barely understandable.

Sirenveli hurried to the carriages and retrieved the wasfought that had been killed. The pack followed, growling dangerously. Two wasfoughts sank their teeth into the fallen and dragged it away.

The pack took one last snarling look at the azheeks before they turned and headed through the flames.

Aven watched them go, his chest heaving. Slowly he turned human, blood dripping down his body. "Where is Chester?"

"I don't know."

"Spread out. Find everyone. Bring them back to the carriages."

Before anyone could reply, Aven turned and ran, leaping into the air. By the time his black feet met the ground, they had turned to paws.

Carriages tore across the tundra, towards the burning forest. Veraion was among them, ushering his horse to go faster as he watched the sun creep towards the horizon. They weren't far now, but he knew the attack had started some time ago. There was no telling how many had survived, but what he did know, what he could feel, was that Chester was alive. And that was all that mattered.

He was riding one of the Sirenveli horses, as they were faster than any other, and as they tore across the tundra, he whispered words of desperation. The beast let out a whinny, every muscle rippling as it stampeded through the barren land.

Thunder cracked through the skies and a patter of rain spread across the tundra. Maina and Theideus sat in the driver's box of a carriage, and as they felt a surge in magic, they looked to the skies.

Theideus stood, turning, looking to where he knew the eastern sea lay. He grabbed Maina by the arm and pulled her up, and as they stared across the tundra, they saw giant beasts rise.

Gangul.

In the sky, an air gangul soared and spun, its body long and swirling, needing no wings to fly. Airstones glowed along its scales, fur billowing from its horned reptilian head like a mane, but the fur had no end. It turned to air like smoke. Great whiskers grew from its snout, the longest flowing about its neck in the wind.

Its claws were huge, arms and legs spaced far apart down its long body. Fur ran down the gangul's spine, from its neck to the tip of its tail, growing long at the end, and like its mane, turned to billowing mist.

Clouds formed around the beast with every movement, graceful and mesmerizing, like a snake dancing in the wind. And beneath the beast of air, rising from the sea, came a water gangul.

Waterstones lined the beast's body, as long and fluid as the creature of the sky. It too had horns on its reptilian head and a mane that turned to spraying water, but down its spine ran spiked webbing. Its arms and legs were just as spaced out along its long, snake-like body, with webbing between each taloned claw. The beast had whiskers fanning from its cheeks, webbed close to the skin, the longest billowing back with every movement.

The water gangul came from the sea, and as it did, it spread its great wings, webbed like a bat's. Seawater sprayed with every beat, and as it joined the air gangul in the sky, the clouds filled with rain.

The gangul circled in the storm, soaring across the tundra, huge and incredible, and as Maina and Theideus watched, their hair billowing about them in the storm, the beasts flew over their heads, tearing for the burning woods.

The patter of rain turned to a downpour.

The gangul circled in the storm, emanating raw magic, the beasts so close to their distant gods. Every inch of muscle and flesh rippled and shone, and as the water gangul beat its wings, dancing with the beast of air, a deafening clap of thunder cracked through the skies. Lightning flashed around the gods' second children.

Light shone from the two, one with greys and purples, the other with brilliant blues, and the colours billowed into the sky, merging with storm clouds, creating rain to put out the forest fire.

The azheeks stared up in silence, tears lost in the downpour.

Lightning clapped and flashed through the clouds, and for a moment they could see the clear silhouettes of the gangul. Then they disappeared into the gale.

Veraion's horse moved faster and faster as he whispered, his voice urging it forward. As they reached the woods, he leapt from the saddle and ran.

Veraion broke into the burning forest, coughing loudly, squinting through smoke. The rain had already soaked his hair and was snuffing out flames. Coal and ash clung to his boots as he ran through the destroyed woods.

As more of the Sirenveli arrived, they flooded through the trees.

"Chester," Veraion whispered, feeling a pain in his shoulder. "*Fuck.*" He slowed, focusing his energy, his brow furrowing. "Tree," he murmured. He glanced around. "Which tree?"

He followed his instincts, racing through the woods until he saw her. She was standing against a tree—stuck, a sword through her shoulder. His face fell and he ran forward. Her head was drooped but her eyes were open, blinking slowly. Her lips looked pale, fingers trembling. Painfully she tipped her head back, and when she saw Veraion, cocked it.

"Am I hallucinating?" she rasped.

"Depends on who you see."

"I thought spirits would be prettier."

He cast her a dry glare.

"What are you doing here?" she croaked.

"I saw it happen."

"Like in a dream? A vision?"

"Yeah."

"Barely an earth azheek, my ass."

Veraion raised a hand to place it on her chest. He looked at her for permission and she nodded. He pressed his hand by the wound and closed his eyes. Chester watched him and snorted slightly, accompanied by a fond, but weak, smile. *Barely an earth azheek, my ass.*

After a moment, he spoke. "Nothing's punctured. Nothing vital."

"How did you see?" she asked. "Not my wound—this. The attack. How did you see what happened?"

He clenched his jaw and glanced at her. "It looks like I care about you."

She snorted weakly. "Are you binding to me, Raion?"

He smiled dryly, holding her gaze. He pressed down on her chest, wrapping his other hand around the hilt of the sword. "First of all, Chester, bonds aren't one-sided." He yanked it out of her.

Chester yelled in pain and fell forward but he caught her, helping her find her footing. She shook, breathing heavily, clenching her jaw. "*Fuck!*"

He tore the sleeve from his shirt and wrapped it around her chest and shoulder, tightening the pressure on her wound.

"You're welcome," he said.

"You saying I owe you one?"

Veraion looked at her fondly, placing a hand upon her cheek. He smiled. "Sure."

Chester snorted, shaking her head, and he picked her weapon up off the ground. Wrapping an arm around her for support, they headed through the woods. She winced, gripping her side, but she had no wound there.

Veraion stared around at the massacre with wide eyes. "What... happened?"

"You didn't see it?"

He cast her a dry glare.

"Aven enlisted a pack of wasfoughts."

They saw the giant through the woods, carrying an injured fire azheek. Aven spotted them and approached.

"I thought you said we shouldn't remove the blade," he said.

"Earth Boy said it was fine."

Veraion then saw a baraduhr suspended from a tree, intestines wrapped around its neck. Aven followed his gaze.

From the hanging corpse, their eyes trailed over the innards, around a branch, and to a body below. But the moment Aven saw the baraduhr's gaping stomach and entrails splayed over the ground, he turned away. A sharp breath left his lips.

"My *god*." Veraion recoiled.

"That was... me," Chester said. But she had seen Aven's reaction, and she came forward with a concerned look, placing a hand upon his arm. "Are you okay?"

He swallowed the knot in his throat and nodded, moving away from the sight. Chester glanced at Veraion, knowing exactly why Aven couldn't look at the gutted corpse. Einmyria.

She limped after the giant.

Chester gasped in relief as she saw Chukuma and Faraji, and the three came together, hugging tightly before they looked to the Sirenveli.

"How many did we lose?" Chester croaked.

"Dead?" Talen said. "Fehir. Hadis, Vefa, Nihan, Timur, and Huri. We're still looking for the rest."

Her face fell with every name. "Yrilim?"

"We haven't found him yet, nor have we found Yenea or Lord Ezaria."

"They wanted lords," Veraion said darkly. "The baraduhr always want lords. The more powerful the azheek, the better. It's why they wait here. For your hunt."

Chester turned and charged through the trees, as fast as her shaking legs could take her. Pain shot through her body with every step, and she stumbled but didn't stop. She moved through the bloodbath until she saw Yrilim's scimitar on the ground.

Chester collapsed to her knees. Picking it up, she looked around frantically. With a pained groan, she rose back to her feet, moving slowly through the pouring rain.

Then she spotted a figure ahead, a man grasping a tree for support. He winced as he yanked armour from his shaking body, feeling a pain in his shoulder that was not his own.

Yrilim clenched his jaw as he fought to stand, but he looked up as he felt Chester approaching.

"You dropped this," she said. He let out a small laugh, and she chucked the scimitar aside.

Chester came forward and grabbed him into a hug, but Yrilim fell to his knees. She caught him, helping him to the ground as he groaned.

"I thought you were supposed to be strong," she said.

"Hey, it's been a while since I've fought," he said, chuckling weakly, but his smile faded as he caressed her face. "We were safe in Foros. We were... safe... in Foros."

More azheeks approached, and Chester waved them over, limping behind as they carried Yrilim to the carriages. She picked up his scimitar and followed.

CHAPTER 20

SUMMONING

Hundreds of azheeks were gathered in the city square. Five funeral pyres surrounded a large stone statue of Atesh, the first lord of fire. Stars filled the sky, a blanket of dark blue and purple swirling above the city, and within it, fire. On every wall, on every building.

On one pyre lay Timur and Huri, for they had been bound, every other tower holding a fallen victim of the Hallows. Hadis, Vefa, Nihan, and Fehir.

All that was heard was the crackling of fire and cries from the crowd.

None of these azheeks had been meant to die. Had they been dying for some time, the moment they passed they would have returned to their element, crossing through to Savai as the gods intended, but these men and women were meant to live. So they were cleaned, wiped free of blood, and dressed in red, placed upon funeral pyres where fire would merge with their bodies and take them to the next world.

Fairo's mother collapsed in his arms, shaking as she sobbed. Fairo stood like a stone, eyes glazed over as he looked at his brother's resting place. Aiyat stood beside them, doing everything she could to stay strong for her son. Behraz held her hand, tears welling in his eyes, lip trembling.

The towers were lit. Flames moved higher and higher up the pyres. Then there came a cry from the crowd.

Behraz ran for his father's tower.

"No!" he cried. He grabbed the ladder and started climbing, fighting to get to where his father lay. But Fairo and Aiyat rushed forward and pulled him back.

"*No!* Daddy! Come back! *Come back!*"

The crowd watched in silence with tears flowing down their cheeks.

"You will see him again," Aiyat cried, holding her son close as he sobbed. "*You will see him again.*"

Chester watched with a knot in her throat. Even once Behraz and his family had disappeared into the throng, his cries were still heard.

Flames consumed the pyres, higher and higher, and when they reached the fallen azheeks, the fires sprang to life.

Flames roared around the azheek bodies, dancing and billowing. Lights rose from the corpses, of red, orange, and yellow, and as fire took their bodies, they became one.

The magic was hauntingly beautiful as the azheeks returned to their element.

A singer in the audience began a sorrowful song, and as she sang, more and more joined in until the cries rang through the city.

"Mother, look down upon us,
Mother, take their souls,
Mother, walk here among us,
Mother, take them home."

* * *

The sun rose to blackened funeral pyres. Veraion and Aven watched from the palace as the towers were taken down.

"Still no word about Yenea or Ezaria?" Aven asked. Veraion shook his head.

"The baraduhr want lords," he said. "They always want lords. The stronger the azheek, the more likely they will survive the torture, but Ezaria… I cannot bring myself to believe that he could have been taken. Just like that."

They shared a look, and Veraion clenched his jaw, letting out a sigh. He returned his gaze to the distant funeral pyres.

* * *

Yrilim stood in his chambers, gazing out of a window overlooking the city. It had been days and there was still no news. The sun rose and fell once, twice, three times, and still there was no word of Yenea or Ezaria.

He could hear whispers from the courtyard, where the others gathered in the night, but he couldn't bring himself to join them. He had been waiting to hear something about his sister, anything.

He now knew how she had felt when he disappeared. Worried sick. Nauseous. *Guilty.*

"Still no sign of Yenea or Lord Ezaria," came a messenger's voice below.

"Keep searching," he heard his father say.

"It's been four days, my lord. We've searched everywhere."

"Keep searching," Ekhrem said. "She's still alive. I can feel it. Yrilim can feel it."

Yrilim closed his eyes, clenching his jaw. He placed a trembling hand on the windowsill.

Chester entered the room and closed the door behind her. She approached slowly, and he smiled as he felt her nearing. The closer she got, the better he felt. She wrapped her arms around him, holding him from behind.

"We shouldn't have gone," Yrilim said. "I should have known better."

"You couldn't have stopped Yenea, you know that."

He sighed, but when he turned to look at her, his face softened. He pulled her into his arms. "Why must we always lose one when we've finally found another?"

"The gods have their plans, apparently." Her words were bitter.

"This isn't the gods," he said. "It's the baraduhr."

"Can you feel her?"

"She's alive. But she's… afraid. Or she was. I felt her fear for days, but today…"

"You would know if she was gone," Chester said. "You might not be blood related, but azheeks still have bonds with those they love, those that are family."

He nodded solemnly. "I'm sorry for what she said at the Hallows."

Chester smiled slightly. "Don't be. She's right. Even I don't know how I left. I don't know why, I just… It makes no sense."

"You share a bond with Veraion, right?"

She glanced at him and let out a soft sigh. She nodded. "Yeah. Although I think it's stronger for him. I think that's part of his powers—he… senses things. He feels things."

"He saw the attack in the woods when it was happening. That's miles from here."

"Yeah…"

Yrilim let out a solemn sigh, closing his eyes, resting his chin upon her head. Then he felt something.

His brow furrowed and he looked to the horizon. Chester sensed the change in him.

"Yrilim?"

"I feel something… I feel…" Yrilim's pupils glowed as he stared to the sky, fighting to see through the darkness. There was something far in the clouds.

Something was moving through the sky, a tiny form. The figure was miniscule, but it was heading towards the city. His eyes widened.

"Yenea."

Yrilim ran from the room and Chester followed. He tore for the courtyard, and the others looked up in alarm as he burst into view. Yrilim stared to the sky and the others followed suit.

The tiny figure was growing closer and closer. As it zoomed towards the city, the details became clearer.

Ezaria, carrying Yenea. She was unconscious, and he was fading too. They throttled towards the palace, moving dangerously fast.

"Oh no…" Yrilim stared.

Aven stepped backwards, his gaze fixed on the incoming lords. He readied himself.

Ezaria zoomed towards the courtyard and Aven leapt up, grabbing the two, flying backwards from the momentum, but he used his own body to break the fall, protecting the lords from impact.

Aven slammed to the ground, tearing across the stretch of grass, uprooting green to leave a channel of dirt in his wake, stopping only once the grass turned to tile. The others rushed forward.

"Aven!" Chester gasped. "Are you okay?"

"I'm fine," the giant winced. "I'm invincible, remember?"

"You're not invincible." She glared.

Yrilim ran towards his sister, cupping her face in his hands. Her eyes rolled back in her head.

"What happened?" Yrilim stared, but Ezaria looked at Veraion.

"*Earthstone. Now.*"

Veraion tore from the courtyard. As he disappeared, Ekhrem rushed into sight, castle hands at his heels.

Ezaria pulled himself up with an irritated wince. He didn't like feeling weak. He leaned against the fountain, silver hair pooling over his shoulders.

"Yenea!" Ekhrem gasped, hurrying to her.

"She's alive," Yrilim said. "She's okay—she'll be okay."

"What happened?"

"We let them take us," Ezaria said.

"Are you *mad?*"

"They took us to their base. A fort within the mountains of Rownen."

"What?" Chester stared.

"There was once a passage that led through the mountains, but it has long been blocked by the shifting earth," he said. "Nobody goes there. It had been decades since I'd flown near. We let them take us inside, to the dungeons. I can still hear the screams." Anger seethed in his eyes, and he looked at Ekhrem. "They're torturing azheeks in there."

He clenched his jaw, closing his eyes for a moment as he fought to stay conscious.

"They knew who we were. They'll know we're coming. The sooner we strike, the less time they have to prepare. But they *will* be prepared."

Ekhrem nodded, his jaw clenched and eyes angered as he held his unconscious daughter.

"We still don't know the extent of what they do or how they do it," Ezaria said. "We don't know what we'll be going into. You don't have to send your people. But I will be going in, and I will be getting those azheeks out."

"I'm with you." Ekhrem nodded. "Sirenvel is with you."

Veraion tore back into sight, throwing an earthstone at Ezaria. It shot into his grasp and he put it on the ground, grabbing a dagger, slamming it hilt-first into the crystal. The earthstone shattered, and he collected the shards in his pallid hands, green lights wafting from them. He raised them, eyes looking to the stars, and inhaled slowly. Lights of the earth rose from the stone, breathing into his lungs.

Ezaria's eyes glazed over. Using the earthstone to enhance his bonds, he called on his distant relative and what little blood relation they shared.

He closed his eyes, an eerie, contained breath leaving his lips.

With what energy he had left, Lord Ezaria achieved *ulu*.

Ezaria's call flowed through crystal and over earth, from the Sirenvel palace, through the city, to igneous tundra. The call travelled over Ianar to the northern woods and over mountains.

It travelled north-west, further and further from the eastern city of fire, soaring for the empire of Zalfur.

The call passed over snowy ridges to Ground Country, through forests of bamboo, pine, willow, and plum. Over fields and farms of cabbage, radish, daikon, and lotus root, it soared by the floating city of Akana.

Over terraces of rice, through fields of durian, mangosteen, persimmon, and rambutan. The call soared over animals, tigers and leopards, red pandas and golden monkeys. Takin and antelope roamed, pangolin scurrying in the night, and lazily, resting through forests of bamboo, were black-and-white giant pandas.

The call flooded over farms of lychee and pitaya, and as it moved north, it pulled higher and higher.

Through mist and clouds, soaring through the air, rocketing for the city of Zeda, the call pulled into the sky until it peaked over the edge and burst from the haze.

Over snowy mountains and frozen lakes, it flowed through gardens and over homes: houses and temples built from stone, wood, and bamboo. Lanterns illuminated the cold night, lining the streets.

Floating islands rested in the air, temples and homes upon them, falling rivers turning to mist in the sky. Leaves swayed in the wind, white and black pine, bamboo, and cherry, pink blossoms flourishing in the cold.

The call shot across Zeda, over pools and lakes, steam rising from natural hot springs.

Further into the city, higher into the air, towards the tallest mountain range of all. A path led through the woods, lined with stone lanterns, but the call soared overhead, into mist, until a castle appeared in the haze.

The walls stood tall, of white stone, with upturned roofs heavy with snow. Towers rose into the air, disappearing into clouds. Guards stood upon watchtowers and floated in the air, polearms in their grasps, robes billowing in the wind. And in the sky, twisting and turning in the clouds, was the great gangul of Zalfur.

The magnificent beast danced in the night, a blur among misty mountains, but as the call soared for the castle, the gangul felt it.

It looked up, eyes filled with light, and heard Ezaria's voice.

Over the first gates and into the castle, the call flowed through a courtyard blanketed by snow, lined with red emperor maple trees.

Into the grounds, through great doors and empty halls, towards an intricately carved round doorway.

Lord Ziang lay asleep, in bed with her ilis.

Ezaria's eyes snapped open, gone behind billowing light of purple-grey. Those around him stepped back in alarm.

Ziang woke with a gasp.

"*Send the army.*"
Ezaria's whisper echoed eerily as though spoken from across the world.

* * *

Yrilim moved through the palace, listening to the voices around him. Soft murmurs echoed through the halls: chatter from the kitchens and laughter from the gardens. It had been three days since the return of Yenea and Ezaria, and finally the city seemed a little more at ease. The loss of another lord hadn't been easy. But the lords were back now, and they knew that soon an allied army would arrive.

He let out a soft sigh as the cool breeze caressed his skin, always warm, always glowing. Even at night, in the dim light of the blood moon, he and his people were radiant.

He felt safe now, at home in the palace, for he could feel his ilis not far away. She was in the courtyard with her closest friends, protected from the world, and as he moved through the halls, closer to his sister's chambers, her presence grew stronger and stronger. That, most of all, helped him feel safe.

The doors to Yenea's room were large, curved at the top, ending in a slight point, and were intricate works of art. Ridged patterns covered them, golden, and the handles were large to match. Mosaic tiles surrounded the doors, and as Yrilim raised a hand to knock, they opened.

"Meha." Yrilim smiled. The castle hand returned the look fondly.

"She felt you coming."

Meha's smile always shone bright, brighter yet when she was around Yenea. Her eyes were large, lashes long, and a colour of deep amber, her nose cute, curved, and her cheeks full. Her hair was long, dark, and pooled down her back in loose waves. Meha usually had her hair in a braid, but at night, with Yenea, the braid came loose. Yrilim raised an eyebrow.

"I hope you've been letting her rest," he said. His words were kind, but she still blushed and stammered, ducking back into the room to hide. Yrilim laughed.

He entered to find Yenea in bed, propped up on a heap of ornate pillows. Her chamber was much like his, with a large bed at one wall, windows overlooking the city, and a great bath at the other end. But her room was more lived in, more loved. There were items here and there, pieces of furniture and many cushions she'd collected over the years, visiting the bazaar. She, like everyone else in the city, had a fair number of colourful lamps. The mosaic lights never failed to make a room look beautiful.

Yrilim snorted as he made his way to Yenea, spotting patches of shaving cream still left on her chin.

"You missed a spot," he said, taking a seat at the edge of her bed. Meha hurried over.

"I'm not done," she huffed. "I never miss a spot."

"My arms aren't broken, you know," Yenea said with amusement, but Meha shushed her and finished wiping the rest away. Meha's hands were wrapped with cloth; they always were.

Yenea was wearing a loose shirt, open down the middle from where Meha had been tending the wounds upon her chest. There was healing paste in some areas, but no cuts were deep.

Torches on walls flickered, illuminating the room with warm light, and Yenea's skin shone radiantly despite her bruises.

"How are you feeling?" Yrilim asked.

"Good." She smiled. "Better."

"Did they hurt you?"

"No, they wanted us strong for… whatever it is they do there."

Yrilim clenched his jaw and sighed, swallowing the knot in his throat. "Why did you let them take you? Why would you…"

Yenea smiled, clear sadness in her eyes. "They wanted lords. And I wasn't going to let them take you again."

He tried to fight the tears coming to his eyes, but it was no use. His breathing shortened and she took his hand.

"Four seconds." She smiled. He nodded.

He swallowed again and again until his throat stopped tightening.

"They knew who I was," she said. "And they knew who Ezaria was. So we let them take us. We pretended to put up a fight, but…" She watched him, unable to look her in the eyes. "The baraduhr started to dissipate after they got us. They were starting to back off. And that's all that mattered."

Yrilim took in a deep breath and nodded, finally looking back at her.

"I'm sorry I didn't come back from Foros," he said. "I knew you were okay, I just didn't… think."

"I've yelled at you enough for that."

He smiled a little and nodded. She watched him before letting out a sigh, gazing over her room.

"I know you want me to say something like 'it was meant to be', or 'you never would have met Chester if you had come home', but I can't."

Yenea held his hand and kept her gaze on him. Her stare was fixating, like she was seeing into his soul.

"I know you love her," she said. "But I feel it in my bones, Yrilim. She's going to be the death of you. She's going to be the death of us."

He squeezed her hand and held her gaze. "She won't. I promise."

"Don't make a promise you can't keep," she said softly. He clenched his jaw and nodded, and she smiled kindly. "Thank you for checking in on me."

"Always."

Meha sat beside Yenea and gave her a comforting smile.

She took in a long breath. "I heard about Fehir. Fairo told me."

Yrilim swallowed the knot in his throat and nodded.

"We'll take care of them," Yenea said. "Aiyat, Behraz. No matter what happens, they have a place here."

Yrilim nodded again. He was finding it hard to find words.

She smiled. "Go to bed, Yrilim. Your ilis awaits. We all need rest."

He nodded again, giving her hand another squeeze, and headed away. Closing the doors behind him, the presence of his sister grew more and more distant as the call of his ilis grew stronger.

* * *

The city of Sirenvel was returning to normal. People trained in the sun and harvested their crops, buying and selling wares in the markets. The bazaar was busy once more. Sirenveli relaxed in the lake, and those that had been injured in the Hallows were milling about with the others. Among them was Talen, sitting in the city square. He was first to notice the black cloud in the sky.

Talen stared up, gaze fixed on the approaching darkness.

A black cloud, moving towards the city of fire. A swarm. Talen tapped Kazim beside him and pointed.

All eyes turned to the sky, widening in fear. But Lord Ezaria saw the militia and rose into the air, hovering above the city. His cold gaze was fixed on the incoming army, his hair billowing about him.

"What the fuck is that?" Kazim stared, looking to Veraion nearby.

"The Zalfuri," he said.

"Make room!" Talen yelled. "Make room!"

He ushered people from the square, helping an old woman push her cart of wares from the open space.

The sun was at its zenith but the city was cast into shadow, rays shying behind a great swarm of beasts, birds larger than any the Sirenveli had ever seen.

The lacian were twice the size of horses, with faces and bodies like eagles and feathers of white, grey, and black. Their eyes were ice blue, beaks large and talons deadly, wings reaching over twelve feet on either side. They carried the Zalfuri soldiers, though some of the riders were not of the army. These riders brought with them supplies.

The fire azheeks stood back, their hair billowing in the disturbed wind.

Ezaria floated above the square's statue, and as the crowd watched, the army of Zalfur rose from their steeds. Air azheeks came from the saddles and plummeted to the ground.

People gasped as the soldiers shot down from the sky, soldiers in black and gold, their faces hidden by terrifying masks. Horned, fanged, snarling and angry, every mask with an eerie smile upon its face. Like cursed spirits of Valduhr.

The Fang'ei stood, spaced out across the square. Then more Zalfuri came from the sky.

Soldiers shot to the ground, one after the other, landing on one knee, heads bowed to the lord above. The army was dressed in armour of black and silver. They stayed in their places until every soldier of Zalfur was kneeling to Lord Ezaria.

The people of Sirenvel glanced at one another uneasily.

Ezaria landed, dust rising about his boots from the force.

"*Rise,*" he commanded in a language the Sirenveli did not know. The Zalfuri stood in unison, bodies rigid.

The lacian circled above them, calling. Their cries were shrill, causing some of the onlookers to wince.

"What are those?" Kazim asked lowly.

"Lacian," Veraion replied. "Creatures of the cold. Lords of the high skies. Only the Zalfuri Skyriders have figured out how to train them. Otherwise, they're as wild as wasfoughts."

Kazim's eyes rested on the lacian, on the riders remaining on their steeds. They didn't wear armour and instead were wrapped with furs, ruffling in the stirring wind. Their clothes favoured greys to blend into the lacian they rode, but upon their chests, decorating their uniforms, were colours of purple.

Kazim looked at a young woman, her long hair billowing about her furred shoulders. He could barely see her from where he stood, but her eyes found him too.

Ziang came forward to greet Ezaria. She was years past her prime, appearing in her fifties, eyes grey and hair black, held up with intricate pins that protruded outwards, decorative pieces dangling from the ends. Just like the rest of the army, dark tattoos marked her skin to mimic Old magic.

As she approached Ezaria, her distant relative, she held her chin high. Ziang nodded, and Ezaria took her forearm into a strong grasp.

Then the Fang'ei pulled back their masks. There were familiar faces among them: Nobaru and Vi'ra.

Vi'ra approached, nodding respectfully. Ezaria watched her, offering his hand. She too took his forearm in a strong grasp, and when she stood back, her barn owl swooped down from the sky and landed on her shoulder.

Ezaria nodded a greeting to Nobaru, knowing to keep his distance or his former apprentice would grab him into an unwanted hug.

A tall air azheek came forward, past his prime, with a body built for war. His long hair was tied back, facial hair upon his chin, and his eyes were a pale blue-grey. He too was Fang'ei, and Ezaria cast him a nod.

"Sanada," he said.

"My lord."

Lord Ekhrem moved through the crowd, Yenea and Yrilim close behind.

"Lord Ekhrem." Ziang nodded.

"Lord Ziang of Zeda, welcome to Sirenvel."

"Did you send scouts to Rownensel?" Ezaria asked Ziang. She nodded.

"Skyriders and a couple of Fang'ei. They'll keep an eye on it and let us know if anything changes."

The Zalfuri soldiers stood rigid, eyes fixed forward. The Sirenveli glanced at them uneasily. They seemed so unreal. They'd have appeared like mannequins if it weren't for the sweat that was already beading upon their porcelain skin.

Ekhrem raised his voice and opened his arms, welcoming his allies.

"Welcome to Sirenvel!" he called. "Please, make yourselves at home. We have cleared space for you to set up camp and have prepared food and drink. Tonight we feast! Sirenvel and Zalfur have long upheld an alliance. Tonight we honour that pact. Tonight we sing and dance and feast. And then... we fight."

A soft buzz sounded among the Sirenveli. Excitement. Nervousness. They watched the Zalfuri, rigid, cold, and finally Ezaria turned to his people.

"*At ease.*"

Only then did they relax, gazing around the foreign city. Most of them were sweating profusely, and granted freedom to move, fanned their faces and wiped their brows.

Nobaru ran to Veraion and grabbed him into a hug, gazing around with a smile.

"It's as beautiful as you drew it," he said. "Now take me to that damn lake."

* * *

Soldiers of Zalfur pulled off layers of armour until they were in naught but comfortable robes, wandering around in awe. The Sirenveli watched as they hovered overhead, exploring the city at different heights.

The camp was set up outside the main hub where there was plenty of space. Kazim wandered over, watching as the air azheeks zipped about, founding tents in record time. They hung banners of the Zalfuri crest, an air gangul upon black fabric. Above the soldiers' tents the gangul was silver, above the Fang'ei, gold.

Those that set up camp did not have any visible tattoos. They were not of the army. Kazim did notice, however, that they had plenty of scars. Scars from beasts. The lacian. Their banners were adorned with purple but there was no gangul upon them. Instead, Azheek Sa'uri that Kazim could not read.

Around camp, the giant birds were resting, ruffling their feathers in the warm air, though many were soaring about the skies. Some were resting outside of the city walls, preferring the colder climate.

Zalfuri sat here and there, eating and wiping sweat from their skin. The packed lunches they ate were triangular in shape, rice wrapped with seaweed, filled with pickled plums or salted fish. Kazim had never seen this kind of food before. He would have stopped and asked someone about it, but his eyes fell on a woman, the same woman he had noticed before. She was busy, setting up a tent, and he couldn't take his stare away.

She was in her prime, with kind grey eyes and soft features, contrasting the scars upon her skin. Her long black hair was braided back as she worked, setting up shelter for the army.

The woman looked up, feeling his presence, but the moment she saw him she averted her eyes, roping a tent into place, and moved away to continue her work.

A smile spread across Nobaru's face as he emerged from the water, as free from clothes as the Sirenveli around him. The azheek compass was tattooed on his lower sternum, right where Veraion had it. He, like all other soldiers, had extended his widow's peak, but now that he was naked, he exposed just how much of his body had been marked.

All of it.

Nobaru was covered: arms, legs, back, and panels down the front of his torso, leaving only a strip down the middle where his compass sat, and as more and more Zalfuri pulled off their layers, more tattoos came into view.

Many soldiers had tattoos to mimic Old markings, dark stripes decorating their arms, legs, and torsos, some even with the markings upon their faces, but greater yet were the tattoos with imagery. Most had large pieces upon their backs, some with art upon an arm, leg, or on their chest, but few were as heavily tattooed as Nobaru.

Their tattoos were stylized: tattoos of women, men, and historical figures. They had lacian, tigers, birds, fish, and flowers, some with mountains and trees native to home, and in the background there were ocean waves, clouds, and black wind bars.

On Nobaru's back was a woman, hair tied up with intricate pins and body draped in loose, extravagant robes. She was lounging, relaxed, stoic, and in her hand she held an opium pipe. The background was filled with cherry blossoms, petals dappling down his arms and legs as the piece merged with all the others.

Nobaru waved to the Zalfuri watching him from the rocky shore.

"Come on!" He beamed.

Veraion and his friends were situated at the shallow ledge, enjoying food and drink Yrilim had brought from the castle. Nobaru swam over, still encouraging his people.

"You'll regret it if you don't at least try," he called. "I can see you sweating!"

They laughed, and it didn't take much longer before the Zalfuri pulled off the last of their layers and dove into the cool water.

Chester watched them from where she sat, noticing two Fang'ei. They were as heavily tattooed as Nobaru.

"Your back makes a lot more sense now," Chester said to Veraion, and he smiled.

Nobaru pulled himself onto the ledge and accepted a drink from Talen, moaning loudly as the taste hit his tongue.

"*Ongji*, what have I been missing out on?" he said.

"I told you." Veraion smirked. "There's more to life than Zalfur."

"Tell that to Dad."

"Please don't call him that."

"He basically is, isn't he?"

"I am not calling Ezaria *Dad*."

"He hates it. It's the best part."

Veraion laughed and shook his head. "I'm still so surprised he's never punished you for your incessant need to push his buttons."

"Oh, he has. But I'm still his favourite apprentice."

Veraion made a high-pitched noise that clearly argued the sentiment. "We all know he favours Vi'ra."

"Okay, well, apart from Vi'ra."

Veraion smiled into his pastry.

"This city is quite sexual, isn't it?" Nobaru said, listening to music ringing through the streets, looking at the barely clothed locals and multitude of pleasure houses he'd passed on the way.

"We aren't ashamed of our pleasures." Talen smiled. "Those of us that enjoy sex are welcome, and those that don't are just as well received."

Yrilim raised his drink to toast to that, his glass met with Maina's and Theideus's.

"Question," Talen said, watching lacian circle the skies high above. "Your lacian, are they going to shit on everything?"

All nearby Zalfuri laughed.

"I'm not answering that question." Nobaru smiled, pushing off the ledge. He floated on his back, closing his eyes.

The sun was hot against his skin, a feeling he welcomed. He listened to the lapping of water and swaying date palm trees, smelling the feast as Sirenveli cooks prepared for the coming festivities.

"I don't know how it can get better than this," he sighed.

"Just you wait." Talen smiled. "It gets better."

CHAPTER 21

PREPARATIONS

The sound of drums, music, and laughter filled the streets. Fire danced in the night to illuminate the city, glowing in the middle of the igneous tundra. The Zalfuri camp was fully constructed. The tents were ready, banners hanging, armour off, and as the lacian rested, riders milled about the city square, eating and drinking what was offered.

Some Sirenveli wandered to the camp and were speaking with the newcomers, curious about their ways... and giant birds. Many were afraid, having never before seen lacian. It didn't help that the beasts' handlers told them it was best to stay away. Being told that lacian don't enjoy the taste of azheek flesh didn't help much either.

The cooks of Sirenvel were busy, now more than ever. With a great host of Zalfuri who could not cook food by hand, stalls were set up all around the square, preparing the best delicacies the city had to offer. And the Zalfuri came with their own gifts.

Rice wine in exchange for Sirenveli wine of red and white grapes. Sweet goods from Usan and Akana that were soft, softer than any of the Sirenveli pastries. Some were baked, made from wheat with fluffy insides, cross-hatched across the top layer of crisp cookie dough, and some were steamed, made from rice, pounded into paste until moulded into shape. These were filled with various flavours—red bean, peanut, and sesame—rolled with tiny seeds or soybean flour.

And then there were the small cakes that were neither soft nor overly sweet. Stunning to look at, the Sirenveli found themselves most curious with these moulded pastries, every one with an intricate design on top, some boasting the Zalfuri gangul crest. The Zalfuri cut these cakes into thin slices, encouraging the Sirenveli to take them with tea. Inside were pastes from red bean, green tea, or white lotus, and in the middle, a salted yolk from a duck's egg. It was an acquired taste, dense and rich.

While many Sirenveli and Zalfuri began the gathering with apprehension, they soon lost themselves in all the sights, sounds, smells, and tastes they had never before experienced. The Zalfuri found themselves laughing at the faces the Sirenveli made upon eating the salted yolks.

In the city square, the people of Sirenvel danced. Most of the fire azheeks were in naught but loincloths, favouring body chains and jewellery that would chime and shimmy with every movement. Belly dancers moved around the bonfire, swaying their hips. They jangled with every step and every shake, adorned from head to toe.

Aven was dancing, a jug of wine in one hand, his peace silk robe billowing about him as he swayed. Talen had tried to decorate him in body chains, necklaces, bangles, and anklets, but after the first time something caught on his forest of body hair, he was quick to take it all off.

Nobaru moved through the throng with a grin on his face. He wore naught but cloth around his loins, twisted and tied about his hips and between his legs to cover only his crotch. Around his waist was a belt, there only to carry a small bottle that was heavy with some form of liquid. Both his butt cheeks were on full display, but he was so heavily tattooed he looked fully clothed.

His hair was tied back in a messy bun and sweat glistened over his skin. He and every one of his people felt as though they were roasting, having come from Zeda mid-winter. He held a silk fan in one hand, doing what he could to cool himself.

"Wine?" someone said. The fire azheek was holding a large jug full of red Sirenveli wine, offering him a goblet.

"Don't mind if I do." He smiled. He took the jug.

Nobaru drank his way over to where Veraion was standing, friends seated at a table nearby. They had cups of wine, plates left with only crumbs, and hookahs filled with flavoured tobacco.

Chester sat, leaning against Yrilim, smoking as the group laughed. The two of them were not drinking, as their wounds from the Hallows had yet to heal, but in the heat of the festivities, surrounded by food and music and laughter, they couldn't resist the double-apple smoke.

"Raion!" Nobaru called. The earth azheek smiled and Nobaru ran over, throwing an arm around his shoulders, planting a kiss on his cheek. "Gods, it's as hot as Atesh's asshole in here."

The table laughed as he drank from his jug.

"Remember, we ride out tomorrow," Veraion said.

"Are you forgetting azheeks don't get sick?"

"Azheeks *can* get alcohol sick if they drink as much as you're drinking."

"I can ride with wine sickness."

"Are you sure?"

"Come on, the horses will just follow the other horses, and I'll shove cotton in my ears. Or, I'm Fang'ei." He fanned himself proudly. "I'll make the Skyriders take me with them. Hide me with the blankets."

Veraion laughed. He glanced at the bottle hanging from Nobaru's belt.

"Don't tell me that is what I think it is," he said. Nobaru cast him a smirk and a wink.

"Of course it is."

"Still?"

"Always. I like to prepare for the best. I'd rather have it and not need it than need it and not have it."

Veraion shook his head, but an amused smile remained upon his lips. The others had been watching and listening and couldn't help but ask.

"What's in the bottle?" Chukuma said.

"Lube."

Everyone laughed. Chester choked on a puff of shisha. Nobaru grinned and remained unbothered, if not proud. He watched Sirenveli dancers in the city square, adoring their full-figured bodies and chiming jewellery that glimmered in the firelight. As beautiful and radiant as every fire azheek's skin.

"I like it here." He turned to Yrilim. "Why did you leave?"

"I'm an idiot." He shrugged. His friends laughed.

"I'm glad you're an idiot." Chester smiled. "And if you look at it, it seems like everything worked out in the end. We all ended up here."

Chukuma and Faraji raised their glasses.

"It's hot," Chukuma said. "But it's nice."

Nobaru was halfway through another swig of wine when he tried to speak. "Mm—earth azheeks!" He pulled away from Veraion and moved to them. "I've never met an earth azheek before."

He shook their hands profusely and both couldn't help but stare. He noticed and smiled. He was ridiculously attractive and he knew it. He loved it, too.

Veraion raised an eyebrow at him. "Never met an earth azheek before?"

"You don't count." Nobaru waved him off. "You can't do anything."

Chester chuckled, but she choked on her shisha smoke and winced as pain shot through her shoulder. Yrilim took the nozzle from her with a laugh and drew in a long puff.

"Can you do cool things with trees and stuff?" Nobaru asked the Forosi.

"We can, yes," Chukuma laughed.

"You still have your powers, right?" Faraji asked Theideus, and the blond nodded. "Do you fight?" He shook his head.

"Theideus only fights when he has to," Maina said, understanding her ilis. "When he has absolutely no other choice."

"But you *can* fight? You were trained?"

Theideus nodded, but it was clear he was uncomfortable. The life they asked about was a life of his past.

"But you can *fly*," Maina said, turning the conversation to Nobaru. "I wish I could fly."

"Technically *I'm* not flying," he said. "I'm controlling the air around me to move me where I want to go."

"So... basically... flying."

"Basically, yeah."

They laughed.

"It's tiring though," he said. "Uses as much muscle power and energy as walking, or running, if you're going fast. It's not like I can just fly all day and feel nothing from it."

"People never really think about that, do they?" Chester said. "And it's not like we create the element—we have to summon it. It's a lot easier for me to steal fire from that candle over there than it is for me to summon fire anew."

"I wish someone had told me that before I became an azheek," Maina said, sighing. "Nobody told me how hard it would be. I'm too lazy to train— I just reap the benefits of not sweating. And being able to eat all the spicy food in the world. That's all I really need."

Theideus laughed silently.

"Everything we do takes work." Nobaru smiled. "Hence why some are stronger, because they train, and some are practically human, because they don't." He pointed at Veraion.

Chester smiled and shook her head. "I wouldn't be so sure about that. Veraion's quite the earth azheek."

Nobaru raised an eyebrow at her, looking to the man. "Did something happen? Something trigger a change in your powers?"

The earth azheek smiled to himself, taking a sip of wine from his goblet.

"Am I right?" Nobaru stood up, looking at him with interest. "What was the catalyst? Or... *who?*"

Maina looked at the tattoo on Nobaru's back of the woman relaxing, smoking opium. "Who's that?" she asked.

Nobaru lowered his voice, speaking in Azheek as he pointed to Veraion with thinned eyes. "*I will get to the bottom of this.*" Then he turned to Maina with a smile. "Zufang," he said. "She was the one that brought Zeda, Akana, and Usan together to become Zalfur."

"Oh, wow."

"This was centuries ago, of course. She was a respected member of court, well loved everywhere she went, the life of the party but also incredibly intelligent and a master with words. She had a way of securing treaties and trades. Zufang was from Zeda originally, and in her later years united the cities to create the mighty empire of Zalfur. Theeennn she retired to the countryside of Akana and smoked opium all day."

The others laughed.

"Hence, I love her." He smiled. "There's a running joke that Zufang only brought the cities together so she could access the best opium, and honestly, that's my favourite version of the story. A true hero."

Nobaru took a puff from the hookah and looked pleasantly surprised. "Oh… that's different."

"So one of your greatest historical figures was an opium addict?" Faraji laughed.

"Excuse you," Nobaru scoffed with comical insult. "Zufang was an azheek. She couldn't be even if she tried."

"But she spent the last however many years of her life smoking opium?"

"A choice. And a great one at that."

They laughed. Nobaru puffed again, enjoying the fruity taste. His voice sounded low as he spoke through a smoky exhale.

"Zufang's children followed in her footsteps, not in uniting cities and being good diplomats, but in lounging around and drinking, and whoring, and getting high. That was until the mighty twins, of course. Zufang was Ezaria's great…? Great? Grandmother?" He looked at Veraion for help, and the earth azheek shook his head and shrugged.

"Don't make me do maths."

"So, while the great Lord Zufang's immediate successors only tarnished her family's reputation, it is safe to say that it was successfully restored."

"It must be weird for Lord Ziang," Maina said. "Being so many years younger than Lord Ezaria, generations younger, but... not looking it."

"The amount of people he has seen grow old and die." Nobaru nodded. "I don't know how he does it."

"Did your tattoos hurt?" Chukuma asked.

"Like *fuck*. Took me ten years to finish all this!" He motioned at his body and the others laughed.

"Why'd you do it then?"

"Because I like the way it looks. And the way others look when they see me. When they see any of us."

"Us?"

"Fang'ei, right?" Chester said. "I've noticed the Fang'ei are the most tattooed."

Nobaru pointed at her with a smile. "Ding!"

"It's a status thing," Veraion said. "You have to earn the right to get tattooed, so the more you have, the more respected you are."

Nobaru stood tall, puffed out his chest, and then bowed deeply. All the while he fanned himself.

"Is this the part where we kiss your ass?" Chukuma laughed.

"I would love that." Nobaru smiled, picking up his jug once more. "Be sure to use tongue—"

Veraion shoved him over as the table erupted with laughter. Nobaru staggered with a cackle, spilling wine as he went, and Veraion shook his head. Still, he couldn't stop the grin upon his lips.

"Will you ever finish yours?" Chester asked him, and he shrugged.

"Look at it," Nobaru said, yanking up Veraion's shirt. "What a sad tiger."

"Maybe it's a white tiger," he said.

"Your skin is brown, you idiot—it's a brown tiger. Until you make it orange."

Veraion chuckled.

"Does Lord Ezaria have any?" Faraji asked, glancing up to where the lord was standing atop a nearby building. He wasn't wearing armour but he looked ready for war. He'd been standing there for a while now, overlooking the party, watching his people. Watching them mingle with the Sirenveli. He himself had established many alliances with foreign azheek cities, but rarely did they ever interact. It was dangerous, bringing foreign-blooded azheeks together, knowing full well what could happen if any of them decided to mate. But he also knew the importance of comradery and how much better armies fought when they cared about one another.

Nobaru followed her gaze to the silver-haired lord.

"Oh, he's *covered*." Nobaru nodded. "How do you think the tradition started? He was the first Fang'ei."

"He makes the Fang'ei get tattooed?"

"No, we do it because we want to."

Faraji was still watching Ezaria in the distance, unsure as to whether or not she was terrified by him. "Does he ever wear colour? Besides bits of gold or silver?"

"Yeah, but it's rare."

"Why?"

"He's worn only black since the day his brother died," Veraion said, and Faraji finally pulled her stare away, nodding.

"He wears red sometimes," Nobaru said. "When one is frequently splattered with blood, you may as well wear it."

Faraji smiled uneasily. "I expected him to wear red. What with the name and all."

"Name?"

"The Red Emperor."

Nobaru's wine flew from his nose. He laughed and then repeated her words like a child mimicking another. "*The Red Emperor.*" He snorted. "*Ongji,* that sounds stupid."

The others glanced at one another.

"Nobody calls him that," Nobaru said.

"Everyone outside of Zalfur calls him that," Veraion said behind his goblet.

Nobaru glanced at the table of foreigners and then shrugged. He looked up to where his lord was standing and the others followed his gaze.

"Does he have any colour in his tattoos?" Maina asked.

"History says he used to," Nobaru said. "But he carved all colour out after his brother's death."

"He what—" Chukuma stared. "He *what?*"

"Carved out—"

"Like with a…" Chukuma motioned as though stabbing himself with a knife and Nobaru nodded. All eyes went wide.

"Hhhhaaaaaaa." Chukuma grimaced, staring at the imaginary blade he was still wielding. His whole body shuddered.

"Fucking Valduhr," Faraji said.

"Are the rest of you not allowed to wear colour?" Yrilim asked.

"Oh, we are." Nobaru swallowed more wine. "But when we dress for combat we stick to black. Helps us disappear into the night. Also helps with not having to worry about blood stains."

Yrilim nodded.

"We'll be taking the silver and gold off our armour before going in," Nobaru said. "It's best when no one stands out. When there's no visual hierarchy—when the enemy can't figure out who to target."

"Says the man whose lord has silver hair," Maina said, laughing.

"Oh, he'll be dyeing it."

"He what?"

"Ezaria, he always dyes his hair black before battle. As I said, it's best no one stands out. Especially him."

"He doesn't want to be targeted?" Chukuma joked. Nobaru looked at him, serious now.

"If our lord, our strongest, is a target, it means he cannot properly protect the rest of us. If he is vulnerable, the rest of us are vulnerable. And now that includes you, too. If you are going into a battle with Lord Ezaria, he is your best chance of surviving."

Chukuma blinked, silent. Corrected.

"He's probably listening, you know," Veraion said. The others glanced at him uneasily.

"What do you mean… listening?" Maina stammered.

"He can make sound travel. Whispers in the wind and such."

"Fuck." Chukuma quickly hid behind his hand.

"Can you?" Maina asked Nobaru. He nodded but was otherwise preoccupied. He had returned to his casual demeanour and was watching a naked Sirenveli woman. Air and water azheeks had bodies that were more slender and streamlined, fire and earth far more compact and curvy, and he couldn't help but ogle at the well-endowed woman as she danced.

"Hey, Raion," he said.

"Hm?"

"Reckon Ezaria used to listen when we…"

Veraion let out an exasperated sigh and closed his eyes, fingers pressing to his forehead.

"I mean, I would," Nobaru joked.

Across the bonfire, Talen and Kazim were waiting in line for food, and though Talen was talking, Kazim wasn't listening. His eyes were fixed on a group of women nearby. Like the rest of the Zalfuri, these women were out of their armour and uniforms, but he could tell what they were. Two of them were soldiers, twins, with tattoos mimicking Old markings, and two of them had no visible tattoos at all. Skyriders.

Kazim couldn't stop looking at them. At one of them. At the woman from before.

"Hey." Talen snapped his fingers in front of Kazim's face. "Are you listening?"

"Mm," he murmured, not looking away from the woman.

She could feel him watching her. She could feel his presence. And though she tried not to acknowledge it, she couldn't help but glance over. She averted her gaze again.

"*Kazim.*" Talen glared. He was holding two skewers now, with potatoes, onions, eggplant, zucchini, and tomatoes, drizzled with yoghurt and honey from the nectar of the city's fruit trees. Kazim finally looked away from the woman when he smelled the food.

"Oh, thanks." He took both skewers and headed off.

Talen stared after him and threw his hands up in defeat. Before someone could move forward, he cut back in line.

"Hi, sorry, one more." He smiled. "My friend just stole mine."

Kazim headed towards the Zalfuri women, and one of the soldiers nudged the lady he couldn't stop staring at. She glanced over, swallowing the nervous knot in her throat.

"Hi." Kazim smiled. "Do you eat… vegetables?"

She smiled, blushing. "I do eat vegetables."

The woman next to her, without tattoos, had a rounder face, and the twins were visibly toned, taller, with angular features. They were a little passed their prime. One of them raised an eyebrow at Kazim.

"Are we all supposed to share those? Or did you just bring one for Rei?"

"Oh…" He blinked. "I'll go back—"

"I'm kidding." She smirked.

"Ji'ah!" Rei smacked her on the arm. Ji'ah only looked all the more pleased with herself.

"Hi, I'm Kazim." He smiled, offering a skewer, and when Rei took it, he offered his free hand to shake. She shook it, and he shook hands with the others.

"I'm Ji'ah," the soldier said. "This is my sister, Ah'ni, and Aina, and your new lover, Rei."

"Ji'ah!" Rei stared.

"Okay, you're drunk." Ah'ni guided her sister away.

"I'm not drunk, I'm an asshole."

Ah'ni and Ji'ah headed towards the lines for food, leaving behind the two Skyriders with Kazim.

"That is… raw." Aina pointed at Rei's skewer. Only then did Rei notice.

"Oh! Right." Kazim laughed sheepishly, taking it back. "How do you want it cooked?"

"Um… I guess… how it normally is?" Rei smiled. "We don't have this in Zalfur."

Kazim's hands burst into flames and they licked down the skewers. Rei and Aina watched in awe, and when the vegetables were perfectly flame-grilled, the fires went out. He held them for a moment.

"I'm not sure when they'll be cool enough to eat… or hold," he mumbled. He offered one to Rei and the other to Aina, and carefully the women accepted. They tried the vegetables that were closest to the top and looked at each other with wide eyes.

"Oh my god," Rei laughed. "This is amazing!"

"Isn't it?" He beamed. The women ate and he stood there awkwardly. "How uhh… how are you?"

It seemed as though Rei was going to give a generic answer, but she changed her mind and replied truthfully. "Hot."

He laughed. "Yeah, I guess I take that for granted. Never sweating."

"You can feel hot and not sweat," she said.

"Oh… I didn't know that."

She smiled, sharing a glance with Aina.

"Do you ever feel cold?" she asked.

"Not that I've noticed. We get tired, but not cold. Our bodies keep us warm no matter what. If it's cold, we just tire out faster."

She nodded. "Makes sense."

Then Ji'ah swooped by, holding a grilled kebab of her own. Her sister raced after her frantically but was a moment too late.

"He'd be nice to cuddle in the winter," Ji'ah cooed into Rei's ear, hurrying away as Rei turned, raising her skewer like a weapon.

"I'm so sorry." Ah'ni shook her head as she hurried by. "JI'AH."

Aina was trying to bite back her smile, failing miserably. "You know, I just realized I really have to… look at that fire. Over there."

She sidled off, leaving Rei alone with Kazim. The two glanced at one another.

"Are you and Aina soldiers?" he asked. "You don't look like it… no offence?"

"None taken." She smiled. "We're Skyriders. We train the lacian. We carry supplies and ensure the army is properly equipped and taken care of. The lacian wouldn't comply if we weren't here."

His interest only grew. "What are they like? I heard they're dangerous, and that only the Zalfuri know how to train them."

Rei smiled. "You want to know a secret?"

"I love secrets."

She smiled a little more and leaned in, lowering her voice. "The trick is that you *don't* train them. They either let you ride them or they don't. They either want to fly with you, or they don't. We just know that and respect that. Those that have no interest in us are free to leave whenever they want, but most return for the food. Still, some feed with us their whole lives and are never ridden."

He blinked. "Whoa…"

"Don't tell anyone that."

"Are they also impossible to kill? I heard they're like wasfoughts."

She laughed. "Lacian bones can be broken, and they decompose over time. They're just… hard to get to."

"Speaking of wasfoughts…" He directed his gaze over to where Aven was dancing drunk in the square. "See that man?"

Rei glanced at Kazim. He was so close to her, and despite her best efforts, her heart was racing.

"The big one?" she asked.

"Yep. He's a wasfought."

She glanced at him again. "We were told there would be a mutant, a wasfought man. Looking at him, I can almost imagine it... but... I'll have to see it to believe it."

He looked at her again, and she averted her gaze with a small smile. She had scars on her face, neck, and arms, more peeking out from beneath her shirt.

"I noticed... most of the Skyriders have scars," he said. "Some of them are pretty bad."

"Oh, many of the lacian are formidable, that's for sure. We may not be soldiers, but we fight an entirely different kind of battle. Every day."

"Do lacian fight?"

"No, they're smart enough not to get involved in our wars."

"Are you... covered? In scars?"

"I am—most are not where you can see them."

"Right now?"

She tried to battle her smile from spreading and looked away, blushing.

"I'm sorry," he said. "I don't mean to make you uncomfortable."

"I'm not, I... I'm surprisingly... comfortable."

"Me too."

They watched Aven for a while, and Nobaru as he danced wildly among the Sirenveli. He grabbed others, dragging them into the throng, encouraging his people to relax and let loose.

"He's funny." Kazim smiled.

"I don't think there's a single person that doesn't like Noba," Rei said. "He has all the characteristics of someone that should be an asshole: good-looking, ridiculously skilled, strong, Fang'ei, favoured by the lord himself—*trained* by the lord himself—lives in the castle, smart, quick-witted, confident... and yet. He's just so *nice*. He makes everyone feel welcome, no matter who you are or where you're from."

They watched as Nobaru took Vi'ra by the hand, and Rei laughed lowly.

"Oh, this is going to be good."

Vi'ra glared at Nobaru as he danced, spinning her around, but soon she couldn't help but break her harsh demeanour.

When Vi'ra laughed her entire face lit up. Her smile softened her cheeks, turning her eyes to half-moons.

She, like many of the other Zalfuri, wore her thinnest robes. The sleeves reached halfway down her forearms, ending almost exactly where her tattoos did, a matching sash tied around her waist. The neckline plunged, exposing Fang'ei tattoos along her chest and the old azheek compass on her sternum.

The silken fabrics reached halfway down her thighs, but like all Fang'ei she had so much art upon her legs they barely looked exposed.

Kazim glanced at Rei as she watched the others dancing.

"Do you want to dance?" he asked.

"Oh, I've never been much of a dancer," she said. "And I... I'm kind of enjoying this conversation. It would be too loud over there."

"This is true... I... I could give you a little tour of the city." He smiled. "Did you have time to look around before? We have a lake—do you like swimming?"

This piqued her interest. "I love swimming. My city is cold most of the year, and we have hot springs, but they're not really for swimming."

"How about cool water in a hot city?"

She smiled, and as they headed away, offered him some of the vegetables left on her skewer. She glanced up to the building where Ezaria had been, fearful of what he would think, seeing her walk off with a man of fire, but he was gone.

Veraion stood in his place, watching the dancers. Vi'ra laughed, and he couldn't help but smile. She had always been a hard one to make laugh, and he was glad to see that Nobaru still had the ability.

More and more people were dancing, allowing the drums to consume them. Chukuma, Faraji, and Talen were among them, and Maina grabbed

Theideus by the hand, heading into the throng, bringing with them their goblets to fill, empty, and fill again.

Chester and Yrilim remained at their table, watching the party with content smiles on their lips. The wound through his side and chest still throbbed, as did the one in her shoulder, and they regretted not being able to dance.

They watched the festivities, laughing as Aven went wild, but Nobaru was by far the most boisterous. Eventually he freed Vi'ra of his clutches and moved around the square, dancing with everyone else, encouraging them to lose themselves in the music.

His smile shone brighter than any fire. In Nobaru's presence, people couldn't help but enjoy themselves. Many also couldn't help but watch him, enthralled by his good looks and full bodysuit of tattoos.

Maina was one of these people, and it confused her. Some of his dancing was innocent and boisterous, spinning people around, but whenever his current partner would initiate, he wasn't afraid to let his hands wander and let theirs do the same. He pulled women against him, marvelling in their beauty, and draped his arms around men, adoring their physiques.

Nobaru collided with Talen, almost flinging him into a nearby fire, but he grabbed the man by the arm and yanked him back to safety. Their faces were inches apart, and Nobaru looked him up and down with a twinkling smile.

"Sorry." He winked before dancing away, throwing an imaginary lasso around Veraion. Talen watched him go with a slack jaw.

"Fucking Valduhr," he muttered. "I think I'm in love."

He was close enough to the tables for Yrilim to hear, and he laughed.

"About damn time!" the lord called.

Nobaru hauled Veraion into the swarm, spinning him around, and the earth azheek laughed.

The music was soft in the palace, far enough from the square to become a distant song. Ekhrem moved through the halls, his robes billowing about his heels. He had spent most of the day with his people, mingling with the Zalfuri, speaking with Lord Ziang, the Fang'ei, and Skyriders, and as the sun set and the true festivities began, he got to head home and relax. He was exhausted, relieved both of his children were home safe, mostly because he never felt right when they were gone. Partly because it meant they could take over his duties and he could finally be an old man.

He moved through the palace, towards Ezaria's chamber. There were mirrors on the floor, leaning against the wall, turned so the reflective sides were hidden. That was one of the first things Ezaria did when he arrived: remove all mirrors.

Ekhrem knocked on the door.

"Enter," came Ezaria's voice, and Ekhrem did.

The room was exactly the same as it had been when Ezaria turned up, the only difference the lack of mirrors. No new decorations or trinkets were to be seen, just the lord's weapons and clothes, and now, brought from Zeda, his battle armour.

He found the Zalfuri lord with gloves over his pallid hands and silver hair half turned black.

"You're smart," Ekhrem said, approaching, knowing exactly why Ezaria did this. The man didn't respond.

They stood by the windows, gazing over Sirenvel, with a view of the palace. They could see people on a palace roof, away from the noise, eating and resting. Yenea and Fairo, doing what they could to recuperate from their injures. They were wise, avoiding alcohol and smoke. With them was the castle hand Meha, and a light twinkled in her eyes every time she looked at Yenea. Aiyat was there too, quiet, and her son, Behraz. Behraz was asleep, but he could never be separated from her, not anymore.

"I cannot imagine what life is like for you," Ekhrem said, watching Ezaria. He meant it kindly. But the cold lord was emotionless as he worked black ink into his hair.

"I am less than half your age," Ekhrem said. "And yet I feel so old and ready to die." He chuckled. "But of course, my body is old. Yours is not."

"If there is one thing I have, it is the will to live," Ezaria said. "There are things I must do before I can die. And I will not die until I do those things."

Ekhrem gazed out the window. "I am sorry I cannot go to Rownensel with you, but there is no denying that I am not fit for battle. Even just a raid. I would be of no benefit to anyone. And with both my children, both lords going, it is my duty to stay and be lord here."

Ezaria nodded. "It is best."

"I don't know much about humans," Ekhrem said. "Sirenvel has been without them, always. We closed our gates as soon as they started being born, thousands of years ago. Sirenvel always was a city of fire. We, here, do not know of their behaviour, but I've heard about it."

"The only source of azheek suffering is humans," Ezaria said. "And the only source of human suffering is other humans."

He was silent for a moment. He shook his head.

"*Humans*," he said. "Impulsive. Destructive. They act on want and not need. They fight for land and power, pillaging and plundering, destroying the very resources they're fighting to get. Humans are never satisfied. Never. All they ever want is *more*. You could give them everything. And they would still. Want. *More*."

Ekhrem watched him, saying nothing. If there was one thing Ezaria could feel, it was hatred.

"If you had a group of people, of azheeks and humans," Ezaria said. "If you gave one azheek enough food for everyone, they would share it with the others. But if you gave it to one human, they would keep it. They would hide it. Hoard it. Use it as leverage and power over the others." He gritted his teeth. "And if you gave a human power, they would devastate entire villages just to have more."

"You know," Ekhrem said, "I have heard that is how the rest of Ianar talks about you. Red Emperor."

Ezaria snorted a little, sneering.

"Before you came here," Ekhrem continued, "all I knew were the stories. But now that you have been here for some time, and especially now that your people are here, I see how much you care about them. Sometimes, when the enemy is terrible, we must do terrible things."

"People believe what they want to believe," Ezaria said. "If it is a villain they want, a villain I will be."

"It doesn't bother you? What people say?"

"I don't care for the opinions of humans. Those that aren't power-hungry aren't any better. They're pitiful. Stupid. *Pathetic.* They spend their lives yearning for respect, desperate for the fleeting high of validation from others. They dedicate every waking moment to pleasing other people, changing who they are in search of acceptance, and they call it living. They lie, manipulate, and cheat, possessive over their partners, and have the audacity to call it love."

"And what would you call love, Lord Ezaria?"

He clenched his jaw. "Ilis."

Ekhrem nodded. There was silence between them, the space filled by the distant song and dance of the feast.

Ekhrem thought of his passed ilis, Mazhar. The pain of losing him had been terrible, but he knew he would see him again, and that was more than enough to feel okay. He gazed over to where his daughter sat, watching Meha look at her with twinkling eyes, and he looked at Fairo. The pain for Fairo was still fresh, and he could see it upon the man's face. They were all holding it together for Behraz, but he knew beneath Fairo's stoic disposition was a man mourning the loss of his twin brother.

He looked at Ezaria. So cold. So broken.

"I have heard about your brother," Ekhrem said. "From history books. They say he was a great man. If I may, humour me... tell me something about him, about Zaoen—something the books won't."

Ezaria was silent for a moment. The he smiled, however slight. "Zao was eight minutes older and one inch taller. And he never let me forget it."

Ekhrem smiled. Having raised his own children, and having seen them interact with others, he could imagine Ezaria, young, with a twin brother that poked and prodded, pushing his buttons. He had seen Fairo and Fehir do the same, watching them grow from Yenea's boisterous friends to men, bound, aging. He had watched Fehir become a father. He sighed.

"The pain of losing an ilis," Ekhrem said. "I know it well. But surely there must be some comfort in knowing that you will see him again? Death isn't as painful for us azheeks. We know we'll see our loved ones again."

Ezaria's smile faded and his cold gaze rested out the window, but he wasn't looking at anything there. His mind was far from Sirenvel.

"I will never see my brother again," he said. "For when I die, I am going to Valduhr."

Ekhrem's brow furrowed. "Are you so sure of that?"

"I have done terrible things."

Ekhrem looked to his city, listening to the far music. He could hear drums and songs, but the sound he loved most was the laughter that echoed through the streets. There wasn't a single person out there, not a single azheek, that hadn't made mistakes in their life. But he didn't know anyone that truly believed they deserved to suffer for it.

"Surely there must be some hope the gods will forgive you," he said.

Ezaria smiled slightly. Cold. Sad. "Even I wouldn't forgive me for what I've done." He looked at the other man. "I know you've heard the stories. I know you've heard I've done terrible things. And yet, you don't know the worst of it."

"Why did you do it?"

"Because I had to." Ezaria picked up more dye from a bowl on the windowsill and worked it into his long hair. "Everything I have ever done, I did for the greater good. Every man, woman, and child I have ever killed was to save countless others. But there are some deaths, some murders, that cannot be forgiven. So I live, and will continue to live, and I will continue to serve my people and better the world, because I have to. And when I die, I accept my fate. I accept Valduhr."

His words were chilling. Ekhrem's face softened.

"You have suffered for hundreds of years," he said. "For the betterment of others. And you are willing to suffer an eternity for it?"

Ezaria smiled again, just as cold, just as bitter. Just as sad. "Those of us who are chosen for certain paths must face whatever it is we come across. I know what I am fighting for. I know what lies at the end of my path. I have seen the future, Lord Ekhrem, and I know, for others, Ianar will be a much better place. If it means saving everyone else, I am willing to suffer."

Ekhrem let out a contained sigh, running a hand over his thick grey beard. "Have you known love? Two hundred years, surely, even with your brother gone... surely you still knew love?"

Ezaria clenched his jaw. "Yes."

"Does it not provide warmth?"

The Zalfuri lord kept his gaze away, but Ekhrem could see sadness in it, now more than ever.

"I am cold because I have loved," Ezaria said. "I have loved men, women, children. And I have watched every one of them die. I have loved azheeks... and I once loved a human."

"I'm sorry... I cannot imagine..."

Ezaria was silent as he continued working black ink into his silver hair.

"You speak to the gods?" Ekhrem asked.

"I have."

"How old were you when you first achieved *ulu*?"

"Eighteen."

Ekhrem stared. "*Eighteen?*"

Ezaria merely looked at him. As unfeeling as he usually was.

"Your daughter," Ezaria said. "Yenea. She has gifts. If she tried, she could achieve *ulu*."

Ekhrem nodded.

"Has she ever tried?" Ezaria asked.

"Not to the extent of my knowledge."

"Would you want her to?"

"Achieving *ulu* is a great accomplishment," Ekhrem said. "I would be proud if she achieved it, if she wanted to."

"But do *you* want her to?"

The Sirenveli lord let out a soft sigh. "Well... I don't know. Would you say that achieving *ulu* made your life better? Or would you say it made your life what it is now?"

Ezaria finally smiled. It was unsettling, a smirk, but hearing Ekhrem's words were truly funny to him.

"It is time for me to rest," Ekhrem said, smiling at the man before him. Ezaria looked younger with black hair, and while he had first thought a young face with silver hair was unsettling, knowing exactly how old and jaded the man was, with a full head of thick black hair, it was almost worse.

Physically, Ezaria didn't look a day past his prime. But the air around him was cold and cursed, tainted by a century of death. Ekhrem felt even older in his presence, as though standing on the edge of the next world.

"Good night, Lord Ekhrem," Ezaria said.

"Good night, Lord Ezaria."

Ekhrem made his way from the room, glancing at the stack of mirrors dejected outside.

Ezaria returned his gaze to the city and watched as a figure headed towards his windows. An air azheek. Vi'ra.

She landed in one of the open windows, looking at her lord. Her cheeks were flush from drink, dance, heat, and laughter, and she smiled at him.

"*May I enter?*" she asked, speaking in his preferred tongue. He nodded, and she stepped down from the sill, lightly, as though weighing nothing. She had excellent control over her powers.

"*Where is your bird?*" he asked.

"*The bird has a name.*" Vi'ra sat in the window.

"*Where is Kono?*" he said. She smiled.

"*That was a test—I didn't think you knew her name.*"

"*I know the name of every man, woman, and child in Zeda. I know the name of every soldier and Skyrider come here to fight.*" He looked at her. "*You were my student, Vi'ra. Of course I know your owl's name.*"

"*Kono is hunting, I presume. It's too hot here for her. She prefers it outside the walls.*"

She watched him as he pushed back his hair, slick with black ink. He looked different like this. Younger, less cold, and yet more intense. It brought out his pale eyes.

"*You're missing the party,*" he said.

"*Oh, I'm not missing anything. I've seen Nobaru drunk a thousand times before.*"

"*Hm. He reminds me so much of Yan'zi.*"

Vi'ra smiled and looked around, noting the complete lack of mirrors.

She came from the windowsill, into the room. She liked the decorations, the patterns on every pillow and cushion. She was patriotic, proud of being Zedai, of being Zalfuri, but she was not afraid to find beauty in other azheek cultures.

There were torches flickering along the walls, none of the colourful Sirenveli lamps lit, so she took a candle, stole a flame, and began to light them.

Ezaria watched her. She was brave, something she shared with Nobaru. It had been a long time since any Fang'ei had felt this close to him, for he kept them at a distance. He should tell her to leave, but as she finished lighting a hanging spiral of lamps, she smiled. Her eyes became half-moons.

He turned away and continued with his dye. She looked at him from behind.

"*You missed a spot.*"

He grunted. That didn't matter.

"*That's why I came here,*" she said, putting down the candle. She reached into a pocket and pulled on a pair of gloves. He looked at her over his shoulder and raised an eyebrow.

"*You always miss a spot,*" she said. "*May I?*"

His expression was as cold as usual, but there was fondness there. He nodded.

Vi'ra waved her hand and a chair zipped across the room. He sat down with a slight sigh as she scooped up black ink and worked it into the areas he had missed.

"*I know why you don't like mirrors,*" she murmured. "*Especially when you dye your hair.*"

He turned his head a little as she continued working behind him.

"*Because you looked the same,*" she said. "*And when your hair is black, it's when you look the most like he did.*"

He said nothing. He sat in silence as she filled every spot he had missed, checking his roots. She was gentle, stroking his hair. She was drunk.

"*Vi'ra,*" he said. She moved in front of him, her gaze resting upon his face.

"*You missed your eyebrows,*" she said.

"*I don't care about the eyebrows.*"

"*But you look stupid.*"

He snorted, and she smiled.

"*You're drunk,*" he said.

"*Yes, but even when I'm sober you'll look stupid. And you know for a fact Nobaru will say something.*"

He did know this, and an amused smile rested on his lips.

"*May I?*" she asked.

"*Very well.*"

Vi'ra took a tiny amount of dye onto the tip of her finger and leaned in, carefully, slowly, wiping it onto his brow. She was gentle, as though tending to each individual hair one at a time.

Ezaria watched her as she worked. She was focused, as she always was. Whenever a task was at hand, Vi'ra gave it her all. She didn't know how not to. She was like him.

His pale gaze rested upon her face, her eyes almost purple in the light of the blood moon and colourful lamps around the chamber. Her cheeks, nose, and lips were pink from the evening, tattoos of Old markings lining her cheeks and neck and over her bottom lip, leading down her chin. Few Fang'ei tattooed their faces, for it was incredibly painful, but she was proud of who she was and everything she had accomplished thus far. And so was he.

"*How long were you in Rownensel?*" she asked.

"*Barely a moment,*" he said. "*We went in, into the fort. Let them take us to the dungeons. That was all we needed. We have the location, and we know they have azheeks.*"

"*So we don't know too much—we don't really know what we're going into.*"

"*No.*"

"*How many do you think we're going to lose?*"

He was silent. She paused her work for a moment and looked at him.

"*I know this is a raid,*" she said. "*Not a declaration of war. And I know you have faced larger numbers. But promise me, my lord, if anything goes wrong, you'll save yourself first.*"

His pale gaze held her. "*You know I will, Vi'ra. But if anything goes wrong, you have to save yourself. That's an order.*"

She smiled. "*You don't give Fang'ei orders, you give us suggestions.*"

"*Because I train you to be smart, and to make the best choices, and you know that if anything goes wrong, Zalfur is much better off if you are still alive.*"

She smiled again and returned to her task, gently wiping dye onto his other brow. He sat in silence, listening to far-off music, listening to the crackle of flames in torches.

Vi'ra finished her work and leaned back a little, smiling.

"*There,*" she said. "*Now you don't look stupid.*"

She stayed for a moment, looking at him. He truly did look like a doll.

Then she smiled and pulled herself away, heading back to the windowsill, removing her gloves.

"*Go back to the party, Vi'ra,*" he said. "*Not all will make it out of Rownensel. Enjoy yourself.*"

She watched him from where she stood. "*I am enjoying myself.*"

"*Go back to the party. This is the last night you can enjoy yourself before war. Don't spend it with me.*"

She took in a deep breath, gathering courage, and walked back over to him. He looked at her from his seat.

"*I have a question for you, my lord.*" She spoke softly. "*I am the best of your Fang'ei. Why do you keep me at arm's length?*"

He rose to his feet and let out a contained breath. "*You are drunk, Vi'ra.*"

"*Answer the question, my lord.*"

He held her gaze. "*Because you deserve to live a good life. And people that get close to me do not live. Good lives.*"

They stood so close, bodies inches apart, but she could feel the wall between them. The wall Ezaria put up between himself and everyone around him, especially those he cared for.

"*Go back to the party, Vi'ra,*" he said. "*That's an order.*"

She smiled, a little sad, a little bitter, but she hadn't expected anything else from him. She took a step back, giving a polite nod and a slight bow.

"*Good night, my lord,*" she said, and headed for the windows, taking into the sky as weightless as a feather.

Ezaria clenched his jaw, swallowing the knot in his throat. Firelight flickered off his porcelain skin and inky black hair, and he pulled off his gloves.

He looked at his palms. There were intricate symbols on them, so faint nobody else knew they were there. Symbols that had once glowed with Old magic. Symbols that had appeared upon his first achievement of *ulu*. The first time he had been shown the Carriers of the King.

CHAPTER 22
THE FEAST

Rei stared around at Sirenveli plants as Kazim loosely tied the horse's reins to a post. She was so enthralled by the foreign landscape, by the flora and fauna she had never before seen, but his eyes were on her. She, like many of the other Zalfuri, was wearing a loose silk robe that was tied about her waist and cut off near the knees. He had noticed the Fang'ei were embellished with gold, the army with silver, and the Skyriders, purple.

Kazim gazed up at the lacian circling in the skies high above them.

"Your uniforms," he said. "They're to blend into the lacian?"

"Mhmm," she said almost absent-mindedly, moving towards an exciting new shrub.

"Then... why the purple?"

She finally looked at him and smiled. "Because sometimes there are instances where sentiment trumps logic. This is one of those times."

She returned to the plants.

They looked so different from what she knew, and she placed a hand upon the rough bark of a date palm tree, gazing up at the spiky green fronds of every leaf and the orange bushels of dates.

There was flora all around her, so strange, so new—like a dream. Small yellow flowers grew in bunches, tiny red clovers swaying in the night's breeze, and curious blooms grew on long stalks. From afar they looked black, but as she moved closer, curious, Kazim smiled and raised a hand. Flames bloomed upon his palm to provide light.

The petals themselves were white, but there were so many veins and dots of purple, it made the flowers look dark.

"Ianar is beautiful," she said, a smile upon her lips. "There's so much beauty to the world."

"It's poisonous," Kazim said. She gave him a look.

"Not to us, it isn't."

"No, but… don't give it to a pet. Or a human."

They shared smiles and headed for the water. He was in pants and nothing else and he pulled them off, racing towards the lagoon. He leapt into the air and did a flip before crashing through the surface. Rei laughed as she was sprayed with water.

She pulled off her clothes, and with a deep breath, threw caution to the wind. She ran, leaping into the air, doing multiple flips, and then dove into the lake. She broke the surface, going from warm air to cool water, and as she came up, a smile rested on her lips. She laughed, shaking water from her eyes.

"This is amazing," she said, floating on her back, gazing at the stars.

"Isn't it?" He smiled.

"I bet it's wonderful living here," she sighed. "Everyone seems so relaxed."

"Surely people let loose in Zalfur? You don't seem shy about nudity."

She chuckled and looked at him. He was resting near the shallow ledge.

"One does not need to be naked in order to let loose," she said. "And one does not need to let loose in order to be naked."

"True."

"We're always naked at the hot springs." She smiled. "But it's not all about nudity. We keep it hidden, for the most part, letting loose. At least in Zeda. Akana and Usan are more relaxed."

"Sounds like you're a professional."

Rei laughed. "Perhaps it's only *hidden* because it's so cold. It's not like it is here, where you can party in the streets fully naked. You'd freeze to death if you did that in Zeda. Especially this time of year." She swam over to him and sighed. "I wish we'd brought more food. And wine."

Kazim hauled himself from the water and hurried over to a nearby tree. He took five steps from it, measuring his way, and then buried into a bush. When he emerged he had two large bottles and a toothy grin.

"My gods," she laughed. "I love this city!"

He raced back over, doing another flip into the water, and when he surfaced, he handed her one.

"Thank you." She smiled, yanking the cork away.

Then came a loud screech and Kazim winced, looking up as a lacian pelted down from the sky. He panicked, searching for cover, but Rei laughed.

"Yongie!" she called. "It's fine, I'm fine, we're having fun. Yong, I'm fine."

The lacian was huge, and when it landed with a loud thud, Kazim's horse whinnied.

"That's yours, I assume?" he asked. He was hiding behind her now.

"Are you using me as a shield?"

"You can take it, right?"

She laughed again. "He won't hurt you. Unless you piss him off."

Rei moved forward, reaching out to pet the beast, giving Yong a fond scratch under the chin.

While Rei did not have any tattoos to mimic Old magic, she had a large piece upon her back. A Skyrider, Kazim could tell, a man and a lacian. The man had long hair and had been tattooed with craft, portraying a stoic and strong image, done in a way where there was still warmth to him. Zalfuri tattoos were quite stylized, and yet he could swear the man was supposed to be Ezaria.

Kazim looked back to the lacian and inched closer. He raised a hand and Yong snapped at him.

"Easy." Rei smirked. "He chose me, not you."

"Noted." He busied himself with wine. She smiled.

Yong clicked loudly, the sound resonating from deep in his feathered throat, and Rei glanced at Kazim.

"Is he allowed to eat a couple of cats?"

Wine flew from Kazim's nose. "*What?*"

"Couple of cats?"

"*No!*"

Rei looked at him a moment longer, trying not to smile, and then turned to her giant beast. "It's a no on the cats."

Yong huffed.

Rei moved in closer and lowered her voice. "Tell the others not to eat any cats."

Yong huffed again and then ruffled his feathers, kicking off the ground to soar into the sky. Kazim stared after the beast with wide eyes, glancing at Rei. Then he peered around to make sure no cats were in sight.

Rei laughed and took a seat by him. "Sorry about that."

"I mean… animals eat what animals eat…"

Rei smiled and looked to the sky, fondly watching the lacian circling above. As Kazim followed her gaze, the lacian moved. They no longer soared over the city, heading instead to the tundra, circling for prey where they were allowed.

"They're smart," he said.

"Very." Rei let out a content sigh. She looked at Kazim and found his gaze upon her back. She gave him an expectant look. "Are you going to ask me who it is or just keep staring?"

"You want me to look at another body part?"

She splashed water at him.

"Sorry, yes. Sorry. Who is it?"

"Zaoen," she said. "The first Skyrider. Ezaria's brother."

"He has a brother?"

"He did. Many years ago. Zaoen was the first to approach the lacian, taking the time to learn their behaviour, learn how to respect them and gain their trust, enough to be allowed to ride one. They say he helped one, one he had found injured. He was the first Skyrider and trained the first group of Skyriders all those years ago."

"What happened to him?"

"He was killed by humans."

"Ah."

Rei smiled sadly. "I never knew him, of course—he lived long before my time—but I know what he was like. He was kind, warm, and funny. Even now, over a hundred years after his passing, every year on the day he died, all of Zalfur mourns. The empire is silent. Nobody goes to work, nobody goes to school. Everyone stays inside, and all day, lacian circle in the skies. Even they remember. And at night, when the lacian return to roost, we release lanterns into the sky and onto the water, saying nothing. Silence, for a whole day and night. For Zaoen."

"Lord Ezaria makes you do that?"

"No, he didn't, and he doesn't. He never said anything about it, but the people loved Zaoen, and that's what the people did the day he died. That's what the people continued to do every year after that. Lord Ezaria... On that day, he goes to the tower of Zaoen and... stands there. Alone. Looking at the place where his brother lay."

Rei smiled sadly, watching moonlight dancing upon the rippling lake.

"People write messages to their ancestors on the lanterns," she said. "Wishes, feelings, letters of love. On that day... the next world feels so close. It's almost like Zaoen comes back to visit Ezaria every year, and when he does, the gates to Savai open and all other ancestors can see their loved ones."

Kazim let out a long, quiet exhale, listening.

"*oras iord ih dahvid ta'e*," she said. "'Day of the fallen brother', or… 'time of the fallen brother'. We call it *dahvid oras* for short. Time of the Fallen, when those from the next world visit." She smiled. "Part of me thinks the silence is so that people can listen, listen for any whispers from their ancestors. I know it sounds like a load of lacian shit, but I swear, the next world feels so close on *dahvid oras*."

He couldn't help but laugh at *lacian shit*, and she smiled, watching him.

"We, the Skyriders, wear purple because it was his favourite colour. We wear his memory with pride."

He let out a long sigh. "I will *never* leave that much of an impact."

She laughed softly. "Neither will I."

They looked up as Yong returned from the skies, ruffling his feathers and clawing at the ground. Kazim looked at the lacian tattooed on her back.

"Do… do all Zalfuri have back tattoos?" he asked.

"Not all, but most."

"Does Lord Ezaria?"

"Yes, he's covered. One giant piece that flows over his whole body. An air gangul—his gangul."

"*His* gangul? He *has* a gangul?"

She laughed. "It's not *his*, but it came to Zalfur when he and Zaoen returned from Elizia. They say that it appeared over Elizia the day he achieved *ulu*, the day the gods told him to return. And it followed them all the way back and has stayed there ever since. It's stayed at Zalfur all these years, circling Zeda mostly, but it also travels to Akana and Usan, and even Port Yan'zi. It really is… gangul of Zalfur. Gangul of Ezaria. That's why the Zalfuri crest is an air gangul."

"My gods," Kazim murmured. "Maybe… maybe if I lived for two centuries I'd be as prolific, too. I'll just tell myself that. That's my excuse."

Rei smiled. "All of that was done before his prime."

"Atesh…"

Rei laughed. "Don't compare yourself to others, Kazim. Everyone's definition of success is different."

"What's yours?"

She smiled to herself. "Happiness."

* * *

Eating, drinking, smoking, and dancing progressed into the night. The music seemed to get louder and louder. Aven drank more and more, dancing with anyone that offered, and there were many Sirenveli that offered. People fawned over him, and as he danced, they poured wine over his colossal body.

With every beat of the drums, he moved. He closed his eye and let the music consume him. He jumped up and down, muscles rippling with every movement, pecs bouncing with every beat. Wine glistened over him, gleaming over his wild body hair, and with an endless supply of drink, he kept going until he was well and truly drunk.

Chester entered the throng a few times to check on him, but every time she did he assured her he was having the time of his life. So she sat with Yrilim, listening to the music, safe in his arms.

Aven danced, jumping up and down, flailing his human limbs, and eventually he started sticking to himself. All the wine was not a good match for his thick body hair and gargantuan muscles. So he ripped off his robe, kicking away his pants, and grabbed a jug of water. He commanded everyone else to do the same as he spread his arms, a jug in each hand, naked as the day he was born.

Then he yelled, "*BATHE ME, BITCHES!*"

Chester cackled from her place, every person around the square laughing as he showered himself with water, and as others did too, he morphed.

Aven cracked and crunched, sloppily, drunk, and people gasped in shock, staggering back as he turned from a giant man into a colossal beast.

"Holy *shit!*" Nobaru yelled.

"I told you!" Yrilim called, raising a hand to his people. "I warned you! It's okay, he's okay! He's friendly! Still the same guy!"

Aven continued dancing as a beast, and as awkward as he had looked dancing as a man, it was even worse now. He spun in circles, leaping around, shaking his wasfought butt as he backed into a belly dancer, and she laughed, pouring water over him.

Chester watched, her cheeks pink and pained from how much she was smiling. It was like watching a child learn how to play, albeit a very large, hairy, and *drunk* child.

"My Little One is all grown up," she said fondly.

Maina and Theideus rushed to join Aven, laughing and dancing with the beast. More and more people joined in, encouraged by Nobaru and the first friendly wasfought they had ever met, and as Nobaru passed Talen once more, he grabbed the man by the hand and pulled him close. Talen had zero objections.

Rei gazed up at the blood moon. She watched it, pink in the night, surrounded by a galaxy of colours and millions of shining stars, and yet, she was distracted by the man that sat beside her. She couldn't see him, but she could feel him so very strongly. Too strongly.

He felt it too, and neither of them knew what to say.

They had moved further along the water, closer to where a thicket of trees grew—farther from civilization and potential eyes. It was quieter here, but they could still hear the distant drums.

She took in a deep breath and turned to him. "Do you feel it?"

He nodded.

"I can't believe it." She laughed to herself. "Is... ilis, it... I haven't known anyone that just *met* an ilis and knew straight away."

He nodded. "Me too."

They both sighed and gazed over the lake.

"This complicates things," she said.

"Are you not allowed? To bind with non-air azheeks?"

"Are you?" she laughed. "Allowed to bind with non-fire azheeks? Look around—there isn't a single person in Sirenvel that isn't a fire azheek. There isn't a single person in Okos that isn't an earth azheek, no one in Elizia, Paradiz, or Volehn that isn't a water azheek. Zalfur has a reputation for our dislike of non-air azheeks, but it doesn't mean we're the only ones. Every major azheek city closed their gates to prevent cross-breeding and human creation—yours is no different."

"I… yeah. You're right. Sorry."

"Sirenvel never allowed humans to happen in the first place, but the za'iri cities, the air azheek cities, did. Humans were accepted, embraced. But it was the humans that ruined that. Your city doesn't know because your city never had to deal with them. With human greed. Human destruction. Not all humans are baraduhr, but all baraduhr are human."

Kazim nodded. "Yeah… every azheek city that closed its gates is content, happy. You only ever hear about turmoil where the humans reside."

"If we bind," she murmured, "if you are my ilis, and I am yours, we'll have to leave our homes. I won't be welcome in Zalfur—I won't be *allowed*. And you? You think you could stay here? You think *I* could stay here? In Sirenvel, the city of *fire*?"

"I… maybe? I'm friends with the lords—maybe?"

She smiled, shaking her head. "Even if they allowed it, I couldn't survive here. It's hot enough right now and it's *winter*. How hot does this city become when the rest of the world is in spring? Summer?"

He clenched his jaw. "Fuck."

"I love Zalfur," she said. "I *love* Zeda. It gets cold, yes, but the people are warm. Our culture is warm."

She moved from him, sitting further away as she started to truly understand what having Kazim as an ilis would mean.

"I'd never get to go home," she murmured.

He clenched his jaw and swallowed the knot in his throat. "But if… if we're binding, it means the gods have chosen this… doesn't it?"

She smiled sadly. "Nobody will think that. Not here, not in Zalfur. The gods can't see humans. Azheeks only get pregnant when the gods mean for them to, but when cross-blooded azheeks get pregnant, the child is always human and the gods cannot see that child. So no one, no one in Zalfur or Sirenvel, will believe that the gods intended for that child to happen."

"I can pull out."

She laughed, going to hit him on the arm, but stopped, afraid of what touching him would do. Her smile faded. "Tell me everything you love about Sirenvel."

He gazed towards his city, listening to the music. "Everything. Everyone. The music, the food, the culture. The horses. The cats. The hot air balloons, the bazaar, the lamps I seem to be hoarding."

He smiled and clenched his jaw, nodding, understanding her apprehension.

"Jealousy is a very human emotion," Rei said. "And yet, right now I'm jealous of them."

"Why?"

She sighed with a smile. "Because if I was a human, I'd be free to do whatever I wanted. Even the gods wouldn't see me, even the gods couldn't hear my thoughts or see my past, present, or future. In a way, humans are more free than azheeks ever will be. There's nothing after death for them, no Valira, no Valduhr. Of course, that is why the baraduhr are so unafraid of being terrible… but it seems freeing. Knowing that this life is the only one you'll ever have."

"I'd never looked at it that way before."

She smiled. "I understand why they're impulsive. This is the one life they have—they *have* to act upon their feelings, upon their wants and needs, otherwise… what's the point of living?"

He watched her. "And if you were human? If there was nothing to worry about, no laws or rules or gods… what would you do?"

She looked at him and smiled. She gazed over his sharp features, his strong brow, pointed chin, and hooked nose—his eyes of fire that seemed to almost gleam in the night.

"What would you do?" he asked.

"I would kiss you"

"Can we be human for a night?"

She smiled sadly. "But if we were human, we wouldn't be feeling... *this.*"

He nodded. She sighed, avoiding his gaze.

"I wasn't supposed to come here," she said. "They didn't summon me. I could have stayed behind... but something told me I was supposed to go. I just felt this pull... and then I saw you."

Kazim looked over to where Yong was resting. "I couldn't stop looking at the lacian, you know. Even when the army were in the square, I kept looking up at them. At you."

"As much as I'd like to pretend to be a human right now, I can't. Because I *feel* you. And if I feel you, if I felt the pull to come here, doesn't that mean... the gods want it?" Then she laughed. "*Ongji*, this is stupid. You hear about this in stories but you never think that upon meeting someone, never knowing them before, that you could feel..." She smiled sadly and looked away.

"Is it common knowledge that Zalfuri aren't allowed to fraternize with foreign-blooded azheeks?" he asked.

"Yes."

"So then why were your friends... supportive?"

"I don't think they realized how serious this was. Ji'ah likes to tease. A lot. They probably think it's just lust. It's not like they knew, it's not like they could feel what we felt. What we feel."

They sighed and sat back, gazing at the lake. The listened to the distant songs, to the distant talk and laughter of their people. They could hear water dripping from their hair, and though they weren't touching, they could feel the pull, the space between them longing to be closed.

"Do you want me to take you back?" he asked. She nodded.

Kazim came from the water, but when his hand brushed hers they both shuddered.

Heat. Electrifying heat, through both of their bodies.

"Fuck," she whispered. It was consuming her. In the light of the moon, their skin looked eerily bright.

She rose to her feet and he followed suit, meeting her gaze. He swallowed the knot in his throat.

He approached. Slowly. When his hand touched hers, lights rose from where their skin connected. She looked at it and smiled, shaking her head in disbelief.

Kazim reached up and cupped her cheek, her skin glowing where he touched her.

"I never knew it would be like *this*." He smiled.

"Yeah, me too." She watched him a moment and then let out a defeated sigh. "Well, what's done is done. Might as well go all the way to Valduhr."

She kissed him, and the moment her lips touched his, lights sprang from their bodies. Lights of red, orange, and yellow rose from his skin, purples and greys from hers, and as they kissed, the lights moved. Intertwining. Connecting.

Aven was back in his human form, already dry from the wine and water. He had danced like a maniac, shaking his wasfought body, spraying everyone around him, and eventually turned back into a man so he could drink more. And more. And more.

He danced with the people that fawned over him, with busty women of Sirenvel, and as their hands roved, they took him by the arm and guided him from the square.

Aven was led to a pleasure house. Music from the feast rang through the open windows, drapes flowing in the wind, hanging from the ceiling and around the great bed situated in the middle of the room. He flopped down, a drunk smile rising on his face as two women climbed on top of him. He raised his great hands and took a breast each into his clutch, smiling as he realized one hand still wasn't enough to hold them.

The people around them kissed and moaned, fondling one another, fondling him, and he closed his eyes with a groan as a mouth closed around his member.

Drums pulsed through the city, through Nobaru as he closed his eyes, moving freely to the beat. Around him, people of Sirenvel danced with one another, unashamed to let their touch wander.

His hands moved down Talen, grey eyes gazing into the man's fiery stare. Talen brought him close, hips gyrating, body chains and gold jewellery chiming. Nobaru draped an arm around Talen's shoulders, their foreheads touching as they both looked down to where their hips ground together. A low groan sounded from the fire azheek and Nobaru smirked.

Nobaru turned around, his back to Talen's chest, grabbing him over his shoulder, by the hair. Talen rested his lips upon the man's neck, hands trailing over his tapered body.

"My pants aren't thick," he murmured into Nobaru's ear. "Everyone's going to see me pitching a tent."

The air azheek smirked, tipping his head back to rest upon Talen's shoulder. He turned his head slightly, lips inches from the other's.

"Then take me somewhere no one else will see."

Aven thrust into a woman from behind, his fingers in another, and around him there were more people having sex. There were so many people touching him, their hands roving over him, kissing him, fondling him between the legs. He felt sensations everywhere.

The world was a blur around him; he could barely make out who was doing what—or who was who. But he didn't care. He closed his eyes and smiled, tasting wine on his lips—then someone's lips. Whose, he didn't know, and he didn't care.

Kazim pulled Rei close, every touch electrifying. His fingers pushed through her hair as she grabbed him, clutching his warm skin, like fire against hers. He picked her up and her legs wrapped around him, longing to be closer.

He moved into the thicket of trees, searching for privacy as glowing colours continued to rise from their skin.

She moaned into his mouth and he lowered to his knees, hands wandering over her body. He pulled away from the kiss to look at her, to push hair from her face. To truly *look* at her.

She was beautiful, the most beautiful woman he had ever seen. Her features were soft and round, her skin pale, so different from the skin he knew in Sirenvel. And her eyes, her grey eyes that looked at him like no one else had ever done before.

Ilis.

She caressed his face, fingers trailing his sharp jaw, her own thoughts mirroring his. The beauty of him, how different he was from everyone she had ever known.

As they held one another, they pushed away the knowledge that from now on, their lives would never be the same.

Nobaru yanked Talen into a kiss the moment the doors closed behind them. They were in Talen's quarters, and he sent a silent thank you to the gods that his house was on the outskirts of the palace, away from prying eyes and ears—away from where he knew Ezaria was staying.

They moved into the living area, knocking into furniture as they went, and as they bumped into a table, a bowl tipped over, sending fruit rolling. Nobaru pulled away and grabbed the bowl, but fruit fell to the ground.

"Damn it," he laughed.

"Fuck it." Talen smiled, already out of breath.

"Wait—are these Sirenveli peaches?" Nobaru grabbed one.

"Yeah."

He immediately took a bite and his eyes rolled back in his head, moaning into the taste. Talen's dick twitched.

"Don't do that," the fire azheek warned. Nobaru smirked.

"Why not?" He took another bite that elicited another moan.

Talen moved towards him, tucking his fingers into Nobaru's tiny piece of clothing. Nobaru looked up at him with a dark smile and took another bite. He let out a low, but quiet, groan.

Talen yanked Nobaru's cloth out of the way and took him into his hand. Nobaru's eyes rolled back in his head once more and another moan escaped his lips.

"Because I want to be the one making you sound like that," Talen murmured into his ear.

"Then do it."

Talen dropped to his knees, taking Nobaru into his mouth, and the air azheek took another bite of the peach. He closed his eyes and tipped his head back as juices dripped from his mouth.

Lights rose all about the forest as Kazim and Rei held one another, their lips connected and hips moving in rhythm. They no longer thought about the world around them, forgetting the worries of their lives. All they knew was here and now, seeing only the other. Their ilis.

She took him by the hands and pushed him down until his back met the earth. She kissed him, her wet hair pooling over her shoulders, a soft moan leaving her lips.

Nobaru groaned loudly as Talen kissed his ear, biting his shoulder as he thrust from behind. Nobaru leaned on the table with one hand, the other reaching back to grab Talen by the hair. He smirked as he drew a moan from the man.

Talen dropped his head into the crook of Nobaru's neck, panting heavily against his skin. Then he kissed him, sucking and biting as he reached around, taking Nobaru between the legs. The air azheek groaned loudly, closing his eyes as Talen stroked him, squeezing and pulling, his thrusts growing sloppy.

The city square was a blur of dancing bodies, food, and wine. Talk was no longer coherent, and all that came from the people were songs and laughter to accompany dancing.

Vi'ra smiled, laughing with other Fang'ei, but when she bumped into Veraion, it faded. He took her hand and spun her around.

"*You're lucky I'm drunk*," she said. "*And that I don't have a weapon on me.*"

He danced with her, words a little slurred as he spoke. "*We both know that if you wanted to kill me, you wouldn't need a weapon.*"

She smirked. Then it turned into a genuine smile.

Aven couldn't see. He could barely even hear what was going on.

Moaning, laughing, groaning, singing, the slapping of skin on skin, and the beating of drums that only seemed to be getting louder.

And louder.

And louder.

He groaned, doubling over as he tensed up, releasing himself into whoever he was currently fucking. He didn't know, and he didn't care.

Then he flopped onto his back, landing on someone. He let out a slurred apology and rolled over somewhere else, and when his back met the sheets, he closed his eyes.

Hands were on him anew, lips adoring his body, and as he lay there, listening to the music, to the drums, someone was on his softening length.

They kissed and sucked until it wasn't soft anymore, and he smiled slightly, slapping whoever's ass it was as they climbed on top and sank down on him.

Nobaru swore loudly, both hands clinging to the table in front of him, arms tensed up as sweat dripped from his nose. It beaded over his skin, wet between him and Talen. The fire azheek was buried in the crook of his neck, groaning, thrusts growing sloppier and sloppier. His hand was wrapped around Nobaru's length, tightly, every movement just as messy.

Their breaths were heavy, loud, panting, mixed with the distant ring of music and chiming of body jewellery. Muscles rippled with every movement, the tattoos on Nobaru's stomach dancing with every breath, changing shape when his abs tensed.

Then the rest of him tensed, seizing as he groaned, curses spilling from his lips, and as he shook, releasing over Talen's hand, the other man hit his climax.

Their groans echoed through the house, off the sandy-hued walls and decorated tiles, flowing out the open windows.

Aven lay still, allowing his partner to do all the work, and he smiled to himself, pushing hair from his sweaty face. He closed his eyes, listening to the ringing music, to the heavy breathing and moaning around him, but as he lay there, the noise began to go away.

Aven blinked slowly, turning his head to gaze at a painting on the wall, and as he looked at it, the world spinning around him, only one piece of the painting came into focus.

A pomegranate flower.

Aven lay still, allowing his partner to do all the work, and his smile faded.

The music was softer in the palace, sounding like a distant lullaby gliding through Yrilim's open windows. Chester lay in his arms, resting in the bath. They listened to the drip of water on water as his fingers trailed gently over her skin.

She looked at him and smiled, leaning in for a kiss. It was soft, but passionate. When she pulled back, he placed another peck upon her lips.

"When we get back from Rownensel, let's have a celebration," he said.

"What, like this?" She nodded her head towards the open windows, to the distant festival they could still hear.

"When people bind, in my city at least, we celebrate it. So yes, like this, but it would be about us."

She smiled. "I'd like that. But when these damn wounds are healed. I want to be able to drink. And dance. And party like a wasfought."

He laughed and nodded, leaning in, and they kissed once more.

Their skin was radiant in the firelight, every scar shining: scars from blades and the occasional beast, and on Chester's breasts, around her nipples and down the undersides, scars from where she had reduced their size. Her priority had always been fighting, and when they grew in, they were possibly the largest nuisance she had ever dealt with.

She smiled, fingers trailing over her ilis, and his trailed over her.

"So we wait to heal," he said. "And then we celebrate."

"Sounds good to me."

"And then we crown you queen of Sirenvel."

She hit him on the arm and he started peppering her face with kisses. She laughed, trying to fight him off, but he kept kissing her.

Finally he stopped and pushed hair from her face, gazing over every feature, softened by her earth azheek blood.

"Stay with me," he murmured. "Stay with me here, in the city. Let them go to war. The gods know we've seen enough."

She smiled. "You know I have to go. We're not even fighting, you and I. We're still injured. But being there will be good for your people, and I'm not letting my friends go in if I can't be there to at least make sure they're okay."

He nodded. She leaned in closer, looking into his fiery eyes.

"First, we kill them all." She kissed him between words. "Then, we stay here."

Yrilim grinned and pulled her onto his lap, placing his lips on hers once more.

"You think Sakhala will turn up for the festivities?" she asked.

"They might."

"Reckon they'll bring another camel hookah? I like that one."

He laughed. "I'll make them."

Chester smiled and wrapped her arms around his neck, her wet hair shining in the firelight, water trickling down the valleys of her back.

Everything felt right.

CHAPTER 23
ROWNENSEL

The gates opened and a legion of horses flooded from the city. Lacian took to the sky, casting shadows over barren tundra. Further and further the army rode from the safety of Sirenvel, racing towards the western woods.

By the time the army reached Rownen Forest, their camp had been set up. The Skyriders got there first, travelling by lacian, reuniting with the first scouts that had been sent to Rownensel. They made base deep in the woods, hidden from the mountain pass. The trees grew tall there, fighting cold winds that swept from the mountains, but still the air was unforgiving.

Tents were erected through the trees, as well as a medical bay prepared for rescued and injured azheeks. The Skyriders had brought with them blankets and furs, and every tent was stockpiled in preparation. Maina, Theideus, and some Sirenveli had gone with them, providing water and fire.

Veraion dismounted his horse, breathing onto his hands in an attempt to warm them. He had found it uncomfortably hot in Sirenvel, but he missed it already.

He ran his hand over his mare's neck, whispering kind words to her, and she snorted fondly, nodding her head. Then he spotted Vi'ra through the trees, tending to her steed, and headed over.

"Vi'ra," he said. She didn't look up from her work, but he could feel a pair of eyes on him. He glanced up to a nearby tree, meeting the gaze of her ever-watchful owl.

"I'm not drunk anymore," she said.

"I know. I wanted to say this to you sober."

She unbuckled her saddle and looked at him.

"I'm sorry," he said. "She loved you. Ilia loved you. You deserved more than a letter saying she had died. I just... I didn't know what to say."

She returned to her work, undoing the straps, removing saddle from horse. "You failed to protect her. I will never forgive you for that."

She put the saddle down and draped a thick blanket over the stallion. When she was done, she returned her gaze to his. Her words had bitten him, and it showed.

Vi'ra looked past him, through the trees, to where Rei and Kazim were speaking. Veraion followed her gaze.

"You might want to remind them what happens when people of Zalfur fraternize with foreign blood," she said. "Before they end up dead."

Vi'ra gave him another cold look before she walked away, to where Ezaria was speaking with Yrilim. He was already watching the odd couple.

Vi'ra pulled Ezaria away, speaking in a low tone, diverting his attention from the lovers. As cold as she seemed, she was still doing what she could to protect her friends.

Chester sat in a tent with Chukuma and Faraji, mixing paint from powder and water. Red for Chester, green for her friends, and white for all of them.

Rising to their feet, holding a bowl each, they took paint upon their fingers.

One by one they decorated each other. Chester and Faraji marked Chukuma with green and white, his face, chest, arms, and legs. They marked his armour and the mask-like shield he carried. Chester and Chukuma marked Faraji: face, arms, legs, armour, and the obsidian war club she wielded. And then they marked Chester. Chukuma and Faraji smeared red and white across her cheeks, forehead, and chin, onto her breastplate and pauldrons. Ekhrem had ensured the three of them were given proper armour for the raid.

They looked up when a great wasfought entered the tent, and Chester smiled. She took red upon her thumb and marked a stripe up the beast's forehead, and he watched her with his single ice-blue eye. Then he transformed to a man, on one knee, and she marked his cheeks.

The air fogged before Veraion as he moved through the camp, nodding to those he passed. He had been summoned to Ezaria's tent and clutched a firestone as he made his way, relieved it could provide some warmth.

The lords' tents were bigger, and as he made for Ezaria's, Sanada, the tall Fang'ei general, emerged from inside. Sanada had aged since Veraion last knew him, and he was so curious to know who his ilis was. But Sanada merely cast him a nod and moved by, heading back for camp. Veraion watched him go, and with a clenched jaw, returned his gaze to the tent. He knocked on the hangings.

Ezaria's voice came from inside. "Come in."

Veraion ducked inside, nodding respectfully. Ezaria's hair was black now, half tied up, ready for war. He wore armour, plated, protected, with the gangul crest in black. All Zalfuri wore the same armour into battle, for every soldier mattered, and every soldier was equal. There was no silver or gold to differentiate the Fang'ei from others, no pale hair to make the lord stand out and everyone more vulnerable.

Around his tent were weapons and armour, piles of furs for warmth, and carpets to block off the cold forest floor. There was a table with diagrams and maps, battle plans having already been discussed, and on top of these was something wrapped in cloth.

"Sit," Ezaria said, and Veraion took his place on a fur-covered bench.

The lord picked up the bundle, pulling away layers of cloth, and when the items came free, he held them out with one hand.

Swords. Fang'ei swords forged from kara'i steel.

The sheaths were black, with intricate gold layering that could be removed for battle. The hilts were wrapped with thin rope, taught and twisted for grip.

Ezaria took one sword by the hilt and drew it. The metal sang. Kara'i steel sounded different, blessed by the gods, and as the lord looked to the sabre blade, Veraion already knew what was on it.

His name.

And he knew, engraved into the other, was Ilia's.

Veraion clenched his jaw, a knot building in his throat. He tried to swallow it as Ezaria looked back to him. The lord turned the blade, pointing the hilt at Veraion.

"You forgot these."

Veraion took in a deep breath and stood, looking at the hilt he had once held with pride.

"You were and always will be Fang'ei," Ezaria said. "You were and always will be worthy of that title. I raise strong, individual minds, not blind followers. I raise wolves, not sheep. You choosing to leave Zalfur was a choice made with everything I had ever taught you. I never give commands to my Fang'ei—you were only ever given suggestions. You earned these, Veraion. Kara'i steel. Unable to rust, unable to diminish. These weapons will live longer than you. You should at least wield them until your time is done. You, for whom these were forged. I know, and you know, that Ilia would want you to wield hers."

Veraion's breath shook and he looked at the blade, hands trembling.

"The choice is yours," Ezaria said. "Always. So, Fang'ei, if you choose to take them, these swords are yours."

Veraion drew in a deep breath, filling his lungs to the brim, and when he exhaled, he was no longer shaking. His hands ceased to tremble and he reached forward, touching his fingers to the hilt. He took it, grip strong, grip so familiar, and Ezaria let go.

Veraion swung the sabre beside him, listening to the metal sing. Like a whistle in the wind. A song just for him, forged in the mountains of Zeda, forged with blessed steel from Elizia. Forged by the Fang'ei of blacksmiths.

This sword was his.

Ezaria turned the other hilt towards him, and he took it, drawing Ilia's blade from its sheath. And together the weapons sang. A matching song, a beautiful duet, like birds playing in the misty mountains of Zalfur.

He stood up straight, looking at his old mentor, and nodded.

"Thank you."

* * *

In the dark of night, the army gathered. Ezaria and Ziang stood in the lead with Yrilim and Yenea. Every non-air azheek was partnered with a soldier of Zalfur.

On Ezaria's command his army took their partners into their grasps and lifted from the ground. Those staying behind—Skyriders, healers, Maina, and Theideus—watched as the army rose into the night, through the forest canopy, soaring towards the mountains.

Freezing wind flowed through the army's hair, but every man and woman not from Zalfur was too distracted to notice the cold. They stared around with wide eyes, looking to the ground far below as their legs dangled uselessly. Among them, Chukuma and Faraji exchanged terrified glances.

In the lead, Yenea raised an arm and flashed a red flame. The army divided.

A quarter swooped left, speeding towards the western face of the Rownen peak. Among them, Ezaria, Yrilim, Yenea, Chester, Veraion, Aven, Chukuma, Faraji, and two Zalfuri twins whose siblings were among the others.

Another quarter headed to the ground, towards the main opening of the mountain pass, and the other half of the army soared to the right, splitting as one group touched down to the eastern face, the other proceeding to the north.

Upon landing, the Zalfuri released their partners.

The ground fighters were led by Fairo and Sanada, and they ducked into the darkness of the mountain pass.

To the west, Ezaria moved for the entrance leading to the tunnels of the mountain. Light flickered from within, the way lit by torches. With a wave of his hand, the fires went out.

Those to the east were led by Kazim and Vi'ra. With them, Talen and his partner, the twin Ah'ni.

They crept towards the passageway and Kazim waved his hand, snuffing out the torches within. Soon they heard the shuffle of a guard's boots. Stepping back, they ducked into the shadows of the mountain. Vi'ra pressed her back to the black stones, listening as the guard came closer.

The human stepped into open air, squinting into the cold night. Then two orange dots appeared behind him. Kazim's glowing pupils. He slit the guard's throat and the man fell to the ground with a heavy thud.

Ziang led the northern army with a fire azheek named Emel, past his prime. They found no passageway to a tunnel and instead peered into a large opening. They could see the entire fort from where they stood.

Ziang nodded to the twins in her party, one of whom was Ji'ah, and Ji'ah closed her eyes, taking in a slow, deep breath.

ulu.

"All clear," she said quietly.

Ah'ni was still, her eyes closed. Vi'ra watched her, waiting, Kazim and Talen exchanging curious glances. Then Ah'ni heard her sister's message and smiled.

"All clear here."

Vi'ra nodded to another Zalfuri twin. Dae took in a calm breath, closing his eyes.

Fairo and his group waited in the darkness of the mountain pass, hidden from the fort behind large rocks. Among them was Dae's twin brother, Liang, and when he received the message, he responded softly.

"All clear."

Fairo watched as another twin, Liu, played her part. Liu was young—too young. But she closed her eyes and murmured a soft message to her own twin.

To the west, Liu's message reached her brother, Oda. He spoke to her softly and then nodded to Ezaria. Wong, another twin, many years past his prime, closed his eyes and whispered to his own brother, and when the last message was sent, Ezaria signalled and they headed into the passageway.

Aven moved in the lead, transforming into a wasfought. He sniffed the air, ears flicking around. His snout crunched back to a half-human face.

"Guards around the corner," he growled. Ezaria flicked his fingers and Nobaru came forward, swinging his bladed tonfas, striding into the darkness of the passage.

"Weren't these fires lit?" came a gruff voice.

"Yeah," another replied.

"I'll get a light."

By the time the man returned with a torch the others were dead. They were sprawled out on the ground, blood pooling over the icy floor. Nobaru was crouched by a corpse, retrieving a small satchel of coin. He stood up, tucking the bag into his person, and cast the staring guard a smirk. Then, in the blink of an eye, he spun his blades and the man's throat split open. The guard fell to the ground, the torch landing beside him.

Nobaru kissed his own hand and patted the guard's cheek with it.

The others headed through the passage, moving further and further from the light of the red moon.

They reached the end of the tunnel to find an opening, overlooking the fort. There was a long set of steps leading to the ground.

Rownensel was huge, stretching across the mountain pass. A fort built of black stone. The outer walls were tall, with watchtowers and ballistae built into place, bolted to the top parapets. Surrounding the front and back of the fort was a moat of perilous spikes, the sides built right up to the mountains.

Guards could be seen walking about the inner ward, others hidden by shadows.

Ezaria looked across the mountain pass. He then nodded to their twins and the two closed their eyes, taking in deep breaths.

"Everyone is in position," Oda and Wong whispered.

The raiding party moved forward. The lords had chosen a select group of soldiers to head into the citadel, and Ezaria spoke with them in low murmurs as they prepared for the task.

Chester and Yrilim were there only to oversee the attack and support the other fighters, but as she looked to him, he was sick. His brows were furrowed, breathing forced. If he could sweat, he would be.

"Yrilim?" she asked. He was doing his best to appear calm, but Chester could feel how uneasy he was.

"I've been here before," he rasped. He glanced at her, then at Veraion, who had overheard. "I think this is where they took me."

"Would you be comfortable joining us?" the earth azheek said. "You may be of help."

Yrilim clenched his jaw and nodded. Veraion hurried over to Ezaria, speaking lowly. Yrilim tried to swallow the knot in his throat, and Chester squeezed his hand.

"I don't remember anything," he murmured.

"You might," she said. "But don't do this if it doesn't feel right."

He smiled, placing his forehead to hers. When they looked to the raiding party, Ezaria gave a commanding nod to Chester.

"I leave you in charge."

She nodded.

Aven moved down the line and pulled Chester in, holding her for a moment. She smiled and looked up at him.

"Be safe, Little One."

He smiled and kissed her forehead. When he moved away, Veraion took his place before her.

"Don't get killed," she said. He nodded, and they closed their eyes, resting their foreheads together. They took in a shared deep breath, and after she squeezed his hand, he and Yrilim moved to the ledge where the rest of the raiding party waited.

"Be careful," Chester said. "All of you."

Ezaria took Aven by the arm and stepped off the ledge.

Pair by pair, the raiding party plummeted to the fort below, disappearing into darkness.

The raiders were led by Ezaria and Yenea, with Aven beside them as a beast. Following them were Veraion, Yrilim, Nobaru, and a handful of other fire and air azheeks. Every Zalfuri chosen for the party was Fang'ei, save for Wong, selected for his ability to *ulu*.

Torches illuminated the halls and passages, shining off wet stone. Every now and then they'd avoid stepping in pools of liquid, and as Aven flared his nostrils, he knew many were blood.

The citadel was eerily silent. Aven couldn't stop his hackles from rising.

"It's too quiet," Veraion murmured.

Ezaria stopped and the others halted. He was trying to get his bearings.

Yrilim leaned against a wall for support. Yenea looked over to see his eyes darting around beneath the lids, his breaths growing shorter.

"Yrilim." She came forward. He opened his eyes and pushed hair from his face with a shaking hand. Looking down the hallway, he returned to his feet.

"Follow me."

Fairo stood with his back against wet stone, breathing calmly as he waited. He noticed Liu beside him, hand wrapped firmly around the hilt of her sword. Her jaw was clenched, fingers trembling.

Fairo placed a hand on hers, using his powers to warm her. "Relax," he murmured. "What's your name?"

"Liu."

"First fight?"

She kept her eyes on her weary hand. There was a moment of silence and Fairo smiled to himself. He didn't want to push the matter and looked away. Then she whispered.

"We weren't supposed to be here," she said, her voice shaking. "But they needed twins."

Surprise filled his furrowed gaze. He didn't know what to say. Instead, he placed a hand on hers and did his best to warm her against the cold night.

"You'll both be okay," he said. "I'll make sure of it."

Yrilim moved in the lead, eyes wide and fearful. No sound was heard but for the crackling of torches and the soft padding of the raiders' boots.

Aven snarled at the same time Veraion grabbed Yrilim by the arm, raising his other hand to signal a halt. Ezaria moved forward and peered around a corner to see a group of guards.

The lord waved his fingers and the guards choked. The humans stared at one another in alarm, gasping for breath, but no sound came from their tightening throats. Ezaria pulled the air from their lungs, fingers tensed and cold eyes fixed on the humans.

They dropped to their knees, clutching their chests. They wheezed for breath, desperately fighting for air, but none came.

They fell, eyes wide and faces purple. The raiders continued on their way.

Aven's skin crawled as he became unable to block out the distant reek of death and decay. Yrilim slowed down. He was going to be sick.

"Yrilim," Yenea said. He had stopped and was breathing heavily. The others halted behind them.

Yrilim looked up at a set of double doors. Aven's hackles rose as he smelled blood and fear, and Veraion clenched his jaw, stepping away as he felt what was inside.

With a shaking hand, Yrilim pushed the doors open.

The others grabbed their weapons, looking for guards and baraduhr, but they found none. Instead, their eyes landed upon a corpse, suspended in the middle of the room. The body was held in place by ropes, on an angle, halfway between standing and lying down. Flayed.

Every inch of skin hung off the mangled corpse like drapes. Legs, arms, torso, and face naught but flesh and slimy muscle. Blood dripped from the carcass, gleaming upon black stone below, dripping into a drain.

Yrilim stood still, his gaze fixed on the body. His eyes were not wide. This did not shock him. He had seen this before.

Tears slid from his eyes.

Now, he remembered.

Ezaria moved forward, stare seething as he looked upon the flayed body. Tiny lights of purple-grey rose from the corpse. An air azheek.

His jaw clenched, the veins in his temples popping. Around him, the others stared at the walls. At the saws and hooks and clamps and blades. They hung from the ceiling, dangling, some stained permanently red.

Thumbscrews, crocodile shears, the cat's paw. The wheel, the rack, and as Veraion looked to a table of torture devices, the pear of anguish.

More skinned corpses were piled in a corner, and Yrilim tore his eyes away, staggering from the hall. Yenea followed, wrapping her arms around him, holding him close, eyes wide and filled with tears.

He fought to breathe. Four seconds. Four seconds. Four seconds. Four seconds.

Yenea clenched her jaw, holding her brother close. This was what he had been through. This was what had happened to their people.

Ezaria came from the torture chamber, teeth grinding, nostrils flared, eyes seething. Aven took in a deep breath, fighting to try and forget what he had just seen.

"I feel death," Veraion murmured as he joined them. "Overwhelming death. We're close."

He moved away from the double doors, following the path to where he could feel hundreds of rotting corpses.

Kazim rested his head against the stones behind him, eyes closed. His heart beat steadily in his chest, breaths calm. Letting out a long sigh, he gazed over to the fort below. His brow furrowed.

The fires around the inner ward were going out, one by one. He turned to Vi'ra, who was watching. There was a dark look in her eyes.

"Was snuffing out the lights part of the plan?" he said.

"No," she murmured. "It wasn't."

Aven heaved a barricade out of the way and raiders opened the double doors, flooding into the dungeons. The mutant was met with a blast of rancid air—the stench of a thousand rotting corpses.

Aven snarled and turned away, fighting to control his morphing body as the others swarmed into the dungeons around him.

He turned back to the prison, tasting rot on his tongue.

Rows upon rows of cells. There were hundreds of them, and none were empty. But no movement came from inside. Some cells had corpses in piles, others holding naught but old bones.

They hurried through the dungeons, eyes wide in horror. Decaying corpses, skeletons with barely any skin clinging to brittle bones. Many were human: azheeks that had been turned human, and humans that had been caught in the crossfire. Any human that had been captured by accident was left here to starve to death.

The corpses of azheeks flickered dimly in the darkness. The bodies of earth azheeks had wavering lights of green and gold, sickly roots growing from them, winding over rock and around bars. Pools of their blood had turned to slimy moss. The dead fire azheeks had turned to coal, embers fading in and out of their skin, flickering lights of fire wavering above their bodies, and the air azheeks were hazy, skin eerily translucent. Pale purple and grey lights hovered above their disappearing forms.

This place was haunted. Even those that had died with their powers were struggling to find the next world.

The raiders spaced out, swallowing their vomit. They were unable to fight the putrid stench of decay, unable to stop tasting it.

So many of the corpses were missing limbs, eyes carved out, tongues severed, fingers and toes removed. They were missing skin, patches where the baraduhr had left them with naught but exposed muscle, others flayed entirely.

Nobaru dropped to one knee as he spotted an air azheek through the bars. Tiny lights wavered above her, her body translucent. He reached forward to touch her hand and his fingers went straight through hers.

Nobaru yanked his hand back with a gasp, watching as her arm dispersed into thin air. Her body was covered in old blood, naked and exposed. He looked to her legs and clenched his jaw. Red had poured from between them.

He swallowed back vomit, tears welling in his eyes. There was a man beside her, another corpse, a fire azheek, and his body was just as mangled as hers. He had been scalped, nose and lips cut off, eyes carved out, and just like the woman beside him, he had been raped to death.

Veraion stood behind Nobaru, sick to his stomach.

"She's gone," he managed to rasp. "But *she* isn't."

He nodded at an earth azheek in the same cell. Nobaru shakily began picking the lock.

Veraion pulled his eyes away from the corpses and focused on the survivor. She had brown skin and long black hair, symbols carved from her left arm. Her naked body was covered in tattoos, patterns marking her arms, back, and legs, and his brow furrowed. He knew these designs.

"She's from the Vaian Islands," he said.

"Isn't that where you're from?" Nobaru asked as he worked. Veraion nodded, placing a hand upon his friend's shoulder before he forced himself to turn away, continuing through the dungeons.

As he moved through rows of cells, his skin crawled. He could feel so much death. He could almost hear whispers of the trapped souls, their breaths sending goosebumps over his skin.

The corpses of azheeks were eerily beautiful among those that had died human.

There was a soft glow in the distance, dim blue light. A trail of shimmering water led away from the others, and Veraion followed, tailing the eerie stream to a cell at the far end of the dungeons.

A child. A little girl. Her blond hair was ridden with filth, her unfed body covered only by a loose shirt that was too large for her. Blue lights drifted around, circling her dying body. Water dripped from her once sun-kissed skin.

She bore Old markings, glimmering with ancient power. The blue light wavered, illuminating her in the darkness, shining along her widow's peak to light her limp hair like a crown. The markings pulsed with the beat of her weak heart.

Yenea approached, eyes wide. "Oh my god…"

"These baraduhr," Veraion murmured. "They have a woman from the Vaian Islands, and they have a water azheek." He shared a dark glance with Yenea.

"Where are they getting all these people?"

He shook his head and moved forward, kneeling before the girl. Her eyes opened.

Her stare shone blue, irises and pupils gone behind billowing light. The sight was so startling, Veraion jumped.

The girl raised a shaking arm, her frail hand touching the bars before her. She looked at Veraion, but her focus was not upon his face. Instead, she looked at his chest, gaze distant as though seeing through him.

"*ma'ale?*" Her words were barely a whisper. "*nim ma'ale? kandr u kom do tad ni? dehe hurd ni, ma'ale. i pend u woud mouriena kom.*"

Veraion's hand moved to his armoured chest as she spoke, and she continued murmuring in her ancient language.

"She's from Elizia," he said. "I know that accent."

"What is she saying?" Yenea crouched.

"She isn't talking to us. She isn't here. She's talking to the gods."

The girl's loose shirt was smeared with blood and shit, drooping off one shoulder.

Yenea looked to the cell beside hers to see a boy, barely twelve or thirteen years old. He had pale skin that looked almost grey, darker about his eyes. He was gaunt, his black, wavy hair limp as it clung to his scalp. The boy was in naught but a pair of grimy pants, curled up in a pool of his own blood and excrement. Yenea looked between him and the young girl. He had given her his shirt.

"Hey," Yenea said, reaching through the bars, and she placed her hand upon his foot. It was the only part of him she could reach. Using her powers, she flooded her warmth through his body.

The boy shook violently. Yenea reached her other hand through the bars and grabbed his foot with both, providing more warmth. Soon his quaking calmed.

He stirred awake, though he was slow to come to. When he opened his eyes, they were a piercing pale blue, a stark contrast to the discoloured skin about the sockets. He blinked slowly and smiled slightly, as though he thought Yenea was a spirit. He had accepted death.

"What is your name?" she said.

"Ivo."

"Ivo, my name is Yenea. I come from Sirenvel, here with soldiers of Zalfur. We're here to rescue you. You're going home."

It took him a moment, but his eyes widened when he processed her words. He sat up, staring around at the raiders moving through the dungeons.

Ivo began to cry. As he did, Yenea saw something on his shoulder: an *X* had been carved from his skin. She exchanged a horrified look with Veraion, and as they turned back to the young water azheek, her shirt fell down one side. Symbols had been carved from her skin. Her open flesh gleamed in the dim light, old blood crusted down her arm.

"Are you warm enough?" Yenea asked Ivo. He managed to nod through his sobs.

She let go of him and stood aside as Aven approached in his mutant form. An air azheek, Jin, came with him, but Ivo's eyes were fixed on the seven-foot beast.

Jin lifted a hand and Aven grabbed Ivo's cell door, heaving it from the hinges. No sound came as Jin silenced the noise with his powers. Aven's snout shortened with unsettling crunches and he crouched down, a human, offering Ivo a hand. The boy stared at him, too frozen to accept the gesture. Aven hauled him up onto his feet.

"Don't fear me, kid." He smiled. Ivo nodded, though he couldn't stop staring. Jin handed him a flask.

"Drink. A potion from our healers."

Ivo took a sip, swaying dangerously. He handed the flask back to Jin.

"Drink more."

"The others need it more than me," Ivo croaked. "Aliath needs it more than me."

They followed his gaze to the young girl, who was still muttering in Azheek, her glowing eyes heavy-lidded.

"The lights," Ivo rasped. "She's dying, right?"

"She'll be okay," Veraion said.

Aven spotted a battle-axe lying on the ground, and he picked it up, handing it to Ivo. The boy struggled to hold it, and while Aven could have helped him, he didn't. He waited until Ivo had it in his grip before he smiled, giving him an approving nod.

He gave the boy a pat on the shoulder, which almost collapsed him, and then a gentle nudge towards the other raiders. Ivo almost fell over, but he hobbled away, staring back to watch as Aven broke into Aliath's cell.

Yrilim slowly walked through the dungeons, eyes glazed over. He swayed, breathing heavily. Yenea hurried towards him, grabbing him as he fell.

"Yrilim," she gasped, helping him to his feet.

"I'm okay," he said. He shut his eyes tight and shook his head, fighting to focus. "I'm fine. I just…"

"I'm sorry," she said, clutching him in her arms. "I'm so sorry. I'm sorry we brought you here."

"No." He smiled weakly. "Don't be. I'm glad I'm here, I'm glad I… I'm glad I know." He squeezed her hand and forced himself to stand tall, taking in a deep breath.

Yrilim moved over to where Nobaru was helping a survivor to her feet, and Yenea watched him go with worry in her bright gaze.

Wong hurried through the dungeons to find Ezaria breaking open a cell door. Not a single sound left the forcefield he created. Ezaria's hand tensed, arm rising, and two unconscious survivors rose from the floor, floating from the cell until he and Wong took them into their arms.

"*My lord,*" Wong said, concern upon his face. "*Message from ame'ulu.*"

"*What is it?*"

"*The torches have been put out. In the courtyard. Darkness.*"

* * *

The raiders moved back through the citadel with what survivors they had found. There were only a handful, ten, maybe twenty. Few survivors could walk, but those that could did their best to aid the others.

They moved through the fort quicker now, coming across no guards.

Ezaria went ahead, carrying two survivors with him. Aven had a grown man draped over each shoulder. As he walked, halfway between man and beast, he sniffed the air, searching for signs of trouble.

"Lucky there are no guards out," a Sirenveli man said. He was carrying the unconscious woman from the Vaian Islands.

"Don't think so lightly of our sudden luck," Veraion murmured.

They continued through the citadel until they reached the mountain pass, stopping just before the courtyard. Ezaria gazed around with distrusting eyes.

"This place should be riddled with guards and baraduhr," he said. "Yet there are none."

The raiders shared dark glances.

"Something is horribly wrong," Veraion agreed.

"Take the wounded," Ezaria told his soldiers. "Get them out of here as fast as you can. Nobaru, stay here."

The Zalfuri each took a survivor into their arms and crept into the courtyard. One by one they lifted from the ground and moved into the open air, disappearing from sight.

Wong and his survivor crashed to the ground, arrows in their chests.

CHAPTER 24

WAR

Wong's brother screamed. Ziang's eyes flashed and she leapt to her feet, grabbing her weapon. Before she could speak, someone hurtled from the northern opening, colliding with a rock, collapsing to the ground—a man, one of the raiders. He was holding on to a survivor.

"My lord," he choked. Blood spurted from his mouth, an arrow through his neck.

Ziang grabbed her polearm and yelled, leaping into the air. "Renji, Ada, stay here! Protect the survivors!"

Then she plummeted into the opening, speeding for the fort.

Chester broke through the waiting numbers just in time to see Ziang's ranks tearing towards Rownensel. A horn sounded, blasting through the mountain pass as Chester grabbed her blades, yelling to her command. An air azheek grabbed her and charged towards the citadel.

The mountain pass was filled with yells as azheeks flooded the air. Darkness broke as Sirenveli drew their flaming blades, fire spreading down their arms.

Flanks of baraduhr were gathered along the parapets, each with a bow in hand, firing at the courtyard below. Corpses were sprawled over the stones: azheeks and the survivors they had been trying to rescue.

Chester yelled, brandishing her flaming weapon, and the pain in her shoulder became naught but a dull ache as anger and fear turned to fuel.

Her partner brought her straight to a line of baraduhr and she slashed at them as they moved down the row, sending humans from their footing, thrown from the edge.

The air azheek let go and Chester hurtled towards a man. He was loading one of the ballistae, and as he heard her yell, he turned around. Her blades struck through his chest, using him to break her fall.

Chukuma and Faraji landed beside her, rolling as they hit the stones. As the three sprang to their feet, their partners tore for the inner ward to aid the raiding party.

Chester kicked a guard in the chest, sending him from the parapets, slicing off the head of another. Faraji leapt into the air, slamming her warclub into a man's head, and Chukuma threw an axe at a guard who had an arrow pointed at the survivors below. The axe hit the guard in the back and Chukuma raced forward, grabbing his weapon just as the man fell from the ledge. He spun and planted the blade into another.

Fairo's numbers tore towards the fort, Zalfuri carrying their Sirenvel partners, and as they zoomed towards the chaos, flames roared down their weapons. Baraduhr along the parapets pointed their ballistae forward, firing at the oncoming numbers, and Fairo ducked, staring back in horror as a bolt speared through azheeks behind him, throttling others off course.

He landed on the parapets and hacked off the head of a guard, kicking another away from the ballista. He charged towards a baraduhr who had a crossbow pointed at Yenea below and sliced off the man's head with one swing of his roaring battle-axe. The axe that had been his brother's.

He wheeled around, gripping the shaft, pupils ablaze, and his hair licked into flames as he swung his weapon. He blasted a guard to the side with one swing, slamming the pommel into another's face, and as a man came for him, he yelled. They swung their sword and he parried it out of the way, smashing his forehead against the other's.

Fairo charged into the fray, making every baraduhr pay for the death of his brother.

Vi'ra threw Kazim into the battle, taking only a moment to ensure he landed safely as she tore through the inner ward. Ezaria was standing in front of the survivors, an arm raised as he held a forcefield around the group, single-handedly repelling all arrows and spears. His eyes were glowing, complete concentration fixed on protecting the others.

Vi'ra ducked around the shield and grabbed the nearest prisoner, leaping back into the air, ripping for the northern opening.

Nobaru, Yrilim, and Yenea had pushed the survivors against a wall and were standing around them, protecting them from oncoming baraduhr. On either side, Aven and Veraion were drawing blood.

Aven ripped men limb from limb as Veraion's Fang'ei blades painted the walls red.

Ziang grabbed a survivor and shot into the air, pelting through the commotion as fast as she could. Higher and higher she flew. There was an air azheek above her, carrying a survivor, but the man was barrelled off course. Ziang shot forward, grabbing the little girl that fell from the soldier's arms, pulling towards the northern exit, staring down as her soldier plummeted to the spiked moat. Impaled in an instant.

When Ziang burst into open air, she let go of her burden, yelling as she shot back for the battle. "Get the survivors to the healers!"

Renji raised his hand and gently lowered the survivors to the ground. His partner, Ada, was completely aflame, providing warmth for the others that huddled close.

Renji cupped his hands to his mouth, about to whistle when a lacian burst into view.

"Rei!" He stared.

Her lacian landed with a heavy thud, and soon more and more Skyriders soared into view with their beasts.

"What in Valduhr is happening?" Rei looked to him fearfully. "We heard the horn!"

"Get the survivors to the healers!" Renji called. He picked up a girl, a water azheek, helping her climb onto Rei's lacian.

Then Jin burst into view, blood pouring from beneath his armour. He collided with rocks, arms wrapped around a survivor. Renji raced forward, but Jin and his burden were already dead.

"Get the survivors!" Rei called to the Skyriders, and the lacian swooped down, landing heavily on black rock and ice.

Aven threw a guard at two others, bowling them from their feet. Baraduhr stared at him in shock, but they drew their weapons and charged.

The mutant grabbed a man by the sword hand and flipped him over, punching him in the gut. As fist broke skin, intestines burst from body.

Aven recoiled, eye wide as he looked at the innards spooling around his arm. Pink. Slimy. Covered in dark veins.

He staggered back with a horrified gasp. As they fell to the ground, he almost saw marble in the place of black stone.

A blade plunged into his back. He roared and wheeled around, mind returning to the battle, and he grabbed his attacker by the head, smashing him face-first into a stone wall. The man fell, head flattened, skull in pieces.

The mutant pulled the sword from his back with a snarl. He looked at the gleaming blade and then threw it. He had been aiming for a baraduhr, but it passed the man and barely missed Veraion. The earth azheek stared back at him with wide eyes.

"Are you *still* trying to kill me?"

"Sorry!" Aven grabbed the oncoming baraduhr and crushed the man's skull with his hands. Veraion shook his head, but then his eyes widened. Before he could yell, a blade cracked against Aven's skull.

The giant exclaimed and turned around. There was an axe in his head. He faced the woman that had put it there and the guard stood back with terrified eyes. Aven grabbed the axe, yanking it from his head. It had broken his scalp but could not mar his wasfought bones.

"Do you *mind*?!" He planted the axe in the woman's skull.

Ivo watched the exchange with wide eyes, clinging to the battle-axe Aven had given him. Blood poured from Aven's scalp, but he grabbed bits of his hair and tied them together, forcing the wound closed.

The light in Ezaria's eyes faded as he returned his stare to the battle.

"Nobaru," he called. "Go!"

Nobaru grabbed Ivo, taking into the air, and finally Ezaria released his forcefield. Nobaru sped for the northern opening, dodging arrows and ballista bolts as he went, and Ivo watched the battle below, eyes fixed on Aven as the giant morphed, ripping people to shreds. He watched as Ezaria shot into the air, using his powers to haul five guards from the courtyard, throwing them into the northern moat.

The fort was in chaos. Fire shone off black stone as every Sirenveli soldier fought with their weapon aflame, almost an exact one-to-one ratio with the Zalfuri. Ivo could see baraduhr with their metal masks, the sight terrifying, chilling him to the bone, and as he was pulled further away, he saw guards loading the ballistae.

The second Nobaru reached the northern exit, he put the boy down. Lacian were soaring to and from the mountain, carrying survivors to the healers. Ivo swayed in place, eyes wide as one of the massive birds landed before him, and the Skyrider grabbed him by the arm, pulling him into their saddle.

Back on the parapets, Talen punched a guard in the face, spinning his sickle sword to slash the man's neck. He kicked the guard over the edge and turned just in time to parry an attack. Lunging to the side, he wheeled around, kicking his assailant in the chest, blocking a blow from another.

Around him, the battle was deafening. The clashing of metal on metal rang through the mountain pass, resonating high above the yells and roar of flames.

Talen darted to the left and right, slicing through skin and parrying blades, setting baraduhr on fire as he moved.

Then came the sound of a great ballista firing, wood creaking and rope snapping, like a whip sounding through the chaos. He watched as an air azheek was speared, throttled from the sky.

He yelled, charging forward, but a man shot by him, passing him in the blink of an eye.

Ezaria blasted through the war, slicing baraduhr as he went, kicking away guards loading the ballista. The strike came so quickly, with so much force, the men flew back, crashing into others.

Ezaria threw his bladed bow like a boomerang, felling more that came from open doors, and when it landed back in his grasp, he threw it to annihilate another.

Ezaria kicked off the stones, into the air, and with a yell, he summoned his powers. His fingers were outstretched and tensed, shaking with the weight he pulled—with the weight of the ballista, bolted to the fort.

Purple-grey light filled his stare, billowing as he forced the weapon from its place. The mechanism trembled, his muscles shaking, and with horrid screeches and snapping wood, the giant crossbow broke from its place.

Ezaria shot higher as the weapon came free, and with a great heave, sent it into the moat, shattering over the spikes.

Chester drove her polearm into a baraduhr's gut, pushing kara'i steel through the man's body. She wrenched her blades free, kicking him off the parapet. Then she swung to slice off the head of a guard, spinning her weapon to cut off another's leg.

Chester moved through the numbers, spraying the walls red. Her pupils started glowing.

She dodged an attack and kicked the man away, but another swung. The baraduhr slammed his blade against her breastplate, and as she stumbled, he grabbed her by the neck. She choked as he lifted her into the air, holding her over the courtyard, and she grabbed the man's hand, sending flames down his arms. He let go with a yell.

Chester fell, grabbing on to the ledge, but her fingers slipped and she plummeted.

The young twin Oda swooped by and grabbed her, lowering her to the ground. Upon her release, he sent her a salute before tearing away. Chester watched him go, face falling as he careened, a spear in his chest.

Ziang raised an arm, lifting one baraduhr into the air, stabbing another. She closed her outstretched fingers to crush the floating human and dropped the carcass to the ground.

She was knocked off her feet as a club collided with her armour, but she swiftly rolled into the fall and leapt back up. Ziang flexed her free hand, the other holding her serrated Fang'ei polearm.

Her attacker charged, and in an instant she leapt into the air, slicing head from body.

More baraduhr ran for her and she spun, kicking her leg up. She kicked air, but the force sent her attackers flying back into stone.

Veraion swung a sword over his head and sliced through a guard's neck. The head fell and he kicked it, sending it straight at another. He swerved an attack, diving between two baraduhr, slicing through legs as he went.

Leaping up, he made quick work to finish them off, wheeling around to plunge his blades through chainmail and into another's chest.

He was fast, moving swiftly through numbers, leaving baraduhr in pieces. He tore between them, closing distances, their swords swinging past him as he moved. With every swing of his sabres, limbs came from bodies.

With every swing of his singing blades, baraduhr screams followed. This, he knew.

Rope-wrapped hilts felt so familiar in his grip, so comfortable. Kara'i steel sliced through skin like it was nothing, through armour and bone like meat, and as he fought with Ilia's former weapon he could almost feel her beside him, guiding him through the war.

Yrilim yelled through pain, yanking his scimitar from a guard's face, blood spraying. A set of double doors flew open and baraduhr poured out.

He charged forward, slicing through their robes with a blazing blade, kicking one of the doors shut. Throwing an arm forward, he sent flames into the passageway, igniting the baraduhr within.

Yrilim slammed the doors closed and placed his hand on the metal locks. His skin glowed red, a burst of fire exploding from his palm. The doors melted shut. The way was sealed.

Yrilim staggered back, falling against a wall. A baraduhr ran at him, but Yenea charged, slamming her foot into the attacker, blasting him off course. She swung her scimitar with a yell and sent head from body.

She stared around, searching for an air azheek, and as Ji'ah landed in the courtyard, slitting the throat of a guard, Yenea waved a flaming hand.

"Get Yrilim out of here!" she called. "He's injured!"

Ji'ah shot forward, pulling Yrilim's arm over her shoulders, wrapping her other around his waist, and zoomed from the inner ward. Ji'ah yelled as arrows pelted for her, deflecting them with her powers, making for the northern exit as fast as she could.

A ballista bolt speared her.

Ji'ah lunged off course, struggling to hold the lord in her grasp. Yrilim stared at her in alarm, fighting to place his hand upon her wound and stop the bleeding.

Ji'ah gritted her teeth, coughing up blood, pulling higher and higher. Her speed slowed, she moved in pained jolts until she was just close enough to throw Yrilim to the opening. He tumbled over rock, staring back at her, lunging forward to grab her arm, but her eyes rolled back in her head and she fell.

He could do nothing but watch as she plunged for the moat.

Nobaru spun his blades so fast his opponents couldn't think. He zipped around, flipping through the air, kicking and punching with ungodly speed. As his spinning blades worked, skin peeled off his enemies.

He leapt up and kicked a guard in the face so quickly and powerfully, the man's neck broke. When Nobaru landed, he pushed hair from his bloody face.

Then he saw Faraji falling from the parapets and shot forward, grabbing her to break her fall. They spared only a second to acknowledge each other before returning to battle.

Chester was splattered with blood, moving so fast one could have mistaken her for Zalfuri, but her polearm roared with flames. Her pupils were alight, shining through the red that dripped from her brow.

Again and again she swung, red hair whipping behind her. Limbs came from bodies and heads from necks. Every time her blades sliced through flesh, her eyes gleamed.

Ezaria spun into the air and shot back for the ground, landing with a fist to the stones, sending a shockwave to throw baraduhr from their feet. He raised a hand, sucking five guards into the air, throwing them against columns and pillars. Drawing two arrows, he felled two baraduhr, swinging his bladed bow to dismember more.

He threw up a hand, commanding control of an attacking guard, and with a yank, closing his fist, the man was wrenched forward and imploded with a sickening crunch.

Guards ran for Ezaria, swinging their swords, and he brandished his bow like a double-ended polearm. The weapon spun as fast as he did, parrying every strike, and he cleaved through the guards as easily as though they were unarmed children.

The guards' blades careened when he swung his own, flesh peeling and limbs dismembered in seconds.

Kicking off the ground, he slung the bow over his body and raised his arms. His eyes disappeared behind purple-grey light, and as another swarm of guards poured from inside, they were taken from the ground. The humans yelled in alarm, kicking their legs, but he rose higher and higher, and so did they.

Eleven of them, grown men and women.

Ezaria's veins popped from the weight, muscles bulging and arms shaking, but he drew them into the air, further from the citadel, closer to the moat.

Ezaria threw down his arms and the baraduhr shot for the spikes, impaled.

He reached for another ballista, yanking the loading guards away with his powers, and with a yell, he wrenched the weapon from its bolts. Veins were swollen beneath his skin as he heaved it into the air, the weight of wood and metal causing every muscle in his body to shake.

He ripped it apart. The ballista shattered.

Kazim moved through the fray, sickle sword curved in a crescent, and as he cut his way through the courtyard, the blade gleamed. The man was small in stature, but as he ran, it worked in his favour. He ducked under swings and skidded across the ground, slicing off legs, pupils blazing.

Nearby, Chukuma, who stood even smaller than Kazim, threw his weight into his shield, careening a baraduhr off course like a battering ram. The baraduhr tumbled over the ground and Chukuma kicked the man in the head, snapping his neck before continuing to the next attacker.

He raised his shield, the mask of Foros dripping with blood, and swung his axe.

Vi'ra yelled, kicking a guard in the face. She spun her swords, slicing through another, and then kicked off the ground, grabbing a baraduhr. Vi'ra shot into the air and threw them down, throttling the masked human to the moat, impaling the woman on a spike.

Then she raised a hand and repelled an arrow. It had come from a guard on a watchtower, and she charged for him. The guard shot another but she caught it, spinning with the momentum, and sent it back. It landed between his eyes.

There was another guard, raising his bow, and she shot forward, kicking him in the chest. The force blasted him back, spine breaking on a stone railing as he flipped, plummeting to the roaring battle.

Vi'ra shot back for the war, landing on the parapets. She sliced off a head and kicked another baraduhr into the courtyard, looking up to see an air azheek plummeting to the moat. She yelled, throwing up a hand to stop the fall, but she was too late and the soldier was impaled on the spikes.

Vi'ra's eyes were livid. A snarl spread across her lips and a blood-curdling cry sounded from her throat.

She threw a sword and sent a man hurtling backwards, swinging to slice off another head. As she raised her free hand, her weapon came loose from the other's skull and returned to her grasp.

Aven tore through the inner ward, his fur bathed in blood. He clamped his jaws around a guard's leg, ripping it from their body, and slashed at another with his claws. He rose onto his hind legs, bones cracking and crunching as he morphed, a mutation of man and beast, and he grabbed a baraduhr, slamming his fist through their mask—through their face.

He threw the man aside, grabbing another, ripping their head off with his teeth.

Veraion rolled over the ground to dodge an attack, slicing through ankles as he went, and leapt back to his feet with ease. His blades spun around him as he moved, kicking a guard in the face, and he disembowelled a baraduhr with a single swing. He moved fast, making quick work of the humans in his way, blood dripping from his scarred skin.

All he could hear was the song of metal on metal and the roaring of flames; all he could hear were the yells of the soldiers around him and the screams of the injured.

Chester slammed her head into a guard's, sending him staggering back. She leapt up and kicked him in the solar plexus. The wind shot from his lungs, and with a spin, her weapon sliced through his neck.

She ran through the courtyard, sliding to the ground to dodge an attack, the blade humming inches from her face. She wheeled up and sliced between the woman's legs, and as she screamed, Chester swung to dismember head from body.

She leapt at another baraduhr, yelling through her clenched teeth. The metal mask gleamed in the firelight. Taunting.

The man beneath laughed, the sound muffled. He shoved her off and sneered. "You just won't fucking die, will you?"

Chester swung her weapon and he parried, kicking her in the chest to send her staggering back.

The man pulled his mask away and smirked.

Rendel.

Chester spat, tearing at him, and their blades met.

Talen darted across the parapets, fast, never moving in a straight line, an impossible target for the arrows that pelted for him. He grabbed a shield from a fallen Sirenveli and threw it at a guard, sending the man from the ledge.

Talen yelled as he swung his bloody sickle sword, slicing a guard's arm, kicking him back to attack another. But as he set a baraduhr on fire, an arrow landed in his chest.

Talen staggered back, and in that second, the baraduhr swung.

Talen's face split open, blood and brains spraying.

Yenea and Fairo watched from the courtyard as Talen fell.

Fairo yelled, casting flames at an approaching baraduhr, ducking as another attacked. Swinging his great axe over his head, he blasted the baraduhr from their feet, his weapon embedded in their sternum.

Yenea ran to where Talen lay, blood spurting with every twitch of his body. His eyes were no longer in their sockets, tongue splayed in half, jaw hanging in shards. Talen's brain fell apart in pieces. The fire in his eyes went out.

Yenea's breathing shortened, eyes wide, and she turned back to the war with a deafening scream. She slammed her head into a guard's, walloping her pommel into another, swinging her scimitar to hack baraduhr apart.

Chester yelled, working her way through guards as Rendel moved back, watching her with a smile. He was moving from the courtyard, making his way towards open doors. Slowly. Taunting.

"Thalamere told me what he was going to do to you," he called over the chaos. "I wonder how much he got to do before his end."

The flames flickered in her pupils, her breaths short and rasping. She yelled, hacking away a guard, slicing off the head of another, tearing towards the man that watched her with a gleam in his eyes. Rendel laughed.

Chester lunged at him and he blocked her blade with his own. His smile was sick as he searched her face.

"There's the answer."

Chester slammed her forehead into his, swinging her weapon, and though he staggered, raising his sword to fight back, he never stopped smiling.

Nobaru leapt into the air and kicked a guard in the head, breaking the man's neck on impact, landing only to do a flip and dodge an attack. He spun his bladed tonfas, slicing the baraduhr's throat, and wheeled at another.

He was fast, mowing through a group of oncoming guards.

Then a piercing pain shot through his body and he fell to the ground. Nobaru rolled over, yelling as the arrow in his leg hit stone, but he raised a hand and sent his attacker away. He grabbed the shaft of the arrow, snapping it with a yell, coughing blood. Rising to his feet, he fixed his eyes on an oncoming baraduhr.

"*andohr sahil, u mida'ar khan*," he snarled through bloody teeth. He threw one of his blades. It landed with a loud *crack* in the baraduhr's face.

Nobaru staggered, raising a hand, and the weapon flew into his grasp.

A blade sliced through his leg and he fell to the ground, thigh severed.

Nobaru screamed, blood pouring from his leg, his dismembered limb lying on the black stones beside him. He stared at it, too shocked to hear his attacker approaching. But a roar of flames sent the baraduhr away and Kazim raced forward, slicing off the human's head.

"Go!" Kazim yelled. "Get out of here!" He turned, hacking down another masked man.

Nobaru forced himself off the ground, fighting through his body's shock.

He blasted for the northern exit, blood spraying from his severed limb. He pelted through the battle until he was met with a flash of cold air and crashed over black mountain stone.

"Nobaru!" Yrilim gasped.

"My leg!" he screamed. "Cauterize my leg!"

The lord stared at him, then to the bloody stump. He was bleeding profusely. If the bleeding didn't stop, he would die.

"I—I don't know how!" Yrilim stared fearfully. "Fire azheeks can't be cauterized!"

Nobaru grabbed Yrilim's hand and looked him in the eyes. Nobaru's grey stare was bloodshot, tears spilling down his cheeks, teeth gritting as he tried to speak through every shake and seizure of his body.

"Burn my leg, bit by bit," he rasped. "Not too hot, you'll damage healthy tissue, but you have to do it—again and again—until the bleeding stops."

Yrilim nodded, reaching for Nobaru's severed limb.

"You have to grab the artery." Nobaru choked.

Yrilim stared at him in horror.

"Artery!" Nobaru shook violently. "Grab the artery!"

Yrilim took in a deep breath and shoved his hand into Nobaru's severed thigh. He screamed apologies as he fought to find the artery that had been cut and was shortening inside of him.

Nobaru screamed, back arching and arms seizing, and Skyriders shot forward to hold him down. Tears streamed from his eyes, his face screwed up in agony, his curses and cries echoing around the mountains.

Yrilim finally grabbed hold of the femoral artery and yanked it back into place, and as Nobaru shrieked, flames burst from the lord's hands.

Screams filled the air. Nobaru thrashed, but Yrilim kept his grip and the Skyriders pinned him down. Yrilim kept his flames from being too hot, careful not to damage healthy tissue, but he had to do it again. And again. And again.

Another burst of flames. Short bursts, one second every time, and the air azheek's eyes rolled back in his head, his body convulsing as he went into shock.

Chester lunged at Rendel, using her weapon to knock his aside. She threw him to the ground. She slammed her flaming fist into his face again and again, screaming through the pain in her shoulder—through the pain in her chest.

She grabbed a dagger from her waist and planted it in his melting visage. Ripping it back, she stabbed him again. And again. And again.

Skin came from bone, blood spraying her face. Eyeballs came from their sockets as mangled pulp, cheeks opening until her blade was hacking up tongue and teeth.

Kicking a flaming guard away, Fairo stared to the parapets above. So many were dead. As he watched, azheeks were sent over the edges and to the courtyard below.

"There are too many!" he yelled. He parried a blade, kicking his attacker, cutting off the woman's head.

Fairo ran towards Yenea, hacking her baraduhr from behind. He yanked his axe out to plant it into another man.

"We have to get out!" he called. "We've lost too many!"

Yenea drove her scimitar through a baraduhr's chest and turned to face the battle. The courtyard was swimming with azheeks.

They stared to the parapets above and her brow furrowed.

"What is that?"

Something was moving under the stones. At opposite ends of the courtyard, spikes were protruding from the darkness.

A grating, closing off the courtyard, trapping the azheeks below.

"Get out of here!" Yenea screamed. "*Get out! Fall back! Get out of Rownensel!*"

Ezaria shot down and snatched up both of them, speeding out of the courtyard. Yenea called out again and Ezaria used his powers to thunder her warning through the mountain pass.

Zalfuri heeded the call and grabbed the nearest fighter, speeding out, fleeing to any exit of the mountain.

Vi'ra hurtled forward, seizing Aven, and with a loud yell, hauled him into the air. Aven grabbed a baraduhr as they went, ripping the man's throat out. He threw down the twitching corpse.

"Chester!" Aven's gasp was barely human, and he stared around, finding Veraion through the fray. "Veraion! Where's Chester?"

Veraion stared around but he couldn't see her.

Chukuma charged through the chaos of the inner ward. He was surrounded by war, unable to see anything but flashes of fire and bursts of blood, unable to hear anything but screams and blaring horns.

"Faraji!" Chukuma yelled, spotting her through the mayhem, and he ran, taking her by the arm. Air azheeks were swarming around him, grabbing up Sirenveli, and as one came for them, he backed away.

"Wait!" he called. "Where is Chester?"

Faraji tore back for the fort and Chukuma followed. The Zalfuri grabbed another soldier and disappeared through the closing grates.

"*Chester!*" Faraji screamed.

Chester was on top of Rendel, stabbing him again and again and again, but what she stabbed could no longer be called a head. There wasn't a single piece of skin left untouched, not a shard of bone that could have been recognized as skull. His eyes were gone, tongue in flayed pieces, hanging from his gaping neck. The arteries in his throat had ceased to spurt blood. There wasn't anything left to strike. But she couldn't stop.

Chukuma and Faraji grabbed her, yanking her off the mangled carcass. Tears spilled down her face, down a mask of warpaint and blood. Her breathing was short, shallow, and as the dagger fell from her hand, she didn't feel it.

She couldn't feel anything. She could barely see.

"We have to go!" Chukuma said, hauling her to her feet. She grabbed her glowing polearm and staggered after him.

Chester shook her head, blinking wildly as she fought to see the world around her. As she fought to hear anything but her thundering heartbeat.

The deep rumbling of the closing grate was almost lost beneath the thunder of war, but when it came to an end, the silence was deafening.

The courtyard was closed. The way was shut.

Azheeks were caged.

The army stared back at the citadel in horror. There were still so many trapped.

At the northern exit, Yrilim screamed. Skyriders swarmed the skies and Rei grabbed him, shooting towards the fort. The second they were close, he leapt from her arms and landed on the metal, staring at his people below.

Around him, more and more azheeks were landing, looking down at their friends in horror.

Air azheeks were clinging to the grating beneath, yelling to their comrades through the bars, but through the fray, Rei saw Kazim. He stood in the courtyard below, hooked sword loose in his hand, eyes fixed on her.

Yrilim turned to those around him, shouting as loud as he could.

"Work together!" he called. "Melt the bars! Zalfuri, tear this thing apart!"

Then he saw her.

Chester.

She stood in the courtyard, face deathly pale. Her weapon slipped from her fingers and fell to the ground.

"No," Yrilim gasped. "*No—no—NO!*"

A deafening bang sounded as Aven crashed onto the grating, every muscle bulging as he grabbed the metal and fought to pull the bars apart. He was roaring, tears streaming down his face. He knew Chester was in there.

Veraion landed near Aven, yelling commands, shouting for the Zalfuri to work together and pull the grating apart. The Zalfuri swarmed the fort, calling on their powers.

Then Veraion saw her.

Everything slowed.

Veraion's eyes glazed over as he blinked, looking around at the chaos.

He couldn't hear them anymore. He could see them yelling, crying, fire all around him and air azheeks summoning power, but he couldn't hear them.

All he heard was the beating of a heart. Chester's heart.

There were so many inside, so many men and women of Zalfur and Sirenvel, and with them, Chukuma and Faraji. He could see corpses of azheeks, Talen's face unrecognizable.

Ezaria hung above the mayhem, his stare wide. Horrified. Livid. The screams of his people rang in his ears, echoing, repeating, so loud he could hear nothing else.

The lord's arms shook as he raised them, fingers outstretched and trembling as his muscles bulged.

Ezaria closed his eyes, taking in a long, deep breath.

The noises stopped. It was silence but for the beating of his heart.

His eyes snapped open, blazing with light. He wrenched his arms back and Zalfuri soldiers were sucked from their places, away from the citadel, to the ground. They landed on one knee, a fist pressed to the stones, heads down, and when they looked back up, their eyes glowed.

Their stares were wide, lost behind billowing light.

Twenty soldiers, identical in the way they knelt, possessed by the lord above.

Ezaria slowly raised his shaking arms, fingers tensed and outstretched, and from the kneeling Zalfuri, he siphoned more strength.

He could hear nothing but his own heart. He could see nothing but the cage he focused on. Blind and deaf, he channelled everything he had.

Pale lights rose from him, from those below, and powers came from their bodies like glowing smoke, leaving their vessels to fuel his.

He pushed his arms forward, hands outstretched as he focused everything on the baraduhr cage, and as he shook, so did metal.

An ear-piercing screech sounded as the grate began to vibrate and tremble.

The veins beneath Ezaria's skin were popping.

Slowly the grating began to part.

"Protect your lord!" Vi'ra yelled. *"Protect your lord!"*

Zalfuri rushed to the sky, surrounding their leader, repelling arrows.

The grating screeched as it shook open, inch by inch.

Trapped beneath, Liu screamed and shoved her hand through the new doorway. Fairo grabbed her arm from above.

Baraduhr emerged on the parapets, wielding staffs, and every crystal head billowed with stolen azheek powers. They swung their weapons.

Zalfuri fell from the sky, and as Ezaria became exposed, an arrow plunged through his neck. He plummeted.

Vi'ra screamed, pelting for her lord, shielding his body with hers. Arrows speared down her back but she didn't stop, tearing forward, grabbing his arm.

Crack.

His spine against stone.

Vi'ra screamed, wrenching him away from the stone ledge. A moment too late.

Blood spurted from his mouth as she pulled him from the war, and she shrieked, screaming through her clenched teeth, covered in her own blood. But he was still breathing. And that was all that mattered. The grate closed. It cut through Liu's arm, snapping around her bones.

Fairo fell back, her severed forearm in his grasp. She plummeted, her screams stopping when she was impaled on a spear.

Veraion couldn't move. He looked around, blinking slowly. Yrilim was smashing a flaming fist into the metal, his body engulfed in fire. Aven was roaring so loudly ears were bleeding.

Yrilim flew back, an arrow in his shoulder. Baraduhr poured into the courtyard, swarming towards the captives, pointing arrows through the bars to fell those above.

"Fall back," someone screamed. *Fall back.*

Tears welled in Chester's eyes. When she looked at Aven, the tears slid down her cheeks.

Sirenveli above the grating were yelling, Zalfuri grabbing them away, dodging arrows that came from below, fighting to escape the powers wielded by baraduhr.

Chester looked at Veraion.

She smiled. It was slight, but it was there.

Thank you.

She nodded, lowering to one knee, and picked up her weapon.

Chester's hand wrapped around the hilt of her great polearm. Ancient runes glowed blue, the crystal shining white among splatters of blood.

As the baraduhr drew closer, she swung.

The world spun back into focus as she slammed her blades into the side of a baraduhr's head, shattering mask and skull, and she wrenched her weapon free, running towards the swarm of haunted faces.

If she was going to die, she was bringing them with her.

GLOSSARY, TRANSLATIONS,

AND PRONUNCIATION GUIDE

DEDICATION

i var vala u iorethe ind uron, nim alyeh larha.

tuma fara doha valira, nim ehan.
i var hava u andal.

kalan u te etheliar. i ihv beranok iord u.

ur vala menid ni imoria.

I will love you forever and always, my little wolf.

Run free through Valira, my son.
I will see you again.

Thank you for everything. I live because of you.

Your love made me immortal.

BASICS

a (ah) . *e (eh)* . *i (ih)* . *ee (eeh)* . *eu (euh)* . *o (oh)* . *u (ooh)*

All Ancient Azheek is pronounced the way it is spelled. Keep in mind that the *u* in Azheek is pronounced like "ooh" as opposed to "uh". Therefore:
-   Zalfur *(Zal-foor)*
-   Usan *(Oo-san)*
-   Anluran *(An-loo-ran)*

With this in mind, traditional Azheek names are pronounced as such:
-   Veraion *(Ve-rai-on)*
-   Theideus *(Thei-de-oos)*
-   Madia *(Ma-di-a)*
-   Aliath *(A-li-ath)*

When vowels are next to each other they do not change in pronunciation. *a* next to *i* is pronounced *a-i. ai. ve-**rai**-on.*
(The *eu* sound uses only one character in written Azheek.)

Names not pronounced exactly as spelled are non-Azheek, such as:
-   Aven *(Ei-ven)*
-   Athos *(Ei-thos)*
-   Einmyria *(Ein-mi-ri-a)*

Most names are not traditional Azheek names as the kara'i are a minority.

The Azheek language has no character for the letter *C* as the same sounds can be created by the *K* or *S*, or a harsh *J* (as in "ch").

All "r" sounds in Azheek are slightly rolled, like a soft "d", unless spoken with a Volehni accent, in which case all "r" sounds are pronounced in the back of the throat, rolled, like a purr.

The Azheek language, when written in Romanization, uses no capital letters as the Azheek writing system itself, *sa'uri*, has no capital letters.

Azheek can be written "elongated" *(loa)*, as seen on Chester's kara'i weapon, or "stacked" in syllable blocks *(poro)*, as is the Fang'ei tattoo on Nobaru's cheek.

Elongated is usually written and read from left to right, whereas stacked is usually written and read from top to bottom.

fang'ei *(loa)*

ianar *(loa)*

fang'ei *(poro)*

ianar *(poro)*

loa azheek is used for proper writing, whether it be letters, scrolls, documents, books, etc.

poro azheek is used for banners, seals, signs, labels, and other instances where one would want to cram as much information as possible into a smaller space.

poro azheek is formal enough for royal banners and seals, but you would not write someone a letter in *poro azheek*.

Unless you are from Paradiz.

The Paradizi usually write with *poro azheek*. When the lords of Paradiz send messages to Volehn and Elizia, it frustrates and often confuses the others because not only is the message written with informal writing, the words themselves are dialect and often slang.

There is a theory that the Paradizi do it just to piss everyone off.

OTHER BASICS

kara : water
kara'i : water azheek(s)
za'ir : air
za'iri : air azheek(s)
siren : fire
sireni : fire azheek(s)
ulo : earth
ulo'i : earth azheek(s)

One-spirit : cisgender
Two-spirit : nonbinary
Swapped-spirit : transgender
Two-formed : intersex

When an apostrophe is used between vowels, it indicates a glottal stop.

THE GODS

Ma'ale Natur *(ma-a-le na-toor)* :
Mother Nature. Creator of the world.

Da'ale Zun *(da-a-le zoon)* :
Father Sun, commonly known as *ir zoon*, the Sun.

Fa'e Lun *(fa-e loon)* :
Sister Moon, commonly known as *ir lun*, the Moon. The youngest of the gods, turned into the Blood Moon the day the Five were killed.

THE FIVE

Natura *(na-toor-a)* :
The first ruler to hold all four elemental powers. A direct descendant from the gods, Natura was two-spirited, two-formed, and came to Ianar already in their prime.
Natura had an ilis, Aisurang, an air azheek. Natura gave birth to the first Ianar-born queen, Aishida.

Awera *(a-we-ra)* :
The first lord of water, one of the Five. A direct descendant of the gods. Two-spirited and two-formed, came to Ianar already in their prime.

Ongji *(ong-ji)* :
The first lord of air, one of the Five. A direct descendant of the gods. Two-spirited and two-formed, came to Ianar already in their prime.

Atesh *(a-tesh)* :
The first lord of fire, one of the Five. A direct descendant of the gods. Two-spirited and two-formed, came to Ianar already in their prime.

Dunia *(doo-ni-a)* :
The first lord of earth, one of the Five. A direct descendant of the gods. Two-spirited and two-formed, came to Ianar already in their prime.

OTHERS

Aishida *(ai-shi-da)* :
The first Ianar-born queen, daughter of Natura and Aisurang.
Aishida was a two-spirited girl. She was only a child when the Five were killed. Since Aishida, the bloodline of the gods has been passed through daughters, whether one-spirited or two.

Savai *(sa-vai)* :
The next world, where azheeks go after their lives on Ianar end.

Valira *(val-i-ra)* :
A part of Savai, a world of light. A place of love.
Where azheeks reunite with their ilis, loved ones, and ancestors.

Valduhr *(val-doohr)* :
A part of Savai, a world of darkness. A place with no love.
Where azheeks never see their ilis, loved ones, or ancestors. A place of suffering. A place for those who caused suffering on Ianar.

MAP TRANSLATIONS

Ianar *(i-a-nar)* :
No translation. Name of the world. Created by the god Mother Nature.

Ilaga Iva *(i-la-ga i-va)* :
North lands. Anything north of Sontar Ivel.
Not to be confused with the Northlands, a vast strip of mountainous land inhabited by humans.

Ilan'gan Iva *(i-lan-gan i-va)* :
East lands. Anything east of Sontar Ivel.

Imog Iva *(i-mog i-va)* :
South lands. Anything south of Sontar Ivel.

Anluran Iva *(an-loor-an i-va)* :
West lands. Anything west of Sontar Ivel.

Sontar Ivel *(son-tar i-vel)* :
Centre City or Country. The capital. Created by the gods the day the Five came to Ianar. A stronghold to house and protect all Azheeks. It is the centre of the world. All land rotates around Sontar Ivel. It is the only place that never moves.
Sontar Ivel is the most magical country on Ianar as it was created by the gods and still holds a connection to them. It is believed to be the umbilical cord connecting Ianar to Mother Nature.

TRANSLATIONS

in order of appearance.

All Azheek spoken throughout *The Rising* is *iren azheek*, meaning Common Azheek. This language is spoken on Elizia and Volehn, but their accents are slightly different. The Zalfuri also speak *iren azheek* as they were taught by the Elizi.

Unless stated to be *paradiz saturi*, Paradiz dialect, all Azheek is *iren*.

(pg. 3)
baraduhr
Masked humans. *barad*, "masked", *duhr*, a slur for humans. *duhr* means "none", as in, azheeks with no powers.

(pg. 8)
vu iar u?
Who are you?

(pg. 12)
ilis
Loosely translates to "soulmate" or "love". An ilis is an azheek's life partner, whether the bond be romantic, platonic, or familial. Azheeks age like humans until they reach their "prime", when they stop aging. It is only after they have bound to another azheek, their ilis, do they age once more.

(pg. 26)
natura's ma'ale, natur
Natura's mother, Nature.
An expression commonly said by those that speak Azheek.

(pg. 29)
aishida

Aishida. The first Ianar-born queen. A common expression.
Sometimes shortened to *aish*, having a similar meaning to "damn" or "ugh".

(pg. 45)
tama iris byan

It's okay.

(pg. 121)
Mahr Ivel

Iron City.

(pg. 126)
Mahriel

Iron heart. *mahr*, "iron", *riel*, "heart".

(pg. 136)
kyale dehen uhr

Kill them all.

(pg. 137)
kanaua'a iord volehnn, fa'ale iord kara, madia

Protector of Volehn, daughter of water, Madia.

(pg. 140)
dahveh?

Do you want to die?
paradiz saturi. Paradiz dialect.
tu u vend do dahv?
Do you want to die?
iren azheek. Common Azheek.

(pg. 141)
mida
Fuck.

(pg. 186)
sahilahk
Shithead. *sahil*, "shit", *ahk*, "head".

(pg. 190)
ulu
A connection to the gods. The ability to pass one's consciousness to the next world, Savai, and speak with the gods or ancestors.

(pg. 192)
ame'ulu
Familial ulu. A connection to one's family member, most commonly a twin. The ability to pass one's consciousness to said family member and speak to them from long distances. Also possible between ilis.
ame'ulu is strongest when used between familial ilis.

(pg. 200)
nim riel
My heart.

(pg. 205)
sikele
Companion animal, from the city of Okos. All Kosi are *ulo'i* and have a companion animal known as sikele. The bond is almost as strong as ilis.

(pg. 304)
shazeu
Fool.

(pg. 362)
mida'ar baba aishida
Fucking baby Aishida.

(pg. 483)
oras iord ih dahvid ta'e
Day, or time, of the fallen brother.

(pg. 511)
ma'ale? nim ma'ale? kandr u kom do tad ni?
Mother? My mother? Have you come to take me?
dehe hurd ni, ma'ale. i pend u woud mouriena kom.
They hurt me, Mother. I thought you would never come.

(pg. 528)
andohr sahil, u mida'ar khan
Eat shit, you fucking cunt.

NAME PRONUNCIATIONS

Ada *(ei-da), two syllables*
Ah'ni *(ah-ni), two syllables*
Aina *(ai-na), two syllables*
Aion *(ai-on), two syllables*
Aishida *(ai-shi-da), three syllables*
Aisurang *(ai-soo-rang), three syllables*
Aiyat *(ai-yat), two syllables, "yat" spoken with a soft "t"*
Aliath *(a-li-ath), three syllables*
Atesh *(a-tesh), two syllables*
Athos *(ei-thos), two syllables*
Aven *(ei-ven), two syllables*
Awera *(a-we-ra), three syllables*
Azhara *(az-ha-ra), three syllables*
Behraz *(be-hraz), two syllables*
Chester *(ches-tur), two syllables*
Chukuma *(choo-koo-ma), three syllables*
Dae *(da-e), one syllable, can be two when spoken slowly*
Dunia *(doo-ni-a), three syllables, can be two when spoken quickly*
Ehl *(el), one syllable*
Eidis *(ei-dis), two syllables*
Einmyria *(ein-mi-ri-a), four syllables*
Ekhrem *(ek-hrem), two syllables*
Elaira *(e-lai-ra), three syllables*
Emel *(e-mel), two syllables*
Ezaria *(e-za-ri-a), four syllables*
Fairo *(fai-ro), two syllables*
Faraji *(fa-ra-ji), three syllables*

Fehir *(fe-hir), two syllables*
Ferhat *(fer-hat), two syllables*
Hadis *(ha-dis), two syllables*
Hamsa *(ham-sa), two syllables*
Huri *(hoo-ri), two syllables*
Ife *(i-fe), two syllables*
Ilia *(i-li-a), three syllables*
Ivo *(ee-vo), two syllables*
Ji'ah *(ji-ah), two syllables, "j" pronounced more like "ch"*
Kazim *(ka-zim), two syllables*
Kono *(ko-no), two syllables*
Liang *(li-ang), one syllable, can be two when spoken slowly*
Liu *(lee-oo), one syllable, can be two when spoken slowly*
Ma'ale Natur *(ma-a-le na-toor), five syllables*
Madia *(ma-di-a), three syllables*
Madias *(ma-di-as), three syllables*
Mahriel *(mah-ri-el), three syllables*
Maina *(mai-na), two syllables*
Mazhar *(maz-har), two syllables*
Natura *(na-toor-a), three syllables*
Nihan *(ni-han), two syllables*
Nobaru *(no-ba-ru), three syllables*
Oda *(oh-da), two syllables*
Ongji *(ong-ji), two syllables, "ji" spoken similar to "chi"*
Rei *(rei), one syllable*
Rendel *(ren-del), two syllables, "r" pronounced the common way*
Renji *(ren-ji), two syllables, "ji" spoken similar to "chi"*
Sanada *(sa-na-da), three syllables, all "a" sounds are the same*
Siran *(si-ran), two syllables*
Talen *(ta-len), two syllables, more emphasis on "ta"*

Tao *(ta-o), one syllable*
Thalamere *(tha-la-meer), three syllables*
Theideus *(thei-de-oos), three syllables*
Timur *(ti-moor), two syllables*
Vefa *(ve-fa), two syllables*
Venhel *(ven-hel), two syllables*
Veraion *(ve-rai-on), three syllables*
Vi'ra *(vi-ra), two syllables, more emphasis on "ra"*
Wong *(wong), one syllable*
Yenea *(ye-ne-a), three syllables*
Yong *(yong), one syllable*
Yrilim *(yi-ri-lim), three syllables*
Zahura *(za-hoo-ra), three syllables*
Zaiera *(zai-e-ra), three syllables*
Zaoen *(zao-en), two syllables*
Ziang *(zi-ang), one syllable, can be two when spoken slowly*
Zufang *(zoo-fang), two syllables*

MAP GLOSSARY

Acolonia *(a-ko-lo-ni-a)*, *five syllables*
Athos's supposed home.

Akana *(a-ka-na)*, *three syllables*
A floating za'iri city in Zalfur. They speak Azheek and Common.
Inhabited by only air azheeks.

Anluran Iva *(an-loor-an i-va)*, *five syllables*
West lands, anything west of Sontar Ivel.

The Cradle
A valley in the mountains of Ilaga Iva, looking like a cradle. It used to be directly beneath the floating city of Zeda. It still holds the frozen bones of the children thrown from the city walls the day Ezaria seized power of Zalfur. Zeda has since moved south-east from the Cradle.
No one dares pass through the Cradle as it is said to be haunted.

The Dead Sea
The eastern sea. None that sail through the Dead Sea return.

Deep South
South of Ianar, this land is too close to the sun to be habitable. It is too hot for any to survive—apart from sireni. But no sireni live in the Deep South as no animals or plants can survive.

Elizia *(e-li-zi-a), four syllables, "z" similar to "s"*
The capital of the kara'i cities. Elizia moves across the oceans, going wherever the Elizi people want to go They speak Azheek.
Inhabited by only water azheeks.

Eloa *(e-lo-a), three syllables*
Also known as the Eloan Islands. A series of islands off the west coast of the mainland. They speak Common.
Inhabited by humans and some earth azheeks.

Endwood Forest
A forest south-east of Zalfur, north-west of Sirenvel.

Foros *(fo-ros), two syllables*
An underground city in Imog Iva. Once a place of earth azheeks, Foros now has more humans than ulo'i. They speak Common.
Inhabited by humans and some earth azheeks.

Great North
North of Ianar, this land is too far from the sun to be habitable. It is too cold for any living being to survive, but it has been rumoured that wasfoughts travel to the Great North to die so that nobody can find their bones.

Ground Country
The land beneath the floating cities of Zalfur, including the port city of Yan'zi. They speak Azheek and Common.
Inhabited by only air azheeks.

Kapadua *(ka-pa-du-a), four syllables*
A land by the south-west coast of the mainland, heavy with jungles and swamps. Once an area of ulo'i, Kapadua is now primarily humans. They speak Common.
Inhabited by humans and earth azheeks.

Ianar *(i-a-nar), three syllables*
The world.

Ikran *(i-kran), two syllables, "r" pronounced slightly rolled*
The main city of a large south island. Known for very spicy food. They speak Common.
Inhabited by humans, fire azheeks, and some earth azheeks.

Ilaga Iva *(i-la-ga i-va), five syllables*
North lands, anything north of Sontar Ivel.

Ilan'gan Iva *(i-lan-gan i-va), five syllables*
East lands, anything east of Sontar Ivel.

Imog Iva *(i-mog i-va), four syllables*
South lands, anything south of Sontar Ivel.

Highlands
A large stretch of mountainous land. The Highlanders and Northlanders have been fighting over each other's land for centuries. They speak Common.
Inhabited by only humans.

Mahr Ivel *(mar i-vel), three syllables*
The Iron City. Athos's supposed home.

Northlands

A large stretch of cold, mountainous land. Close to the Great North. The Northlanders and Highlanders have been fighting over each other's land for centuries. They speak Common.
Inhabited by only humans.

Ocean of the Moon

Northern oceans of Ianar, this sea is closest to the Moon.

Ocean of the Sun

Southern oceans of Ianar, this sea is closest to the Sun.

Okos *(o-kos), two syllables*

Once the ulo'i capital, Okos is the only earth azheek city to remain uninhabited by humans. All Kosi have a companion animal known as sikele. They speak Common.
Inhabited by only earth azheeks.

Paradiz *(pa-ra-diz), three syllables, "z" similar to "s"*

A kara'i city that moves across the oceans, going wherever the Paradizi people want to go. They speak their own dialect of Azheek.
Inhabited by only water azheeks.

Rownen Forest *(rau-nen), two syllables*

A forest in Ilan'gan Iva.

Rownen Mountains *(rau-nen), two syllables*

A stretch of mountains in Ilangan Iva.

Rownensel *(rau-nen-sel), three syllables*

A fort within the closed mountain pass of the Rownen Mountains.

Sakhala *(sa-kha-la), three syllables*
A sireni city. Once close to Sirenvel, Sakhala has moved from Ilan'gan Iva, through Imog Iva, and is nearing Anluran Iva. The land broke off in a large island and is close to the Deep South. They speak Common.
Inhabited by only fire azheeks.

Sirenvel *(si-ren-vel), two syllables*
A sireni city situated inside an extinct volcano. The volcano erupted the day the Five were killed and has been extinct ever since. The original city of Sirenvel was destroyed but was rebuilt. The capital of sireni cities. They speak Common.
Inhabited by only fire azheeks.

Sontar Ivel *(son-tar i-vel), four syllables*
The capital, the heart of Ianar. Created by the gods, it still holds immense magic. They speak Common.
Inhabited by humans, earth azheeks, fire azheeks, and air azheeks.

Usan *(oo-san), two syllables*
A floating za'iri city in Zalfur. They speak Azheek and Common.
Inhabited by only air azheeks.

Vaia *(vai-a), two syllables*
Also known as the Vaian Islands. A series of islands off the south-west coast of the mainland. They speak Common.
Inhabited by humans and some earth azheeks.

Volehn *(vo-len), two syllables*
A kara'i land that moves across the oceans, going wherever the Volehni people want to go. They speak Azheek.
Inhabited by only water azheeks.

Vora *(vo-ra), two syllables*
Once a sireni city, Vora is now an unhabitable land. The city of Vora was situated in a dormant volcano, and the day the Five were killed, the volcano became active. It is still active to this day.

Yan'zi *(yan-zi), two syllables, "zi" similar to "tsi"*
A port city in Zalfur, part of Ground Country.
Once the port city of Amora, the Amorai were wiped out by the Zalfuri and the port was rebuilt and renamed Yan'zi after the lord Yan'zi, who was killed in the fight. They speak Azheek and Common.
Inhabited by only air azheeks.

Zalfur *(zal-foor), two syllables*
An empire of all za'iri cities. Zalfur includes the floating cities of Zeda, Akana, and Usan, as well as Ground Country and the port city of Yan'zi. They speak Azheek and Common.
Inhabited by only air azheeks.

Zeda *(ze-da), two syllables*
A floating za'iri city in Zalfur. The capital of za'iri cities and the capital of Zalfur. They speak Azheek and Common.
Inhabited by only air azheeks.

AZHEEK SA'URI

(characters of the written Azheek language)

"ah"

"yah"

"eh"

"yeh"

"ih"

"yih"

"eeh"

"yeeh"

"euh"

"yeuh"

"oh"

"yoh"

"ooh"

"yooh"

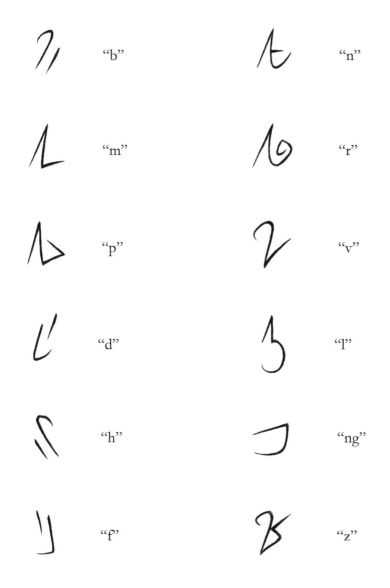

"b" "n"

"m" "r"

"p" "v"

"d" "l"

"h" "ng"

"f" "z"

⁊	"k", soft	𝓃	"t"
𝓣	"k", hard	𝓃̆	"th"
》	"g", soft	M	"j", like "jump"
𝈂	"g", hard	M̆	"j", soft, like "Asia"
𝓍	"s"	M̄	"j", hard, like "ch"
𝓍̆	"sh"	𝒐	Silent. Used for *poro* writing when a syllable contains only one vowel. This silent character goes first.

PUNCTUATION & STRUCTURE

goes between each word,
loa & poro

comma, *loa*

full stop, *loa*

apostrophe, *loa*

comma, *poro*

full stop, *poro*

apostrophe, *poro*

1	2

| 1 | 2 |
| | 3 |

| 1 | 2 |
| 3 | 4 |

Stacked Azheek, *poro*, uses syllable blocks.

Every block is one syllable.

Each block contains between two and four characters, no more, no less.

The characters are read in the order as shown above.

Elongated Azheek, *loa*, is written the same as Common.

Mahriel

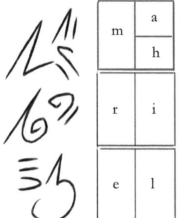

m	a
	h
r	i
e	l

Veraion

v	e
r	a
	i
o	n

Aven

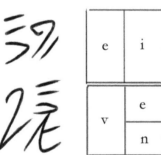

e	i
v	e
	n

Ezaria

–	e
z	a
r	i
–	a

Theideus

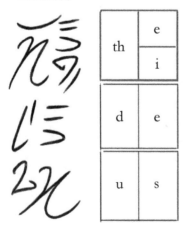

th	e
	i
d	e
u	s

Ziang

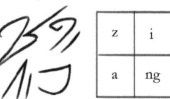

| z | i |
| a | ng |

CAPITAL CITIES - WRITTEN

LOA

elizia

okos

sirenvel

zalfur

PORO

e

li

zi

a

o

kos

si

ren

vel

zal

fur

PUNCTUATION EXAMPLES

kanaua'a iord volehn.

kyale dehen uhr.

ka

na

ua

'a

i

ord

vo

lehn

kya

le

de

hen

uhr

ᛚᚾ'ᚾᛃᛝ : ᛃᛚᛝ · ᚾᛗᛝᛘ · ᛉᚾᛉᛝᛈ · ᛚᛞᛝᛝᛚ :

ᛚᚾ'ᚾᛃᛝ : ᚾᛗᚾ · ᛚᛝᛝᛗ · ᛃᛉᚾᛝᛘ :

ᛚᚾ'ᚾᛃᛝ : ᛉᚾᛝᛖ · ᛝᛘᛝ · ᛘᚾᛝ · ᛚᛞᛝᛝᛚ :

ᛚᚾ'ᚾᛃᛝ : ᚾᛗᚾ · ᛚᛝᛝᛖ · ᛝᛚᛝ :

ma'ale, loi atis uouhr pehim,
ma'ale, ota deht lua'is,
ma'ale, uahn isi sa'e pehim,
ma'ale, ota dehen ide.

Mother, look down upon us,
Mother, take their souls,
Mother, walk here among us,
Mother, take them home.

AZHEEK SYMBOLS

z"ir   kara   ulo   siren

For more information, maps, artwork,
and character portraits, visit
www.azheek.com

Lightning Source UK Ltd.
Milton Keynes UK
UKHW011111260821
389520UK00001B/219